THE
BILLIONAIRE
BAD BOYS
CLUB

EMMA HOLLY

OTHER TITLES BY EMMA HOLLY

The Prince With No Heart

The Assassins' Lover

Steaming Up Your Love Scenes (how-to)

The Billionaire Bad Boys Club

Hidden Series

Hidden Talents

Hidden Depths

Date Night

Move Me

The Faerie's Honeymoon

Hidden Crimes

CONTENTS

Chapter One   1

Chapter Two   14

Chapter Three   18

Chapter Four   35

Chapter Five   45

Chapter Six   57

Chapter Seven   67

Chapter Eight   83

Chapter Nine   100

Chapter Ten   109

Chapter Eleven   123

Chapter Twelve   143

Chapter Thirteen   157

Chapter Fourteen   178

Chapter Fifteen   198

Chapter Sixteen   210

Chapter Seventeen   223

About the Author   233

CHAPTER ONE

ℑ

The Bad Boys Club

Trey Hayworth had a choice. He could jack off to his dog-eared Victoria's Secret catalogue or rely on his stash of torn out underwear stud ads. The Victoria's Secret women were soft and curvy, the Calvin Klein men as ripped as gym rats in their groin-hugging briefs.

Both made Trey's eighteen-year-old cock swell up and harden.

He could have used both to masturbate to of course, but he preferred to save that treat for his last climax. Privacy was precious. He liked to make a full meal of it.

Trey's father was a pharmaceuticals rep for a drug company. Twice a month he traveled out of town on sales trips. When he was home, he kept too close an eye on his son for Trey to risk breaking his anti-sex edicts. When he was gone, Trey had more leeway. His sort-of pal Kevin Dexter had shown him how to feed fake footage into his dad's spycams, which gave him multiple days and nights to revel in freedom.

He could pretend he was normal then. Crawl the mall. Crash a party if he knew of one. He wasn't popular enough to be invited. The other seniors at Franklin High smelled the freak on him—his indeterminate sexual preference, his home situation, the whole "his mother killed herself last year" thing. Whether they were jocks or nerds, people steered clear of making friends. Trey didn't fit their boxes. They didn't know what to make of him. His saving grace was that he was decent looking and owned a car. Waiting tables sixteen hours a week meant he could buy non-lame clothes and keep his rusty

Mustang running.

His father believed allowances ruined kids.

But that was fine. Trey was happier not relying on him. Safer too, probably. Trying to please her spouse had led to his mother giving up on everything.

He pushed that thought away. Remembering how his mother had checked out made him feel like he was choking. Determined not to waste his time alone, he scooted beneath the box spring to retrieve his inspiration from its well-concealed hiding place. His cock woke up as he did, twitching like Pavlov's dog from the familiar feel of his back sliding over the cool floorboards.

The sound of a raised male voice froze him there with the dust bunnies.

Zane Alexander's father was on a tear tonight.

In some ways, Trey's next door neighbor was the opposite of himself. Zane was a golden boy. Captain of the football team. A zillion friends. A Porsche. A girl for each arm and leg if he wanted them. In one important way, however, he and Trey had too much in common.

Trey squirmed out from under his bed and crawled to the windowsill to peek out. His pitch-black hair was long—too long, according to his father. Thus far, he'd avoided his father's scissors. As a result, he had to shovel it out of his eyes to see. A strip of grass separated the two ramblers, maybe fifteen feet in all. The night was dark and the shades were pulled. The light from a single lamp silhouetted Zane and his father in their living room. Divorced for a couple years from his beauty queen of a wife, Zane's father had been Franklin's hometown hero once, a football prodigy like his son. An injury sidelined his career, leaving him to simultaneously hate and need to live through his son—who he liked to pimp out at the sporting goods store he owned. Mr. Alexander was big and beefy but not as tall as Zane. As if he didn't want to remind his dad of that, Zane's shoulders were hunched in.

"You forgot?" Mr. Alexander's drunken voice shouted. "You *forgot?* You want to tell me how you could be such a stupid shit you couldn't remember one simple thing!"

Zane's answer was inaudible. Truthfully, it didn't matter what he said, no more than it mattered what he'd forgotten. What happened next was inevitable.

His father's arm uncoiled, his meaty fist smacking Zane in the temple. Trey flinched and gripped the window tighter. Zane didn't let out a sound. Again came the fist, and again Zane took the blow. If reflex made him jerk away slightly from the swing, experience kept him from blocking it.

Defending himself would be the opposite of helpful.

He'd made the right choice. Mr. Alexander was finished then, his anger a storm that had blown over.

"No sniveling," he instructed before he left the room. "You take your medicine like a man."

His son stood there by himself, his chest going up and down, his fists opening and closing with some struggle. *Shit,* Trey thought, not sure what was happening but concerned. Zane's body language said he was about to explode. Trey sucked in a breath, wondering if he should call out. Zane and he weren't friends by any stretch, but maybe something he could say would help.

Before he could decide, Zane turned sharply and headed for the door.

He was out of the house in seconds, striding down their front walk on jerky legs. Probably he wanted to walk his upset off. Trey had done the same lots of times. As he went, a circle of streetlight lit up his chiseled face. Trey winced. The cheek Zane's father hit was bruising. It made Zane's expression seem even more set and grim. His eyes were a blue so bright it was electric.

He looked like he might do anything.

Despite suspecting it was a bad idea, Trey swung out of his bedroom window, hung by his hands, and dropped the remaining distance onto the lawn. Because he was no champion athlete, the landing stung.

By the time he'd rounded the house's corner, Zane had reached the end of their cul-de-sac. Still reluctant to call out, Trey sprinted as stealthily as he could after him. If Zane intended to throw himself off a bridge, Trey was going to stop him.

Mr. Martin's head jerked up as he dashed past in his half crouch, startled from the engrossing task of watering his boxwoods in his robe and slippers. Trey nodded as if everything were normal. Thankfully, the surprised neighbor didn't say anything.

God, this was stupid. Zane wasn't a bully, but—just on principle—he'd beat Trey senseless if he caught him stalking him. The guy was a beast, 6'2" already and solid with muscle. He was quick as well, or he'd never have pulled off playing quarterback. He'd make mincemeat of a sparely built guy like Trey.

Zane didn't seem to know he was being followed. He didn't look around as he led Trey out of their suburban neighborhood and along the shoulder of the two-lane blacktop they took to school. Zane's hands were shoved in the pockets of his dark blue hoodie, his long strong legs apparently tireless. Though Trey ran a couple miles most mornings, he was beginning to get winded.

Then again, his breathlessness might have been arousal. Masochist that he was, he'd had a boy crush on Zane for years. The occasional glimpses he'd caught of his neighbor changing spurred more fantasies than a truckload of underwear models. Trey knew for a fact Zane woke up with morning wood.

As he'd expected, Zane turned in at the high school's grounds. He headed for the track, which was empty at this hour. The chain link fence that surrounded it wasn't tall, and Zane vaulted it easily. Empty or not, the track was lit. If Trey wanted to follow his example, no way could he miss being seen.

He hesitated in the darkness. Zane unzipped his hoodie and pulled it off, revealing his monster shoulders under a white T-shirt. He crouched down to stretch his thighs. He was going to run—an activity Trey could conceivably join him in.

His heart drummed behind his ribs as he told himself not to pussy out.

"Hey," he said like he'd only then walked up and noticed Zane. "You come out here to run?"

Zane turned his head and snorted. His blackening eye confronted Trey, managing to convey sarcasm in spite of swelling up. "Don't be a tool. I knew you were tailing me since you climbed out of your window."

Trey hadn't known his cheeks could blaze quite that hot. A second later, a fierce sexual tingle streaked up his spine. If Zane had known he was there, why hadn't he stopped him?

"I was worried," he said as steadily as he could. "I heard you and your father fighting. I didn't want you to do anything crazy."

Zane let out a ragged laugh. "I guess Horny Hayworth knows a thing or two about crazy."

The nickname wasn't Trey's favorite. He wasn't as big a slut as that. He just tried not to waste opportunities. But at least Zane wasn't saying to take a hike. Trey approached the fence, stopping when he was close enough to grab its top rail. "You want to talk?"

"Fuck. What is there to say?"

"Nothing. Anything. Who cares as long as you know you're not alone?"

This might have been too touchy-feely. Zane dropped his arms and frowned. Still he didn't tell Trey to fuck off. "Your dad hits you too?"

Trey pulled up his flannel shirt to expose a fading bruise. It crossed his ribs in a purplish stripe. Maybe it wasn't appropriate to compare right then, but Trey was aware his six-pack wasn't as ripped as Zane's.

"Shit," Zane said. His fingertips touched the fence as if he'd reach through and stroke the mark. "I never hear him yelling at you."

"He's quiet. Likes to tell me I'm going to hell in a 'rational' tone. Also he doesn't drink. He avoids leaving bruises where they might show."

Zane grimaced at the reminder of his black eye. "I'm going to have to stay home from school until this looks better, and I'm already too behind. I'll lose my football scholarship if I'd don't graduate. Stupid guidance counselors are starting to give me looks. I know my dad will drag me to some other town if they confront him. This shit is so close to being over. I only have to get through this year."

Trey wrapped his fingers farther through the fence links. "You could say I did it. My GPA is okay. I'd survive a couple days suspension."

Zane's eyes widened. They were close now, not even a foot apart. Trey could smell the sweat on him from his rapid walk. "Won't your dad go ballistic?"

"He might do that anyway. It's not like he needs a real reason. If I catch shit for fighting, at least I'd know I was helping out . . . someone."

They both knew he'd avoided calling Zane a friend. Zane gnawed his full lower lip, stirring a longing to suck it that was painful.

"It'd help," he admitted. "I'm no dumb jock, but I can't miss more classes and still keep up."

"So we'll do it," Trey said. "We'll say you called my Mustang a piece of crap, and I got in a lucky shot."

"A lucky shot . . ." Zane's tone was amused.

"Wouldn't work otherwise. Everybody knows you'd take me in a fight."

Zane's gaze measured him up and down.

"Maybe," he said as Trey tensed with self-consciousness. "Maybe not. You're a fast damn bugger. I've seen you running here before."

Zane had seen him running? Zane had bothered to notice him among the usual morning crowd?

Trey took a second to close his gaping jaw. Zane wasn't paying attention to his amazement. He crossed his arms, big guns bulging under the sleeves of his white T-shirt. "You should be on the team."

"Me? Play football? You've gotta be kidding."

"I'm serious. Tony Ciccone blew out his knee last week. Coach would let you try out if I asked him to."

Only Zane could say this like it was no big deal. "No offense, but I don't think I'm the team sports type. More to the point, I'm pretty sure I'm not theirs."

"I have to pay you back somehow. I don't like being in people's debt."

Zane's bright blue eyes were stubborn . . . and maybe something else.

"You *want* me on the team," Trey blurted without thinking.

The faintest wash of color darkened Zane's cheekbones. "I wouldn't mind having someone as fast as you to back me up."

His gaze held Trey's a bit too determinedly—as if he were resisting a temptation to scope out other parts of him. Trey knew that trick. He'd used it more than once himself. Being attracted to guys *and* girls wasn't always convenient. Recognizing the look in Zane set his blood on fire, his prick stiffening so swiftly it hurt.

"Shit," Trey breathed at the inescapable conclusion. "You're bisexual like me."

Zane didn't try to deny it, though he did heave a sigh. "Don't tell," he said, sounding more resigned than anxious. "My life is complicated enough."

"Sure," Trey said, disappointed but understanding why. If his quirks hadn't tended to out themselves, wouldn't he have tried to pass for one or the other? Sometimes being bi felt the same as believing in Santa Claus. People assumed he was actually gay and trying to pretend. "Look, you mind if I join you on that side of the fence? I feel silly talking through it this way."

Zane scrubbed his short sandy hair, then waved for him to come on. Trey didn't vault over as picture-perfectly as Zane, but Zane wasn't watching anyway. He'd moved to a nearby set of bleachers to sit on the bottom bench. Trey dropped beside him, not too close but not too far. Just because Zane was bi didn't mean he wanted to do him. A trio of dry brown leaves blew across the track's asphalt, the skittering sound a counterpoint to his not-quite-normal breathing.

He knew it couldn't be normal with Zane sitting next to him.

"Sometimes I don't know who I want to kill more," Zane said. "Him for hitting me, or my mom for cutting out."

Trey wasn't sure what to say to this. Everyone in Franklin knew Zane's mom had run away to Trenton to live with some greasy guy who sold bargain mattresses. Sometimes his commercials played on late night TV.

Fortunately, Zane didn't require a comment. "What's the bruise from?" he asked.

"Belt. My dad caught me watching *Baywatch*. He's got issues about sex. No," he added in response to Zane's raised eyebrows. "Something happened when he was a kid. Now he's convinced sex is evil. He'd stop the world from having it if he could."

"Good luck with that." Zane leaned forward, forearms braced on his knees. His legs looked sexier in those worn gray sweatpants than most men's did naked. He turned his head to give Trey a sidelong glance. "I never."

Trey squinted. "You never?"

"You know: with a guy. I knew I wanted both since I was a kid. I didn't actually realize that was weird until it was too late."

Trey prayed he wasn't giving away how much this confession excited him. "You could try it out with me," he offered as casually as he was able. "See if it's worth the trouble. Unless you'd rather not."

Zane's stare was not as informative as Trey would have liked.

"If you aren't attracted to me, that's okay," he added hastily. "I know I'm not everybody's type. We can still be, well, maybe not friends exactly but—"

Zane put his hand on Trey's knee and squeezed. "You're my type," he said huskily.

Heat rolled through Trey in searing waves—up his thighs, down his chest—every drop of blood in his body trying to squeeze into his cock. His prick was so hard it was about to bust his jeans. "Really?"

His voice broke, and Zane laughed softly. His fingers squeezed Trey's knee again. "Really. I'm sorry I treat you like you're invisible. I'm sorry I didn't go to your mom's funeral last year."

Sanity-stealing lust fought with confusion inside of him. "Why would you? Even if we're neighbors, we don't really know each other."

Zane leaned over and kissed him.

That surprised him. In his experience, guys didn't always go in for kissing. Trey was glad Zane did. His lips were soft but they pushed firmly, molding over his mouth and urging it open. Trey didn't resist, a thrill shivering through him as Zane's warm wet tongue slid in. Hoping he wouldn't spook him, he cupped Zane's face. The hold steadied Zane's lean jaw, allowing Trey to participate with a minimum of good form. Since he had the chance, he took Zane's sweet lower lip and sucked.

Zane surprised him a second time by moaning.

Trey smiled at the throaty sound, which made Zane draw back an inch. "You've got a good mouth," he said defensively.

Trey snickered. "I'm glad you think so."

"You'd moan too if you'd never kissed a guy before."

"Kiss me more and I'll moan for you."

Zane gave him a disgusted look.

"Make me m-o-o-an," Trey teased, sensing he wasn't really ticked.

Zane laughed in spite of his annoyance, got a grip on Trey's ears, and went in for the kill. He kissed Trey like actors kissed women in movies—deep and hard and starving. The force he used was overwhelming but kind of great. No one had ever kissed Trey until he went dizzy.

"Crap," Trey gasped when Zane let him loose for air.

"Moan louder," Zane ordered, pushing him backward onto the bleacher to take his mouth again.

Trey was already making noises. When Zane settled over him and started grinding their hips together, they definitely turned to moans. Trey drove his hands under Zane's T-shirt, feeling up his big back muscles and urging him closer. He wanted to grab his ass, but settled for kneading the fans of muscle above it. Zane was doing fine without more encouragement. The ridge of his cock was thick—long too, from the feel of it under his sweatpants. He worked it up and down Trey's prick like he wasn't shy at all. His humping was a little awkward, but his enthusiasm felt amazing. Trey absolutely had not expected this lack of inhibition. More than happy to let all the tigers out, he bent one knee up to give Zane more access.

"Shit," Zane cursed, abruptly jerking his hips away.

Okay, maybe he'd overestimated Zane's readiness for this.

"Was that too much?" he panted. "Do you not want to feel my cock?"

Zane let out a growling noise. "I *love* your cock. I'm gonna come if we keep that up."

"So?"

"So I'm not gonna fucking rush this." Zane sat up, leaving Trey splayed on the bench. His erection throbbed like a Learjet behind his jeans. Zane looked at the giant hummock and then at him. "Unzip yourself."

Zane seemed sure, so Trey squeezed the top button free, gingerly dragging the teeth open. He'd never felt like this only from unzipping—as if every nerve was cranked to maximum sensitivity. Once his jean front was spread, Zane took over, digging into his briefs to pull his cock up and out of the stretch cotton.

The first contact of his fingers was electric—and not just for Trey.

"Oh man," Zane said, hands sliding greedily up the rod. "God, this is so gorgeous."

Trey wasn't convinced his prick was gorgeous. He was a good size, but his glans was flattish, his shaft oddly bulgy in the middle. He did pay attention to his grooming. As black as his hair was, his bush bugged him otherwise. Zane seemed to like its manscaped darkness. He combed his fingers through the short curls, then returned to fondling his dick. His thumbs rubbed a dangerously tingling circle around the head.

"Easy," Trey said shakily. "I'm close to coming too."

"Sorry." Zane let go to shove Trey's shirt to his armpits. Trey would have been disappointed, but then Zane bent to lick his breastbone, a big wet swipe like he wanted to taste his sweat. "Mm," he said, veering sideways to stroke Trey's tight left nipple. He latched on and sucked, thrumming it fast and hard with his tongue.

Trey gasped, hips thrusting helplessly upward as unexpectedly strong sensations zinged from his nipple to the knob of his cock.

"Do you like that?" Zane broke free to ask. "Girls usually seem to."

Trey barely had breath to laugh. How many times had he imagined having someone compare exactly these notes with him? This was going so much better than he'd dared fantasize. Saying *yes* with his body, he dug his fingers into Zane's hair, the way he'd dreamed of for fricking forever. Zane rotated his neck with pleasure as Trey massaged his scalp.

"That feels good," he said. "You really make me feel things when you touch me."

"You do too," Trey panted. "I guess we've got chemistry."

Zane rolled his eyes—no hearts and flowers for him—but his lips were smiling.

"Do the nipple thing again," Trey suggested. "I felt that all the way down my dick."

"Will you do it to me later?"

The hint of shyness in Zane's voice got to him even more than his oral skill.

"I'll do anything you let me," Trey promised hoarsely. "Any damn thing you can dream up."

Flashing a brilliant grin, Zane bent back to his chest.

He made Trey squirm and himself chuckle with enjoyment. "I'm going for this," he warned, beginning to move his kisses down Trey's abs.

"Uh," Trey said. Muscles in his stomach jumped from the swirly Zane's tongue drew around his navel. Zane couldn't mean he was going to blow him. That wasn't how beginners wet their toes. Then again, maybe Zane didn't care. He caught Trey's cock again, driving the sweaty heel of his palm up its underside, pushing the length into his stomach. The stroke felt amazing, especially when the edge of his hand compressed the tip.

It felt even better when Zane's tongue followed the same path.

"Zane," Trey said, his voice strangled. "We can just give each other hand jobs. You don't have to go this far your first time."

Zane licked the killing spot underneath the rim, where his foreskin would have attached if he hadn't been circumcised. "I want to. Just let me know if I screw it up."

He tucked his fingers under the shaft, tipping it back toward him. As if he knew it would make his mouth slide better, he wet his lips. Trey hitched up on one elbow so he could watch. Despite his intention to memorize every lick, his eyes nearly closed with bliss the moment Zane's sexy mouth closed on him. He had just the head in there, cradled between his tongue and his hard palate. His hand fisted Trey's root—good thing, considering how badly Trey wanted to pinball to his tonsils. When he was able to drag up his eyelids, Zane was staring at him, his mouth stretched open by Trey's cock. That visual set Trey's heart thumping harder. He wrapped his hand over the one that was straightening him.

"Keep your hold here," he rasped. "And maybe push the skin down. I like the feel of getting sucked when my dick is tight."

Zane's eyes widened, his breath speeding up. Maybe the idea that other people's mouths had been where his was turned him on. His grip grew stronger, stretching the surface of Trey's cock better than he could himself.

Trey arched his neck and groaned. "Jesus, Zane, that's perfect."

It wasn't half as perfect as when Zane slid his hot mouth down him.

Both men and women had given Trey blowjobs. He'd never failed to enjoy them, but this was an ecstasy of a different order. Zane blew him like it was a Hail Mary play he'd been visualizing. His tongue knew just where to go, his full lips forming the ideal ring for suction. Trey's nuts drew up so quickly he had to squeeze pretty hard through his jeans to pull the right one down. He'd learned the tactic helped him hold off if he felt too close to coming. When Zane saw him do it, he grabbed the other half of his sac himself.

Trey writhed like a fricking eel. Zane's pressure wasn't gentle, but Trey enjoyed an edge of pain. The entire center of his body—from his diaphragm to his thighs—sizzled with fireworks. Zane sucked him slower and wetter, his magic mouth drawing easily up and down. Trey groaned, his head rolling back and forth on the peeling paint of the bleacher bench. His left hand dug hard into Zane's hair, his right clawed around his own balls. Zane hummed around his dick like he loved every inch of it.

"Pull off," Trey warned, though he didn't truly want him to. "I haven't jacked myself in a week. I never come a damn teaspoonful."

Zane made a sound around his mouthful that sounded like *nuh-uh*. In case Trey had any doubts about his meaning, he shook his head from side to side.

The motion felt better than Trey was prepared for. It twisted Zane's tongue and lips around him like the stripes on a barber's pole.

"Fuck," he cursed. His left hand tightened on Zane's head, but Zane resisted that urging too. He stuck to his slow pace, letting his tongue caress Trey's underside tenderly. The sweetness of it killed him. Zane was into this. Maybe Zane was actually into him.

"That's good," Trey forced his vocal chords to push out. "God, Zane, that's really nice."

Zane pulled up him until the head popped out. His seductive lips shone with saliva. "I want it," he said, his pupils liquid black in the blazing blue of his eyes. "I want you to shoot down my throat."

The expression on his face made Trey's penis throb violently. Zane pushed down again before he could think what to say. His hand had slid behind Zane's neck when the football star pulled up. Now he forced himself to stop fighting, telling his body to relax and roll with Zane's motions. He caressed Zane the way Zane's tongue caressed him. Everywhere he could, Trey rubbed gently against him: inner thighs brushing ribs, fingers massaging nape. Zane uttered a little noise, like he loved the kindness and like it hurt him at the same time. Maybe the jock would be embarrassed after, but Trey didn't care. His eyes stung with feeling, his heart clenched enough to ache. The edge of the gargantuan orgasm he was riding wasn't as big as his emotions.

If he missed out on this moment, he knew he'd kick himself.

"Do me," he crooned, the words completely different ones in his head. "Do me, Zane. Make me come for you like you want."

Zane groaned and took him deeper, his wetness and his suction increasing. Trey's climax gathered, his cock twisting tight with its last warning. Zane must have felt the shaft contorting inside his mouth. His cheeks pulled close, soft, his hand releasing Trey's trapped testicle. Heat rushed outward from the freed spot. Trey gasped as his ejaculation shot from him.

It felt like a flood to him, but Zane didn't seem to mind. He sucked right through the contractions, his tongue doing things that kept Trey's climax as sharp as it could get. When it ended, Trey didn't recognize his own sigh. It was low and melodic, like he was singing his pleasure, like every muscle had released a tension he hadn't known it held. His legs lost their grip on Zane, the soles of his running shoes slapping the compacted dirt beneath the bleacher bench.

The sound seemed to wake Zane from his sucking. He let Trey's cock slip free, the thing so exhausted he couldn't even mind. With a casualness Trey found reassuring, he wiped his mouth on his T-shirt's sleeve. Then, clearly not disgusted, he turned his head to rest on Trey's sweat-streaked stomach.

"Shit," he murmured, lungs going up and down. "That was hot."

He lifted a second later, one arm reaching between his own legs to tug himself comfortable. Trey's eyebrows shot upward. "You didn't come?"

Zane looked at him and grinned. "I did. The second your big hot dick slid into my mouth. I just got hard again."

Trey was happier with this answer than he knew how to say. "You are a crazy mother. How'd you know to suck me so well?"

"It was good?"

"It was incredible. I can't believe that was your first time."

Zane hunched his shoulders, the gesture both mischievous and bashful. "I'm a big reader."

"Come on."

"Okay, maybe I watch a lot of porn. And sometimes I practice on a dildo when I jack off." Zane hid his face against Trey's stomach to laugh silently.

Trey couldn't remember ever being so entertained. "Your practice paid off." He gave in to the temptation to stroke his sandy locks. Zane used some sort of product to spike his hair, but it was still silky.

For half a minute, Zane lay still under his petting. Then he sighed and sat up. He looked down at Trey, flushed from sex but not speaking. His powerful thighs V'd around the bench, his hard-on sticking up nice and prominent in his sweatpants. Trey scratched his stomach, searching for the best approach to get a crack at it.

"I'm not as good at oral sex as you," he tried, "but I surely do like it."

Grinning, Zane slid his hands down his own torso, skirting his erection to cup and hike his balls. The lift pushed his junk forward. "I bet whatever you did would feel good to me."

Mesmerized, Trey watched his erection wagging behind the cloth. "If I did suck you, I'd get hard again."

"If you got hard again, you'd have to teach me some other way to play."

Trey had never been accused of having a poker face. Easily reading his approval, Zane dug into his sweatpants. His championship hands emerged with both his cock and balls. Trey licked his lips at the tasty sight. Zane's family jewels were as sizable as the rest of him. Even better, the big flushed head was sticky from having come. His own goodies began stirring between his legs.

"You're getting hard right now," Zane whispered.

Trey loved how awed he sounded but didn't grab for him straight away. He had a couple issues he wanted to get clear first. He sat up too, hoping this would help him think. His cock bounced higher as their knees bumped. Ignoring it, he gripped the stretch of bench between them. Zane looked at him questioningly.

"I need to know," Trey said. "Is tonight the only time we'll do this? 'Cause if it is, I'm not letting you go till dawn."

Zane dropped his hold on his cock, his fingers wrapping next to Trey's. He hesitated. "I don't want it to be. You just shouldn't expect me to, you know, ask you to go to prom."

"No," Trey agreed, though the reckless freak in him would have liked if Zane wanted that. "What I'm asking is if you want to fool around again—in private."

Zane's hands covered Trey's, squeezing them on the bench. "Yes, I really do want that."

Trey had to smile at his seriousness. "Good. I really want it too."

"So . . . it'll be our secret?" Zane's fingers stroked the dips between Trey's knuckles—as if he thought Trey needed bribing to keep quiet. Trey couldn't let this pass without teasing.

"Yup," he said. "We'll call it the bad boys club."

Trey knew Zane would think this was stupid. "We're *not* calling it that," he huffed.

"I think we are," Trey contradicted, prepared to do some bribery of his own. Amusingly, neither of their cocks was bored by the conversation. Both were sticking up and bouncing. He reached for Zane's, wrapping it in his hand and pulling toward the head. As susceptible as a virgin, Zane shuddered and closed his eyes. When Trey squeezed his fingers tighter around the rim, Zane's breath sighed out pleasurably. Deciding he had the jock where he wanted, he switched hands and pulled again. To his surprise, the pressure revealed that Zane was uncut. Trey was able to stretch his foreskin at least an inch higher. A shiver of titillation rolled down his vertebrae. He'd never had a guy with a hood before.

With some effort, he dragged his focus back on topic. "You know why we're calling it the bad boys club?"

Eyes still closed, Zane shook his head tightly. His expression was enraptured, but even rapture could be improved. Trey licked his palm, slicking it good and wet for his next caress. This time Zane squeaked as it tugged up him. Given his reaction, Trey couldn't doubt his was the first male hand to pleasure Zane's equipment.

"Why?" Zane gasped, rolling his hips higher.

"We're calling it the bad boys club so this can be our secret handshake."

In spite of his distraction, this tickled Zane's fancy. He laughed and his eyes flew open. "You're crazy."

"Crazy for you." Trey wagged his brows to make this a joke as well.

Since he hadn't minded it before, Trey smacked a kiss on Zane's mouth. Then he bent to the part of Zane they both wanted him swallowing. Zane's cock was oven-hot, his skin as smooth as satin. Trey's tongue did a happy dance over him.

"God," Zane moaned, the volume of the cry exciting. His pelvis jerked, shoving half of him inward.

Trey took him eagerly. He discovered this was extra good when you had a thing for the other person, when you weren't just sucking a cock but a cock you'd been dying for. Trey wanted to devour Zane, to pull on him with his mouth until he popped like a champagne cork. His tongue went crazy along his shaft, his hands searching out the sweetest places in the vicinity. His thumbs dug between Zane's balls, pushing through to where his cock rooted. Trey loved having his perineum rubbed. Luckily, this wasn't just a hot zone for him. Zane punched his groin upward.

He groaned Trey's name, hands urging his head closer.

"Please," he gasped, totally thrilling him. Trey sucked him harder, and Zane let out a wail.

He came like Trey had, in a burst so big it couldn't be contained, tremor after tremor milked out by his suckling. His final sigh echoed Trey's, his fingers combing Trey's hair over him.

Trey pulled gently up him, leaving one last kiss on the warm wet crown. As if it had been waiting for the salute, his cock sagged downward immediately afterward.

"Wow." Zane's breathing was ragged. "You're better at that than you gave yourself credit for."

His hand was on Trey's shoulder, gripping it like he was a teammate who'd scored a goal. Trey wanted to hug him but decided not to push. He didn't know what Zane was feeling—apart from more relaxed.

"So," he said carefully. "You want to try this again tomorrow?"

Zane flashed the devilish grin that made all sorts of heart flutter. "Screw tomorrow. Tonight isn't over yet."

CHAPTER TWO

Bad Girl

Rebecca Eilert was dreaming. Same as thousands of other girls, she danced with a famous actor who'd invited her to prom. *You look so pretty,* he said. *There's no other girl like you.* She didn't believe him. She wasn't that special, but she liked hearing it. When she laid her head on his shoulder, he rubbed her back. *Let's ask your parents if we can run away.*

The fateful words yanked her from her slumber, the slap of reality causing her heart to pound. She had no parents, and she couldn't run away.

Her mother was dead.

Her father was permanently "off on business."

Her two seven-year-old brothers only had her to take care of them.

Though no one had celebrated, her sweet sixteen had come and gone yesterday.

Oblivious to her distress, Charlie and Pete were locked in their usual morning war. Who got to use the bathroom first was a favorite squabble, along with Pete's habit of stealing his twin's backpack. Charlie *knew* which one was his because it had no rip in it. When Pete yelled at Charlie for sticking his toe across the duct tape that split their room, Rebecca wanted to yell too.

Their house had three bedrooms. None of them had to share. The problem was, not sharing meant giving up on the pretense that their father would return.

Her final image of him came back to her. He'd been standing by the front door, his overnight bag zipped and bulging by his feet on the penny tile. He was handsome—maybe a little weak, a little less pulled together since his wife had gotten too sick to spoil him. Her funeral had been a week ago to the day.

I can't handle it, Rebecca, he'd said. *Your mom being gone. You. When you try to cling to me like this, all I want to do is run.*

He'd actually shuddered. He'd been too disgusted by her needing him to hide his repulsion. In that moment, if there'd been a knife in her hand, she'd have shoved it into his heart.

How dare he make her feel like she was the needy one? Like it was her fault he was abandoning them.

Call child services, he'd said. *There'll be someone who wants the boys.*

Clearly, he couldn't conceive of anyone wanting her.

So it was on her now: taking care of the boys, of herself. As Pete and Charlie's turf war hit a new crescendo, she yanked her flowered comforter over her head. She wished she could stay under here forever, pretending everything was all right. She knew they were lucky they had the old brick row home. She wouldn't hold her breath about her dad sending money, but their mother's insurance payout covered the mortgage. They could keep the house they were used to—even the same bedrooms. As long as no one got sick and the roof didn't spring a leak, they were safe from starving.

Probably anyway.

On the bright side, she was getting really good at forging Sam Eilert's signature.

Before her stomach had time to clench, her bedroom door burst open and banged against the wall.

"We're hungry," Pete announced, finally in agreement with his brother.

Rebecca sat up and glared at him. Though she was tired and angry, her heart twisted. Pete *looked* hungry. Like his brother, he was skinny as a rail— pale too, with pinchy shadows around his eyes no boy his age should have.

"Sorry," he said guiltily, though her glower had faded. "Forgot to knock. Charlie ate the last of the cereal yesterday."

Without their mother to cook for them, cereal and milk had become their go-to meal.

I'm screwing up, Rebecca thought. *If I'm going to keep them out of foster care, I need to do better.*

"I'll make breakfast," she announced, immediately wondering if she could.

Charlie skidded down the hall in his socks and bumped into his brother. He and Pete were blond like her, but not identical. Charlie was a hair taller and had a wider, more anxious mouth. He hung his pointy chin over Pete's shoulder.

"Pancakes?" he said hopefully.

"Yes," she said with as much firmness as she could muster. "Whole wheat with syrup."

Throwing off the covers, she swung out of bed in her Dalmatian-print pajamas. She tried not to think about her mother shopping for them with her. Paula Eilert been sick already. That trip to Macy's was one of their last outings.

"We don't have syrup," Charlie said.

"I'll make that too," she declared.

Her tone must not have been as confident as she'd meant. The boys exchanged doubtful glances with each other.

"I *will*," she said. "Go set the table so I can dress."

The twins must have found a smidgen of optimism. By the time Rebecca reached the kitchen, they'd put out the plates and silver. Praying she could whip this together before the elementary school bus arrived, Rebecca set to work.

To her relief, pancakes turned out to be a cinch. She'd watched her mother prepare them so often she needed no recipe.

The syrup was trickier. Sugar dissolved in water didn't taste right at all. Trying to think fast, she chopped and threw some apples in the saucepan. Maybe a pie-filling thing would do. She'd seen her mother make them too. Muttering to herself, she rummaged through the pantry for ingredients that might work. The boys watched her dash around with big eyes, reminding her to flip the pancakes as they fluffed up and browned.

"We don't *have* to have syrup," Charlie said, trying to be helpful.

"I'm not giving up," Rebecca growled, though her apples had gone mushy. Cursing, she strained them out with a slotted spoon. That disaster discarded, she noticed the remaining juice had thickened. It smelled pretty good. Hoping to salvage something, she blew on the spoon and licked. The miracle that hit her taste buds had her gasping with excitement.

Completely opposite to her expectations, her apple syrup was delicious.

Not only that, it had an amazing texture: smooth and rich on her tongue and a zillion times better than store-bought. With a sense that the magic would disappear if she didn't hurry, she ladled her creation over the boys' pancakes.

"Eat," she urged, setting the portions in front of them.

Possibly she was acting crazy. The boys looked at her, then the food, then picked up their forks and started shoveling.

Pete was the first to pause. "Mmm," he said, a sound she wasn't certain she'd heard him make before. The noise wasn't simply pleased; it was shocked. She'd made him pay attention to what he was eating.

"Mmm," Charlie agreed, nodding emphatically. "This is better than Mom's, Becca!"

They were seven, so those were all the compliments she was getting . . . unless you counted them literally licking their plates clean.

Delighted by their reactions, she almost forgot to eat herself. When she did, she found her brain ticking through adjustments to make the dish better.

She wasn't even trying, and her mind just did it. She hadn't known it would. It seemed important. Actually, it seemed epic. Rebecca was okay at lots of things. This suggested there might be something she maybe was great at.

I could learn to really do this, she thought.

"Five minutes till the bus," Charlie broke in to say.

Charlie lived in fear of missing his ride to school. Sympathetic to the worry—because if anyone needed safe routines it was them—Rebecca handed him a damp washcloth. While he mopped the stickiness from his face, she herded her brothers out of the kitchen and down the entrance hall. On the way, she checked Charlie's precious non-ripped backpack.

"Everything is here," she assured him. Apprehension that he'd forget something was a recent tick of his. "All your books and all your supplies."

More relaxed than his sibling, Pete slung his matching sack over his shoulder. His boniness made her gladder that she'd fed him. When his clear gray eyes met hers, they seemed eerily grown up.

"We'll remember," he said before she could start her spiel. "Dad is working in Cincinnati. He called us all last night."

"Right." She bent to kiss his head. She kissed Charlie's too, holding both of them a little longer than usual.

"Bus!" Charlie said in a panic.

"All right," she surrendered, letting go to open the door for them. "You two have fun today."

They galloped down the steps without looking back, exactly like they used to with their mom. *Those boys,* her mother would sigh. *They'd run straight off a cliff if it looked fun enough.* Back then, Rebecca's brothers had seemed like pests. Today she understood her mother's concern. Pete and Charlie needed someone to be their safety net. Like it or not, she was it.

*I **will** do better,* she told herself.

From then on, whatever it took, she'd be a real parent.

CHAPTER THREE

ፆ

The Night They Met

The last four years had been the best of Zane's life. Finally free of their fathers, he and Trey had gotten into Harvard. Zane's way was paved by a football scholarship, Trey's by a special economics prize. Trey might have been more surprised than anyone that he'd won it. His essay on the correlation between macro and micro markets had been submitted by one of his teachers at Franklin High. Though Zane wasn't stupid, when he'd tried to read the doorstopper of a paper, he'd understood one word in two. The experience taught him an important lesson about his friend.

Trey Hayworth's smarts were easier for him to downplay than his sexuality.

Zane didn't hesitate to say *yes* when Trey tentatively suggested they room together off campus. Not only was this convenient for their continuing sexual hookups, but if Zane got lost in his classes, he had a built-in tutor. The arrangement turned out better than either predicted. For four years they worked and played with equal fervor, each one giving the other whatever hand he needed.

No longer a social outcast, in the university's broader atmosphere Trey blossomed into the king of the eccentrics. His gentleness attracted people . . . and his big brain. He brought his coterie of geeks and Goths to cheer Zane on the gridiron, in return for which Zane made sure every one of them was welcome at jock-thrown parties. Zane discovered his own knack for economics by starting a lucrative bookmaking enterprise. Obviously, he couldn't make book on Harvard football, but what his scholarship didn't cover, his sideline did. Even professors placed bets with him, his reputation for always paying off a matter of pride with him.

As far as it was possible for two individuals to rule a place like Harvard, Zane and Trey did. They were a familiar sight strolling Harvard Yard's leafy paths, generally shoulder to shoulder. They both liked clothes, though not the same styles of them. Zane favored Tom Ford suits while Trey was more Abercrombie and Fitch. Because Trey was Zane's odds maker, once their extracurricular work took off, they could afford to shop. They didn't pretend to be privileged; they just naturally looked it. They learned about living well by doing it—*living free*, they called it. From the best place to eat scallops to the best place to ski, they were interested. If they didn't know, they researched. Before they'd been on campus a month, people mistook them for grad students.

Neither ever went home on breaks, and both were aware they weren't missed.

Rumors cropped up now and then about the true nature of their friendship, something they chose not to comment on. Girls they enjoyed aplenty, though none of them lasted. By mutual if undiscussed agreement, the only men they slept with were each other. That source of gossip cut off, too many females heaved too many sighs over torrid trysts for anyone to conclude precisely what they were.

That was the way Zane liked it. What he felt for Trey, what he did with Trey, was his business. Well, his business and Trey's. Somehow they'd never got around to spelling out the rules exactly.

He assured himself that was his preference too.

At the moment, contrarily, he wished their association were more defined. Graduation was a week away, their classes finished, their futures twinkling brightly in front of them. Trey had accepted a position at a prestigious economics think tank in DC. Zane had played decently for the Harvard Crimson, but not at a level to turn pro. He was moving to Seattle, having been headhunted by an alum to help start a chain of fitness clubs. The work would be exciting, the responsibility more than most of his peers could boast. Nonetheless, from the moment he'd said *yes* to the CEO, depression had gripped him.

He didn't want to work for other people. He had his own dreams to chase. The fact that Trey didn't seem to mind them parting increased his dejection. He actually tried to turn down Zane for dinner, claiming he had a mountain of packing to start on. Zane had to coax him a full five minutes to get him to accept.

"We haven't tried this place yet," he said, physically tugging the moving box out of Trey's hold. "*Boston Eats* gave it a five-fork rating."

"Fine," Trey huffed. "But you're picking up the tab."

Zane had planned to. He always did when the restaurant was his choice.

Grumpy enough to bite more than food, he grabbed the keys to his Mercedes CLK and his portfolio.

"Oh no," Trey said, attempting to yank the leather case from his hand. "If I have to quit packing, you're not bringing along work."

"It's not work," Zane snapped, his patience pushed to the limit. "It's an idea I've been meaning to show you."

That shut Trey up long enough to complete the short drive. Wilde's Bistro was on Brattle in Harvard Square, housed in a less-than-lovely concrete and glass complex. The atmosphere was so-so, but the food had been drawing raves. Trey's years of waiting tables in high school had given him an interest in fine dining that Zane enjoyed sharing. They'd made it their tradition to go somewhere nice, just the two of them, once a week.

Zane damn well hated that this might be their last time.

Trey was sloppy chic tonight in tan pants and a navy sweater vest with a rumpled white shirt beneath—tails hanging, naturally. He doffed his sunglasses as they went in, his grin and wink for the very gay maître d' scoring them a window table. Tonight, that also made Zane grumpy, though—to be fair—he didn't shy from using his looks to earn a perk or two.

"You boys enjoy yourselves," their escort cooed, handing them the prix fixe menus. "I'll send your server right over."

Annoyed by the special treatment, Zane glowered at the entrees.

"Your face . . ." Trey exclaimed, chuckling. "Why do you get angry if I let some guy think he has a chance with me?"

"I don't."

"You do," he insisted. "And you don't care half as much when I flirt with girls."

Zane flipped the page back to appetizers. "I don't care about either."

Trey sat back and heaved a sigh. His hair flopped over his broad shoulders, the glossy black locks as outrageous as ever. Women went wild for the silky strands—just like they did for the Celtic tat he'd had inked onto his neck. He'd gotten the black-work knot freshman year—to prove his skin was his own, he'd said. Because Zane understood the appeal of that, he'd shut his trap on his objections. Afterwards, he'd admitted the thing was hot, but only to himself. Trey didn't need to start thinking he knew best about everything.

Clearly, he was thinking that now. "You care," Trey said quietly.

"What do you want?" Zane asked in exasperation. "Me to hold your hand in public?"

"What I want is for you to feel like you can, to not to care if people get the wrong impression—or the right one, for that matter."

"I'm not you."

"You don't need to be. Just be okay with who you are."

"Fine," Zane snapped. "Who I am is still uptight."

Trey laughed and shook his head. "Point taken," he surrendered.

Zane's irritation melted, as susceptible to Trey's grin as the maitre d'. Trey was an amazing person, and he'd gotten more so in the five years that they'd been friends. Truth be told, he was sexier at twenty-two than he'd been when they were eighteen. He was taller, more filled out in the chest and shoulder. His green-gold eyes held a self-acceptance Zane wasn't certain he'd ever share. Zane felt compelled to push life into the shape he wanted. Trey seemed content to let it unfold.

Trey leaned forward now, lightly touching the gold-haired muscles of Zane's forearm. "What did you want to tell me?"

For a couple seconds, Zane couldn't remember. Trey's expression was gentle, his eyes familiar and trustworthy. His lashes were thick and dark, his eyebrows heavy slashes above them. Those brows made him look more dangerous than he was—not unlike the masculine stubble he rarely shaved completely. Then again, maybe Trey's gentleness was the danger, sucking a person in, letting him think he'd stick around forever. A tingle spread from the place Trey brushed with his fingertips, pleasant sensations sliding smoothly across his skin until his cock gave a good hard twitch.

If they'd been alone, he'd have French-kissed Trey, then fucked him like a sailor over the nearest chair.

"The portfolio?" Trey reminded. "You said it wasn't work."

"Oh, excuse me," said a soft female voice. "If you're not ready to order, I can come back."

Trey glanced at the waitress before he did. Because Zane was looking at Trey, he witnessed the subtle shock that snapped through him.

"*Hello,*" Trey said, his eyes widening.

Zane jerked his gaze to the waitress too. She was on the small side; younger than they were, he thought—though he couldn't be positive. Zane and Trey usually came off as older than their years. This girl had gamine cut blonde hair, big gray eyes, and a mouth so soft and pink it could have been candy. Her Wilde's Bistro apron made it hard to tell, but he thought her rack was good.

"I'm Rebecca," she said. "If you like, I can tell you the specials."

"*Please,*" Trey said, like it was really important.

Zane looked at him sharply. His roommate's voice had dropped lower than normal.

Rebecca rattled off the specials, then pushed her pencil eraser into her bottom lip. In spite of the situation, interest zinged along Zane's nerves. She truly did have a stellar mouth. "I'm not supposed to tell you this, but you really shouldn't order the lobster."

"We shouldn't," Trey repeated.

The short waitress shook her head. "There was a screw up with our purveyor. All we've got today is frozen."

Trey planted his elbow on the tablecloth and his chin in his hand. The position turned him toward Rebecca, silently declaring: *I'm all yours, sweetheart.* "Frozen lobster so close to Maine is blasphemy."

Flustered by his attention, Rebecca pulled her order pad to her cushy chest. "The striped bass is good. And the duck breast, though it's not on special. One of the senior line cooks makes it. He's got a knack."

Trey's smile couldn't have been more salacious if she'd been discussing sex. "You seem familiar with the kitchen."

He must have been giving her his best smolder, because the girl's breath hitched. "I cook on the line for lunch. I serve dinner because the tips are good."

"People *are* more generous once they've survived a day at work."

Trey wasn't simply playing his fellow wait staff card, he was crooning at her. The girl began to flush, but stopped herself with a laugh. "Alcohol doesn't hurt either."

Trey smiled at her humor. For all the pair noticed, Zane could have been invisible. He'd watched his friend flirt before, but disappearing himself was a new experience.

"We'll take the duck to share," he cut in. "And the smoked cod tartine to start."

"Oh." The girl shifted her gaze to him, her smile faltering as she recalculated them being a couple. Recovering, she scribbled down what he'd said. "And you?" she asked Trey. "Would you like an appetizer?"

"The terrine of foie gras." After all these years of fine dining, the French pronunciation rolled off his tongue. "We'll get back to you on the wine." His tone was soft, his penetrating green eyes reclaiming their intimate hold on hers. The girl's soft mouth parted, as if she saw something in his consideration that perplexed her. For a couple seconds, the pair stared at each other.

"I'll . . ." She cleared huskiness from her throat. "I'll put your tickets in right away."

As she spun jerkily and walked off, Zane struggled with his shame. "She was cute," he observed, some part of him unable to leave dogs sleeping.

"She was," Trey agreed, now perusing the wine list. His manicured index finger trailed as smoothly down the page as it could stroke an erection. He didn't mention that Zane had effectively cock-blocked him.

That meant Zane really was obliged to act mature.

"You could probably get her number."

Trey looked up and smiled. He seemed to know what had just happened —even if Zane preferred not to sort it out. "What's in the portfolio?"

"Oh. It's . . . a business proposal I wanted your feedback on it."

The weird exchange with the cute waitress seemed to be over. Trey traded the wine list for Zane's zippered leather case. He opened it, pulled out the stack of bound pages, and flipped through them. Though his movements were swift, Zane knew his friend was reading.

As he did, his expressive lips began curving. "You want to call your business The Bad Boys Club?"

"It conveys a feeling. Exclusive but still fun."

"I agree." Trey turned a few pages back and forth. "This is a big plan, Zane. A magazine. Luxury vacation properties." His saturnine eyebrows quirked. "A fleet of fractional jets?"

"I want to create a brand. I wouldn't try to do everything at once."

Trey closed the neat report. "You'd start with the magazine."

"Yes." Zane was relieved he saw it the same way. "I know magazines are risky, but this one is designed to be ad heavy. We'd do articles on the coolest expensive watches or the best wines for impressing your girlfriend. So many people are insecure about spending money. Whether they have a lot or a little, they want to know they're buying the right things. Of course there aren't 'wrong' things, but they want someone to guide them. People who won a bet were always asking my opinion on how to celebrate. It was like they needed my approval."

A grin slanted Trey's mouth. "That's because you're the lucky stiff whose shoes they wished they could walk in."

Zane didn't take offense. He knew Trey's teasing was meant fondly. "I want The Bad Boys Club to represent a lifestyle. Work hard. Play hard. Look good while you're doing both. I was thinking . . ." He hesitated, because this pushed the edge of his comfort zone. "Every so often, we'd do a spread with skin appeal: the best nude beaches in Europe, the hottest soccer players with their shirts off. We'd draw in male and female readers. Everybody likes visuals."

"You mean everybody likes eye candy." Trey laughed, patting the tablecloth to either side of Zane's report. "You'd totally have to be the first cover boy."

"Me?" Zane jerked straighter. He hadn't thought of this.

"Absolutely. You *are* the brand you're talking about: the guy women want to bed and men want to hang out with. I can completely see you pulling this off. Like Oprah with testicles."

Zane choked on the water he'd been sipping. "Thank you for that image."

Trey leaned across the table to grip his hand, passion animating his eternally interesting face. "You can do this, Zane. This is so not beyond your capacity."

"I want you to do it with me," Zane admitted.

Trey's jaw dropped, his eyes gone round. His throat moved like he was having trouble deciding how to respond. Abruptly nervous, Zane pulled his hand back from him.

"I know you're excited about working in DC. You'll probably be advising senators before the week is out. The thing is, you'll have more fun if you stick with me."

Trey sat back and blinked at him.

"Full partners," Zane went on stubbornly. "You wouldn't be working for me like you did on the bookmaking. We'd be an equal team."

Trey's green eyes welled up. "Well," he said, blinking them again rapidly. "I wasn't expecting this."

"Think about it," Zane said gruffly. "We don't have to stop being partners just because we're leaving school."

"Right." Laughing softly—possibly at himself—Trey picked up his napkin and pressed it to his face.

"Uh," said the waitress, choosing then to come up. "Did you decide on the wine?"

Trey laughed harder and dropped the shield for his expression. "Rebecca," he said, looking at her directly despite his emotion. "We'd love it if you'd bring us a bottle of the Les Belles Filles Burgundy."

Zane reminded himself Trey usually remembered server's names.

"That'll complement what you ordered." Rebecca sounded like she knew . . . and like her customers ought to care. Evidently, she had confidence in her taste. "Shall I bring the bottle with the main course?"

"Please," Trey said. The pair traded smiles, not as flirtatious as before but like they approved of each other and were enjoying it.

Zane bit his tongue against interrupting their mutual admiration society. If Trey wanted to make time with this girl, that wasn't his concern. Because of who they were sexually, they couldn't supply each other with everything they craved. Given a choice, neither would give up women as bed partners.

"I'll take care of it," Rebecca said, tapping her pencil crisply against her pad.

Maybe consciously or maybe not, as she walked off, Trey turned to watch her butt twitch in her plain black trousers. When she'd disappeared past a couple tables, he returned his gaze to Zane.

"I'll think about your offer. I expect you could use an answer soon."

"Soon would be good," Zane conceded, "but take the time you need."

Privately, he'd expected—hoped?—Trey would jump at the opportunity. Did his delay mean he was searching for a way to refuse? Would Zane feel half as excited about his dream if his best friend weren't living it with him?

Uncomfortable with his doubts, he squirmed like a five-year-old through dinner, which—despite being tasty—couldn't hold his attention. Trey *mm*'ed and savored per usual. The waitress and he didn't share any more moments. Zane couldn't decide if he felt relieved or guilty.

Since Zane was paying, Trey left the tip. Zane believed in being generous, but the pair of hundred dollar bills Trey pulled from his wallet raised even his eyebrows.

"The service was good," Trey said as he stood. "Plus, she seemed like she could use it."

His gaze evaded Zane's, not a reassuring development. Just how sparked by this girl was he?

"Okay," Zane said, wondering if he should say more. In the end, he decided no comment was safer. They walked out onto the street where the sun had set and the temperature was cooling. The commercial area was popular. Shoppers and diners came and went. Zane paused on the sidewalk, squinting through the streetlights to see if he could spot stars. They were blurry, but he found a transparent three-quarter moon.

Please say yes, he thought silently to his friend.

Trey stepped closer to him, the back of his hand brushing the back of Zane's. Traffic rolled by, some of the cars recognizably driven by students. In a what-the-hell reaction, Zane wove their fingers together.

Trey bumped his shoulder companionably.

"I want to do it," he said. "The thing is, I'm sure I haven't saved as much money to invest as you."

Zane's heart jumped inside his chest. "Your brain is worth more than mine."

"True," Trey agreed.

Zane turned to him, wanting to kiss his sly smirk so badly he hurt.

"Careful," Trey teased, the smile deepening. "You look like you're on the verge of a PDA."

Zane growled deep within his belly, beginning to tug Trey urgently toward their parking spot. He hadn't realized he was getting hard while it happened, but now his cock pounded. Trey laughed, guessing exactly where the night was going.

Zane was so eager it took two tries to unlock the silver convertible.

"I can drive," Trey offered, not hiding his amusement.

"I'm faster," Zane refused.

Trey didn't wait for Zane to get through the next intersection before he reached past the armrest and manhandled his erection.

"Crap." Zane's foot slipped off the gas pedal, causing the car to jerk. Because he was an excellent driver, he recovered without an accident. When Trey curled his fingers tighter and massaged, he was prepared for the knee-weakening wash of bliss.

"Just trying to help," Trey purred, rippling his hold again. "You looked like you were having trouble . . . containing your excitement."

"When we get home," Zane warned, "I'm going to fuck you so hard your head will spin."

This was no dissuader for his roommate. Trey squirmed closer on the seat, leaning toward Zane until his lips brushed his ear warmly. "Promise I won't be able to walk straight?"

"Yes," Zane confirmed through clenched teeth.

He drove carefully enough not to kill them. Trey's hand never left his crotch—squeezing, kneading, dragging all ten fingernails over the hardened ridge. Only when Zane's breath hissed inward did Trey's technique gentle. He rubbed Zane's erection gently with the heel of his palm. A quick check of Trey's lap told Zane he was sporting a big hump too.

Sweat broke out on Zane's forehead.

"I could suck you off while you're driving," Trey whispered in Zane's ear. "I could just lean over and unzip you with my teeth."

Zane's hard-on throbbed as if a very pleasurable knife had stabbed it. They were two blocks from the old triplex in which they lived.

"If you make me shoot before we get behind closed doors, I'm fucking going to kill you."

Trey was a master at knowing when to back off. Smiling like the Cheshire cat, he released Zane's tormented dick and lounged against his door.

"I have my own surprise for you." He slid one hand down the bulge in his smooth tan pants. His fingers were together, his palm absolutely flat. The ridge he pushed against barely budged.

"I've seen your prick before," Zane said even as his mouth watered.

Trey rubbed his hand down and up again. "You haven't seen my prick like it is tonight. Trust me, you're going to beg to give me a blow job."

Zane shuddered as Trey's tongue swept around his lower lip. Dragging his attention back to the street, he gripped the steering wheel white-knuckled. Their neighborhood in Cambridge was residential, many of the old three-story houses providing rentals for students. Short on driveways, parallel parking was the norm. Miraculously, Zane got the Mercedes into its spot with one try.

Continuing to look at Trey seemed like a bad idea. As he jogged up the steps of the old house's wooden porch, he felt as if a foot-long hammer were wedged in his underwear.

"Get the lead out," he called to Trey, who was strolling more leisurely behind him.

Still on the middle of their front walk, in full view of any neighbors who might be peeking out their windows, Trey reached into his trousers to adjust his boner.

The wave of heat that rushed to Zane's core seared him.

He fumbled over opening the deadbolt just as he had the car. Luckily, he and Trey rented the first floor. They didn't have any more stairs to run up or doors to unlock.

When Trey finished sauntering to the porch, Zane grabbed his wrist and yanked him in after him. Trey stumbled, but only until Zane caught him. Their combined weights slammed the door behind them.

The kiss that ensued was equatorial. Zane flattened Trey against the wood, grinding their groins together and eating at his mouth. Zane was only a little taller and barely had to bend his knees to match up their erections. Rarely shy about touching Zane, Trey climbed him with one leg and clutched both octopi arms around his back.

Zane relished the way they groped him.

"God," Trey sighed, his neck arching back, his right hand urging Zane's ass to rock harder. "I am so fucking hot for you."

Past waiting any longer, Zane tore free and started ripping off his own clothes. As he did, he backed toward the living room. He loved fucking Trey over the arm of the button-tufted leather Chesterfield, the height being exactly right for them. He toed off his black Pradas, then braced on a chair to peel off his socks.

"Hurry," he said to Trey, because he was barely done unbuttoning his shirt.

Zane shucked his trousers, leaving himself in nothing but underwear.

Seeing this, Trey pressed his hand to his heart and smiled. "You wore my favorites."

The boxer briefs were black Calvin Kleins with a white waistband. Zane preferred Hugo Boss, but Trey had fetishized the former brand during his teenage jack off days. Exploiting this, Zane teased his fingers under the stretchy band. "Why don't you finish stripping and then help me?"

That spurred Trey to undress with greater efficiency. He left his briefs on like Zane: white snug cotton that glowed against his bronzed hair and skin. Because he'd adjusted his cock outdoors, the head of the thick stiff rod—now leaning slightly to the left—stuck out above the top. Zane loved everything about Trey's penis: the slightly flattened breadth of the crest, the strength of the veins, the way his shaft swelled in the middle when he was extra excited. It was swelling now, behind the soft cotton. His cock was big, maybe bigger than Zane's. Since Trey was leaner, it seemed so.

Zane couldn't take his eyes off the sexy monster as Trey approached.

He touched Zane's waist when he arrived, fingers rubbing his skin softly. His tenderness might have been the only thing that could drag Zane's gaze upward.

"Take yours off first," Trey said. "My surprise is under mine."

"You've really got a surprise."

"I really do," Trey said.

Zane kissed him, lips molding over his lover's gently, hands flattened for balance behind his shoulder blades. The girl-soft kiss was more Trey's style than his. When he let go, Trey was starry-eyed. Pleased with himself, Zane shucked his briefs, spun them around one finger, then plopped himself bare-ass naked on the couch.

"All right," he said, arms and legs akimbo on the leather, "show me what you've got in there."

Trey shoved the white briefs down his legs. Zane noticed his bare cock first, this being the natural magnet for his interest. He took a moment to realize Trey's pubes were shaved.

Then he saw the outline of the ornate monster.

"Holy fuck," he said, scooting forward on the cushion.

Trey had a new tattoo, a black Chinese dragon a bit smaller than Zane's hand running up the left half of his abdomen. This was no press on. The skin around the design was pink from healing. The dragon's tail curled around the hefty base of Trey's erection, the final pointy tip extending onto his penile skin on the underside. Zane's breath hissed in at the thought of artist's needle shooting ink into him there.

Getting this tattoo must have burned like a mother.

Zane's penis lurched out so hard it felt like it was burning too. His hands seemed to find their own way onto Trey's thighs, stroking the hairy muscles there. He swallowed, more turned on than he knew how to describe.

"It's not complete yet," Trey said, his voice softened by shyness. "I could only stand to have one color done for the first session. You'll see the letters more clearly once the green and red are there."

There were letters? Trey's erection cast a shadow from the light on the end table. Zane pushed his shaft gently to the side so he could see better. He was panting and couldn't seem to stop. Somehow, he thought Trey would forgive him.

And there they were: an intertwined *Z* and *T* worked into the dragon's body. The lettering was fancy, hard to read unless you knew to look for it.

"It's for me," Trey said. "To always remember us. No one else will guess it's there."

Zane throat threatened to close up. Fuck, Trey was sweet sometimes. He didn't know how to thank him, though he was going to try. He looked up, knowing his emotions shone naked in his eyes. "When did you get this done?"

"Last week. I kept wondering if you'd notice I was avoiding you in bed."

"Oh I noticed." Zane laughed ruefully at himself. "Why do you think I've been in a shit mood lately?"

"Because you thought we were going our separate ways."

"Didn't that upset you?"

"Yes," Trey said. "Why do you think I wanted a memento—especially one that was guaranteed to get you hot under the collar."

Zane frowned, but Trey wasn't fooled.

"Come on," he said. "You think I haven't noticed how much you like my neck tat? You hardly ever nuzzle the other side. It's always the inked one you're licking up."

Zane shook his head. "You are too smart for me."

Trey didn't say *of course*, just tipped his head endearingly to the side. "Want to christen my cock art?"

In case Zane couldn't figure out what he meant, he poked the tip of his tongue out. That this was a cheap trick didn't matter. Zane's groin tightened with excitement.

"Yes," he said huskily. "I want to lick you until you're dripping . . . and then I want you to fuck me."

Trey's grin had been widening, but at this it faltered. "Really? I thought you didn't like being fucked."

Zane had a thing about pitching versus catching, but maybe it was time he got over it. Trey taking him wouldn't make him less of a man. Trey couldn't make anyone less than they were.

"I want you to," he said, his ass going weirdly hot. "It wouldn't hurt you too much, would it? Since your tattoo is still healing?"

"Oh boy." Trey dragged his thumb and fingers down the sides of his expressive mouth. He had long creases there when he smiled, like dimples on steroids.

"What?" Zane asked, because Trey looked sheepish. "Should we save this for another night?"

Trey shook his head and laughed breathily. "Here's the thing: If fucking you hurts me a little, it'll get me extra hot."

Zane didn't think of Trey as a guy who kept secrets. His face gave him away too easily. Zane's obvious amazement must have embarrassed him. Trey's face turned redder than his cockhead.

"I don't mind that," Zane hurried to reassure him. "I'm just surprised you kept this to yourself."

Trey didn't explain why he had. He grabbed Zane's hands, hauling him off the couch and kissing him thoroughly. Zane enjoyed that, but didn't forget his agenda.

"Phew," he said, disengaging his tingling lips. Their groins were plastered together, their long naked cocks squashed as close as possible. Zane wondered if his curls were chafing Trey's waxed skin—and if this was good or bad. Whatever the answer, Trey was revved. His slit was leaking a steady trickle of pre-cum.

Loving that, Zane rubbed the moisture slowly across their side-by-side dick heads.

Dropping his gaze to watch, Trey bit out a breathless curse.

"Stay," Zane ordered, sitting back on the couch himself.

He kept his hold on Trey's hands, fingers locked to form conjoined fists. Normally, he'd have gripped the base of Trey's penis before he went down on him, but he trusted him not to over thrust. The gamble had a nice payoff. Trey's fingers tended to telegraph every shift in his tension. They tightened like iron when Zane's mouth sank over him.

Trey sighed as sweetly as if it were his first time.

Zane never lost his enthusiasm for this act. Sucking Trey's cock was his idea of heaven. Tonight, it looked like his friend wasn't destined to last long. His moans grew louder, his fingers clenching Zane's as his thighs knotted. Taking pity, Zane switched to lapping the flat of his tongue up him.

Trey's body undulated from knees to chest.

Laughing, Zane sat back with his legs sprawled. His cock could have been a pole planted at his crotch. "You're not up for teasing right now, are you?"

Trey shook his head and panted.

Zane was going to do it anyway. Sliding off the couch, he kneeled on the carpet to nip and kiss Trey's hipbone. Trey had a sexy muscle that swooped and fell around it. Zane mouthed his way along it until he reached Trey's dragon. With a little prayer that he hurt him the right amount, he pulled his tongue across the slightly hotter skin where the tattoo artist had performed his magic.

Once he'd left a trail of wetness, he blew on it.

Trey shuddered, fingers gripping Zane's hard enough to hurt. Zane's cock began to tremble, sympathetically excited. The tattoo made this better, the knowledge that his lover could not only take the pain but actually got off on it. Maybe this said weird things about Zane's kinks, but he couldn't help enjoying that Trey was tough. Again Zane licked, a longer swipe this time . . .

Then he dragged his tongue to the very tip of the dragon's tail.

"Stop," Trey begged, a mere breath of air. "I'm too close to going."

Zane stopped. He wanted Trey to last too. "You ready to take me then?"

"*I'm* ready," Trey said. "You need a bit of prep."

Zane and Trey's two-bedroom apartment was their sanctum. They didn't bring female dates here, and only close friends hung out. Because of this, they didn't hesitate to stock every room with supplies. Considering how much they liked sex, they never knew where the mood would strike.

Trey reached into the end table drawer for KY and Trojans. Tossing them to Zane, he shifted the lamp and table out of their way. Making sure they didn't trash their belongings was usually Zane's job. Watching Trey's arm muscles tighten with the familiar task sent an odd thrill through him.

"Stand," Trey said. His voice was every bit as authoritative as Zane's could be. "I'm going to fuck you over that couch arm."

Zane stood. His legs were stiff as he moved into the specified position, his forward bend on the padded leather unavoidably awkward. This was Trey's place, exactly to a T. Zane rested his weight on his elbows, craning his head around as his friend stepped closer.

"Good," Tray praised, sliding both hands around Zane's butt cheeks. His palms were warm, his caress admiring.

He took the lube away from Zane's hand.

Zane had engaged in butt play a time or two—a thumb crooked into his hole to excite him, a lick that skirted the forbidden. Until tonight, that was as far as it went. Trey had never stuck a finger all the way in before, much less one coated in warm lube. Zane must have been readier than he knew. His body didn't resist the smooth intrusion.

"God," he said, squirming helplessly. His interior tingled around Trey's knuckles, and his cock had begun to drip. "Jeez, Trey, that feels so good."

Trey bent over to kiss his nape, hot breath stirring the short hairs there. "Want to try another finger before you take my dick?"

Zane did and didn't, his every erotic nerve suddenly impatient. "Yes," he said, because he had to give some answer.

Trey pulled out, squeezed more lube down his crack. His way prepared, he pushed two fingers into him. That was even better. Zane groaned, his spine arching with pure need. Seeming to understand what he wanted, Trey moved his slick fingers. He curved them to match Zane's passage, their probing almost too gentle. Gentle or not, they felt incredible. In and out they rubbed —deep, slow—sending waves of feeling through his body.

Zane gritted his teeth with pleasure, helpless to keep his moans inside. "Tell me, Trey. Why did I . . . wait so long to do this?"

Trey laughed and pulled his fingers out, eliciting a small whine from Zane. Paper ripped. Trey had grabbed a towelette packet to wipe his hand.

"Nothing wrong with waiting until you're ready." To Zane's relief, Trey's voice was thick with anticipation. "You're bound to enjoy it more this way."

Zane was already enjoying it. He still held the box of condoms, his tensed-up hand having crumpled the cardboard. Trey rescued the squashed package and took out what he needed.

Unable to resist, Zane turned his head to watch. As graceful as a sculptor smoothing a length of clay, Trey rolled the latex on.

"Now I know I'm big," Trey said, stroking his shaft more than he had to. "I promise you, though, you can take my mighty sword. You don't have to worry about swooning."

"Fuck," Zane said, startled into a laugh.

Seeing his joke was appreciated, Trey grinned broadly. His *mighty sword* sheathed and ready, he cruised his hands gently up Zane's back. "I love you," he said. "I'm really glad you're ready to try this."

He said this as easily as Zane would wish him luck on an exam. He seemed not to realize hearing it would stun Zane. Trey loved him? Trey wanted to say it? Zane knew they were best friends; more than friends, truthfully. Nonetheless, those words rocked his foundations.

"Shush," Trey said, amusement crinkling his eyes. "That's a freebie. No need to think about it too hard."

"I—"

"Shush," Trey repeated before he could stammer. "New rules are I get to say what I like when I'm fucking you."

"You're not fucking me yet," Zane returned weakly.

Trey leaned down to nip his shoulder. "Hairsplitter," he mocked him.

He drew his hands to Zane's ass, pulling his cheeks apart. "Push out a little," he said. "My cock is wider than my fingers."

It was wider, but by God it felt good. Being taken was different than being the one in charge. Something in Zane, something not of the body, felt like it was giving way. He was trusting Trey, more than he ever had before. Maybe it should have alarmed him, but that pleasure was as intense as the rigid pole pushing into him. Trey obviously liked penetrating him. Zane heard the hitch in his breathing, the little moan of bliss that caught in his throat.

"Okay," Trey panted, once he was halfway in. "Your erection might flag a little, but trust me it will come back."

Caught beneath the Chesterfield's soft roll arm, Zane's erection was solid as granite. "Um," he said, "I think my libido is skipping past that part."

He arched to take more of Trey, the shift in angle allowing the other man to glide in all the way. That felt so awesome they moaned in chorus.

"You okay?" Trey panted.

"Yes." Zane couldn't help squirming. Stretched by Trey's huge erection, he couldn't decide if his back passage itched or just felt wonderful. "You?"

Trey's ragged breathing broke up his laugh. "My tattoo stings a little. It's really making me hot."

Him saying so made Zane's toes dig into the plush carpet. He swung one arm back to latch onto Trey's hip. "Please don't wait. Please fuck me right away."

Trey trailed his fingertips up Zane's arm. "Okay," he said, bending to kiss Zane's shoulder. "You don't have to hold me, though. I promise I'll get you where you need to go. Your first time, you should just relax and enjoy."

Zane let go reluctantly. Leaving everything up to Trey didn't sit naturally with him. With a quiet grunt of approval, Trey slid one arm beneath Zane's chest, hugging him firmly for leverage. His other hand gripped the couch cushion. Something about the sight was unbelievably sexy. Their bodies situated, Trey retreated to Zane's brink. Zane sank his teeth in his lip, dying for the pulsing organ to drive back in.

Trey rocked forward with the perfect amount of *oomph* to push a gasp from him.

Trey didn't ask Zane if this felt good. Zane wasn't *his* first, and he knew what he was doing. He repeated the thrust instead, building speed, building force, until Zane's moans began sounding crazed. Trey had found his prostate. The flare of his glans ran repeatedly over it, the fatter center of his shaft adding a wonderful extra pressure to the proceedings. Zane even liked the smoothness of Trey's shaven groin slapping him.

"I can . . . rub your cock," Trey offered, his chest wall tight behind him. "Sometimes taking it in the ass . . . isn't enough to bring guys off."

In Zane's experience, it was always enough for Trey.

"There's no wrong answer," Trey assured him when he hesitated. "Ask for . . . whatever seems good to you."

Zane didn't get a chance. Trey shifted his legs apart, maybe to improve his balance, or maybe just because. The move stretched Zane's legs wider. His feet were stuck in the broadened stance, held in place by Trey's weight and position. The sensation of being trapped heightened his awareness of Trey pumping inside him. Zane's throat went tight, his lungs struggling to get air fast enough.

Did Trey know what he'd just done to him? If he did, he'd done something to himself as well. His thrusts came harder, his hips slinging jerkily inward. The leather couch cushion creaked from the strength with which he gripped it. He was breathing as raggedly as Zane.

"Hold my cock." Zane panted out the order, sensing Trey didn't have much longer. "Hold it . . . really tight and don't rub."

Trey released the couch cushion, fumbling under his partner to get a grip on him.

Trey's fingers tightened and Zane cried out. His next cry was even hoarser, because of course Trey wasn't satisfied with a simple hold. He'd always been fascinated by Zane's foreskin. Now he cinched it with thumb and forefinger, forcing the retracted hood back above the flare. He shimmied it around Zane's glans, pleasure stinging the sharpest nerves he had.

"Take it," Trey urged, his hips and his voice gone wild. "Fucking take your climax. Fucking come over my fingers."

Trey's own words did a number on himself. He shoved hard, his cum flooding Zane with heat. The final jump and swell of his cock pushed against Zane's prostate.

"Zane!" Trey cried, pulling back two inches and slamming in again.

Zane's heart thumped a mile a minute, the ache in his lower torso deliciously suspenseful. About to die if he didn't come, he threw back his head and bucked as hard as he could into Trey's next thrust.

The orgasm seemed to explode inside his brain.

He spurted over Trey's fingers, spraying the couch, the rug—hell, maybe half of Boston. This was a colossal ejaculation, more than could be accounted for by the week he'd gone without. Trey had touched off a switch inside him, and possibly in himself. That they'd been fucking each other five years now didn't seem to matter. The twists and turns of their kinks still had some surprises left.

They both were shaking when Trey sank over him.

"Jesus," he said, dragging his lax mouth across Zane's sweat-streaked skin. "Tell me I didn't hurt you at the end."

"You didn't hurt me," Zane slurred obediently.

Trey pulled out with a groan, dropping from where he was to sit on the floor. "I don't think I can stand up."

Without his weight, Zane felt as light as air. He squirmed fully onto the couch, then turned himself around. Trey's damp dark head was near enough to pet.

"Thank you," Zane said. He meant for everything: the last five years, tonight, the future they were going to share together. Zane might not have cornered the market on introspection, but he knew this was a rare moment. In this moment, his life was very close to perfect.

As if he sensed his thoughts, Trey drew Zane's hand down and kissed its palm.

Emotion overwhelmed him. How could he deserve this man? Trey's kindness alone was humbling, his ability to forgive. Trey never held back his affection, no matter what Zane did. In the face of that, Zane had no right to deny him anything he wanted.

"We could go back to Wilde's tomorrow," he offered impulsively. "See if the lobster is fresh yet."

Trey hesitated for one heartbeat. "No," he said. "I expect we'll be too busy to try their food again."

CHAPTER FOUR

Chef

Rebecca's heart pounded way too fast as she opened the passenger door and hopped out of the delivery van. Her head chef Raoul was driving, taking time off to help her. She owed him big for this, especially since—strictly speaking—he didn't work for her anymore. In the back of the van was his strapping son Dominic. They'd double-parked in the financial district, a busy area of Boston that mixed Colonial buildings and skyscrapers. Because Raoul couldn't leave the wheel, Dominic was helping her offload her two shrink-wrapped six-foot-tall supply carts. Neatly packed onto the steel shelves was everything she needed for today's menu. She knew this because she'd checked the contents as obsessively as her brother Charlie used to check his backpack for school.

She couldn't afford to forget anything today. Every detail had to go perfectly.

She wiped sweaty palms on her clean black trousers, then grabbed the back end of the first cart to guide it down the van ramp with Dominic. He grinned at her, a nice kid who adored his talented father and seemed likely to follow in his footsteps. Once the second cart joined the first on the hot sidewalk, he flipped the ramp up and slammed the doors.

"Knock him dead, chef," Raoul called out the driver's window. Though they were friends, he often called her that. Coming from him, the title was a cross between "boss" and "hon."

Grimacing at the butterflies in her stomach, she acknowledged his well wishes with a wave before he drove off. God, she hated being this nervous.

"You'll be fine," Dominic assured her like he was sixty and not sixteen. "You've done this sort of thing, what, two-and-a-half zillion times?"

"Pipsqueak," Rebecca retorted as they shoved the carts toward the entrance of TBBC's corporate headquarters. She might have done this a zillion times, but never with so much riding on the result. "If their kitchen sucks, I'm not letting you forget it for a year."

The building's doorman trotted over to open the non-revolving door. His charcoal gray uniform was sharp, his buttons bright enough to blind. Trey Hayworth and TBBC didn't do anything half-assed. She'd need her A-game to get this job with him.

Inside, the circular air-conditioned lobby was just as intimidating—soaring steel and glass and Carrara marble stretching to a hundred-foot atrium. Her mind boggled at the thought that two Jersey boys who'd barely cracked the age of thirty were responsible for Beantown's latest architectural marvel. The spread she'd read in *Boston Magazine* claimed the pair had been integral to the design process, and that Hayworth in particular had caught an engineering miscalculation that would have resulted in large stretches of windows popping out in high winds. If she'd been applying for an architectural position, she'd probably have quailed before she set foot inside.

You're a genius at what you do, she tried to remind herself. *No one cooks for Bostonians like you.*

Unless they did, and she'd been deluded all this time.

The stupid thought sank her stomach. God, please, let her not screw this up. She couldn't beg that bastard Titcomb to take her back on staff, not if it meant working under the dumbass dickhead he'd hired to be her supposed boss. Titcomb liked the guy because he'd won some reality TV show. However he'd managed that, it wasn't by cooking well. The only thing sadder than his overworked, over-seasoned dishes was watching him try to impress Wilde's crew with his "credentials." She knew the veteran cooks were hoping she'd get this job and could bring them over. Titcomb would be lucky if the new guy didn't drive him out of business within the year.

Not that she'd be there to see it.

Molars grinding, she pushed her cart beside Dominic's across the shiny lake of imported stone. The wheels bumped slightly at the lobby's center where the company's elegant gold logo was inlaid.

"Ms. Eilert?" said a security guard in a suit. He'd stepped out from behind his desk before they could reach it. He was trim and polite, his wireless earpiece adding to his professional air. "We're holding the freight elevator for you if you'd like to follow me."

"See," Dominic murmured. "No way is this place's kitchen going to suck."

Rebecca smiled, amused by his confidence—despite her ability to be neurotic under almost any conditions. Calm at least for the moment, they and their carts made it to the twentieth floor before her palms broke into a sweat again.

She forgot they were damp the moment she caught a glimpse of where she'd be working.

"Whoa," Dominic said, coming to a halt behind her.

TBBC's corporate kitchen was a palace. Impeccably equipped, every pot, every burner, every inch of burnished steel worktop was spotless. Rebecca's entire brigade from Wilde's could have cooked here with room to spare— assuming she still had a brigade, of course.

"The walk-in is that way," the suited guard informed her, gesturing toward its door. "Feel free to use anything in it. Mr. Hayworth has cleared his schedule for 1:30. If you suspect your food won't be ready, please use the phone on the wall to warn his assistant."

"I don't think that will be a problem." Rebecca was slightly breathless from the lovely toys around her.

The guard smiled at her. "Good luck," he said, exiting politely.

"Am I staying?" Dominic asked, hardly containing his eagerness.

The terms of Rebecca's tryout allowed her an assistant. She'd been planning to do everything herself. When you had her experience, creating a tasting menu for just one person wasn't overly difficult. On the other hand, Dominic had sufficient training from his father to carry off simple sauces and fine chopping. Seeing his pleading look, she remembered how eager she'd been to learn when she was his age. If he stayed, she'd have to keep her nerves wrapped up for his sake—which might not be a bad thing.

"You'll do what I say?" she asked, pointing her sternest chef's finger. "No getting 'creative' with my instructions?"

Practically bouncing, Dominic crossed his heart.

"All right," she said, swallowing back a surge of adrenaline. "God help me, you're my sous-chef."

~

A tasting menu's purpose was best described as *amuse-gueule*: amusement for the mouth. Small portions kept taste buds in a state of attention, while creative presentation seduced the eyes. Flavors could be subtle, but they had to communicate. *I am basil. I am lamb. Do I not blend magically with my companions?* Ideally, courses took diners on a journey: from surprise to delight, from pungent to delicate. Childhood memories could be evoked or exotic global trips. If food was emotion, a tasting menu was a tale packed with adventure. Creating one proved a chef possessed imagination as well as skill.

The journey Rebecca had devised mixed comfort and surprise. Naturally, preparation didn't occur without hiccups. Adjustments invariably had to be made en route. In the end, however, when the minute hand on the wall clock clicked to 1:29, she felt as confident as she was capable of.

She smoothed the front of her chef's whites, polished a faint smudge from the first plate's cover, and turned to face the door. Dominic had set up the little table at which her sole guest would eat. Rebecca believed in working clean. Although later dishes were still in process, very little chaos remained.

At precisely 1:30 and ten seconds, Trey Hayworth entered the kitchen.

He and his business partner Zane Alexander were among Boston's most glamorous bachelors. In addition to making their mark in commerce, they supported numerous charities. Rebecca had seen shots of Hayworth in his tuxedo climbing out of limos too many times to count. She knew the young CFO was hot stuff.

She hadn't known meeting him in person would stop her heart.

He was tall and tan and shaped from shoulder to hip like a pro athlete. His black hair was long enough to tie back and as smooth and shiny as if he'd just brushed it. The cuffs of his beautifully fitted Oxford shirt were rolled up to his elbows. An expensive watch gleamed on one wrist, but his soft suede shoes were as scuffed as if he'd kicked around in them for years. The overall effect was one of effortless stylishness, suggesting weekends in the Hamptons or maybe Ralph Lauren ads. He literally looked polished.

Maybe he buffs himself with money, she joked, trying to recover her humor. From what she'd heard, the bad boys had enough of it.

Her cynicism shredded the moment his gaze met hers.

Clear and bright, his surprisingly hot green eyes were the color of bottles deposited on a sunny shore. Glints of amber increased their intensity, as did their lush frame of dark lashes. His thick eyebrows were crazy-sexy— brooding, manly—unavoidably sinking their hooks into her where she was most girly. His gaze seemed to penetrate her soul . . . evidently as preparation for wetting her panties.

"*Hello*," he said with a smile that hinted at unfairly deep dimples.

Squirming already, Rebecca experienced the oddest shiver of deja vu.

"I'm Rebecca Eilert," she said, aware that her voice wasn't quite steady. Annoyed with herself, she offered him a hand that damn well was. "Thank you for giving me this opportunity to show you what I can do."

The panty-wetter took her hand in both of his, holding rather than shaking it. Again, Rebecca quivered with arousal—an inconvenience she could have done without. Hayworth's palm was unexpectedly callused, possibly from rowing. Her college-age little brothers were on a crew and had similar rough spots. For a second, Hayworth seemed to be waiting for a response from her. Whatever it was, Rebecca didn't know how to supply it.

"Would you like to begin?" she asked politely.

His mouth was well-shaped but not full. At her question, it slanted to one side—as if he were enjoying a private and slightly rueful joke.

"I'd be honored," he concurred.

Dominic took his cue with a smoothness that would have done his father proud, pulling out the single chair for Hayworth. Hayworth took it, then let the young man spread his napkin and pour his water. That done, he looked expectantly at her.

Rattled but not—she promised herself—shaken, she set the first plate in front of him.

Hayworth's *ah* of pleasure as she removed the lid was exactly what she'd hoped for.

Two fluffy golden potato blinis sat on a clean white plate, one picture-perfect little pancake tipped rakishly atop the other. This base was surmounted by a glistening scoop of tomato confit, which she'd seasoned lightly with roe of cod. Rebecca explained the dish's contents, stepped back, and allowed him to dig in.

Hayworth did so, then swallowed his mouthful. "Oh my God," he moaned gratifyingly, spooning into the dish again. "That is amazing."

His appreciation was just beginning. He adored her creamy Maine lobster bisque, and pronounced her lamb chops with cassoulet wicked. Her palate-cleansing cucumber fraiche was praised, and her squab with foie gras and figs. By the time she was ready to serve dessert, her newly anointed sous-chef was grinning from ear to ear. Dominic knew he'd helped her prepare a hit.

Rebecca gave thanks the teenager's heels remained on the floor.

For the final 'taste' she'd made upside-down apple tart with dollops of homemade cinnamon ice cream. This was a signature dish for her. Served in a small ramekin, the dessert mingled sweet and spicy, playing off the textures of creamy and toothsome. The tart and tender apples complemented the crispy puff pastry as if God had invented them for this pairing. Buckwheat pancakes with apple syrup it was not. All the same, for her, the tastes and scents brought back that first success. Unbeknownst to her guests, each time she served it, she shared her heart with them.

Hayworth scraped the ramekin with his spoon, then sat back in his chair and sighed. Though the amounts she'd served were too modest to have stuffed a big man like him, he wove both hands together over his flat stomach. His eyes were shining, his smile as satisfied as any guest she'd seen.

"That was killer," he declared.

His tone was husky, causing her to speculate how he'd sound in bed. Mesmerized, she noticed a small Celtic knot tattooed on his neck. She'd seen these sometimes on Harvard students—book boys trying to act badass. Hayworth wore his differently, his toughness maybe not put on. The possibility added a whiff of mystery to his buffed stylishness, reminding her people got inked for other reasons than showing off.

Maybe Trey Hayworth was more than a spoiled tycoon.

"So Rebecca gets the job?" Dominic broke in, the sixteen-year-old no longer able to restrain himself. "You'll hire her to be in charge of your restaurant?"

Dominic was too excited to notice the repressive look she shot him. Thankfully, Hayworth was amused. "I believe your chef and I need to discuss that privately."

"Shoo," Rebecca added, giving the boy a gentle shove toward the door.

"She's awesome," Dominic called over his shoulder. "She only yells for really bad screw ups. All the line cooks love her."

He was still trying to cheerlead as the door swung shut behind him.

"High praise," Hayworth murmured, rubbing his lower lip.

"I can do this," Rebecca said, because he seemed undecided. "I've done everything in restaurants, from scrubbing toilets to expediting to stocking up on wines. I know the profit margin on every plate and what it doesn't pay to be stingy on. I've hired and fired and trained servers to make sure every guest walks out the door as happy as possible. I'm more than a chef, Mr. Hayworth. I'm the entire package. You'd be lucky to have me."

"That I have no doubt of," he said with a wry mouth twist.

He could have been suggesting a double meaning. Before she could color up, he sobered. "You're my top candidate, Rebecca, but I have to consider this. You've never run a place this big before."

Rebecca clenched her jaw. Was he going to call Titcomb? Would Wilde's new owner trash her for the huffy way she left? Calling his handpicked chef a pompous A-hole might not have been her most brilliant career move.

"I can do it," she repeated a smidgen more softly. "I've studied what TBBC is about. You want a showstopper *and* a place folks can be comfortable eating in. You want the food critics slavering for a chance to slam you . . . and then to go home beaming. That's what I *do*, Mr. Hayworth. You won't find anyone better suited to creating a restaurant you and your partner will be proud of."

Hayworth rose, which she interpreted to mean the time for arguing was over. She was five foot nothing, and he towered over her. He also smelled good, like soap and sweat and some faint cologne too expensive for her to know its name. She steeled herself against its appeal. As if he felt sorry for her, he dropped one warm hand to her shoulder.

Despite the kindness of the gesture, the amount of testosterone he exuded was distracting. He rocked his sexy beard shadow like nobody's business.

"You're my best candidate," he said, giving her incredibly tensed-up muscle a light squeeze. "I promise I'm taking your application seriously."

She needed this job, not only for her pride and to rescue her crew from Wilde's, but to continue paying Charlie and Pete's tuition. The twins covered books and rent with work-study, but Harvard was expensive. She'd been as proud as a peacock when they got in—as if their braininess proved she'd been a good caretaker. She wasn't sure she could bear for them to transfer somewhere cheaper.

She truly couldn't bear it if somewhere cheaper was far away. Her little brothers were her family twice over. She already hated going home to an empty house.

She couldn't say that of course. Trey Hayworth was a big mogul. He wouldn't care why she needed him to hire her.

"Thank you," she said, inclining her head stiffly. "I'll wait to hear from you."

~

Trey left Rebecca in the kitchen to gather her equipment. As he rode the executive elevator to the top floor, he was aware he'd treated her shabbily. That she could handle his latest project he'd established in five minutes. The woman radiated motivation, not to mention competence. The reasons he hadn't dropped to his knees to beg her to take the job had nothing to do with her.

He thought he'd prepared himself for today. Naturally, he knew who she was. He'd recognized her name the instant her resume crossed his desk. Some might argue he should have forgotten it after all these years. Who had she been except a waitress with a nice pair and a pretty smile? There had to be thousands like her in any big city. That didn't seem to matter. The night they'd met, the night she'd imprinted herself on his memories, was a life changing one for him.

That was the night Zane admitted he wanted them to stay together.

Trey had never regretted accepting Zane's offer—business or otherwise. Zane might not have said the words, but Trey knew he loved him. Pursuing a girl like Rebecca would have road-blocked all the good things that came after. She wasn't a woman he could sleep with and then let go. Trey didn't know if it was genetics or hormones or some weird subconscious awareness. He just knew her eyes had warned him; the way his chest had tightened at her nearness. She was his thunderbolt, possibly the only woman he could fall for as hard as Zane.

With a heavy sigh, he pushed into his big office.

Zane's office was next to his. Most days, if he heard Trey come in, he'd say *hello* with a friendly drumroll on their shared wall. Today he couldn't. He was on his way to Hawaii, to visit a resort they were considering bundling into TBBC's collection. His partner being so far away didn't lighten Trey's mood at all.

Zane tried not to be possessive. He liked their arrangement. At least once a month he indulged his alternate erotic interest with a female. His revolving door for dates amused Trey, but it served a purpose. Rotating women as he did, Zane avoided encouraging any particular one to believe she'd stick around. Though Trey stepped out less frequently, his methods were similar. Hardly anyone got a repeat, and nobody slept over. Other men were off limits entirely. Trey understood his partner needed to come first with him. Sharing Trey with another love of a lifetime would be a deal breaker.

He dropped into his desk chair, swiveling toward the long expanse of windows to stare at the city. August's sunshine shimmered in sparks and sheets off the old and new buildings. He could see the waterfront from this direction, the wharves and the bright harbor. Boston was never all one thing or another: neither all modern nor historic, neither completely land nor sea . . . kind of like him, when it came down to it.

He remembered the day, two weeks after his and Zane's fateful dinner, when he'd given in to temptation and returned alone to Wilde's. He'd purposefully gone during lunch, when Rebecca had said she worked in the kitchen and not out front. He'd emerged with her last name and a pounding long-term hard-on. Simply coming as close to her as that had sent a storm through his libido.

The reaction was enough to shock him to sanity. He hadn't tried to contact her. He'd pushed the thought of her behind him, telling himself his crazy ideas about her had to be in his head. Love at first sight was silly. What he felt for Rebecca Eilert wasn't any more than a crush.

Eventually he'd stopped dreaming about her sad gray eyes. Eventually he no longer wondered if anyone but him had noticed how profoundly alone she was.

Being more romantic than Zane didn't make him an idiot.

Or maybe it did, because when he saw her application for the executive chef's position, he hadn't torn it up. The letter she'd sent along had been literate, humorously thorough, and inadvertently neurotic. The things she didn't realize she was saying charmed him as no female had for years. He had his assistant schedule her to cook before he could stop himself.

He'd changed his clothes twice this morning, taking extra care to close-trim the stubble most women seemed to love. As they rode in the limo—Zane to the airport and he to work—Zane had accused him of having a hot lunch date. He'd been teasing, but Trey had blushed like a teenager. He hadn't told Zane he was interviewing chefs, though they both had a stake in the future Bad Boys Lounge. Truthfully, he couldn't tell him. Rebecca was the only applicant he'd seen.

Trey was acting like a cheating husband. He needed to cut it out. He'd almost convinced himself he would when he stepped into that kitchen.

His heart had jumped in his chest like it had at Wilde's. *It's her*, sang his imagination. *She's in the same room with me.* His skin had tingled at her presence, his every cell humming with aliveness.

Her littleness was a mule kick to his breadbox.

She had the same short blonde haircut, like she'd settled on a style and couldn't be bothered to change it. Her eyes were still huge, still haunted by shadows and mulishness. She was wirier than he remembered, as if she didn't —or maybe couldn't—leave a restaurant's heavy lifting to underlings. The tension in her handshake astonished him. She was like a racehorse who never, ever allowed herself to relax. He shouldn't have found that sexy. He shouldn't have wanted to strip her naked and massage her all over.

"I'm insane," he said aloud to the high ceiling.

He'd been disappointed when she didn't remember him, though he'd been a solitary restaurant patron in Lord knew how many. That should have convinced him he was deluded. If they'd been soul mates or whatever nursery tale he was spinning, surely she'd recognize him too.

He let his head thunk forward onto his blotter. Maybe if her food hadn't been so fracking amazing, maybe if he hadn't watched her glow like a sun at his praise, he'd have been able to stop flirting with disaster. Unfortunately, Trey had eaten a lot of world-class meals, from Paris to Sonoma. Rebecca's was right up there with the best of them.

She deserved this job. Hell, she'd be great at it. Worst of all, to go by what his research had uncovered about her leaving Wilde's, Rebecca needed it.

It wasn't fair to turn her down just because he found her treacherously attractive.

"Crap," he said, caught in the quandary.

Unused to being indecisive, he sat up to absently rub the ache in his crotch. Too late he realized where his hand had gone. She'd done it to him again. He was as hard as a teenager, his horny cock a pole in his underwear.

Had it been like that when he ate her food, when he'd squeezed the knotted muscle at her shoulder?

He groaned at the memory of how it felt to touch her. He'd been so focused on her he couldn't have sworn what his own body was doing.

What if she'd seen her effect on him?

Heat seemed to explode in his groin. Sometimes his kinks really were ridiculous. So what if she'd noticed his hard-on? Rebecca was a grown woman —and attractive. Men had to throw wood for her now and again.

Other men throwing wood for her wasn't the most helpful topic to calm him. Giving in to what he couldn't fight, he unzipped his trousers and shoved a hand inside. God, handling himself felt good, especially when—apparently —he'd needed to for a while. He didn't bother with the jar of Albolene in his bottom drawer. He kept the infamous jack off aid there for Zane. Trey enjoyed the chafing of his bare palm, the sexual burn that edged on discomfort. Gritting his teeth, he pumped his erection quickly, concentrating the strokes toward the top where his nerve endings were thickest. He was too impatient to tease himself, besides which he had a conference call in ten minutes. He needed this release now.

She was here, he thought, his mind running a bit away with itself. *I had her hand in mine. I could have bent down and tongue-kissed her.*

He saw himself slamming her naked against the stainless steel walk-in door. She was so petite he'd have no trouble trapping her with his weight. Off her feet would be good, her thighs hugging his waist, her lush pink mouth pressed tight to and sucking his. She'd gasp when he slid his throbbing penis inside of her. Compared to her, he'd feel really big. Maybe he'd have to saw in and out to get in; maybe tease her clit so her wetness would ease his way. He wished he knew what her pussy looked like, wished he knew how she kissed.

Pressure built in his scrotum, balls jerking toward the base of his erection. He yanked his flesh harder from his body, abusing it, willing the tension that rose in him to crest.

She'd called him Mr. Hayworth. Maybe he could tie her to a worktop and force her to call him Trey.

The thought of her strong little wrists and ankles bound up in leather sent his excitement rocketing. Maybe he'd truss her all over, from thighs to waist to dark crisscrosses between her breasts. He pictured suckling her nipples, imagined rolling them on his tongue. His breath came from him in hard quick pants as he ground his ass cheeks into the office chair. The extra friction on his tailbone made all his sensations better; made him picture her in even more detail. Knowing he was nearly there, he tugged his cock faster. Though it wasn't smart, the fantasy was so good he couldn't let go of it.

I remember, she'd cry. *I couldn't forget you!*

Then Zane would come up behind Trey and bugger him breathless.

He snapped so suddenly into climax he didn't have a chance to grab a tissue. He spurted across his blotter, a long white arc that felt incredible shooting out. His cock blazed with pleasure at the contractions, then virtually melted with contentment. He wasn't certain he'd ever felt as good before.

The good feelings couldn't last, of course, not when he had so little chance of living out this scenario.

Hell, he thought. He was in big trouble.

CHAPTER FIVE

Temptation

The line cooks of the world formed an effective spy network. They worked everywhere, knew everyone, and—most importantly—were bonded by a fellowship of incredibly grueling work. They were like cops in a way, only with knife rolls instead of badges. Nobody understood a cook as well as the guy who stood shoulder to shoulder with him at a blazing hot grill station.

Having spent a sleepless night that strengthened her resolve not to give up too easily, Rebecca stumped to her kitchen wall phone at daybreak. Her targets also roused early, so this was a good time to call. Within fifteen minutes, she had the information her plan of attack required.

Trey Hayworth's limo driver, who bought his daily bagel and a cup from a cafe in Faneuil Hall, was ferrying his boss to his new restaurant's site today. The decor was nearly finished, and Mr. Hayworth wanted to check on it.

Rebecca dabbed concealer on her under-eye circles and dressed herself for battle.

In her case, this meant throwing a light summer jacket over her standard white shirt and black trousers. Also, she swiped on lipstick with actual color. If she were careful, she wouldn't gnaw it off too quickly.

She took it as a good sign that her old Nissan Versa agreed to start.

The address she'd been given was on Charles Street in Beacon Hill. Beacon Hill was quintessential old Boston, the most sought-after neighborhood for elite Victorians. People sought it out today as well. Cobbled streets delighted tourists, sidewalks were paved in brick, and Federal-style residences all seemed to sport historical black shutters. Here on Charles Street, swanky shops and restaurants were as common as ivy.

Rebecca thanked the parking gods for helping her find a spot just a block away.

The Bad Boys Lounge inhabited the lower floors of two adjoining brick row houses. An old fashioned wooden sign swung above the sheltered entry. The custom painting showed a pair of rakes in Colonial dress, escorting two buxom ladies in for dinner. The scene was happy rather than leering, and Rebecca smiled at it.

The door beneath was propped open by a potted topiary tree.

No need to knock then, and no chance to be tossed out before she had her say. Cautiously, she stepped inside the big dining room. Morning light slanted in from the front windows, cutting through the dimness inside. Her eyes took a moment to adjust. The soon-to-be restaurant was empty, a scatter of construction and design clutter indicating it wasn't yet finished. Free to humor her curiosity, Rebecca looked around. As she did, her heart sighed within her breast.

However she might resent testosterone-based entitlement, the bad boys had a rep for doing things top-drawer. She'd known that when she applied to work for Hayworth—counted on it, in fact. What she hadn't prepared for was this exceedingly mellow place.

The atmosphere was upscale men's club with a soupcon of modern edge. Dark plank floors threw their gloss to dark leather, which blended beautifully with aged wood. Antique tin tiled the ceiling, where tiny industrial lights hung down between exposed pipes. For color, stacks of fat coffee table books were in the process of being shelved in recesses at horseshoe booths. To her left, an elegant archway opened onto a softly glittering bar space. She couldn't see a single bad table, and the traffic paths for wait staff appeared to be well thought out. The end result was comfortable and stylish. Men would salivate at these surroundings, but women would as well.

A bad boy who took his date here seemed likely to get lucky.

The covetous urge that seized Rebecca was impossible to throw off. This leather-scented little kingdom ought to be hers to rule. She wanted *her* savory clam chowder served at the round tables, her fresh lobster with butter sauce. Wilde's most regrettable trait was its sad lack of ambience. Even unfinished, The Bad Boys Lounge had enough for three eateries.

Damn, she thought. *I could spin magic here.*

Since wishing wouldn't bring this about, she continued along the just-wide-enough back hall to the kitchen's logical location. The wainscoting in the passageway was black oak, the carpet protected from deliverymen by taped-down brown paper.

She saw no one until she reached the pass-through window. This was where wait staff would hand in their tickets and pick up plates. The shelf was sturdy, the height good for servers to dip their knees and cheat a heavy tray onto their shoulders. At first, Rebecca thought the kitchen was empty. The lights were off, and it was shadowy inside.

Then she noticed the tall man rubbing his bottom lip in front of the brand new grill.

A hot prickle slid across her breasts. She didn't simply recognize Trey Hayworth's profile; she recognized his whole shape. Considering she'd just met him, she found this disquieting.

"Mr. Hayworth," she called softly before her nervousness could worsen.

He spun around at her voice like a gun had gone off.

"Fuck," he said, which didn't strike her as promising.

"Sorry," she said, stiffening a little but aware she was trespassing. "The entrance was open. I was hoping for a chance to talk to you one more time."

He stared at her for a moment, then shook himself.

"That's okay," he said with a surprising lack of anger, considering. "You just startled me." He walked toward the pass-through. Then—belatedly remembering he could—he veered aside to open the kitchen door for her. "Please come in and have a look."

His politeness knocked her off balance more than his curse.

"Thank you," she said. "I know I shouldn't have showed up like this."

He'd invited her to have a look, but didn't seem inclined to give her one. He stood in front of her, too tall to see around, hands shoved in his pants pockets. When you were a big-deal boss, she guessed you could dress as you pleased. Today he wore a pale green polo shirt that stretched over broad shoulders. His jeans appeared to be faded in all the right places. Rather than check them out and confirm, she kept her eyes on his face. His dark brows screwed together as he gazed down at her. He seemed so boyish any second Rebecca expected him to start rocking on his heels.

"What—" He cleared his throat. "What did you want to say to me?"

His strange reception had made her forget her prepared speech. She retrieved it with an effort. "I thought it might help your decision to know why I left my last position."

"Not a mystery," he said. "Latest owner brought in a new executive chef and demoted you. You were perfectly right to quit. I'm sure you can cook rings around that yahoo."

"I don't know about *perfectly* right," she admitted wryly. "I could have waited to leave until I had another job."

Hayworth smiled, his eyes warm with understanding—unnervingly warm, actually. He seemed weirdly happy that she was here. Rebecca tried to ignore how that unsettled her. Nothing she'd read about Trey Hayworth suggested he was this eccentric. But that didn't really matter. Plenty of good bosses were quirky. With her responsibilities, she couldn't afford to be picky.

"What do I need to do to get this job with you?"

"Ah," he hemmed, rubbing his lower lip again. "I *want* to hire you . . ."

"But?"

He looked at her, seemingly unable to answer.

"You could try me out," she offered. "Let me work for a month for free."

"That wouldn't be fair."

"Then what would be?" she asked, her determination unshaken. "Because my gut tells me this combination of The Bad Boys Lounge and me would work out."

His grin burst out like sunshine, momentarily dazzling her. His dimples were as deep as she'd expected. "Really?" he said, like she'd given him a gift.

"Really. I have no trouble imagining me and your restaurant being a big success."

"Me too." He put his hands on her shoulders, their size and warmth unavoidably perking up her hormones. "I can picture you here. I can picture us having fun."

Okay, that was a strange response. Her mind said *um*, but her temporarily fractious libido urged her not to protest. His lovely hands chafed her shoulders, comforting little rubs like he thought she was cold. Though she shivered at his touch on her linen jacket, she was anything but chilly. Tingles pulsed between her legs, fire spreading through her clit and beyond. Her nipples tightened with a vengeance, practically punching against her bra. Hayworth's gaze dropped to the sharpened peaks like they were magnetized.

When he licked his lips, her shiver grew bigger.

"Rebecca," he said, his tone as serious as the grave, his eyes rising with difficulty to lock on hers. "Believe me when I say I know I'm being inappropriate."

Her mouth fell open as he leaned down. Suddenly, her hands were on his front, not pushing him away but curling into his polo shirt. Boy, if this was how she reacted to a bit of attention, she needed to date more. She was tugging him toward her, and his arms slid warm and strong around her. His chest was broad and steely. As his head came closer, she rose on tiptoe.

He licked a swipe up her parted lips, his tongue as soft as a rose petal. Rebecca's breath shuddered out of her.

"God," he whispered and sealed their mouths together.

He tasted like sun-warmed cherries.

Rebecca wished he'd kiss her forever.

"Mm," he hummed like he had over her food yesterday. "Mm, Rebecca."

"Mr. Hayworth—"

She lost her breath as he hiked her butt onto the worktop. The seat brought their heights closer. He angled his head and kissed her a second time, his tongue sliding sleekly into her waiting mouth. She didn't stop him any more than she had before, her fingers tightening helplessly on his shirt. His kiss was yummy—sliding in, drawing out, sucking gently at her tongue to coax it into playing. It seemed like ages since any man had held her, and he was a fine one. She moaned at the heat he stirred inside her, cream filling her sex so swiftly it spilled out. She squirmed on the stainless steel even as his mouth pulled free.

"Please call me Trey," he said.

"Mr. Hayworth—"

She wasn't trying to be funny, but he laughed. His hand came to stroke her face, those rowing calluses—if that's what they were—undeniably erotic. His gentleness silenced her, both in his touch and eyes. The pad of his thumb slid across the top her cheekbone. She supposed he noticed the shadow under her concealer, because he clucked his tongue.

"Were you losing sleep over this?" he murmured. "I didn't mean to make you do that."

"You are . . . a very peculiar man," she pushed out breathlessly.

He smiled, a shade of melancholy in the curve. She couldn't look away from his gaze, nearly colorless in the shadows but conveying mysterious multitudes of feeling. His narrow waist spread her knees, and her thighs were as tense as stone. Through everything, her hands had remained on his chest. She noticed they'd started rubbing in small passes up and down his pecs.

Trey noticed too. His eyes went dark, his respiration quickening.

"I'm kissing you again," he warned.

No one could mistake the way she wrapped her arms around him for anything but encouragement.

Her participation seemed to embolden him. He groaned, his kiss turning more aggressive, which felt completely great to her. He pulled her off the counter and fully onto him. Though she clung like a monkey, the difference in their heights meant her pussy rocked against his waist—not the target it craved. Rebecca tried to wiggle lower, which somehow resulted in Trey pushing her into a cement block wall.

That put the huge hump of his erection exactly where she needed it. Heedless of what it said about her, Rebecca threw all her strength into rolling over it.

Trey wasn't offended. He shoved his hand into the back of her trousers and under her panties. "Fuck," he said, feeling how wet she was. "Jesus, Rebecca."

Her name sounded funny when he said it, like he knew her better than was possible. In that moment, she didn't care. He was hot and hard and she wanted him like she couldn't remember wanting a man before.

"Yes," she gasped, tugging greedily at his shirt.

Trey tore it over his head himself. "You," he said.

Understanding him perfectly, Rebecca returned the favor. She had a jacket to wrestle off, plus a button-down collar shirt. Naturally, she took longer than he had, but he panted flatteringly while she worked, his attention glued to every move she made. He panted harder once her shirt was gone. Her bra was satiny and white with small push-up pads to give her some cleavage. With her usual habit of sticking with the comfortable, she had drawer full of others just like it, bought on sale at a bargain store. She was sure he'd seen nicer—both in lingerie and breasts. If he had, he wasn't complaining.

"Oh God," he moaned, staring down at her pebbled nipples. Before she could stop him, he hiked her farther up his body. Nuzzling down into her bra cup, he latched his mouth over at least half of her right breast.

Rebecca's bosom was too small to be her favorite part of her body, but the way her nerves caught fire as he drew on her certainly increased her fondness.

"Can I?" he broke off to ask, already bending toward the floor. "Rebecca, can I get inside of you?"

His knees hit the tiles, and he rolled her under him. His weight felt good, his heat and the ragged in and out of his ribs. She drove her hands up his naked back, fingertips digging like a cat into its firm muscles. His skin was hot, as smooth as if he'd come to her from a spa treatment. Without a second thought, her legs had spread to make room for him. He looked at her, propped above her on his forearms. The expression on his face shocked her, like if she said *yes* it would mean the world to him. Who was she that a man like him would look at her that way? Whatever the reason for it, his urgency was catching. Rebecca was so excited she couldn't seem to take a full breath.

That she wasn't in the habit of hopping into bed with men she barely knew was hard to remember.

"Okay," he said, sensing her lingering indecision. "I won't ask you that yet. Just open and unzip my jeans. Just take me into your hand."

"Will you take me?" she asked.

He smiled so wickedly she blushed. That made her feel silly. She wasn't a mouse. She could ask for what she wanted in plain English.

"I mean will you take my pussy into your hand? Will you get me off too?"

He ducked his head to kiss her, deep and wet and dizzying. When he finally released her, she knew her eyes were starry.

"Sweetheart," he said, his voice a fusion of sex and smoke. "If you let me, I'll get you off each and every way you desire."

This was quite a promise. Rather than express doubt, Rebecca reached for the metal button of his blue jeans. He lifted his hips for the unzipping, his hot dark gaze holding hers. His bulge pushed out as the tab lowered.

"You're big," she breathed.

He flashed his dimples at her again.

"Oh fine," she said, eyes rolling at his smirk. "It's not the size that matters. It's what you do with it."

He started to laugh, but her hand was just then sliding into his cotton briefs.

He sighed long and low with pleasure, lashes sinking as her fingers roved over him.

"Oh boy," she said, loving all that velvety rigid heat. "Oh boy, you are a handful."

She pulled her hold up his shaft, and he writhed like the sort of dancer who gets paid in dollar bills. She guessed he was sensitive. She thought she was being careful not to grip too tightly.

"Fuck," he said with his teeth gritted. "God."

Remembering what he'd promised, he worked his own hand into the front of her panties, two long fingers pushing her lips open. The heel of his palm settled on her clit, giving it a firm grind that spilled more cream from her. He curled his fingers to their second knuckle into her wet entrance. Once there, he didn't rub or thrust. Instead, he used his fingers to exert pressure on the wall where her ache of wanting was most tender.

Rebecca's moan betrayed how much she liked that.

The longing sound brought his eyes open, their lustrous surface catching stray gleams of light. "I have a condom," he said huskily. "I really want to be inside you, if you think you'd enjoy that."

She knew she shouldn't let this go any farther, but she couldn't say *no* to him. He got to her in places she hadn't known she had: emotional places, places she wanted to throw open for the first time. Never mind she'd probably smack herself tomorrow. Today she wanted to know what being taken by him was like. Resistance dissolving, she smiled before she answered.

"Okay," she said, giving his hard-on a friendly squeeze. "Why don't you show me what this bad boy can do?"

She spoke as humorously as she could, knowing better than to be too serious with a guy—no matter how sweet he was acting.

"I'm not asking if you're sure," he warned, reaching hastily into his back pocket. He pulled the condom from his wallet, using his teeth to rip the corner off. She didn't bother asking how old it was. Given his looks and charm, the answer had to be not very.

"Do you want me to help?" she asked.

He smiled and shook his head. "Already got it on."

He kneeled back to show her. Though his cock was worth ogling, something else caught her eye. The Celtic knot on his neck wasn't his only ink. A tattoo stretched up the side of his ripped stomach: a Chinese dragon, it looked like. She guessed the thing was old news to him. Before she could reach to touch it, he pushed her legs up his front. He removed her boring comfortable shoes and dragged off her trousers. This was a skilled bit of undressing. Rebecca tried not to worry if her most recent shave had been recent enough. To judge by the way he rolled forward and rubbed her thigh, having access to her booty was what he cared about.

She still wore her satiny panties, but they weren't much of a barrier.

"Sorry it's cold," he whispered, meaning the kitchen tile.

She ran her hands up his clipped chest hair and struggled not to purr. He was manscaped just the right amount for her. "Sometimes a girl's gotta do what a girl needs to."

"You could be on top."

This time she shook her head. Her refusal seemed to please him. Maybe he preferred the superior position? Smiling, he curved one hand under her bottom and lowered his hips to her.

The thickness of his erection settled over her labia.

"Say when," he said, "and I'll be inside you in two seconds."

She wasn't sure what he meant until his pelvis began rocking. He was warming her up again, sliding his length up and down the silky gusset of her panties. The friction felt really good, and even better when he compressed her nipple between his thumb and finger. He pulled the bead out, and a zing shot straight to her pussy.

"God," she gasped, hips jerking with pleasure.

"'When' is the word," he reminded her.

Jeez, he was cute. She stretched up to kiss him, hands starfished on his back, tongue saying *thank you* and *please do me*. He jerked with surprise before kissing her back just as hungrily. The way he gulped for air when she let him go was a treat of the first order.

"*When*," she teased, her voice rough with arousal.

Excitement flashed across his features. His hand shifted between them, thumbing aside her panties and fitting his cock in place. Though his tip was broad, she was very wet. He rocked it inward to test her, and she grew steamier.

The sound she made was probably a whimper.

"Yes," she said to the brief question in his expression.

He closed his eyes and pushed with his ass muscles.

She saw everything on his face as his cock slid in: pleasure, wonder, a flicker of being overwhelmed when being wrapped in warmth felt a bit too nice. Then *she* couldn't keep her eyelids up. The sensation of being filled had to be savored.

He didn't rush his penetration, at least not until the end. Then he groaned and shoved harder, taking the last inch of her.

Rebecca thrust upward to grind them both closer.

He let out a growling noise, like this was the far side of too much. Even then, he didn't start thrusting.

"Please," she begged, short nails curling into his shoulders. "Don't make me wait for more."

His laugh was at least half moan. He did something with one knee that lifted her butt off the hard cool tile. "Hold on tight," he said. "God, I want this so bad."

She didn't know why he did, just that she was grateful. He drew back, and then—thank the Lord—he went at her fast: quick strong pumps that tugged her inside and out. She'd never gotten so much clit stimulation from plain old intercourse. Maybe this was due to his thickness, or he just had a good technique. Whatever the reason, her excitement climbed faster than she expected. He hadn't been driving at her even two minutes before she hovered on orgasm.

Her neck arched off the floor with its imminence.

"Shit," he said, reading the tremors inside of her. The fingers that gripped her bottom dug in harder. "Breathe for me . . . just . . . hold on a little longer and I'll catch up."

He went faster, using longer strokes that somehow didn't push her past the brink. They did plenty for him. His breath huffed out, the center of his thick shaft swelling.

The pressure the extra girth created was inspiring.

"Rebecca," he gasped. "Don't tense your thighs like that."

She hadn't known she was doing it. Probably her body didn't want to wait for its climax. He massaged her butt, no doubt coaxing her to relax. The caress felt really good to her. She couldn't help wriggling around him, couldn't keep from thrusting harder into his next down stroke.

He grunted and slung a second bent knee under her. Rebecca's eyes flew open as her world shifted. Though she was lying down, Trey had sat up to thrust. His hands held her hips like steel, controlling her movements. Ironically—given her control freak streak—him restraining her pushed really good buttons. Her body seemed to think it could react more freely if he was driving it. She tried to distract herself by focusing on him. His bare chest looked like a god's, muscles rippling under the sheer dark fur. He was close to the peak as well, his beautifully interesting face tightening with pleasure. With a groan of need, he shifted directions the tiniest bit.

The new angle he pumped into her was even better than before.

"Take it," he panted. "Take what you need from me."

He stretched his thumbs to her labia, rubbing into the nerves beneath while at the same time pushing the folds closer to his striving cock. His veins had a texture, popped up as they were with blood. Wonderful sensations throbbed crazily through her groin.

"Trey," she gasped, startled by how sharp her feelings were. Desperate for an anchor, she slapped her hands around his wrists.

When his eyes slitted open, they should have been shooting flames. Had she done something to him, cuffing his arms this way? His stare was too hot, too intensely impassioned.

"Almost," he rasped, muscles in his jaw clenching. "Al—"

Rebecca's peak uncoiled.

He let loose with her, his loud groan of pleasure pitched lower than her wail. Like exclamation points to his ejaculation, the head of his cock dug repeatedly into her, the deep percussions against her cervix reverberating through her as after-orgasms. Before this, she'd have sworn she didn't care if she and a man came at the same time. What did it matter, as long as they both enjoyed themselves? With Trey, she had to rethink her attitude. The warmth that flooded her as they peaked was incredible, the sense that they were truly sharing the experience. He deepened the feeling by pulling her upward after and hugging her.

It seemed normal that her head settled on his shoulder, that her hands rubbed his back like his were rubbing hers. The scent of his cologne and sweat were heady. If she weren't careful, they'd become her new favorite smell. He let out that hum of his, his all-purpose happy sound.

"Sweet," he said, pressing soft lips to her hot temple.

Somewhere on the wall a clock ticked, the second hand going tock-tock-tock. Rebecca's breath gusted out on a reluctant sigh. With every *tock*, sanity returned.

"Sorry," she said. "I swear I didn't sleep with you so you'd give me the job."

Trey pushed back slightly to look at her. "I swear I didn't sleep with you so you'd take it."

He sounded annoyed. In her experience, guys who just came were in good moods. "Are you angry?" she asked.

"Are you really sorry?" he retorted.

"Well, that was enjoyable—as I'm sure you noticed, but if you're planning to hire me, you have to agree it wasn't smart. Bosses and employees shouldn't sleep together."

His expression was a study in irritation, perhaps because he couldn't dispute her point. "Damn it," was all he finally said.

Taking this as her cue, Rebecca pushed gently off of him. Her shoes were halfway across the kitchen, her trousers caught on the edge of a lowboy refrigeration drawer. Shoving her legs back in them, she did her best to hide her disappointment that he didn't argue more. Calling what they'd done *enjoyable* was an understatement, to say the least.

She took comfort in him muttering to himself as he stood and yanked up his pants. The word *idiot* peppered his diatribe.

He waited to speak to her until she was buttoning her shirt. She noticed he'd smoothed his hair back into its ponytail.

"I *am* hiring you," he said grimly.

Rebecca's heart gave a little skip. "Truly?"

"Truly. Full pay from the start and no arguments. I—" He paused to grind his teeth. "I reluctantly agree we shouldn't do that again."

She smiled in spite of herself. *Reluctantly* agreeing was sweet of him.

~

Watching Rebecca dress in her borderline frumpy clothes was an exercise in frustration. Could Trey have backed himself into a worse corner? After all those years of fantasizing, now he knew how amazing real sex with Rebecca was . . . and he'd conceded they shouldn't do it again. She was right of course. Sex in the workplace led to messiness and complications—neither of which he'd have shied from if his workplace weren't already complicated from loving Zane.

One quickie with her on a cold hard floor had worsened his longing by a gazillion times. He couldn't wish it hadn't happened; he wasn't smart enough for that. He *did* wish it hadn't been quite as earthshaking.

There was something between them, some out of the ordinary emotional chemistry. Trey was willing to bet she'd never come like that with another man. Her eyes in those final moments had been too damned surprised.

When she laid her head on his shoulder, he'd nearly asked her to marry him.

Knowing he'd lost his mind for certain, he handed her the thick-soled shoes he'd taken from her earlier. While it was true restaurant work kept people on their feet, surely she could do better. Telling himself not to be a fashion snob didn't kill his urge to toss them in the trash.

"Thanks," she said. Dropping the hideous things to the floor, she braced on the worktop to push her cute feet into them. He'd rushed through stripping her, though he had noticed her legs were nice—lent charm by muscles as well as curves. He was sorry they'd disappeared into her uninspired black trousers. Honestly, she had to be trying to look dowdy.

"Do you even own a dress?" he blurted.

She straightened and looked at him pinchily. "I don't see how that's your business."

It *might* be his business. Being named The Lounge's executive chef could conceivably involve a photo op or two.

He clamped his mouth on the words. Being in the right wasn't always strategic. "I'll have Elaine email you a contract to look over."

"Elaine is your assistant?"

"Yes." Stubbornly, he didn't pass Rebecca her tan jacket—yet another supremely boring garment—but held it up for her. Though she grimaced at him playing gentleman, she turned and slid her arms into it.

When she would have moved away, he dropped his hands to her shoulders, once again as tense as before they'd worked out their kinks on the kitchen floor.

"Don't be sorry about this," he said, his frustration creeping into his tone. "If you'd just eaten a great meal, you wouldn't regret it afterward."

She turned to him, and he let her. Her features were delicate—extra pretty with flushes from sex and kissing staining them. Ten heaps of boring clothes couldn't hide that her lips were luscious, her elfin hair improved by tousling. Clearly ignorant of her gorgeousness, she cocked her head to one side. "You're not sorry for what we did?"

"Never," he declared, meaning it.

She smiled, probably because he sounded so earnest. She patted his chest, immediately making him regret having covered it with a shirt. He hadn't forgotten how she'd enjoyed combing his chest hair.

"All right," she said. "No regrets for the world class meal."

Perhaps he shouldn't have, but he felt better at her calling it *world class*.

CHAPTER SIX

The Darling Boys

Rebecca walked down the block and sat in her Versa, staring at nothing. She'd promised Trey she wouldn't be sorry, but that was easier said than done. He was going to be her boss—probably, hopefully—which meant their relationship ought to stay professional. Now that she'd felt his athletic body pressed up to and into hers, she couldn't imagine how she'd accomplish that.

Not wriggling on the seat was impossible. Having Trey only once would never satisfy her. He'd been an amazing lover: vigorous, intense, with a knack for knowing what she wanted almost before she did. All he had to do was look at her with those hot green eyes, and she'd melt into a puddle.

She dropped her head to the steering wheel and groaned. His cock had been lovely: its silky heat in her hand, the skill with which he used it to pleasure her. Her fingers curled at the thought of stroking his shaft again. Worse, they curled at the thought of embracing him.

He'd cradled her at the end, as if she were precious. She'd felt safe in his arms. She'd wanted to stay there.

Absolutely nothing about that was smart.

Over the years, she'd struggled to be smart about men. Until she was twenty-one, she'd done without dating. She'd been a single parent without a support system. She couldn't risk anyone revealing her and the boys' situation to an adult. That was too likely to result in them being split up, and she'd committed herself to keeping the three of them together. Just as important, if anything had happened to the twins while she was out having fun, she

57

wouldn't have been able to live with it.

"Hey, lady!" called a voice from a nearby car. "You coming or going?"

"Sorry," she said, realizing the man was hoping to claim her parking spot. "I'm leaving now."

The other driver backed up to give her room, polite enough now that he knew she was moving. Grateful for the distraction, Rebecca focused on the tasks required to get on the road.

She *almost* didn't think about Trey Hayworth as she drove home.

When she arrived at their house in Cambridge, a shock awaited. A battered pick-up sat in the driveway behind her delivery van, the logo for a firm called Alcott Construction on its door. Equally troubling, a large green dumpster hulked on their small front lawn. Broken drywall and wood were piling up on one end.

Rebecca flew out of her car almost too quickly to park it first.

"Ex*cuse* me," she said to the hulking young man who came up her basement steps, dragging a roll of stained carpet behind him. "What the fuck are you doing in my house?"

Rebecca wasn't big, but she could do scary, no problem. The young man paled at her clear fury.

"Uh," he said, halting in his tracks while keeping his hold on the rolled-up rug. "Your brothers hired me to reno your cellar?"

"My brothers!"

"Becca!" Charlie called, hurrying frantically down the front steps. "It's okay. This is Jesse. He goes to school with us. His dad is in construction. We wanted to surprise you."

As soon as he was near enough, Rebecca punched his shoulder.

"Ow!" Charlie said, rubbing it.

Pete stuck his head out the front door too.

"You," she said, pointing her finger of doom at him. "Go back in the kitchen and wait for me."

Pete made an *oh crap* face and disappeared. Rebecca looked at the boy named Jesse. To his credit, he seemed to have retrieved his nerve. He squared his bulky shoulders and answered her. "They told me you'd come around once they explained what this was for."

"Fine." Rebecca moderated her tone a tad. "Please don't trash my house any more until I talk to them."

The boy opened his mouth. Charlie stopped his protest with a head shake. He knew when his sister's temper had hit its red zone.

"Inside," Rebecca ordered, shooing him ahead of her.

"We're not being crazy," Charlie started babbling on the way. "Pete and I both agreed this is a smart idea."

"Well, as long as you *both* agreed," Rebecca snapped angrily.

Always calmer than Charlie, Pete stood his ground at the kitchen table. At nineteen, the twins were still gangly, but probably their full height. They weren't as blond as she was—her hair having a little help—but the bright summer sun had streaked their shaggy waves. Naturally, she thought they were handsome, something girls their age were beginning to discover. Their recent rowing obsession had filled them out. To her surprise, Pete's formerly spindly biceps looked impressive in his ragged gray T-shirt.

When did that happen? she wondered.

"We have a plan," were the first words out of his mouth. Pete knew his older sister as well as Charlie did.

He slid his open laptop across the well-used butcher-block table. The screen displayed a neat black and white blueprint. Reserving the right to lose her temper later, Rebecca stepped closer to look at it.

"It's an income suite," Pete said. "One bed, one bath, with an open kitchen and living room. We've planned a stacked laundry in the hall closet, so you won't have to share yours. I talked to a rental agent. With the right finishes and all the students here who need housing, you should get a thousand a month for it."

"*Pete*," she said, appreciating his pitch but aware this transformation would take dollars she didn't have.

"It's *smart*," he insisted. "The ceilings are high enough to be legal, and the plumbing's in decent shape. The only thing you had down there was Charlie and my old junk."

"Pete, converting basements into apartments costs money."

"You *have* it," he said. "The house is worth way more than the mortgage. And if you don't want to go to the bank for a line of credit, Charlie and I are working on a way around that."

"We are," Charlie agreed, nodding to support his twin.

"Guys," she said. "You can't just grab some friend of yours to come here and tear things up. You have to discuss these things with me."

"You'd have said 'no,'" Pete justified stubbornly. "You know how you are about this house. Anyway, Raoul told us about you quitting Wilde's. You shouldn't have to worry about everything yourself. Charlie and I can help support the family too."

"Raoul told you!" she exclaimed, annoyed for a new reason.

"Exactly," Charlie said. "You wouldn't tell us that, but we're supposed to tell you. We're almost grown-ups, Becca, and you treat us like babies."

They were babies to her, though she couldn't admit that. "How much is this 'income suite' going to cost me?"

"Only eighteen thousand," Pete replied. "Maybe a little more if that crack in the foundation turns out to be something."

"Jesus."

"That's not so much," he and Charlie chorused in unison.

They made her laugh, her beautiful darling boys. "Could I convince you to stop if I told you I might have another job?"

"No!" Pete said.

"No!" Charlie seconded.

"*Do* you have a new job?" Pete asked.

"I think so. I haven't seen the contract yet."

"A contract," Pete said, sounding excited. "Can I read it before you sign?"

Her slightly older younger brother was at least half lawyer. "I'll read it first," she said. "Then I'll consider letting you."

This was good enough for Pete. He rubbed his lean hands together. "We should celebrate."

"We should finish tearing out the drop ceiling first," Charlie corrected. "The permit guy said Becca's new between-unit insulation has to be sound and fire-rated."

As much as a brother could be, Charlie was her soul mate. If an activity counteracted worries, he was all for it.

"Why don't we do both?" she said. "I expect your friend Jesse will like celebrating too."

~

They spent a few hours on demo, getting disgustingly sweaty. After that, Rebecca showered and cooked a nice lunch for everyone. She expected the twins knew this would calm her, because they didn't volunteer to chop. Their friend Jesse ate more than he talked but seemed knowledgeable about construction. He was a class ahead of Pete and Charlie, and they obviously looked up to him. Just as obviously, he looked up to his father—whose firm Rebecca planned to Google the second the boys left.

She didn't bring up the obvious: that Pete and Charlie could save her money by moving home again. They paid for their housing with part-time jobs because their independence was important. No matter how much she missed them, she had to let them practice leaving the nest.

That, however, wouldn't come to pass today. Relaxed now and happy to have them near, she lingered with the three of them at the kitchen table, sipping coffee while Pete and Jesse teased Charlie about a girl he liked. Given their circumstances growing up, having a guest in the house was a relatively new pleasure.

It made them almost seem normal.

"You can't take a girl to the library on a date," Pete was instructing.

"That wasn't supposed to be the date," Charlie protested. "That was just where we arranged to meet. I can't help it if the stacks turn her on."

"Do you date much?" Jesse turned to ask her quietly.

Rebecca's mouth fell open. The faint flush on Jesse's sturdy face said he asked this out of more than idle curiosity. She supposed he was a good-looking kid. Compared to Trey, though, he seemed awfully unformed.

"Hardly ever," Charlie said as she searched for a safe answer. "Becca barely owns a dress."

"I do too," she said, thinking twice in one day was too often to be accused of this.

"It's a *beige* dress," Pete informed Jesse. "Buttons up to her neck like a nun's habit. I think she bought it back in '06."

"I did not. It's only, like, three years old. And it's a perfectly nice shirtwaist. Anyway, why do I have to wear a dress on a date?"

"You don't have to wear anything," Jesse assured her earnestly, which sent her brothers into fresh fits of snickering.

The boys proved they all were too young to date by throwing balled-up napkins at each other. Maybe sensing he wasn't coming off as mature, Jesse volunteered to help clean up. Rebecca's kitchen was old and didn't have a dishwasher. Not quite by the by, Jesse mentioned he could get her a deal on a kitchen reno . . . once her income suite was finished.

Rebecca avoided grinning by a hair. Jesse might be young, but he certainly was working out the paths to a woman's heart.

Pete seemed to think his friend had made too much progress. As the others went down the front walk later, he hung back in the entry. "Watch out for him," he said, cocking his head toward Jesse's departing back. "He's a nice guy, but he's got a string of older women he dangles after him."

"Ah, the lure of a hunky young handyman," she mused.

"I'm serious," Pete said. "Not that you shouldn't date. You should. Maybe someone fun your own age. It isn't right for you to give up having a life for me and Charlie."

Rebecca absolutely wasn't going to mention the *fun* she had that morning. She hugged Pete instead, loving the easy way his arms came around her. Neither of her brothers had outgrown showing affection.

"I shall ruminate on your advice," she promised him humorously.

Pete pushed her back to arm's length, his almost-adult face concerned. "You don't have to be alone so much, Sis. The time when the three of us had to hide things is over."

Before she could speak, he trotted down the front steps after the other two, leaving her with her eyes stinging. Sometimes Rebecca wished the twins weren't so awesome. If they hadn't been, maybe she wouldn't dread the day when they *would* be grown up.

~

Zane and Trey had come a long way from their student digs in Cambridge. Their place in Lexington was a 1930's era mansion set on sixteen acres of walled-in greenery. Their needs were seen to by a small and loyal staff, perhaps the only people in the world who knew Zane and Trey rarely used the second of their two bedrooms. The house itself had twenty, plus a library, an indoor pool, an outdoor lagoon, and a huge garage with room for fifteen cars.

They sometimes threw weekend parties, which could get racy. Then the rule was what happened at Buck House—as the estate was known locally—stayed at Buck House. Thus far, they hadn't had problems. The friends who came to play also valued privacy.

Most of the time, they enjoyed the place on their own. It was too big for two people, but it was peaceful. Zane loved coming home to it, whether from a day in Boston or a longer business trip. Few residences could have reminded him less of the 1960's rambler he'd grown up in. He could be a different person here entirely—not abused, not boiling so helplessly with anger he feared he'd turn patricide. Here he was free and calm. Here he and Trey ruled what they surveyed.

Owens, their relatively new driver, dropped Zane off at the tall columned portico. Owens would park the limo, pass Zane's luggage to Mrs. Penworth for laundering, after which he'd retire to his apartment over the big garage. The man was settling in. As a nephew to Mrs. Penworth, their house manager, he'd known what to expect of the job.

With no suitcases to haul in, Zane let himself in the wide front entrance. The hour was past ten. The house was quiet, nothing brighter than wall sconces burning in the main hall. To Zane's left, the paneled door to the library was ajar.

"Trey?" he called, his heart beating faster at the thought of greeting his closest friend. Per usual, his eagerness to see Trey made him slightly uneasy. Pushing that aside, he swung the library door open. A single black-shaded sconce near the door illuminated the long book-lined space. Naturally, the A/C was blasting. Trey liked the house chilly.

"You in here, Trey?" he asked.

"Here," he said from the other end of the room. He'd been hidden within a wing chair in the half-circle of French windows that overlooked the back lawn. Tonight, a bright half moon cast squares of light through the panes. Trey seemed to have been daydreaming. A magazine lay open on the carpet at his feet. On the table beside him a bottle of Bordeaux—half empty—and a glass—half full—showed how he'd spent the time.

Zane wondered if he were drunk, not a common state for him. Trey turned his head to watch him approach without rising. "How was Hawaii?"

"Unproductive. The resort wasn't up to TBBC standards."

"Mm," Trey said vaguely. He picked up his wine and sipped. "Meet any interesting women while you were there?"

Trey never asked him that. Zane couldn't imagine why he was asking now. "No. Wasting my time put me in a bad mood. I didn't feel like chasing skirts."

"Sorry," Trey said absently.

"You okay?" Zane dropped his hand onto Trey's shoulder. "You don't usually sit in the dark drinking wine."

"The moon was nice." Trey let out a laugh Zane couldn't interpret.

Because he hadn't gotten up yet, Zane bent down to kiss him. Trey touched his face and returned the slow lip lock. The kiss was nice. Trey didn't kiss any other way. Despite this, when Zane drew back, his uneasiness had returned. Something was off with his friend and, because of that, something was off with Zane.

"Did something happen while I was gone?" He stiffened as a possibility occurred to him. "You didn't get another letter from your aunt, did you?"

Trey's father had killed himself six months earlier. According to the police, he'd left no note and no warning signs besides a general depression. Mr. Hayworth had simply parked in his closed garage and let the engine run. This, as it happened, was the same method his wife had used to commit suicide. Trey hadn't gone to the funeral. His father hadn't contacted Trey after he went to college, nor had his son called him. His aunt, on the other hand, had been writing to her nephew ever since her brother's death. Her persistence was one of few things Zane ever saw upset Trey.

"No," Trey said, squeezing Zane's hand in reassurance. "And it wouldn't matter if I had. I know all she has to say: that her father didn't abuse my dad when he was a kid, and if my dad ever told me differently, it was a pack of lies. I don't think she realizes she confirmed what I'd only suspected until she wrote me that first time."

Zane sat on Trey's chair arm, letting their sides rest companionably together. "Why do you suppose she keeps at it?"

"God knows." Trey wiped his hands down his face, dragging the muscles with his palms. "After all these years, I think she's having trouble believing her own story. If she can convince me, the lie will be shored up. She was older than my dad. Maybe part of her thinks she should have protected him."

"Maybe she wants forgiveness."

"I can't forgive her for something she won't admit happened. Hell, I don't even know her. Dad kept me away from his relatives."

"Bet you didn't guess the fucked-up way he raised you was kind of a favor."

Trey laughed, the streak of black humor about their childhoods a trait they shared. He pushed out of the wingchair, maybe not drunk, because he didn't sway.

"Come." He reached for Zane's hand. "Walk in the moonlight with me."

"Romantic," Zane accused, not minding that at all.

"You bring it out in me. Always have and always will."

Zane's body stirred for his lover, waking as it hadn't for the beaches or the beauties of Hawaii. Aware this was liable to turn into more than a walk, he opened one of the French doors. Perversely, Trey resisted his tug toward it.

Grinning, he pulled out the drawer in the little table his wine sat on. Digging through the clutter, he retrieved a pair of wrapped condoms.

"In case I get lucky," he explained, flashing his dimples.

"In case *you* do." Amused and finally feeling he was home, Zane bumped his shoulder. Hand-in-hand, they strolled onto the lush green lawn. Crickets creaked and ivy rustled on the back wall. The night was sultry compared to the over-cranked A/C, the warmth as soft as velvet against his skin.

"Welcome home," Trey murmured, fingers rubbing his gently.

Zane ignored his worry that Trey was the only person in the world who made him this happy.

~

The email with Rebecca's proposed employment contract arrived later that evening. It was long, but if she understood the legalese correctly, it was weighted more in her favor than TBBC's. The salary seemed astronomical, the signing bonus overkill. She supposed Trey's company paid the most to get the best, but could this be normal? She read the thing three times at the kitchen table to make sure she wasn't overlooking a hidden catch. Maybe he'd lied about not sleeping with her again. Maybe she was secretly agreeing to be his sex slave.

You're neurotic, she reminded herself. *Can't too good to be true really be true sometimes?*

Constitutionally unable to bring herself to sign so quickly, she went down the steps to the cellar to mull over her alternate concern. Funnily enough, the gloomy old cellar looked better torn back to studs. Being her, she couldn't resist carrying a flashlight to the crack in the foundation. Now uncovered, it ran in jags from the wall's top to its bottom. Though it was dry at the moment, she saw signs water had seeped in. According to Jesse, her outside wall might need excavating—which could cost additional thousands.

She touched the crack and gnawed at her lip. How long had the break been here? Since their mother's death? Since their father's abandonment? Maybe it was a blessing she hadn't known. If she had, she wouldn't have slept a wink in years.

She shivered, suddenly aware how alone she was down here—no one in the house above her, no close ties to her neighbors. Her mind flashed back to the feel of Trey's arms around her. She wished someone were there to hold her now, to tell her: *I understand why you're upset the twins' clothes and toys are gone.* Yes, maybe other kids could use them, but she'd liked knowing they were here.

Sighing, she plunked her butt on the cellar steps.

What had Trey been like as a boy? And how did boys grow up to be tycoons? He seemed the type for whom business would be an interesting challenge, but not an obsession. His partner, Zane Alexander, was usually the one the press interviewed. Was he more ambitious or just better at talking? They looked as if they liked each other when they were photographed, as if they were good friends. What would it be like to have a friend that long? Raoul was her friend, but they didn't hang out and drink beers. He invited her to his house sometimes, and she ate barbecue with his family. Though they cared about each other, she couldn't imagine telling him anything truly personal.

She couldn't imagine telling him she'd had wild monkey sex with her brand new boss on a kitchen floor.

She hoped the wild monkey sex wasn't the reason for the generosity of her contract.

"You have to sign it," she said, admitting it. If she didn't, how would she pay for this maybe-not-crazy project the boys had roped her into?

To her surprise, the decision eased the semi permanent knots of worry in her shoulders.

She continued to feel better when she woke up the next morning, though she did wish she were going in to work. She'd faxed the signed contract back last night. When she checked her email, she had a response from the as-yet-unmet assistant Elaine. She asked if Rebecca was free to meet Mr. Hayworth on Wednesday, to discuss her ideas concerning hiring and menus. While Rebecca appreciated the implication that her opinions were valuable, it seemed to her Trey could have sent his own answer. Was he that busy? Or did he intend this distance to cool things between them? She couldn't forget him saying he pictured them having fun together at the restaurant.

Odds were, she shouldn't hold her breath on that.

To keep herself occupied, she cooked up a care package for the boys, everything assembled in pans with reheating instructions. They rented a house with six other students, and it had a full kitchen. She wondered if she should throw in candles to help the romantically challenged Charlie with his new girl. Was it weird to admit she knew he and Pete were sexually active?

The kitchen phone rang as she slid the finished dishes into her fridge. Her heart jumped into her throat. What if Trey were calling her?

"Pete," she said, recognizing his voice after she picked up. She swore she wasn't disappointed. That would have been stupid.

"Bec," he said, the super-shortening of her name a signal that something was up. "Glad I caught you. I need a favor for Charlie. Can you bring his anti-anxiety meds to the Common?"

"Boston Common? What are you doing there? And why does Charlie want his meds? I thought he decided not to take them anymore, on account of the side effects."

"He did, which is why he left the last of his supply in the medicine cabinet in our old bathroom."

Her knees now a little shaky, Rebecca sat on the old vinyl barstool beside the phone. Leaving the pills here was pure Charlie. For him, preserving one final shred of his security blanket made it easier to let go.

"He probably won't need them," Pete assured her. "If you just bring them out, he'll feel better."

"But what's wrong?"

There was a pause while Pete covered his cell phone. When he came back, his voice was hushed. "It's that girl he likes. She came to watch the photo shoot."

This answer was pure Pete. "What photo shoot?"

"We told you," Pete said, which he so had not. "Charlie and I and a couple others got picked to be this year's Hot Men of Harvard. You know, for *Bad Boys Magazine*. They're paying us real money. We're putting it toward the income suite. The thing is, we have to strip down to Speedos, and Charlie doesn't want to get too nervous and look like a dork in front of Caroline."

Rebecca squeezed her temples, her brain trying to process too much information simultaneously. "*Bad Boys Magazine?*" she repeated, experiencing a neck-tickling prickle at the coincidence.

"It's that magazine with the fancy cars and the watches. It's national, not skeevy. The guys who own it are these cool self-made billionaires."

This Rebecca was aware of. "Right," she said aloud.

"You'll come, won't you?" Pete continued. "I don't want Charlie to be embarrassed. This girl is really cool."

"I'll come," Rebecca promised. "And I'll bring Charlie's pills. I'm just not sure they're supposed to be used like this."

"Thank you!" Pete exclaimed. "Like I said, once he knows you've brought them, he'll probably feel better."

"Fine. Just give me time to change. All I've got on is jeans and an old T-shirt."

"Uh," Pete said. "Your jeans look good. I mean, they're fine. Most of the people here are wearing them. Maybe it's better you don't make Charlie wait."

His tone was weird, but he hung up before she could question him. She shook her head at the receiver. She felt more comfortable in work clothes, but if Charlie were having a crisis, she'd go as she was. In a way, she found Pete's call reassuring. She guessed her little brothers weren't independent yet.

CHAPTER SEVEN

Common Ground

*Well, **hello**,* Zane thought, his inner skirt-chaser perking up. A little blonde was hurrying toward him on the Public Garden's pedestrian bridge. The temperature was near ninety, for which he was grateful. The pint-sized bit of booty wore a strappy Harvard T-shirt with a shelf bra built in. She had great arms, slim but muscled, and truly mouthwatering tits. Jiggling on her ribs with the energy of her strides, they were no bigger than oranges but beautifully shaped and high. Her lack of stature aside, her legs and hips were great—precisely the sort of limbs faded blue jeans were meant to drape. Her hair was a Peter Pan pixie cut. Cute, he thought, and ideal for showing off her cheekbones.

Observing that she seemed to be looking for something, Zane stepped politely into her path.

"Need help?" he offered when she jolted to a stop.

She had big gray eyes, startled at the moment and unexpectedly piercing. Without warning, his throat tightened. For a second, he had the odd sensation that he knew her.

"Oh," she said, lashes blinking fast as she took him in. As usually happened with women, her gaze took a detour over his chest. Shaking that off sooner than some did, she clutched her canvas shoulder bag closer to her side. "I'm looking for a photo shoot. My brother is one of the models. He told me they were posing in Boston Common, but no one's there."

"We *were* there," Zane said pleasantly. "Now we're setting up near the swan

67

boats."

"Oh. You're with them. That's great. I really need to find Charlie or Pete Eilert."

"Of course," he said, realizing why she seemed familiar. "You must be Rebecca. I see the family resemblance. I'm Zane Alexander, by the way. It's very nice to meet you."

This appeared to fluster her. Her cheeks flushed up an adorable pink, a color that went well with her luscious mouth. Her upper lip was shorter than her lower, creating an effect that was both succulent and girlish. Added to the big eyes and the gamine hair, she looked impossibly innocent.

Zane sent up a silent prayer that this was misleading.

She accepted the hand he held out dazedly. "I— I'm sorry," she said. "I should have recognized you. You're the Zane Alexander who owns the magazine."

"I am." He was pleased she didn't seem star-struck. Skirts that belonged to groupies weren't his favorite to chase. Rebecca's little hand was cold. He experienced a need to chafe it he truly couldn't resist. "Why don't I take you to where they're setting up?"

She was gaping at him, but at this she shut her mouth. "Yes," she said, retrieving her hand from his. "That would be nice of you."

He'd waylaid her on the stretch of bridge that crossed the narrowest point of the park's lagoon. Having lost her hand, he took her elbow to lead her down the small jog of stairs to the bank. If she'd taken ten steps farther, she'd have seen the set-up herself. The crowd of boys in Speedos had gathered near the swan boats, which the magazine had taken over for the time being. The photographer and his assistants were there as well, adjusting reflectors and blotting sweat as required.

"Group photo," he explained as the dozen underdressed college boys clambered joking onto the wooden seats. The pontoons sploshed at their shifting weight. "It's kitschy, but I expect readers will like it."

On the bank now, Rebecca searched the faces for ones she knew. Zane's hold remained on her arm. He felt her stiffen as she spied who she sought.

"The little bastard," she murmured. "He's perfectly all right."

Zane followed her line of sight. One of her brothers had thrown his head back with laughter at something another model said. He wasn't certain which twin it was, but he took a wild guess. "That one's Charlie?"

"It is," his sister confirmed. "Apparently, Pete called me out here for nothing."

Her delectable pink mouth flattened into a line. "Not for nothing," he coaxed, secretly enjoying the angry set of her jaw. "It's a pretty day, and I'm happy to meet you."

She gave him her full and startled attention. Zane struggled not to laugh. For whatever reason, this cutie wasn't expecting to be flirted with. No doubt his amusement showed in his eyes. Rebecca's brows drew together in confusion. "Why are you here exactly? Aren't you too important?"

He did laugh then. "I usually do the interviews for our annual Hot Men of Harvard piece. *Bad Boys Magazine* has its own staff these days, but now and then I get nostalgic. When we started, I did everything from layout to selling ads. Anyway, I like to see what the latest generation of Harvard lights is up to. Your brothers were standouts. Very well spoken and personable. Their account of how you raised them is inspiring."

Rebecca let out a gasp so sharp he couldn't miss hearing it. "They told you that?"

"Shouldn't they have?" His answer was the pallor that swept her face. If that weren't enough to clue him in that something was wrong, one of her knees buckled. She looked as if she were going to boot or faint.

"Hey," he said, quickly getting an arm around her. "Let's find you somewhere to sit."

He grabbed a bottled water from a passing magazine staffer, not wanting to pause more than that in guiding his distressed damsel to a shady spot. The nearest he saw was under a huge weeping willow. Rebecca was shaking as he settled her on the bench. He handed her the water, which she took a sip of.

"Sorry," she said. "I'm all right. That just took me by surprise."

Zane sat next to her, figuring she could use his warmth. She seemed to be in shock. Her side was actually cold.

"Look," he said, laying his hand gently on her knee. Despite being attracted to her, he tried to keep the touch platonic. "If you need me to pull the interview, I will. Your brothers didn't act like they were breaking a confidence, and God knows my tiny journalist streak will cry—as human interest goes, the story is great. I will kill it, though, if it bothers you that much. We'll find something else to sell issues."

Rebecca rubbed her forehead. "I guess it's not a deep dark secret anymore. They're too old for anyone to take them away from me."

Zane's throat tightened the same way it had when he first saw her eyes. "Your brothers should have warned you they were going to spill the beans."

To his surprise, she laughed. The sound was nice, low and a bit throaty. "Pete and Charlie know me too well to ask permission about some things. They must have decided I'd been holding on to that too long."

"So you don't mind? God knows I'd like to run the piece. Their stories of how you tried to pretend your father was still around were hilarious."

Rebecca laughed again. "Did they tell you about our Christmas Eve with the mannequin?"

"How Charlie stayed up all night and moved it from chair to chair to convince the neighbors that it was real?"

"What about the Brazilian fry cook I hired to impersonate our dad for parent-teacher night? He had gray eyes, which was perfect, but he barely knew

English. We pretended he had laryngitis and couldn't speak."

"That one I didn't hear."

Rebecca leaned back against the bench, her shoulders almost relaxed. "He was illegal and really sweet. I promised I'd sponsor him for a green card as soon as I was old enough and had a job where I could."

"And did you?"

"I did. He works in LA now for Wolfgang Puck. That frosts me a little. He was a damn good cook. I'd be happy if he was still with me."

Her smile was wry but totally beautiful. "You must have been scared," he said softly. "Raising two boys by yourself at sixteen."

"Terrified," she said humorously. "Sometimes I still am."

They smiled at each other, and something inside his chest swooped like a wave dropping. He'd had Trey to help him through his nightmare years. This woman had no one. "Your brothers were lucky to have you."

"Oh no." She shook her head in disagreement. "I'm lucky to have them. They're such great kids. I don't know how they turned out so good."

Zane knew. The love she felt for them shone like a sun from her. Whatever mistakes she'd made, her brothers wouldn't have doubted that. To him, who'd been anything but loved, it was no wonder they'd flourished. He wanted to touch her, more than the hand he'd left resting on her knee. Her cheek looked like it would be soft to stroke, her lips a dream to kiss.

"Would you have dinner with me?" he asked before he'd quite planned to.

She jerked in surprise. "Oh. I—"

"Coffee is fine too, if that seems lower key."

She laughed and covered her lips. "It's not that . . . I don't know if you know this. It's kind of a funny coincidence. Your CFO, Trey Hayworth, recently hired me to run your new restaurant."

Zane sat straighter, drawing his hand back from her knee. "The Bad Boys Lounge on Charles Street?"

"That's right. So I don't know. Maybe you're my employer too?"

Zane supposed he shouldn't be taken aback by not knowing. The restaurant—their first that wasn't part of a resort—was more Trey's project than his. It was odd Trey hadn't kept Zane in the loop, but not overly. "I'm . . . more of a silent partner there," he said. "I'm pretty sure us having dinner wouldn't break any rules."

Rebecca stuck a thumbnail between her teeth, obviously considering this. Zane wasn't accustomed to hesitation, certainly not from women who showed signs of finding him attractive.

"Should I reiterate the coffee option?" he offered, trying not to sound insulted.

Rebecca removed the thumbnail she was gnawing. "Sorry. I—" She squared her shoulders with a crispness that would have amused if it hadn't been *his* ego that was stinging. "I'd be very happy to have dinner with you. I just feel obliged to warn you I'm not in practice for dating."

Not in practice sounded like Rebecca wouldn't be his usual speedy catch-and-release conquest. But maybe that was all right. He hadn't lied to Trey the other night. He was tired of chasing females, only to leave them by the roadside. Admittedly, if this one let him bed her right away, he wouldn't turn her down, but maybe actually talking to a woman on a date, with no expectations beyond that, wouldn't be awful. He could relax and let her relax too. If she were as tightly wound as today's exchange suggested, she needed it.

~

Like his CFO, Zane Alexander packed an extra punch in person. For one thing, he was plain old big—6'4" or 5" with muscle packed onto his muscle and shoulders she was certain could still play quarterback. Staring at him from her height-challenged state easily could have overwhelmed her.

Rebecca was fortunate she was ballsier than she looked.

Her hormones had a harder time digging in their heels. He was a hunk and a half. Great body. Great face. Killer smile and blue eyes. If Trey was quirkily good-looking, Zane was flat out handsome. His hair was a thick sandy color, expertly styled to create a just-rolled-out-of-bed, finger-combed casualness. He wore the same uniform as the rest of the magazine staff: straight-legged jeans topped by a short sleeve Henley with the *Bad Boys* logo on the left breast. No one looked bad in it, but as he leaned forward over his knees on that willow-shaded bench—the better to meet her gaze—he was drool worthy.

The gray waffle cotton hugged his torso lovingly. Even the sweat marks beneath his arms didn't lessen his sexiness. From where she sat, his body's reaction to the August heat just made him smell better. He and Trey both had good taste in cologne.

The fact that Zane had asked her out—and that she'd accepted—somewhat astonished her.

Should she have said *yes?* Would having dinner with him create more complications between her and Trey? Not that there necessarily was anything between them apart from a work relationship. They'd both agreed their hot-as-Hades indiscretion in the Bad Boys kitchen shouldn't be repeated.

Crap, Rebecca thought, her insides melting like flambé—both for the hunk in front of her and the one she'd just remembered. A bead of sweat rolled down the small of her back. Could a woman cream through a pair of panties *and* blue jeans? That would be embarrassing.

"Rebecca?" Zane said like he was about to laugh. The back of one big knuckle brushed the side of her leg. It was a light touch, really, but it raised a pulsing tingle inside her clit.

"What?" she asked, aware she'd missed something.

"Is tonight okay for dinner? I could pick you up around six."

He could pick her up, and they'd sit across from each other at an intimate table. She'd stare at that full-lipped mouth, watching it grin, watching it eat, wondering how it would feel eating her . . .

"Tonight is fine," she said, slightly strangled. She didn't have to sleep with him. Probably he wouldn't want to once he realized what an oddball she was. She'd wrestle her hormones into submission. Rebecca was no stranger to self-control.

"Good," he said, smiling at her and giving her thigh a pat.

That settled, he sat back and rolled his big shoulders. The way this shifted his chest muscles fascinated her. Despite his magazine-perfect grooming, he seemed as much animal as man. Rebecca truly couldn't look away. He didn't appear to have the same problem.

"Ah," he said, his gaze directed toward the lagoon and the photo shoot. "Here are your brothers now."

Rebecca jerked her much too X-rated attention away from him. Her brothers were indeed coming over. For some reason, the twins were dripping from head to toe. They'd been supplied with Bad Boy brand robes to wrap over their skimpy Speedos. Soaked state aside, they looked happy.

"Hey, Becca," Pete greeted her. "Hello, Mr. Alexander. We were going to introduce you two, but I guess you took care of it yourselves."

Rebecca's head had a lot going on in it right then. Nonetheless, a light bulb did turn on. This whole thing—Pete's claim that Charlie needed his meds, asking that she not change out of her snug old jeans—was the boys' idea of a fix-up.

"Glad you're feeling all right," she said dryly to Charlie.

"Oh sure," he said. "I don't mind being tossed overboard with Pete. The other guys were only horsing around."

"I meant you've recovered from your anxiety attack."

Her slightly younger little brother had sufficient conscience to blush. "Oh. Um, that was a false alarm. Caroline didn't show up after all."

"That's too bad." Rebecca ladled on the sympathy. "Why don't you invite her for Sunday dinner? I'll meet her then."

"Uh," Charlie stammered. "I don't— She might—"

Pete covered his snickers with his hand.

"I haven't decided how to pay you back yet," she warned him.

"Pay me back for what?" Pete said with his sweetest smile.

Zane stopped her answer by rising. "I see you've got family stuff to talk about. Go ahead and take a break, boys. I'll see *you*—" he pinned Rebecca with a sexy smile "—around six o'clock tonight."

"He'll see you?" Pete repeated as soon as Zane was out of earshot. "He asked you out already?"

He seemed both delighted and surprised.

"That's quick work," Charlie said in a similar tone.

She wasn't mad enough to scold them. The flattering aspects of having a date with a guy like Zane were making her giddy. On principle, she pretended to be annoyed.

"You two," she said, "are lucky you're too old to be grounded."

~

The photo shoot was duller after Rebecca left, but Zane stayed until the end. Rebecca's brothers waved goodbye to him as they straggled off with the others. Their gawky man-boyishness amused him, while their innate niceness reminded him of their big sister. She flitted in and out of his thoughts as he returned to TBBC's headquarters. Work reclaimed his attention there, mostly. He had one meeting, two calls, and a boring report to review. To lessen the drudgery of that, he read the document on his tablet between showering and changing for dinner. Spending long hours at the office made it handy for him and Trey to share a trio of rooms behind their offices. They had a full bath, a walk-in wardrobe, and a quiet space with a napping couch.

Trey came into the bathroom as Zane scraped five o'clock shadow from his cheeks. Stubble didn't suit him like it did Trey.

"Going out?" Trey asked, sounding a bit surprised.

Zane rinsed the razor under the tap. "Yes. With the older sister of some kids who were in the shoot today."

Trey leaned against the doorway. "Pretty?"

"Yes." He started on the other side. Part of him suspected he ought to tell Trey his date was Rebecca. She was his employee, and he might worry Zane would mess that up. The thing was, Zane didn't want to be told to watch his step with her. The chances they'd have a second date were small—or that this one would go so badly she'd feel a need to flee the state. In any case, Trey hadn't told Zane he'd hired her. Maybe Zane was being stubborn, but he shouldn't have to get Trey's approval.

"Missed a spot," Trey said, taking the razor from him. He tipped Zane's chin sideways with his fingers, dragging the blade carefully up his throat. His touch was pleasant and familiar, creating a heaviness in Zane's groin that wasn't quite an erection. Finished, Trey set down the razor and smiled at him. "Now you're perfect."

His green-gold eyes were fond. Emotion rose inside Zane, strong as a summer storm. "You're perfect," he said back.

Trey laughed and kissed his cheek. "You have your car, right? I can take the limo home without you?"

"Yes. I don't think I'll be home too late. This woman is no sure thing."

He spoke without considering how the claim would sound. Trey lifted his dark brows. "Not losing your touch, are you?"

"Doubt it." Zane grinned even as a prick of guilt for holding back information urged him to be honest. "This one is nice to talk to is all. We had some common ground."

"Well, good," Trey said, but as if he wasn't sure it was. He hesitated. "Have a good time."

He left before Zane could figure out how to close the odd little distance that had opened between them. He shrugged as Trey shut the mini-apartment's outer door. He probably shouldn't worry. He and Trey were solid. Nothing stayed off between them long.

~

By the time her cheap bedside clock ticked to six, Rebecca was ready to admit her brothers were right about her wardrobe. She had nothing date-appropriate to wear—not her work clothes, not her jeans, not her suddenly sorry-seeming beige shirtwaist dress.

It was just her luck that the doorbell rang while she was in it.

"Screw it," she said to her reflection. She'd showered and shaved her legs and slapped on both lipstick and mascara. This was as good as she got. If Zane Alexander didn't like it, she couldn't help that now.

When she opened the door, the warmth of his smile nearly wiped out her nervousness.

"You look so nice!" she exclaimed, unable to hold it in. He was wearing pale linen trousers with a thin designer-y black T-shirt. His narrow leather belt probably cost more than her dress, and never mind his sharp-looking shoes.

"Thank you." He bent to kiss her cheek, wafting the scent of soap and cologne over her. "You look pretty nice yourself."

"Ugh," she said, at which he raised his brows. "All right, I'm supposed thank people for compliments, but I know you're lying. I'm afraid this is the only dress I own."

"You could have worn jeans."

"I considered them, believe me. This is what I was in when the doorbell rang."

He laughed, seeming to enjoy her neurotic honesty. "I could mention that, to me, you'd look good in a sack."

"Hm." She gazed at him sidelong. "You're pretty good at this lying thing."

He laughed at that too, further lightening her mood. With a flair she couldn't help but appreciate, he presented her with a bent elbow. "Ready to go?"

Sliding her arm into the crook of his was a pleasure she wasn't prepared for. His skin was warm, his golden body hair like silk. Her arm was bare against both. She shivered, and then he did, and then he laughed again.

"See," he teased. "You don't need fancy dresses to get to me."

Rebecca didn't know if their destination was his original choice, or if he'd switched gears to make her more comfortable. Whichever it was, he took her to The Cellar Pub, a local hole in the wall that offered a dizzying array of craft beers and burgers.

"This okay?" he asked as she scanned the menu posted outside the entrance.

"Perfect," she said, only to be surprised by how genuinely pleased his smile of response was.

The place was crowded with young people—*of which you are one*, she reminded herself. Zane got them a booth in a back corner. Rebecca decided he was one of those people who felt at home anywhere. Like a big slouchy cat, he relaxed against the seat, arm stretched along the back and knees sprawled casually. Rebecca wished she could imitate him. Her limbs all felt as stiff as pokers.

When the waitress came, he convinced her to bring them a tray of small samples for the beers. "With labels," he said, slipping a folded hundred into her hand. "I know it's a hassle, but we'd really be grateful."

"How did you know I wanted to do that?" Rebecca asked.

"Just a guess," he said, pleased again. "Chefs like to taste things, don't they?"

"They do," she said, pleased with him as well.

By the sixth tasting sample, Rebecca's neck unkinked.

"So . . ." Zane said on a teasing note. "What's the story about that dress?"

"Oh God."

"I told you I didn't mind but, seriously, only one? What do you wear on dates? And don't tell me you never go, because you're too pretty."

"I guess I don't go on date-y dates."

Zane put his elbow on the table and his chin on his hand. He was silently —and grinningly—inviting her to go on.

"Oh fine. I feel most comfortable in work clothes. My closet is full of black trousers and button-up white shirts."

She turned the shot glass she was currently sampling from in a circle. Zane reached lazily out and covered her hand with his. His touch stilled more than her fingers. She could actually feel her pulse slow. "Why do you feel most comfortable in work clothes?"

"You don't really want to know that."

"Yes I do." His thumb rubbed the side of hers, stirring hot sensations his knowing eyes seemed completely aware of. Rebecca tensed her thighs. "Does it have to do with raising your brothers?"

She sat back but left her hand where it was, under his. "Work didn't just save us," she admitted. "It saved me. I'd lost my mom. My dad had walked out." She grimaced, but let the memory go. "I needed something to keep me from constantly worrying. I could cook, and restaurants aren't always fussy about who they hire. I made money to cover bills, and I found a calling. Putting on my chef's whites is my idea of dress up."

He took that in, his blue eyes steady and quiet.

"Tell me about you," she said.

The waitress returned with their loaded burgers. They were delicious, charred and juicy and rare on the inside. Good though they were, Rebecca wasn't going to let a little thing like eating get him off the hook.

"Tell me about you," she insisted.

"That's a long and unsavory tale."

"So?" she said around a bite of red meat.

He thought for a moment. He was such a charmer, he must have a standard answer, one that would relay amusing and evasive truths. Rebecca hoped that wasn't the answer she'd get. He set down his burger and faced her.

"My father used to beat me."

That she wasn't expecting. "Like . . . as a regular thing?"

"Once a week, I'd say. Depending on how much he was drinking and if I 'made' him lose his temper. Starting when I was ten or so."

"And your Mom?"

"She wasn't in the picture. She ran off with the Mattress King, ironically enough."

"The Mattress King?"

"He owned a warehouse store in Trenton. Wore a bad toupee and ran loud commercials on late night TV. We lived in a small town. My father didn't much like having been thrown over for a bad joke."

"Wow," Rebecca said, picking up her food again.

Zane did as well, though she doubted he tasted it before he swallowed. "I don't talk to him anymore. When Trey and I left for college, I never looked back again."

"That was probably smart," she said, though she knew people did look back—whether they wanted to or not.

He nodded and looked down. He didn't seem like a mogul. He just seemed like a person. Rebecca wondered if she should touch him the way he had her. Giving in to the impulse, she rubbed his strong-boned wrist. He didn't pull away.

"I'm okay," he said. "I had Trey to get me through. We had each other."

Something in his voice said this hadn't been an ordinary friendship.

"You two are close."

"Yes," he said and lifted his gaze to hers.

She couldn't read what was behind it but sensed she was seeing a side of him he didn't show most people. How did souls connect? People talked about it in books: The eyes were the window to and all that. Pete and Charlie were part of her, but other folks were a mystery. Was Zane's soul talking to hers as he stared at her? Did hers understand the secrets that weren't coming out his mouth?

Okay, she told herself. *You've had too much beer.*

Maybe he thought so too. He broke the tension with a gentle but charming smile. "This is too serious. I should be asking you your favorite movie or where you wish you could go on vacation."

"To work," she not-quite-joked. "Obviously."

"You could cook your way around Europe," he suggested in the same vein.

"Mm," she said. "That would be fabulous."

~

Rebecca lived in a single family two-story Victorian. The residence wouldn't have been fancy even when it was new, but Zane supposed it had character. When he picked her up, she'd explained her brothers' basement apartment plan. Zane had assured her the strategy wasn't stupid, and that she'd have no trouble learning how to be a landlord.

"You're a boss already," he'd said. "You're used to keeping on top of things."

The dumpster hulking in her front yard was less obvious in the dark. As he parked his old silver convertible in her driveway, Zane reminded himself she had a lot of pressures on her: new job, changing home, boys becoming more independent and expecting her to let them. For a person as tightly wound as Rebecca, this wouldn't be easy. She might not be in the mood to hop into bed with him.

This, needless to say, wasn't a thought he was used to having about women.

Overall, tonight had left him off kilter. He wondered why he'd told her about his father hitting him. Because she was different than his usual arm candy? Because her brothers had opened a window onto her equally non picket-fence childhood?

Unable to answer, he shut off the engine. By this point, he was half-hard, though he knew better than to look too eager to be invited in. He didn't want to push Rebecca past her comfort zone. Hell, maybe he didn't want to push himself. He was seriously attracted to her, more than he'd been to any woman recently.

Ignoring the whiff of danger, he turned in his seat and looked at her. She was sitting forward with her knees together, her thumbnail stuck between her teeth again. The nervous gesture shouldn't have struck him as so endearing. The compulsion to put her at her ease was strong. One thing he knew for sure: he didn't want the night to be over yet.

"You know," he said, his wrist draped over the steering wheel. "I think when Trey and I were students, we lived less than half a mile from here."

She twisted to face him. The Mercedes' top was down and the nearest streetlamp lit her fine features. "Really? We could have met and not known it?"

This seemed to intrigue her. Smiling and oddly happy, he reached to brush a pixie wisp from her smooth cheekbone. "I'm just glad we've met now."

"Oh you're full of it," she said good-naturedly. "A guy like you could date a different woman every night of the week if you wanted to."

"A guy like me."

"You know: gorgeous, successful, in command of himself."

He liked her description. Enjoying the feel of her downy cheek, he continued stroking his finger over it. "Why can't I want to date you?"

"Because I'm weird."

"Maybe I like weird."

She smiled, her shoulders visibly relaxing. How did she get through every day so tensed up?

"You like *cute*-weird," she corrected, teasing him.

"I'm glad your self esteem is sufficient to admit you qualify."

She laid her adorable blonde head on the seat back, the change in position causing his hand to cup her ear. She might as well have groped his cock. His half hard-on lengthened inside his trousers, swiftly stiffening all the way.

"I had a nice time tonight," she said. "I liked talking to you."

"Me too." He was surprised how much he meant it, and how strongly the need to get inside her surged up in him.

"Will you kiss me good night?" she asked. Her manner wasn't quite shy, but it wasn't bold either—as if she wasn't certain he'd want to.

Zane wanted to kiss her, and a hell of a lot more besides. Chest rumbling with a growl he didn't mean to utter, he slid as far over as the small car required. She moved toward him simultaneously, her own cry as their lips met completely flattering.

Oh kissing her was good. She was small and strong and she poured her whole body into answering his passion. There was plenty of that, wave after wave rolling through him, until his dick ached with it. Groaning, he pulled her on top of him. He couldn't keep his hands from running over her. Her back, her arms, the curve of her narrow waist, all called him to admire them. Her tight little butt obsessed him—its firmness, its roundness, how he could cover half of it with his palm. Her ass made him long to take her in ways he'd only taken Trey until now.

Actually, her ass kind of made him want to spank her.

He counted himself fortunate she couldn't read his mind. "Mm," she hummed, wriggling as his hand slid under her wretched dress and over her slightly nicer satin panties. Half Zane's blood tried to race to his cock at once. She was wet, her gusset soaked where he pushed the cloth between her labia.

She broke free of his kiss and gasped.

"Too much?" he panted, feeling like a teenager who'd tried to steal third base.

"Maybe." Her Cheshire smile was at odds with her breathlessness. "Why don't I even things up a bit?"

His size and the car's lack of it didn't allow her much room to move. He debated suggesting they take this show inside when her surprisingly firm hand wrapped his erection. He arched, the top of his head bumping the window frame. The way his scalp tingled had more to do with her rubbing him than the possible concussion.

"Fuck," he groaned, feeling her touch so intensely he could hardly believe it. One more squeeze, and he swore he was going to come.

"Too much?" she asked.

Maybe she was joking. Tit for tat, and all that. Zane didn't wait to find out. He shoved her seat fully backward on its track, then flipped her down onto it. At the cost of a couple curses and bonked body parts, he twisted into a hunched position where he could shove her dress up and latch his mouth over her pussy. The pleasure he took in this improved the second he ripped away her panties. Her clit was so swollen he had no trouble zeroing in on it.

"Jesus," she said, ineffectually pushing at his head. He licked up her creamy button, and she whimpered. "Zane, the top of your car is down."

"Gaze at the stars," he laughed, drunk with the taste of her. "And for God's sake, don't be loud enough to disturb your neighbors."

"Oh God," she groaned, because he'd brought his thumbs into play beside his mouth. He wedged his shoulders beneath her thighs, spreading them wider. Her hands forked into his hair, her hips jerking closer in spite of her embarrassment with the exposure. "Zane, I can't—"

He found a hot spot to the left of her clit and worked it in a circle with the pad of his thumb. Apparently, it was a good nerve cluster. Rebecca groaned and thrashed and clutched his head harder. "We're outside," she said, trying to whisper. "I can't . . . relax enough to come."

He was pretty sure she could. She was hot enough to burn him, the moans that caught in her throat ramping up his excitement. Now that he'd got himself where he was, he was damned if he wanted to cut this short.

An idea sprang into his mind that—in the moment—seemed like genius. Possibly it was evil genius. His cock thudded like a demon as it came to him.

"I can help you keep quiet," he said, hands flying from her sex to his belt buckle. "Then you'll be able to relax."

His belt whipped free of its loops with a telltale metallic rattle.

"Zane," she breathed in shock. "You can't fuck me out here."

She would have let him. Her temperature had jumped ten degrees. "Not the plan," he assured her, despite the temptation. "Give me your wrists."

"What?"

"Wrists," he repeated.

She stared at him with her mouth open. Her pupils were dilated from more than the darkness. His instincts were on target. Whether she knew it or not, this game excited her.

"I promise," he swore harshly. "I'll stop the second you ask me to."

She swallowed and then offered him her wrists. She looked so obedient, so surprisingly natural. Zane's heart rate sped up wildly. He was doing a number on his own arousal as well. Trey had trained him to like these scenarios. Struggling not to shake, he wrapped his belt in figure eights around her slender wrists. The leather wasn't tied, but it would stay where it was.

"Bite it," he said. "Or hook it behind my neck. Whatever helps you feel in control."

The suggestion that binding her wrists would increase her sense of control sent a shudder through her body.

"Okay?" he asked, because she seemed unable to speak. She nodded, a quickened pulse beating in her throat. Satisfied, he bent back to her pussy.

She was twice as wet as before, twice as wild and responsive. She was also quieter. Only gasps and tiny strangled mewls came from her. When he rolled his eyes up, she had the belt clamped between her teeth. The sight did incredible things to him. He forgot how uncomfortable his hunched position was. Aroused beyond bearing, he wanted to make her come so hard the belt would be all that prevented her from screaming.

He sucked her until she tensed every muscle with her longing to go over, until he knew all she needed was a bit more pressure. He drove his hands up the front of her body, underneath her loose dress to the wire bottom of her bra. His fingers pushed it easily upward, each hand covering one round breast. Her skin was feverish, her hardened nipples perfect for scissoring between his knuckles.

She hissed and arched for how good that felt. Then, as if she needed it too much to remain inhibited, she finally slapped her belt-bound wrists behind his neck.

This was a signal he had no intention of disregarding. As she urged him closer, he lavished all his oral skill on her clit, sucking it with force and directness: lips, tongue, everything brought into play.

She came without screaming, but she came hard. When her thighs relaxed at last from their spasm of pleasure, he shifted up her body. The move kept her arms behind him, tied wrists limply hugging him. Her eyes were wide, her pulse still trembling within her cushy lips. He kissed her softly, and she returned it the same way. He loved that as much as he'd loved her earlier aggression. Her kiss conveyed a depth of caring he shouldn't have been hungry for. He *had* that in his life. Trey gave it to him in spades. Ruthlessly shoving that consciousness aside, he lowered his hips to hers.

The stiff ridge behind his zipper couldn't be overlooked.

"Zane," she murmured against mouth, definitely not an objection.

He didn't open his trousers. He liked his hands where they were, fanned and kneading her warm soft breasts. Rebecca's legs were parted around him, her panties torn away. He began to rub against her slowly, getting her wetness on the linen, teasing his prick with prospect of getting off. Her bound hands fisted in the small of his back, her calves moving restlessly behind his.

"Are you going to come like this?" she asked in a hushed tone. "Without even unzipping?"

He looked into her big gray eyes, into her shining black pupils. "Do you want me to?"

Her pelvis arched to him. "Yes, please," she whispered in answer.

He needed the release bad, but he didn't rush. He waited until tension rose in her again, wanting her to go with him. Then he dropped his head beside hers on the car seat and ground hard and quick into her mons, making sure to strafe the swelling at its apex. Growls of pent-up longing escaped him, his cock as trapped by his clothing as her wrists were by his belt. The constriction pleased his nerves, the perversity of doing this like he was back in high school. As excited as he was, the friction got to him in no time.

He had to let go, and he did. He gasped at the intensity of the orgasm, hot kicks of ejaculation driven hard from his cock and balls. Rebecca went a second later, her involuntary cry muffled against his neck.

He suspected he'd remember the sound of that for a while.

"Whew," Rebecca said after a long moment.

Zane covered her mouth with his sweaty hand. Someone was coming toward them on the sidewalk—walking a dog, he thought.

"Stay still," he instructed her very quietly. "I don't think they'll notice us."

The person didn't seem to, talking nonsense to his dog and humming an off-key show tune. By the time he was gone, Rebecca was biting her lip against laughing. She'd unwrapped his belt already to free her wrists, so he rolled off her. She straightened her dress and wriggled her bra back on. She tried to get the convertible's seat up, but she needed his help for that.

Her amusement remained apparent through all of it.

"We're both completely crazy," she declared.

Her hair was sticking up all over, actually more stylish than it had been before.

"Maybe," Zane said, giving in to the urge to smooth it, "but I'm pretty sure we need to do that again, preferably in a bed."

To his astonishment, her smile faded.

"Maybe we shouldn't," she said.

~

Rebecca saw she'd dumbfounded him, though he tried to act like it was no big deal. "Why would you say that?" he asked calmly.

She wasn't certain how to explain. What were the guy rules for two friends fooling around with the same woman? As to that, what were the girl rules for pointing out they had? She did her best not to squirm under his regard.

"I don't want to cause trouble between you and your partner."

"Trey and I don't run each other's sex lives. I mean, he wouldn't like me upsetting his new chef. Other than that, I don't see why he'd care."

He wasn't telling the complete truth. She knew that from her experiences riding herd on the twins. Maybe he saw the suspicion in her eyes. "Call me crazy," he said, turning it back on her, "but you seemed to enjoy what we did."

She'd more than enjoyed it. She'd been as shocked by his ability to divine her unsuspected kinks as she'd been by Trey's. "Of course I enjoyed it," she said aloud. "Maybe this is just too fast for me."

"I can slow down. I . . . like you, Rebecca. Why don't you take tonight to think about it? I'll call you tomorrow."

In her admittedly limited experience, guys rarely meant they *would* call when they said that. If Zane didn't mean it, it would let her off the hook of this dilemma.

"All right," she said, opening her door and getting out. "Call me tomorrow."

I won't be disappointed if you don't, she swore to herself as she went inside.

CHAPTER EIGHT

On the Menu

Trey had Elaine arrange his Wednesday appointment with Rebecca. He told himself it made sense to talk at the Lounge. Rebecca could confirm that the kitchen and dining room were set up to suit her. Yes, Zane was back in Boston and, yes, he might read something in Trey's body language if he saw him with her. That wasn't why Trey didn't want Rebecca at headquarters. He had no plans to pursue her. Anything Zane might misinterpret was moot.

Aware the excuse was slim, he shook his head and opened his laptop at one of the dining room's finished booths. He'd come early, and Rebecca wasn't there. Possibly, he should have had sex with Zane more than once this morning. The thought of his new chef arriving made his libido feel antsy.

He'd left the street entrance open, but Rebecca knocked anyway. Trey's palms broke into a sweat as he went to greet her.

"Hey," he said. "Glad you made it."

This wasn't very bosslike, but he was grateful anything came out of his mouth. His pulse was going haywire, his eyes trying to drink in every part of her at once. It wasn't normal to be this happy about another human being's presence.

"Come in," he said, stepping back to give her room.

She came, ran her gaze around, and turned back to smile at him. "It looks great," she said delightedly. "It's more finished than last time."

He reminded himself she was delighted because she'd be cooking here, not because she was with him. His cock wasn't listening. It was throwing a little party inside his Calvin Kleins.

"Should we sit?" he offered, gesturing toward the booth he'd chosen.

She jerked as if her thoughts might have wandered too. "Sure," she said. She held up the computer tablet she'd been clutching to the side of her crisp white shirt. "I brought some suggestions for the menu. I realize you're a foodie and probably have your own ideas. I promise I'm not married to what I'm proposing."

She wasn't married to what she was proposing. Trey's mind had trouble processing that plainly. "I want your ideas. I'd be wasting your expertise otherwise."

They slid into the booth at almost the same moment—and with very similar awkwardness. Trey's legs were longer and his foot ended up against hers. He pulled it back, but the contact rattled her as well. She fumbled over opening her computer, a hot red tide rising up her cheeks.

He wanted to lick the color, or maybe just fuck her senseless over the tabletop. He was so hard he hurt, his prick a fricking missile seeking the heat of her.

Sheesh, he thought. *I'm a maniac.*

The remainder of their discussion unrolled along the same road. Being this close to her might have been easier if he hadn't known she wanted him too. Because he did, it took twice as long to rough out a menu, considering they weren't at odds over it. Rebecca's vision of classic Boston favorites given a luxury twist was very much what he'd had in mind.

He noticed the longer they sat, the tighter she pressed her knees together. When she crossed them under the table, he wanted to break into tears. Truly, he deserved industrial strength credit for the sacrifice of not chasing her.

"I, uh, need to put the word out," she said. "But I should be able to pull a crew together within the next two weeks."

"You're going to steal some line cooks from your old employer."

Her sly smile was a welcome break from tension. "A couple. But they already told me they'd follow me to a new place."

He grinned back, and a small silence fell. Rebecca stroked the edge of her computer like it was something else. Trey tried not to get any harder at the unconsciously sexy movements of her fingers. Wrenching his eyes to her face didn't improve matters. Her lips were so tempting . . . and her eyes . . . and that delicate stubborn jaw . . .

"Uh," he said, his voice unavoidably husky. "We should plan on a dress rehearsal, after you've got the staff up to speed."

She'd stopped fondling her tablet, but seemed to be staring at his mouth. "Right. You'll want to invite local celebrities and press."

"Friendly ones. That way we can get buzz started off on the right foot."

"I'm not afraid of critics. Not if I've got a good team. Your special guests and their taste buds won't know what hit them."

He loved her confidence . . . and agreed with it.

"Rebecca—" he said just as she blurted out his name.

"Sorry," she apologized. "I didn't mean to interrupt."

Trey didn't know what he'd been about to say. Something crazy, chances were. *Please strip naked* or *where would you like to honeymoon?* "That's all right. What did you want to tell me?"

"Only that . . . I'll shop."

She said it like someone else would have promised to see a dentist. "You'll shop?"

"For clothes. That I can wear to greet VIPs. Your signing bonus was generous. It's fair for you to expect me to look like a top-drawer chef."

God, she amused him, enough that his chest warmed with it. "Do you hate it that much?"

"I don't hate it exactly. I worry I'll buy the wrong thing."

Worry ought to be her middle name. He wanted to take her shopping in the worst way. He would have loved to watch her change into or out of anything.

"I know a stylist," he said instead. "She's not a bully so much as a guide. I'm sure she'd be happy to work with you."

Sybil would be perfect. She shopped for Trey and Zane when they were short of time. She knew how to pinch a penny or empty out a mint—as her clients preferred.

Trey tried to look reassuring, but Rebecca hesitated. "Could I get back to you maybe? I might have someone I can ask."

He was more miffed than was rational. She had someone she could ask? Why would she when he had the ideal answer? Evidently, if he couldn't sleep with her, he *really* wanted to help her out.

"Sure," he said, doing his best to hide his annoyance. "I'll have Elaine email you the stylist's info, in case you change your mind."

"Great," she said.

It might have been Trey's imagination, but she sounded miffed then too.

~

The call was close, but Rebecca escaped The Bad Boys Lounge without jumping Trey Hayworth's bones.

He's your boss, she repeated. *Sleeping with your employer is asking for trouble.*

Too bad she wanted to ask for trouble. And ask and ask and—

"Shut up," she snapped to her rearview mirror. As she pulled her car into traffic, her face was hot—not merely from arousal but also annoyance.

Trey would have Elaine forward his stylist's info? The man couldn't peck one email with his own fingertips?

Oh Lord, what was her problem? An email wasn't a lock of hair. And she didn't need a memento of her non-relationship with him. Maybe most absurd, because she'd refused Trey's referral of a stylist, now she was hoping Zane *would* call her. It *was* tomorrow. Twelve hours into it, to be precise.

Stopped by a red light, she glared at her shoulder bag, which she'd thrown on the right-hand seat. Her cell phone was in there, and it wasn't ringing.

She could ask the twins for fashion advice, but they wouldn't be as useful as Zane. He'd founded a magazine around what people ought to buy. He must know his Gucci from his Dior.

"You are so transparent," she muttered. How could it be a good idea to fight her attraction to one man with her yen for another? Trey and Zane were friends. The phrase *sailing close to the wind* was invented for this sort of thing.

When her cell phone buzzed, she jumped a foot in the air. Knowing better than to talk and drive, she swung her car into a miraculously open spot at the curb. She dug the phone out before it stopped buzzing.

"Yes," she said.

"You're there," came Zane's voice. "And you're answering."

She wasn't coy enough to pretend she didn't recognize him. "Hi, Zane," she said as her nipples tightened and her panties dampened yet again. "How are you doing?"

"Hopeful," he said, his charm apparent even through the phone speaker. "Could I tempt you to a picnic on my boat? The skies are supposed to be clear tonight, and I anticipate a breeze."

Rebecca squeezed her temples. "That sounds—" *ridiculously romantic?* her girly side suggested "—really nice, but I sort of need to ask a favor."

"A favor." He sounded curious rather than displeased.

Was asking this the lesser of two evils? Rebecca jumped in before she could decide. "I need to add to my wardrobe. Nothing crazy like a bunch of ballgowns, but a couple outfits I can wear for the public aspects of my new job. You seem to know about women's clothes."

"I know about them intimately," he agreed waggishly. He was silent for a moment. "Suppose we both get what we want tonight?"

His tone ran through her like melting caramel. "Is that a trick question?"

"Maybe." He laughed. "Meet me at this address at five. I'll take care of everything."

"You could explain what you mean."

"No I couldn't," he twitted her. "You're going to have to trust me to take *all* your needs into account."

He texted the address and then he hung up, leaving her gaping at the little screen. She should trust him and show up? Did he realize who he was talking to?

He did, of course, and presumably this was why he thought it was funny.

"Zillionaires," she muttered, maneuvering her car away from the curb.

Thought they could arrange the world. A cab let her into traffic, and she lifted her hand in thanks.

She'd go on Zane's mystery date. She'd squeezed herself into a corner where she more or less had to.

"I *didn't* do that on purpose," she said.

Her protest wasn't convincing. She knew she was excited to find out what he'd planned for her.

~

Naturally, the address Zane gave her was a boat slip in Boston Harbor. Which of the small yachts belonged to him couldn't be mistaken. For one, his was the biggest, and for two, the name painted on the back was *Bad Girl.*

Rebecca grinned when she saw that. Really, she couldn't help herself.

Zane trotted out to greet her as she walked up the pier, an indicator of eagerness she was too flattered by. Zane probably treated all his dates nicely —the ones he hoped to sleep with anyway. In spite of knowing this, she couldn't suppress a flutter as he handed her up the ramp. This was heady stuff for someone who'd once washed dishes to cover grocery bills.

"Welcome to the *Bad Girl,*" he said with a brilliant smile. "We're nearly finished setting up."

We referred to him and a nicely dressed older woman who stood by two long racks of clothes. The living room was spacious enough that the racks weren't close to filling it.

This was a home Rebecca had entered. Teak wood, highly varnished, gleamed in narrow planks on the floor. A long white sectional—one she suspected wouldn't have fit in her house—stretched beneath a broad window. An open stairway led up to a second level: sleeping cabins, she presumed. To her right, she caught a glimpse of a kitchen with white marble countertops.

She had no doubt it was better equipped than hers.

"This is Sybil Spaulding," Zane said, after she'd finished her quick gawk. "She's a personal shopper. I'm sure you'll find something you like among what she's brought to try on."

Sybil shook Rebecca's hand. "I've taken the liberty of laying out a few selections in one of the upstairs bedrooms."

"Great," Rebecca said, returning her gentle grip. "Maybe I could meet you up there."

The minute she disappeared, Zane came over and kissed her.

"Mmph," she said, pushing at his chest as she tried to fight the inevitable melting of her spine. Zane's kiss was comprehensive, to say the least. "Zane, I want to talk to you."

"I know." He angled his head for another sleek penetration, which she admitted she enjoyed. He pulled back and smiled. "Now that you're not so tense, maybe you'll listen to what I say."

She *was* more relaxed, especially since his big hands were smoothing up and down her back. It didn't hurt that the kiss had affected him. A definite bulge nudged her from behind his pants.

"All right," she surrendered. "Explain yourself."

"Sybil is aware your budget isn't as big as some. As long as you don't go crazy and snap up everything she brought, you're not liable to break the bank. And, much as I hate to restrain myself, I'm only asking you to accept one small gift from me in return."

"Zane. That isn't— I can't—"

"I know. " His smile was warm, his blue eyes seeming to glow with genuine affection. "Accepting gifts from men you barely know isn't appropriate. Please just indulge me this little bit."

"*Zane.*" Her treacherous hands rubbed his chest, the muscles of which felt awesome beneath the navy silk shirt he wore.

"Think how much time you'll save shopping this way," he coaxed. "And how much surer you'll feel about your purchases once two people have approved."

"That," she said, "really is dirty pool."

He smiled unrepentantly. "Go upstairs. I'll wait here for the fashion show."

He pushed his luck by swatting her bottom.

"Do not try that again," she warned, shaking her finger. Zane's expression was angelic.

Upstairs, in a hallway paneled with dark wood and hushed by a thick carpet, she counted five cabin doors. The final one on the left was ajar. Striding toward it, she grumbled about Zane's highhandedness . . . at least until she saw the clothes that lay on the bed.

Zane must have given Sybil instructions. Everything the shopper had selected was a transformed version of Rebecca's everyday work wear. Dark pants and skirts were paired with light-colored button tops. The difference was that the styles and fabrics were heaps nicer.

"Silk," Rebecca said unsurely, stroking one pale blue shirt. The cloth felt delicious against her fingertips.

"It's washable," Sybil assured her. "And you can wear a camisole under it. I also brought a selection of accessories. Dress up any of these outfits with jewelry, and you can go anywhere short of a formal ball. That shirt you're touching certainly suits your fair coloring."

Tears stung Rebecca's eyes. This was so thoughtful . . . and so smart! She looked helplessly at Sybil, unable to say a word.

"Why don't I select a combination you can start with?" she said.

All the clothes Rebecca pulled on fit. More than that, everything flattered her.

"He guessed my size," she blurted, twisting back and forth in front of the full-length mirror.

A moment later she realized Zane must have scads of practice guessing women's measurements.

"Would you like to model this outfit for him?" Sybil suggested politely.

"Oh no," Rebecca said, braced by the reminder of who Zane was. "That's too damn *Pretty Woman*. If you think these clothes are all right, that's good enough for me."

Sybil might have hid a smile as she helped her remove the blouse again.

In the end, Rebecca chose five outfits, a simple cultured pearl necklace, and two pairs of low heels she expected her calves would tolerate. Sybil presented her with the total and accepted her credit card. If she noticed Rebecca's tiny wince, she was too tactful to let it show.

The shopper had been professional, pleasant but not chatty. To Rebecca's surprise, Sybil touched her arm to stop her before she left.

"Zane's gift for you is hanging in the closet. I'm sure he'd be pleased if you put it on for him. Maybe I shouldn't tell you, but this is a first for him. Although I've shopped for him and Mr. Hayworth, you're the first female he's called me in to help. I'm sure he doesn't mean his present to come with strings attached."

"You like him," Rebecca said.

Sybil blushed even as she lifted her chin slightly. "Mr. Alexander is a gentleman. You don't see that often these days."

Rebecca supposed you didn't—especially not in a man of so much privilege.

With Sybil's testimonial to goose her on, she opened the room's closet. A fragile dress hung inside, mid-thigh length and lovely enough to steal her breath. The fabric was a silver silk so shiny it shimmered like water. The matching sandals were tall enough to kill her if she weren't careful.

She saw at once it wouldn't be possible to wear underwear with it.

Oh boy, she sighed privately. She wanted to put that dress on; wanted to show Zane how she looked in it as much as she wanted to see herself.

He's earned this, she thought, *sitting patiently in the living room all this time.* Maybe he was hoping she'd put out in return or maybe, as Sybil Spaulding claimed, he wanted her to have it without strings.

Unable to resist and feeling disconcertingly as if she were sixteen again, Rebecca stripped naked and dropped the dress over her.

It was beautiful. She was beautiful. For the first time in a decade, Rebecca acknowledged that. Her face held a hint of the girl she'd been, but her body was a woman's. She looked seductive in the thin clinging silk: firm where she ought to be, soft where a man would like. She was better than naked wearing it. She was enchanting.

Squeezing her feet into the teetering sandal heels brought her back to reality, but she was determined not to do this half-assed. She'd always taught the twins the best thank yous were wholehearted.

As a precaution, she gripped the handrail when she went down the stairs. Zane was in the living room, working on his laptop. He looked up at the clack of her sandals. His reaction was priceless. He rose to his feet, hand on heart, as if she were a bolt of lightning that had struck him.

"Wow," he said and swallowed.

"I have to keep this," she confessed, laughing. "It looks too nice on me."

"It looks *amazing*." He took her hands as she reached the bottom, holding them out from her sides.

"Thank you," she said. "You did a thoughtful thing."

"You didn't mind too much?"

"No. It reminded me I used to look forward to buying clothes. My mother loved taking me each fall before she got sick. She could pinch a penny, but she was into it. She'd pour over *Seventeen* before we went. She called it our girls day out."

He dragged his eyes up to hers, simply staring at her. He seemed to understand she'd revealed something personal. "I, um— Wow. I'm having trouble remembering what I meant to say. Our picnic boxes are in the fridge. I told the captain we could cast off soon. We'll eat on the aft deck, if you like."

"We have a captain?" She was startled by this idea.

"We do. I can operate the yacht but, generally speaking, drinking and boating isn't a good idea. I wanted to share a glass of wine with you and watch the sunset."

Her fingers were tangling with his, their thumbs stroking together with a suggestiveness that made her knees tremble. "What time is sunset?"

A smile spread across Zane's sensual mouth. "Not for hours yet."

"We could maybe work up an appetite before we go admire it."

Rather than speak, he scooped her into his arms. He carried her up the narrow stairs without clutching the railing or tumbling them to their deaths— a testament to his athleticism that she was grateful for.

He didn't miss that she'd taken a tighter grip on him.

"You're safe now," he teased as they reached the top landing.

"It's simple neurotic reflex," she assured him. "I knew you had me."

"Not yet." He carried her to a new bedroom at the top of the quiet hall. "I'm hoping to have that privilege soon."

The master cabin was bigger than the one where she'd tried on clothes. Decorated in brown and gold, its bed was custom-carved and king size. Zane laid her gently on the gold coverlet. He didn't follow her down, but started unbuttoning his silk shirt.

"Please." Rebecca rolled onto her knees. "Let me help you with that."

Zane stopped working on the buttons. "Thank you," he said—almost seriously.

Rebecca grinned and took over the task for him. She loved being this close to him. Smelling him, feeling his heart beat hard and strong under her fingers. The center of his chest appeared, its furring of golden hair narrowing to a line that dove into his trousers. His erection reshaped the front admirably.

"I remember this belt," she said, releasing its buckle and pulling. "But I don't think you'll need it tonight."

"Want your hands free?" he suggested.

Rebecca opened his waist catch and pulled his shirttails free. He helped her get the garment off his powerful arms, at which point she truly had to caress him.

As she did, a low sound of pleasure broke in his throat.

"You're a fine looking man," she said, palms and fingers exploring his rib cage. "Only a foolish woman wouldn't want her hands on you."

Zane was breathing harder, his big chest going up and down. He didn't interfere with her petting by trying to touch her. "Have I mentioned how much I like you, Rebecca?"

"Only the once." Amused, she bent to brush her lips across his peaked left nipple. "You could say it again any time you want."

He caught her face in his hands, straightening her, looking into her eyes. His expression hovered between a smile and something more intense, something that might have been wonder. "I like you," he repeated. "You're smart and funny and so damn sexy my cock is crying."

He kissed her before she could answer, deep and hard, his long-fingered hands holding her in place. The slide and draw of his tongue, so like the motions of lovemaking, caused her body to react.

"Oh," she gasped, breaking free. "I need to take off this dress before I get it wet."

Zane's handsome face darkened, muscles in his cheeks tightening with lust. "Rebecca," he growled.

"It's silk," she said, though she didn't think he was arguing. "I don't want to ruin it."

He released her so she could pull it off, hands curling at his sides as he watched. She crawled off the massive bed, draped the pretty silver dress on a chair, and then turned to him.

"There," she said, completely naked and only a little shy. "Now I'm ready for anything."

He laughed then. "You're a character."

She hopped back onto the bed, one more concern rising while it still could. "How far away is your captain?"

Zane's eyebrows arched. "I hope you don't think we need his help."

"Oh no." Heat touched her cheeks in embarrassment. "I just wondered if it was safe for me to be noisy."

Zane's slow smile of answer was anything but safe. "The cabins are soundproofed. You can say—or scream—whatever you like to me."

She leaned back, not quite brazen enough to stroke herself. "Well? Hurry up and make me."

As if it were a race, he shucked his trousers and briefs, giving her a too-short flash of his tall nude body before clambering onto the bed over her.

"Wait!" she cried, pushing him to his back. "Let me look at you."

Clearly happy, he grinned up at her from where he'd tumbled. "'Hurry up.' 'Wait.' Make up your mind, Rebecca."

He wasn't too shy to touch himself. He took his hard-on in hand, pointing its flushed tip at her. The other hand he wrapped warmly around her breast.

"Oh," she said, liking the way his thumb circled her nipple.

Naturally, when he pulled his fist slowly up his shaft, his erection was all she could stare at. The length of it was solid, his own personal monument. Thinking of things she could do to it, her tongue curled over her upper lip.

"You see how he likes you?" Zane purred. "How he beads up and cries when I cup your breasts."

Rebecca put her hand lightly over his, fingertips caressing the dips between his knuckles. "I like him too. I want him inside of me."

Zane stretched up until he could kiss her. He pulled his cock again, tugging slowly enough that her hand rode his to the crest. She guessed being on the bottom wasn't his thing. He rolled until she was beneath him, dwarfed by the size of his big body. He didn't lie on her yet. With a longing moan, he dipped his head to suck her nipple.

"These are gorgeous," he murmured, dragging his head across to the other breast. He must have shaved, because his cheeks were smooth. "So round, so perfect, I could suck on them all night."

Her hands fluttered to his hair, fingers sinking into thick waves. Though she didn't think of her breasts as perfect, the way he nuzzled at them and groaned almost convinced her. He pulled at her, flicking the stiffened tips with his tongue. That got to her a little too well. She was aching terribly.

"Zane," she said, rubbing the inside of her thigh against his waist.

He lifted his head, blue eyes lasering at her. "You don't want to wait anymore?"

She shook her head, and he smiled. He reached across her, pulling open the bedside drawer, strafing her pleasantly with his chest hair in the process. His hand returned with a condom. He sat back on his bare heels.

"You put it on," she said shyly. "I like watching you touch yourself."

He must have believed tradeoffs were fair play, because he took one of her hands and placed it between her lolling thighs. "You don't have to put on a show," he said, urging her fingers into a curve around her labia. "Just hold yourself while I put this on. Just feel what watching me does to you."

He opened the condom wrapper but didn't roll it on. "Cup your breast with the other hand. Don't cover the nipple. I want to look at that."

Rebecca did as he asked, since it was simple enough. Watching her watch him, he pushed the pad of his thumb across his penis slit, employing more force than she'd have thought comfortable. Moisture welled from the opening. Rebecca shivered as he spread the fluid across and around his tip. His skin grew redder, his shaft standing more upright. He rolled the condom over himself, smoothing the latex until it clung to him. His veins bulged starkly under it.

"Wow," she said, unused to finding this sexy.

When he smiled and lowered his gaze meaningfully, she noticed she was gripping her pussy considerably tighter than before. Her whole sex was pulsating: lips, clit, the soft wet parts that were inside her. She wasn't quite masturbating, but she was close.

"You'll have to move your hand out of the way for me," he said.

She did so with surprising reluctance.

When he came over her again, she knew there'd be no more waiting. His face was intent, focused on her and what they were about to do. He propped himself on his elbows and aligned his hips with hers. God, his shoulders were broad. She slid her hands over them, then down his sides to where she could hold on. His cock rested on the line of her pussy lips, hot and thick and pulsing with excitement.

Its weight felt amazingly good to her.

"We'll take this easy," he assured her.

She wasn't worried. She and Trey had managed . . . and then she realized maybe this wasn't the most appropriate comparison to make. She couldn't help it. Trey was leaner overall, but erection-wise, they were around the same size.

The image of Trey's highly aroused penis rolled into her mind: the wider flare of his cap, the dragon's tail circling his root. Her pussy contracted, embarrassing her.

Being turned on by the memory of another man wasn't appropriate either.

Thankfully unaware, Zane smiled at the increase in her wetness. Tipping his cock down between her labia, he angled it to notch her. To her delight, he bit his lip as he pushed inside.

This, of course, wasn't her only reason to be happy.

"Oh boy," she said, palms sliding up his back. "Oh wow, that feels good."

He entered her in one slow glide, working his right hand beneath her bottom to ensure his cock squeezed in all the way. All the way felt incredible, like she was filled and then some. Rebecca bracketed her legs around him, leaving her heels on the mattress. When her hips cocked up to get closer, he chuckled.

"My cock's still crying," he informed her. "You are so fucking soft and tight around me."

"Better move," Rebecca advised. "Give your friend what he's crying for."

He didn't need to be asked again. Zane moved like he was the boat rocking her: slowly, smoothly, long ins and outs that left them both moaning. When one position got him too restless, he shifted into another. He rolled her to her side for a while, then on top of him. As she sat above him, his fingers plucked the aching tips of her breasts. When that no longer addressed his needs, he pulled her down to kiss her shoulders and urge her mouth tight against his neck. His hands stroked her everywhere, even the crack of her butt cheeks. Nothing felt wrong to her. His touch was magic no matter where it went.

Patience fraying yet again, he eased her off him and onto her stomach. Rebecca clutched the edge of the mattress as his cock plumbed her sheath from behind.

"Zane," she said, arching her ass to him. "You can go faster."

Zane gave a little grunt. "I want this to last."

Apparently, he thought their latest mutual torment could be improved on. He shifted her more onto her side and crooked her top leg up, thrusting in from a close rear spoon. With his left arm pushed beneath her, he was able to wrap her up with both. That was a nice position, the spots his cockhead knocked against and rubbed over delicious. The way he held her felt marvelous, the nuzzling of his face against her shoulder. The only drawback was the incredible wound-up tension in their bodies.

"I need you to go faster," she admitted. "And I can tell you need it too."

He moaned out a sound of protest, but his next shove surged in harder.

"Yes," she urged, tightening on him.

He shoved again, harder still.

"God," he gasped, letting her know this felt as great to him as it did to her. He wrapped one hand around her mons veneris, shifting his weight a bit more on top of her.

His next thrust was hard enough to make her cry out.

"Good," she praised for fear he'd think he'd hurt her. She fumbled back to grip him behind the thigh. "Please, Zane, do me more like that."

Her plea made him growl, made his erection stiffen and swell in her. When she clenched her sheath around him, he cut loose. He fucked her then, no other word for it. Both their right knees dug into the mattress, his forcing her leg higher and more open. The stretch felt wonderful, being overwhelmed by all that big male power. His abdomen slapped her butt like it was spanking her.

"You're . . . too small for this," he gasped even as he went wild.

"I'm not," she promised, groaning with pleasure. Heaviness gathered in her pussy, an ache only he could cure. "Zane, Zane—"

The pad of his middle finger dug firmly into her clit and rubbed. She came with a spike of feeling that blinded her. Zane cried out, churning into her so fast it was insane. Then, with a cry and a good hard slam he crashed over the edge as well.

His cock throbbed inside her, his ejaculation so distinct, so strong she couldn't have missed it. Finding that sexy beyond belief, she came again.

"Re . . . becca," he said, her name broken by panting.

His cock slipped from her as his body relaxed.

"Mm," he hummed and—as easily as that—he was unconscious.

Caught beneath half his weight, Rebecca laughed softly. She'd had men fall asleep after sex before, but never so abruptly. Coming had felled Zane like the proverbial tree. She wriggled around beneath him until she lay face up. Zane's cheek settled on her breast. Still asleep, he snuggled to her, one long arm and leg wrapping her. His slumbering self seemed determined not to let her get away.

Rather than allow the rubber to get them both messy, she reached between them to peel it off. Zane grumbled as she stretched to discard it. Finding a luxury brand tissue on the nightstand to stroke him dry earned her a melodic sigh. She was done then, free to enjoy his snuggling and his warmth and the oddly pleasant intimacy of his nakedness and hers. Like Trey, he smelled incredible after sex, a combination of personal chemistry and what was probably hundred dollar an ounce cologne.

Now that she wasn't occupied with Zane, she could look around. The space was bigger than her bedroom at home, the furniture in it equally oversized. Like the bed, the wall panels were dark wood. Whatever sealed them left them with a glossy shine, an effect echoed in the nightstands and the portion of the elegant en suite bathroom that she could see. The counters there were white-veined black marble. Apart from the bedroom rug, which glowed in subtle desert hues, everything her eye fell on gleamed softly. She might have been shut up in a very expensive box—a protective box, it actually seemed to her. Nothing bad was allowed to happen here.

Extending from the wall above the bed was a wooden half-moon canopy. Two reading lights were recessed within it, suggesting—in case she'd ever doubted—that this bed hadn't been designed for one person to sleep in.

Oh whatever, she chided. She'd known Zane wasn't a monk. Maybe she should simply savor being here tonight. She had plenty of time to remind herself not to get used to it.

She closed her eyes, smiling at her temporary worry sabbatical. Not intending to fall asleep, she didn't realize she had until the dream came to her.

Night had descended. She was waitressing on Zane's boat. Its spacious dining room was packed, Boston's skyline twinkling behind the long windows. She was serving her own food, and for some reason all the courses were on her tray at once. Knowing that was wrong, she debated returning to the pass-through. The last thing she wanted was to humiliate herself in front of all these people.

"Here," Zane called, signaling her from a table. "We're ready for dinner now."

Trey sat across from him in a gorgeous all-white tuxedo. That was awkward. What if Trey realized she'd slept with his closest friend? Unlike Zane, her new boss wasn't smiling.

"I tipped you," he said sternly, pointing to a pair of hundred dollar bills that lay across his bread plate. "The least you could do was leave him alone."

This was an odd way to put it, she thought.

"Don't listen to him," Zane said. "He has no claim on me."

Zane's formal wear was black and white. He reached across the table to hold Trey's hand—which seemed to contradict his words.

"I'm confused," Rebecca said. "Do you two want me or not?"

With a simultaneity that had to be practiced, the men unzipped their tuxedo trousers and pulled out erect cocks. Rebecca gasped, suddenly painfully aroused. The men turned in their chairs to face her and began to stroke themselves. They'd spread their legs very wide. She could see into their trousers down to their testicles.

The display was too much for her. She wanted to drop to her knees before them, to suck one reddened cock and then the other until they exploded. They'd like watching each other. Somehow she just knew that.

Her heavy tray trembled on her shoulder. She realized she forgotten to pull on panties beneath her brand new skirt. Hot cream from her arousal was trickling down her leg.

"We *would* want you—" Zane began.

"—if you weren't *so* needy," Trey finished.

"I'm not needy," she objected. "I work like a dog. I take care of everyone!"

Zane shook his head sadly. "You only pretend. We know how much you want to cling."

"Fuck you," dream Rebecca swore. "I'll serve your food to someone else!"

She stormed away with her tray—or tried to. People kept bumping her, sticking their elbows and shoulders out from their seats. At last, she reached an empty table on the edge of the room. She set the courses down on the tablecloth. The plates were cold, an embarrassment to serve. All her hard work was ruined. She wanted to cry but refused to.

A shadow came up behind her. She didn't turn. She already knew who it was.

"They see the real you," her father said. "I'm not the only one."

Rebecca shuddered awake. Her heart pounded in her chest, fear and anger surging through her in sickening waves. What was she doing with Zane tonight? How could she imagine nothing bad could happen in this room?

Bad things could happen anywhere.

Settle down, she urged herself, conscious that the nightmare still had a grip on her. Then again, just because a dream was a dream didn't mean she should ignore the reality check. She eased Zane's head from her shoulder and sat up. The sky outside the porthole window was nearly dark. They must have slept a while.

Night was the time she worried most. About work. About the boys. Anything she could dream up. Especially since the twins had gone off to college, she felt vulnerable sleeping in the family house. The big man lying beside her tempted her to think differently. For countless reasons, that was a mistake. At the most, she and Zane would enjoy a fling. At the worst, she'd screw up the job she'd just won. That message from her subconscious was crystal clear.

She looked at Zane slumbering. He'd grabbed a pillow to hug instead of her and seemed happy enough with it. He was a good-looking man—a decent one, from what she could tell. What he wasn't was a person she could afford to lean on.

She'd let his past and some excellent sex seduce her into thinking they had a bond.

He was a billionaire CEO. She was a fancy cook. He bought women thousand dollar dresses. She baked bread as gifts.

He was smoother than a 24-karat egg.

She couldn't be trusted not to blow a gasket over undercooked salmon.

She eased naked from his luxurious bed, padding down the hall to the cabin where her real clothes lay. They felt rough as she pulled them on, as awkward as a hair shirt. She thought about writing a note for Zane, then decided he must be used to this sort of thing—though possibly not from the receiving end. Did people leave notes after one-night stands? Hell if she knew what was expected.

She crept like a thief down the stairs and across the dark living room. Fortunately, they hadn't pulled away from the dock. Maybe Zane hadn't had a chance to issue that order. Maybe the captain had given up and left. Whatever the case, no one challenged her as she slipped away.

~

Okay, Zane was human. Now and then he fell asleep after sex. Usually he only relaxed that much with Trey. Sometimes he intended a second round with a woman and woke up to find her gone. If the first round didn't bear repeating, he wouldn't fall asleep at all. He'd get up, pull on clothes, and make polite noises like, "Gee. Early day tomorrow. Maybe we'd better get to our own homes." Women didn't always like that, but most appreciated that it saved face.

He wasn't sure what Rebecca's disappearing act was supposed to save.

Zane hadn't consciously decided he wanted Rebecca to spend the night. It was only when he woke to an empty bed that he knew he had. He was annoyed then, and insulted, and maybe a little sad. That was good sex they'd had. Sweet sex. The kind where you thought you'd made a real connection to someone.

Just in case she wasn't gone, Zane pulled on a pair of boxers, got up and looked around. Her clothes weren't in the guest bedroom any longer, and the yacht's living room was dark. The kitchen hadn't been entered, not even to make coffee. She'd left in a hurry . . . and silently.

Seeing it was 9:10, Zane called her on his cell.

She picked up after four rings, long enough to be considering not answering. "Uh, hello, Zane," she said.

"Where are you?" was his admittedly gruff answer.

"Home. Were you expecting me to stay?"

"Yes," he said, only stretching the truth a bit.

"Should I have left a note?"

"You should have woken me. At the least I'd have made you coffee."

"It's nine at night."

"I'd have made decaf!"

A soft laugh came through Rebecca's end, informing him this conversation was stupid. He imagined her rubbing her brow in that way she had, as if so many thoughts were in there they needed to be soothed. "Sorry," she said in a less uptight tone. "I guess I'm having second thoughts about taking this any farther."

He didn't miss the irony that this was typically his line. "We can talk about that."

"I'd rather not."

Zane stared at the phone in disbelief. "You'd rather not?"

"I like my independence. I need it, if it comes to that."

"Was I acting like I wanted to chain you up?" His dick twitched with left-field interest in that idea. Rebecca would look adorable shackled to a wall.

"No," she admitted. She was silent for a moment. If she said it wasn't him, it was her, he was going to reach through the phone and strangle her. "I just don't feel *comfortable* with this hookup, given who you are and who I am and the fact that your business partner is my boss. I shouldn't have let my hormones run away with me. I should have been more sensible."

"Rebecca, I think—" Zane hesitated, every self-protective instinct urging him to shut up. With an effort, he ignored them. "I think this could be more than a hookup."

"I can't," she said. "Look, Zane, I really have to go."

And then she hung up on him.

"She hung up on me," he marveled to no one. He didn't dial her back. He had sufficient pride to restrain himself that much. He didn't break out his black book either. Replacement sex with some other woman only would have proved how much realer making love to Rebecca was.

He went back upstairs to dress. Forget taking the boat out tonight. He'd go home. Hopefully, Trey would be in. They'd do something, or nothing, and they'd go to bed together.

He was pulling on his trousers when he noticed what was draped across the back of the bedside chair: Rebecca's skimpy silver dress, the one that had stopped his heart when he saw her in it on the stairs. He'd bought that for her, to show her how beautiful she was. He was pretty sure he'd succeeded. She'd admitted she couldn't resist keeping it.

"Fuck," he bit out.

If she'd left this behind, she truly didn't mean to see him again.

CHAPTER NINE

Idle Hands

Rebecca had plenty to keep her busy in the wake of cutting things short with Zane. She pulled her semi-new crew together, putting them through their paces in the fully loaded Lounge kitchen. Her friend Raoul bounced around like a kid in a candy story. Trey's choice of equipment—and his willingness to buy more—made him her head chef's new hero.

"Finally!" he crowed. "Everything is how you like it. We'll throw mud in the faces of those *culos* at Wilde's Bistro."

Rebecca secretly hoped so but merely smiled when he said this.

She and the crew tinkered with her recipes: cooking times, temperatures, this ingredient or that. The results Rebecca achieved by herself, with every detail under her control, weren't the same as what a busy brigade of line cooks produced. Rebecca's crew was skilled and proud of it. Nonetheless, some needed coaching to reach her high standards. Those who weren't used to her methods tried her patience, but they worked through it. They all knew consistency was key. They weren't aiming to be Joe's Diner. At this level of play, one crappy plate could tarnish a reputation—and forget a crappy night.

Rebecca heard everyone's input at group tastings, including wait staff and busboys. She wanted them to feel they had a stake in the restaurant's fate, though it went without saying she had the final word.

If a trial went well, she grew cautiously excited about their prospects. If it sucked, she tried not to dwell on it.

When she went home, it was to an abandoned construction zone. The twins' friend Jesse had excavated one side of her house and patched the foundation. This was followed by what she believed was called dimple-boarding, repairing the drainage system, and filling the trench again. That done, Jesse's crew had moved inside. Every night she'd go down to survey progress, hating that she couldn't tell if the work was done correctly. The basement apartment *seemed* to be moving along okay, enough that she didn't regret having signed some darned big checks.

As she'd expected, Pete and Charlie's contribution had only gone so far.

You have to trust them, she reminded herself. The twins were young but not idiots. They'd taken their friend's measure in deeper ways than she could by Googling.

She tried to ignore the fact that the thought of having a boarder in her home made her stomach lurch. Zane had temporarily managed to calm her on that prospect. On her own, she didn't have the knack.

Zane hadn't tried to contact her again, aside from shipping the infamous silver dress to her. He'd included a scribbled note in the FedEx box. *No one but you would look right in this*, it said, a statement she was irritatingly unable to interpret. Was the message meant to be angry or romantic? And what right did she have to care? He'd signed the note Z, like he was Zorro or something.

One night, Jesse "happened" to stay later than his crew. When she made her usual foray to the cellar, he'd asked her out for a beer. Rebecca turned him down politely, then went upstairs and cried. She knew she'd been stressed lately but, even for her, this was ridiculous. She also knew it wasn't Jesse she was sorry to have refused. What she did regret didn't matter. Staying away from Zane was the reasonable choice.

Pulling herself together, she dove into getting the restaurant ready even more determinedly.

~

Trey stared out his office window in a futile attempt to stop obsessing about Rebecca. As he did, their executive assistant knocked on the open door.

"Sir," she said. "I thought you'd like your mail."

Elaine was attractive but blissfully uninterested in men. Dressed in a smart brown suit, she set the short stack in his inbox. "The latest *Bad Boys* is in there," she informed him.

The magazine was more Zane's baby, but it had been TBBC's first successful project. Elaine knew he liked to keep up with it.

"Thanks," he said. "Any plans for the weekend?"

"Gardening," she answered. "And possibly a movie."

He didn't ask what she was growing or which movie. Elaine didn't invite her bosses to get familiar. Now and then, he and Zane invented stories about her wild secret life, but the truth was they found it easier not to know. Elaine was efficient, trustworthy, and never complicated their lives. Right then, that trait seemed more precious than rubies.

"Mr. Hayworth?" she added before she left. "I sent the list of responders for Monday night to your computer. It looks like most everyone you asked is coming."

"Good," he said. "Thanks for doing that."

Trey didn't want to think about Monday night, their scheduled preview for The Bad Boys Lounge. If he thought about it, he'd wonder how much Rebecca was worrying, which was sure to lead to wanting to go to her.

Rather than succumb to temptation, he pulled the mail toward himself. Yet another letter from his aunt got fed straight into the shredder. Sending them to his office was her new tactic, one that wasn't any likelier to entice him to open them. He set aside a business proposal to read later.

The latest issue of *Bad Boys* was next. He did a double take when he saw the cover. A pair of eerily familiar faces grinned at him from the glossy front.

"MEET HOT HARVARD TWINS PETE & CHARLIE EILERT," urged the headline.

Eilert was Rebecca's name. Trey's research had focused on her work history, but he recalled she had younger brothers. What a strange coincidence that Zane's magazine had picked them as cover boys.

Unable to resist, Trey flipped straight to their interview. His eyes were drawn to a block of text in the middle of a column.

> *"Charlie always was intense," Pete said jokingly of his brother. "Even at the age of ten. He decided the neighbors wouldn't be convinced Dad was home for Christmas unless he animated the mannequin we'd dressed up as him. I was recruited to help. I conked out at midnight, but Charlie crawled the floor until daybreak, shifting the dummy from chair to chair. He wore himself out so well he fell asleep facedown in his pancakes the next morning."*
>
> *"Rebecca cooked more when I woke up," Charlie said. "Though she did tease me."*
>
> *"She teased you worse when you tried to invent a way for the mannequin to drive us to school."*

Trey set down the magazine, blinked, then began again at the start. He was so amazed by what he learned that he went through it twice.

This was extraordinary. Rebecca's childhood read like a Dickens novel. Mother dies. Father abandons family. Teenage daughter raises brothers while keeping father's absence secret. No wonder she was uptight. She'd spent a good portion of her life looking over her shoulder.

He'd been right to sense a sympathy between them on that long-ago night at Wilde's. They were kindred spirits, more than he'd realized.

He rose from his chair, his head buzzing with odd thoughts. Did discovering this about her change anything? Was she less of a soul mate if there was a rational cause for his reactions? He slapped his palms to his brow, barely aware he'd done it. Kindred spirits or no, given his own dysfunctional childhood, could he trust his feelings?

Stop, he thought. No one could prove soul mates existed or what being one entitled a person to. All Trey knew for sure was that Rebecca called to him. So did Zane, and he valued Zane too much to risk losing him.

He sat and looked at the article again. His hands flattened the magazine's open pages, a bit too close to stroking them.

He couldn't think straight—not a preferred state for him. Popping up again, he grabbed his jacket and strode across the hall to Elaine's nice but small office. She looked up at him startled. The clock behind her said four thirty.

"I'm going out," he said. "You can leave whenever you're ready."

"Yes, sir," she said, too circumspect to ask questions.

He felt better out in the sunshine. The afternoon wasn't sweltering, more fall than summer for the time being.

Jacket slung over his shoulder, he walked in the hopes of the exercise settling him. Past the Old State House he went and then down Tremont Street to the Common. The lush green park reminded him how much he loved living here. The people of Boston were a wonderful mix of blue- and white-collar—in every shade of the rainbow. On any corner, he might see ivory tower academics bumping elbows with cops and dog walkers. Trey belonged here as much as anyone.

He crossed the Common with meandering steps, eventually landing on Charles Street. He could check on the restaurant. It was only a few blocks off.

"Crap," he muttered under his breath. His subconscious had done this on purpose.

She'd be there of course, but so would everyone else, a whole horde of cooks and bottle washers much too busy to speak to him. She'd been training her crew as if their first night were an Olympic event. He could stick his head in, as any owner might. Rebecca didn't even need to know he'd come.

As soon as he decided, an undeniable excitement fluttered in his stomach.

To his amazement, when he stepped through the door, the only soul in sight was her. She sat in the dining room, sipping from what he thought was a pint bottle of porter.

"Where is everyone?" he asked.

"Sent 'em home," she said. "We were getting over-prepped. I told them to enjoy the weekend, and I'd see them first thing Monday."

"*You* sent everyone home."

She seemed to recognize this was out of character. She poured beer into the glass she hadn't been drinking from. "Sit," she said. "Taste. I think this will complement our spin on Boston beans and bacon."

This was one of their appetizers, served on lace-thin triangles of sourdough toast. Unsure what he was getting into, Trey sat and sipped. "Yes," he said. "That combination ought to work."

When she said nothing, he studied her. He was irrationally content to be in her presence, though he disapproved of the dark circles beneath her eyes. She looked thinner than the last time he'd seen her, and she couldn't afford to miss the weight. That bothered him. This job was supposed to ease her burdens, not add to them.

"Are you okay?" he asked.

She let out a ragged laugh. "I had a moment today when I was convinced everything was crap. I honestly thought I needed to toss out every recipe and start again from scratch."

"Ah," Trey said. "That's when you sent your crew home."

"I wish. I sent them home an hour later after my head chef told me I'd better. When every other word I say is 'fuck,' he knows it's time to rein me in."

"Smart man."

"Good man." She took another swig from the bottle.

"You know, Rebecca, Monday night doesn't have to be perfect."

"Sure it does. Trying to be perfect is what keeps me sane." She said it wryly, but he sensed it wasn't a joke. Worried, he wrapped his hand on her bare forearm. He didn't like that she eased away.

"Sorry," she said. "I shouldn't be laying my doubts on you."

"Why not? Can't we be friends as well as employer and employee?" Though he strove to say this lightly, he wasn't certain he'd pulled it off.

Rebecca's big gray eyes rose to his. The steadiness at her center seemed to look straight into his heart. Fuck, he wanted her. His cock was abruptly aching, his chest tight with longing to nestle her against it.

"Can men and women be friends?" she asked.

"Sometimes," he answered cautiously.

"Do you have any?"

"You've got me there," he confessed ruefully.

"Raoul is my friend, but he's married. And older. I think I'm kind of a daughter to him. Maybe men and women can be friends as long as they don't want to have sex."

She made him sadder than he could say—not for philosophical reasons, but because he craved a tie to her. If friendship were all she'd give him, he'd take it.

"I like to think," he said, "that with the proper motivation, people can set aside one sort of desire in favor of another."

Rebecca burst out laughing. "I think I'm drunk," she said. "That actually sounded good to me."

"Maybe I should take you home."

She looked at him. Her pupils were dark with wanting and something else, something that went deeper than attraction. Did she know it was there? Would she let it matter? She reached out, fingers brushing the hand he'd flattened on the table. Though her touch retreated almost at once, tingles radiated up his arm.

"That's nice of you," she said, "but I'm pretty sure a taxi would be safer."

~

Zane was doing a piss-poor job of forgetting Rebecca. He'd tried not thinking about her, but whenever he let his guard down, she crept into his thoughts. This annoyed him immensely. Screw the woman if she couldn't realize they might—*might*, he emphasized—have the makings of a special connection.

Might doesn't pay the mortgage, his father had liked to say, usually as a prelude for pimping Zane out at Alexander Sporting Goods. God, he'd hated those workdays. High school football hero stuck with his dad's jokey arm around him, hawking number jerseys to kids while his latest bruises throbbed on his back or thighs. He'd loathed being used that way, knowing if he said *no,* he'd get a worse beating. *A real man earns his keep,* his father would say. *Don't tell me you aren't one.*

Grimacing, Zane shut down the computer on his desk. Things were bad if he'd started down memory lane with his shit of a dad.

"I'm here!" Mystique announced, appearing at his office door in a cloud of Dior and expensive hair products. "Don't everyone stand up and clap at once."

Her real name was Missy Kroner. Mystique was what she went by for modeling. Fluent in French and English, she was amusing, sexy, and an undeniable hard worker. Zane had seen her intermittently over the last three years, though he took care not to date her too often. Mystique's ambitions most definitely included becoming Mrs. to a high-profile wealthy man, someone who'd add luster to her mystique—if you'd pardon the pun—without overshining it.

"Hello, Missy," he said, getting up to kiss her soft cheek. Even in her stilt-heeled white go-go boots, he was taller. Humming with catlike pleasure, Missy twined slender arms behind his neck. She was fully made up and, as a result, didn't tongue-kiss him.

"I forgot what a lovely big brute you are. Clearly, it's been too long since we've seen each other."

She pouted, which wasn't his favorite expression, though her expertly painted mouth was beautiful. *Not as beautiful as Rebecca's,* his treacherous memory pointed out.

"Oh, you know," he said vaguely. "We moguls get caught up in doing mogul stuff."

"More like bad boy stuff," she quipped. "I can't believe I convinced you to come away for the whole weekend."

Zane was having qualms of disbelief about that himself. "I like Montreal." He stepped back slightly to stroke her shining brunette waves over her shoulders. "And you know I enjoy having you polish up my French."

"I'll show you what I'll polish," she teased, slapping one perfectly manicured hand around his crotch.

It was six thirty on a Friday. They were in the empty hall outside his and Trey's executive offices. With the exception of the janitors and him, headquarters had cleared out. Zane let Missy back him leggily into the nearest wall. As she intended, a few squeezes of her fingers got a rise out of him.

"You're a naughty girl," he said, palming her narrow butt. Continuing the theme of the go-go boots, she wore a sixties style flowered minidress. Under it, he discerned a teensy thong.

"The naughtiest," she assured him, her voice husky.

Missy loved sex and he liked having it with her. Nonetheless, when she batted her fake eyelashes, he couldn't help thinking of centipedes. He was shamefully grateful when a shadow moved in Trey's office, distracting him from her. Trey had left earlier. No one ought to be in there.

"Excuse me," he said to Missy, pulling free of her groping hands. "I need to check on something."

Trey's office was closer than his to the elevator. He must have forgotten to lock up, because the door was open.

An older woman in a yellow polyester pantsuit was rifling through Trey's desk. The papers on top were scattered, and she had his bottom left drawer open, the one where he stashed rubbers and Zane's favorite hand job assister. Clucking her tongue, she thunked the box of prophylactics and Albolene onto the clutter.

Zane categorically refused to blush over them.

"Who the hell are you?" he demanded. "And how did you get in here?"

"She came up with me," Missy answered from behind him. "She said she'd forgotten her ID and could I let her up."

The guards knew Missy and that she was expected. No matter how harmless this white-haired old lady looked, they shouldn't have let her sneak past them.

"You're Trey's aunt," he said, hard and cold as she gaped at him. "Constance Sharp."

"You're a dirty man," she returned querulously. "You and my nephew both."

This did bring heat into his face, though he fought it down. "That's enough," he said, striding in and taking her by the arm.

She was seventy if she was a day. She couldn't hope to resist his strength. She fought though, going so far as to cling to edge of Trey's desk. "I need to be here," she cried. "I have a right to speak to my own nephew!"

Zane wasn't in the mood for this. As carefully as he could, he wrapped his arms around her middle and lifted her off her orthopedic shoes.

"Zane!" Missy said, shocked at him. "She's a little old lady."

"Get the elevator," he ordered.

He must have sounded stern enough. Missy ran ahead to press the button.

"You're dirty too," Trey's aunt said to her, devaluing whatever stock she'd earned with the model.

Thankfully, the elevator came quickly. Missy squished herself into a corner to accompany him to the ground floor. This was due to Trey's aunt having decided her best strategy was to spend the journey kicking his shins like a two-year-old. She repeated her claim that Trey ought to talk to her, adding that her father was worth ten of them. Zane couldn't tell if she had dementia or was just crazy. Truthfully, he wasn't sure he cared.

The security team rushed over the minute they exited, wide eyed and apologetic and seemingly wondering if they ought to pull their guns.

Zane handed his thrashing burden over to two of them. "Find out where she's staying. Get her there safely and make sure she doesn't gain entrance here again. If I hear she's gotten ten feet into this lobby, all of you are fired."

The guards assured him they'd take care of it.

"Sorry," he said to Missy, vibrating with tiny tremors as Trey's relative was carried out of sight. He was so angry for his friend's sake that his heart thumped wildly. Trey was too good a person to have to deal with this.

"That's okay," Missy said, a little shaken herself. "You know what they say about family. Can't live with them. Can't make them go away."

He laughed at her joke, hugging her with genuine gratitude. "I'll make this up to you," he promised.

Liking that, Missy smiled coyly at him from under her fake lashes.

~

Somehow Rebecca made it to Sunday night without imploding, no easy task after she'd ordered her crew to relax over the weekend. She'd heard through the line cook grapevine that Neil Montana—the jackass whose hiring had driven her out of Wilde's—was predicting an epic fail for The Bad Boys Lounge. As celebrities went, he was a nonentity, destined to be forgotten as soon as *Monster Chef's* next winner was announced. For the moment, he had a soapbox, and some people would enjoy hanging on his words.

To anyone who'd listen, he dubbed the Lounge "Beantown Boredom"— his idea of scathing wit.

Rebecca longed to call Trey and sound off but restrained herself. Venting equaled bonding, and she and Trey didn't need any more of that. So what if he'd have settled her in two minutes? He wasn't responsible for her mental state.

Too keyed up to sleep and hoping to blank her thoughts, Rebecca switched on the TV in the living room. A gossip show was on. What was Miley up to? Who were the latest Kardashian love interests? Soothed by the inanity, Rebecca was debating which of her new outfits she'd wear tomorrow when a familiar face appeared onscreen.

She slid forward on the couch so fast she almost fell off.

She couldn't tell if the footage was live or taped; she hadn't been paying enough attention. Whenever it had been filmed, the piece showed Zane Alexander emerging from a French nightclub, looking like expensive sex incarnate in a royal blue shirt and black trousers. A woman hung on his arm laughing. She was nearly as tall as him and drop-dead stunning. Rebecca recognized her as a famous swimsuit model. Mystique, she thought was called. Though Rebecca thought Zane was more intriguing, the video paparazzi were there for the brunette.

"Did you enjoy the band?" one reporter called to her, sticking out his microphone.

"How could I not," she cooed, "with a fine man like this to keep me company?" She hugged Zane's arm, and he smiled down at her.

Face and chest flaming with embarrassment, Rebecca seized the remote and snapped the TV off.

Boy, Zane hadn't taken long to get over her dumping him—if *dumping* was the right term. And so much for what they had being more than a hookup!

She lobbed three couch pillows in swift succession against the wall. The final was aimed so wildly her framed poster of a Parisian *boulangerie* fell down. Didn't people say Paris was for lovers? How nice for Zane to be there with his!

She might have descended into a tantrum, but her own growl of rage shocked her.

"They're not yours," she reminded. Not Zane. Not Trey. And what sort of idiot was she to want to claim them both?

The answer to that was simple: a female idiot with a pulse.

Rebecca's chest hitched as if gearing up for a crying jag.

"No," she growled for a new reason.

She wasn't allowed to fall apart. Not over this, not the night before the Lounge opened. She forced herself to breathe—one breath in, one breath out—until she'd calmed as much as she was going to.

CHAPTER TEN

♀

Opening Night

The Bad Boys Lounge put its most beautiful face forward. Flickering candles and fragrant flowers softened the men's club atmosphere. The fat coffee table books were shelved in their built-ins, the glassware polished like crystals. Everyone who stepped through the entrance looked glamorous. Here was a female anchor for local TV news; there a player from the Bruins with a date so stunning she could have been the celebrity.

Some of the guests congratulated Rebecca on her brothers' recent interview—either because they assumed it was smart promotion, or because they admired her courage in raising the twins alone. She accepted the slightly discomfiting compliments with the best grace she could. Mercifully, they were infrequent. Rebecca bought the "Best New Wines" issue every year, but at more than ten bucks an issue, the subscription base for *Bad Boys Magazine* wasn't huge. She expected this was deliberate. Neither Zane nor Trey was afraid of appearing exclusive.

Then again, who was she to talk? She might not be a high flyer, but she wanted people to feel privileged to eat her food.

Given the crowd, she was grateful she'd splurged on the pearl necklace to dress up her ivory silk blouse and black skirt. Though the outfit reminded her of Zane and his fickleness, at least she didn't stick out like a sore thumb.

Her feet already ached in the two-inch heels.

"Thanks so much for coming," she said for the umpteenth time. She'd stopped offering her hand a while ago. The coldness of her fingers had shocked people.

She and Trey stood ahead of the hostess's podium, greeting guests as they came in. Rebecca was no stranger to schmoozing dining rooms. Having faces to associate with a restaurant personalized the diners' experience and made them feel valued. She simply wasn't accustomed to being away from her true job so long. She longed to be with her crew, heading off the million and one disasters that might be unfolding.

Barring that, she wished she could focus on the action behind her back. Early sitters had ordered and received their first courses. The noise of talking and laughter obscured what she *believed* were hums of approval. The wait staff seemed slightly harried as they passed to and fro, but no more than a filling house and first night jitters could account for.

God, let them stay steadier than she was.

A gap between arrivals allowed Trey to sneak his fingers over to chafe her wrist. "Stop agonizing," he scolded. "If the kitchen were having problems, someone would have come out to get you."

"Only if they realized the problems were happening," Rebecca gritted from the side of her mouth.

Trey was spared from trying to counter this by the arrival of her brothers.

"Look at you!" she cried, hands flying to her lips. "All dressed up in your suits."

Pete wrapped her in a bear hug and then stepped aside for Charlie. Next to him was a little redhead with horn-rimmed glasses. Rebecca saw at once how a girl like this might drive Charlie to anxiety attacks, fictional or otherwise. She was the precisely the sort of nerdalicious siren smart boys dreamed about. Ordering herself to act like a sister ought, Rebecca fought not to recall Charlie's story about snogging in the library stacks.

"This is Caroline," he said, pride mixing with nervousness. "My friend from school."

"So nice to meet you," Rebecca said, taking the girl's hand. "Charlie's mentioned you."

"Sorry I couldn't make it to your Sunday dinner," the girl responded politely. She looked down as if surprised. Too late, Rebecca remembered she shouldn't have touched her. "Wow, your hands are like ice!"

Pete laughed. "Our big sis is a perfectionist. Leaving her crew to cook a new menu by themselves is her idea of a trip to the guillotine."

"Pete!" Rebecca chided, though what he said was true.

"You know Raoul can handle it," he returned.

He squeezed her arm as the busy hostess came back to lead them to their table. Wistful, Rebecca craned around to watch them go. Her brothers were so tall now, handsome in their gangly way. Suddenly, she could see why the *Bad Boys* editor had chosen them for the cover. They had a presence most young men didn't, a lively . . . interestingness. Other diners glanced at them as they passed—including at shy Charlie.

"Well, well, well," said a voice she wished she didn't recognize. "Enjoying your fifteen seconds in the spotlight?"

Reluctantly, Rebecca turned back toward the street door. Neil Montana stood before her, backed up by a circle of his cronies. He wasn't quite six feet tall. His build was skinny but soft, his pasty face not improved by his trying-too-hard-to-be-fashionable beard scruff. She'd worked for him all of six days before quitting—which was six days more than any chef with standards should have had to take.

Had Trey invited this idiot? Or maybe Neil had bought one of the tickets whose proceeds were going to charity. God, it didn't matter. Rebecca forced her shoulders straighter and her jangled brain together.

"I *am* enjoying myself," she confirmed. "Though of course I prefer working in the kitchen to all this attention."

Neil let out a skeptical snort. Attention was what he lived and breathed for.

Thankfully, the hostess appeared to lead him and his gang away. "Enjoy your meal," she called after them before hissing, "Did you invite him?" to Trey.

"I believe he's Gordon Hewitt's guest. I sent him a handful of tickets."

Gordon Hewitt was the editor of *Boston Eats* and a well-known food critic. Her head whipped around to confirm he was with Neil. Sadly, he was, his short form dashing in a rumpled jacket and bow tie.

"Crap. I didn't see him. Hewitt must think I'm completely stupid. Why did he bring Montana? He can't possibly like his food."

Noting her horrified stare, the dapper food critic smiled and lifted two fingers. Weakly, Rebecca returned the greeting.

"Crap," she repeated, jerking forward again.

"It's okay," Trey soothed. "Hewitt has a reputation for being puckish. He probably invited Montana in the hopes of inciting a drama."

"Just kill me now," Rebecca moaned.

Trey laughed underneath his breath. She was glad he was taking this in stride, though—strictly speaking—she should have followed his example. God, she wished she were in the kitchen. Her nervous energy would have served a purpose there.

She was so overwrought she didn't immediately identify the striking woman who swung legs first out of a limo that had pulled to the curb. A chauffeur handed her out, a service the woman seemed used to. Her dress was Marilyn-esque: white, pleated, its flowy skirt poised to lift at any convenient draft. Though her hair was dark, its waves were styled to resemble the iconic movie star's. Her pouty red lips glistened with reflections from the Lounge's decorative outdoor lights. Strings of the twinkly bulbs spiraled around the entrance.

"Mystique," Trey said when she reached them. "I didn't know you were in town."

"Oh you know." She waved a hand whose glossy manicure matched her lips. "Spur of the moment thing."

"Well, I'm glad." He accepted her air kiss. "It's always nice to see you."

The tilt of the model's head struck Rebecca as dubious. Did she think Trey *wasn't* glad to see her, and if so, why not? Rebecca realized she hoped Trey disliked her. Bad enough Zane and she were cozy.

She probably had a weird expression on her face when Mystique shifted her gaze to her. "You must be the chef. Congratulations on the big night."

She showed no awareness that she knew who Rebecca was—not that she was worth mentioning by Zane.

"Thank you," she said, her spine inescapably poker stiff. "I hope you enjoy the meal."

Sensing her tension, Trey laid his hand in the small of her back.

"I'm sure I will," Mystique said pleasantly.

She continued in, stirring murmurs even among the ritzy crowd. Zane hadn't appeared behind her, so perhaps the couple was meeting here. Hardly steady to begin with, Rebecca's pulse began skittering. She knew he'd probably attend tonight, but she been trying her hardest to compartmentalize that knowledge. Could she bear seeing Zane in person with his beautiful arm candy? Did she have the nerve to face him with Trey no more than six inches from her side? For that matter, could this situation get any more uncomfortable?

"Jesus," Trey murmured, looking at her. "You've broken into a sweat."

"Sorry," she said. "I just really want to oversee the kitchen."

He rolled his eyes. "Fine. Oversee. I'll take care of the rest of this."

Rebecca hurried off as if she *were* escaping a guillotine.

A server stopped her in the back hall. "Chef," she said, a smile on her face. "Your clam chowder is a hit. Folks are scraping their bowls!"

"Great," Rebecca said. She moved aside to let the waitress pass. Though glad to hear the accolade, she wondered if it meant her other appetizers were simply *meh*.

Steady, she ordered, grabbing her chef's whites. Even as she shoved her arms through the sleeves, she pushed through the kitchen door. There she found the sort of chaos she didn't like to see.

Raoul was haranguing two of the newbies with the Spanish version of *get your asses into gear*.

"What?" she said to get his attention. "Are we in the weeds?"

"No. Just slow getting off the mark. These two—" he narrowed his eyes at the flinching cooks "—need to get over their fucking quivers at turning up the heat."

"You," Rebecca said to the newbie she knew had quicker hands. "Go help plate. I'll take over your station."

"Yes, chef," he said, already trotting off despite looking unhappy.

"Fast and pretty!" she yelled after him. "Presentation is important. Don't send anything hot out cold!"

"You're staying?" Raoul asked, seeming relieved by this. Apparently, they were closer to the weeds than he'd wanted to let on.

"Yes." She took control of the departed newcomer's sauté pans. "You're overseeing the grill?"

"Yes. Lorenzo's expediting."

She'd seen this on her way in. Lorenzo was one of their senior men. Once they picked up speed, he ought to have no trouble keeping the train on track.

"Focus," she reminded the sweating newbie beside her. "When Lorenzo calls an order for your station, let him know you've got it. If someone is working on the other half of your dish, keep him in the loop on how far along you are. *Everybody communicate!*" she finished with a bellow.

"Yes, chef!" the kitchen bellowed back.

She smiled at that, and turned back to work. For the next ten minutes, the kitchen's chaos became the nimble dance it was meant to be.

Then the lobster started returning.

Lobster couldn't be rushed. You had to cook it gently or you'd lose its exquisite taste and texture. The Lounge's version was butter-poached with creamy broth and orzo. Topped with savory Parmesan "crisps," it made a memorable small entree, the sort diners would come back for . . . assuming, of course, that it was actually cooked.

In spite of the hubbub around her, the second server to call for a re-fire put Rebecca on full alert.

"Crap," she said. Adrenaline poured through her as she signaled the second newbie to take her pans. Fearing the worst, she headed straight for the pass-through. Lorenzo was poking the rejected food in befuddlement.

"They're raw in the middle," the server insisted, which Rebecca could see for herself.

"Why are you letting them go out like this?" she demanded of Lorenzo. "You're supposed to check every plate."

"I—" Lorenzo stammered, his big brown eyes filling up with tears.

Rebecca's brain went into panic mode. The senior man was built like a wrestler and normally tougher than alligator hide. She hadn't cursed him out yet, so the problem had to be personal—a fight with his girlfriend, or some such thing. "Christ," she said, too stressed out to be sympathetic. "Don't do this to me tonight."

"Sorry, chef." His eyes welled up even worse, tempting her to slap him out of it. "I'll pull it together."

"Damn it. You're my best expediter after Raoul, and he's better than you at meat. Don't make me take you off this post."

Lorenzo dragged his sleeve across watery eyes. "Yes, chef. I'm sorry."

Rebecca didn't want *sorry*. She wanted her crew to straighten up. "Seafood!" she called over her shoulder to that station. "Give your fucking lobsters more time in the oven."

The smattering of *yes, chefs* she got back didn't satisfy.

"Fuck," she snapped in her deepest drill sergeant's voice. "You know that bastard from Wilde's is out there. He's dying to see us fail!"

"We never fail, chef!" Raoul roared back at full volume.

Her head chef was grinning, which put her nearer to an even keel. She slapped Lorenzo's shoulder to let him know they were all right, then pointed to the newbie she'd shifted to plating. "We're a team here," she said in a quieter tone. "You be Lorenzo's back-up if he needs it."

"I'll tell the guests new plates are coming," the waitress assured her.

Nodding curtly, Rebecca strode back to the sizzling cooktop and her orders. As a rule, she didn't relish blowing up. She was so wired now her hands shook. Her entire life seemed to be trying to overwhelm her at the same time: the twins, her house, her fucking sweetheart of a boss and his fucking too-sexy-to-stand best friend. Her breath caught in her chest as if an ogre had her around the ribs. Emptying her lungs required a conscious effort.

Focus, she ordered. *Just like you told the crew.*

The newbie at her elbow glanced at her sideways. "You okay, chef?"

"I will be," she promised him grimly.

~

Zane was having a bad Monday.

This, he decided, was a fitting follow-up to his shit weekend—not to mention every crappy minute he'd suffered through since waking alone on his yacht. If Rebecca had tried to put a whammy on him, she couldn't have done a better job.

The trip to Montreal had begun as merely uncomfortable. Missy had been a smidgen too curious about why Trey didn't want to see his aunt.

"I know so little about you," she'd wheedled on the Bad Boys jet. "I'm not some on-the-make groupie. You can trust me with your personal life."

Except he couldn't. He liked lots of things about Missy, but trust wasn't in the mix—not on his own behalf and certainly not on Trey's. Maybe she'd have kept the gory details about their childhood to herself. Maybe she'd have let them slip the next time she wanted to seem in the know in an interview. Zane couldn't predict what she'd do and didn't care. He didn't *want* to share his past with her.

Few realizations could have clued him in more clearly to the lack of substance in their relationship.

Because he'd agreed to join her for the weekend, he tried to be a decent companion. He squired Missy around to her parties, listened to her chatter about her dramas, and only made a single call to check on Trey and his upcoming opening night.

Missy knew something was up anyway. They had sex once, the night they arrived in the hotel. Missy wasn't a stranger. Zane had expected going to bed with her would be a step up from his recent one-night stands. Instead, it had been worse, not just soulless but dishonest. Sleeping with Missy had felt like misleading her.

She must have noticed his heart wasn't in it, because she didn't press for more. Zane's relief was premature. Missy saved her big confrontation for the return flight.

Why was he so withholding? Couldn't he see she cared about him? Didn't he feel anything for her?

"You have more real emotion in your voice when you talk to Trey," she accused. "I deserve to be more than a convenience."

Zane choked back an urge to declare that it wasn't her, it was him. He said other soothing things, no doubt just as annoying, basically admitting that she was right. She *did* deserve better than he was offering her.

"I understand," he said. "If I were you, I wouldn't waste any more time with me."

This wasn't the response she'd been looking for. They were the only passengers in the private jet's cabin. Missy gaped at him from the leather seat opposite his, her mile-long legs crossed and her high-heeled shoe jiggling. Her perfect nails worried the label on the designer water she was drinking.

"There's someone else," she said.

This was one straw too many for Zane. "Saying there's someone else suggests we have the sort of relationship where I could cheat on you."

He said this gently, not betraying his temper. Maybe he should have lost it. Missy gasped as if he'd struck her.

"I'm not giving up," she said, graceful hand to her graceful throat. "I believe we have something even if you don't."

"You're kidding yourself, honey. You and I were never more than a bit of fun."

He said this gently too, but it sank in deeper. Missy tossed her head and glared out the window. He hoped he'd gotten his point across. Missy did have a habit of believing what suited her.

They touched down around six thirty that evening. Zane handed Missy off to Owens to drive in the limo to the hotel where she was staying. Not as experienced as some TBBC employees, Owens jaw dropped at the sight of his glamorous passenger. Zane concluded his presence wouldn't be missed. He took a cab instead, thereby avoiding last-ditch debates about what he and Missy had. The taxi dropped him at the home of a friend, a lawyer he'd met at Harvard. Fortunately, Evan was free to see him. Unfortunately, he didn't think they had grounds for a restraining order against Trey's aunt, or that such an action would necessarily stay out of the media.

"You and Trey are public figures," Evan warned. "When you go to court, people wonder why."

Zane had a bit more sympathy for Missy as he left. He wanted to deny what he'd been told in plain English. To top off that disappointment, between calling another cab and going home to change, he was late to Trey and Rebecca's big event. When he pulled up on Charles Street in his old Mercedes, groups of guests were coming out. He threw the convertible's keys to a valet, but doubted the minutes he saved would help. From what he saw, the Lounge's maiden voyage was over.

He went in anyway. A last few tables in the back were in the process of getting up. Trey stood among them, seeming at ease with what was being said. The guests were in a good mood, so Zane guessed the evening hadn't been a disaster. Trey laughed, the sound carrying. He looked good in his dark gray suit with the white shirt collar unbuttoned. His hair was tied back so you couldn't tell it was shoulder length. His sexy stubble showed off the planes of his cheek and jaw.

All grown up, Zane thought, remembering him in more casual getups. Affection expanded in him so fiercely the sensation was uncomfortable. He knew he was walking a slippery slope with Rebecca but couldn't seem to drag his feet off it. She felt like the antidote to every forgettable woman he'd slept with, like proof he could connect to one with a deeper part of him than his cock. Wasn't there a way to hold onto Trey and have a shot with her? And how would he know if he never tried?

He didn't call out to Trey, whose back was to him. Doing nothing to draw attention to himself, he slipped down the hall to the kitchen.

"Where's Rebecca?" he inquired of a busboy.

Because he'd asked like he had a right to know, the young man pointed to a door marked "Staff Only."

Inside was a combined break room and overflow storage. Metal shelves stacked with dry goods lined the walls. Zane spied a small coffee station, a large round table, and the door to the staff toilet. In the middle of the floor, on the tweedy brown carpet, he found Rebecca.

She lay on her back with her knees bent up. Her left forearm shielded her eyes. Her right was flung out flat, as if the ground beneath her were unsteady. She wore her precious chef's whites, the front now dirty from her labors. Zane's restless emotions settled even as his heart beat harder. God, he was glad to see her.

"Is there a reason you're lying on the floor?" he asked.

Rebecca twitched but didn't rise. "My back is trying to seize up. It's a stress thing. I took a couple ibuprofens. It'll stop in a minute."

Weirdly amused, Zane crossed the room to drop down next to her.

Rebecca shifted her forearm to look at him. The look in her narrowed eyes was not friendly. "Why aren't you with your girlfriend?"

"My girlfriend?"

"The one you took clubbing in Paris. The one you thought it was perfectly okay to bring to my opening. The *swimsuit model*."

The last description he understood. His mind took a moment to sort out the rest. "Mystique was here? I didn't bring her. I just arrived myself. Anyway, we weren't in Paris. It was Montreal."

"Whatever." Rebecca hid her eyes again. "At least you didn't tell her you slept with me."

This seemed as much a complaint as a statement of gratitude. The smile Zane was fighting grew stronger. "You're jealous."

"I'm stupid," she retorted, her sumptuous lips pressed thin. "I know I have no right to be angry."

"She's not my girlfriend," Zane said, to which she responded with a snort. "She isn't. She's a woman I've dated on and off for a couple years. This weekend decided me to switch her to 'off' for good."

"If she showed up here, you need to convey your decision more clearly."

Sensing a grudging reduction in her annoyance, Zane coaxed Rebecca's arm away from her face. Her hand fit nicely between his. Turning her head without lifting it, she looked at him with her big gray eyes. The vulnerability he saw there touched him. Funnily enough, so did her prickliness.

"I wouldn't do that to you," he said softly, "even though we only slept together once. Deliberately shoving her in your face would be childish— especially on your big night."

"It wouldn't be my business if you did."

He stroked her cheek with the back of his hand. "You could make it your business in two seconds."

"I told you—"

"I know what you told me." He slid his arm beneath her back, helping her to sit up without straining her muscles. "How did tonight go?"

"Oh," she said, "we had a couple bumps. The guy who replaced me at my old job showed up with an important food critic. Half a dozen lobster plates went out raw and—evidently—my big tough expediter falls apart over fights with his roommate."

Zane eased her toward him until her brow rested on his shoulder. With extra gentle fingers, he massaged the back of her neck. Her skin was warm, the short hair at her nape like silk. "What went right?"

"Almost everything else," she admitted. "My crew pulled it together after they bobbled. I don't think The Lounge will get panned."

Zane was willing to bet it would get rave reviews. Smiling, he gave in to temptation and kissed her hair.

"Zane . . ."

"Shh." He moved his lips to her temple. "I've been thinking about doing this for days."

She pushed back, head lifting, lush mouth opened to protest. Zane kissed it softly and silenced her.

He could have kissed her all night. She melted into him like a dream, pleasured noises breaking in her throat despite her misgivings. He came erect in surges, letting out a groan when she rubbed his chest. Craving a lower hold, he dragged her hand downward to his bulge. She wasn't shy about exploring, her fingers strong from the work she did. Once he knew they'd keep at it, he slid his hand up to cup her breast. God, he loved squeezing it. Its tip was a hard tight button beneath his palm.

"Rebecca," he pleaded, "say you'll give this a chance."

She sucked in a breath but didn't get a chance to answer.

"Damn it!" Trey cursed from the door.

~

Rebecca pulled away from Zane so fast her back went into cramp mode. "Shit," she hissed, trying to ease the spasm by thrusting her arm back there.

Poised in the doorway with his hands braced on either side, Trey looked both angry and hurt. Somewhat to her surprise, Zane was the person he directed his fury to.

"I held back," he said. "All these years I wanted to pursue her, but I held back for you!"

"What are you talking about?" Zane asked, which could have been her line. "You barely know Rebecca."

"I held back ten years ago!" he spat out.

"What?"

"The waitress at Wilde's. The night you asked me to be your business partner: your partner for real, I thought!"

Obviously, Rebecca was missing a couple checkers from this game. "I waited on you at Wilde's?" she asked, choosing the safer of her two confusions.

"Yes." The sparks Trey's eyes were shooting shifted to her instead. "You warned us not to order lobster because the purveyor delivered frozen. You looked at me like you saw my soul. You knew I wanted to ask you out. I didn't because of *him.*"

Memory stirred: Two Harvard boys at her table, their clothes and their confidence setting them apart. She recalled the piercing green-gold of Trey's eyes, the vibe between him and his friend that she couldn't figure out. She was no expert on souls, but the floor had rocked beneath her at Trey's stare. She'd been disappointed when he simply left later. She'd have broken her no-dating rule for him. She'd have broken a lot of things.

I dreamed this memory, she thought, *that night on the yacht with Zane.*

"You left me a two hundred dollar tip," she blurted.

"No," Zane said. Apparently, this triggered his recall. "That was her? God." He shoved his hands through his hair, gaping at her and then at Trey. "You could have asked her out. You didn't need my permission."

"Like hell," Trey bit out. "You didn't want me sleeping with anyone I might fall for. It's why you hate me flirting with other men. You think they're more of a danger. You think I'm gayer than you."

Zane's glance shot to the open door. He didn't want anybody to overhear, which he'd hardly mind if what Trey said were false.

"Oh, boy," Rebecca said, the pieces falling together. "You two are a couple?"

"We're *not* gay," Zane clarified in a lower voice. "We're bisexual. But, yes, we're a couple."

He didn't seem to like admitting it. Rebecca rubbed her back, which was still knotted up.

"We both like women," Trey said, stepping farther into the room. "We don't want to give them up, so we came to an arrangement."

"And now you both want me."

"Apparently." Trey's anger seemed to have run its course. He looked from her to Zane. If gazes could see into souls, theirs were doing it then. Rebecca sensed Trey asking his lover a silent question.

"No," Zane said categorically.

"What if she were willing?"

"*I* want her," Zane objected.

"You want me too," Trey said. "I know we've never done it before, but you can't tell me it's never crossed your mind."

"Guys," Rebecca interrupted, suspecting they were trying to steer her fate without her input.

"Wait." Trey lifted a hand to silence her. "I'll ask you too. I need to settle this with him first."

When he and Rebecca turned their attention back to Zane, his face was completely red. "Why would she agree to that?"

Trey's quirky mouth slanted with amusement. "Some women like the idea of two men making love to them."

"But we're not just— We'd—"

"Yes," Trey agreed in answer to Zane's stammers. "She'd see us touching each other. No way could the pair of us be naked and not betray our attraction."

Despite the pain in her back, Rebecca's breath caught with arousal.

Zane's flush-brightened face jerked to her. "You wouldn't mind that?"

"Uh," she said, her own cheeks hot. Her pussy was wet enough for her clit to swim. The way the little rod was throbbing it could have been trying to.

She cleared her tightened throat. "As long as you guys were comfortable, I expect I'd like it."

Zane rubbed his face up and down. "Honestly?"

"She just said she would," Trey reminded with a soft laugh.

"I didn't say I'd sleep with both of you," Rebecca broke in hastily. "I said the idea didn't offend me. You're still my boss, Trey. And there's still the matter of me not wanting to cause a rift between you and Zane. No offense, but from the looks of things, you can't promise I won't do that. Trey, you were ready to take Zane's head off when you walked in on us kissing."

The two men exchanged another look.

"I want to try," Zane said.

"Me too," Trey agreed, like it was settled. "In spite of being mad, watching you kiss her was kind of hot."

"Hey," Rebecca said, a mix of panic and elation spiking inside of her. "I get a say in this."

"She could use a good tumble," Trey pointed out to Zane.

"And how," Zane responded. "As tense as she always is, she could probably use a lot of them."

"I need to *think* about this," she protested.

Zane cocked his head at her. "I'm not sure letting you think is a good idea."

~

Though Trey was the one to suggest he and Zane both pursue Rebecca, nervousness flooded him. This was a giant risk. If things went south, he could lose everything.

Zane's attention was directed toward more practical issues. "Help me get this off her," he said.

This was Rebecca's white chef's coat.

"What's wrong with her?" Trey asked, kneeling down on her other side.

"Back spasm. I think it must have hit her once the pressure of the night eased off. Delayed reaction or whatever." He swatted Rebecca's hands. She was trying to work the buttons instead of him. That this hurt her was obvious from her winces.

"Shouldn't we call a doctor?"

"I'm fine," Rebecca snapped. "I've had this happen before. It'll go away."

"If you stop fighting me, it will." Zane looked across her at Trey. "Hold her hands. She's being an idiot."

Trey took Rebecca's hands. She struggled in annoyance, but his hold on her wrists was firm. Her little tugs sent sensation pinging to his groin. To judge by the twitching between his legs, he was getting an erection. This might not be the best issue to raise right then.

"Zane's not trying to hurt you," he said.

Rebecca frowned, but stopped pulling away. "I haven't said 'yes' to your proposal."

"I know," he acknowledged.

"Then why are you manhandling me like I did?"

"Jesus," Zane muttered. "*That* isn't manhandling."

Rebecca looked startled by his sureness. Her distraction allowed Zane to get her sleeves fully off. She wore her pretty silk blouse beneath, the one Trey had been pleasantly surprised to see her in. Zane seemed surprised for his own reasons.

"Hey," he said, stroking the collar smooth. "This looks nice on you."

"Your shopper knew what she was doing," she admitted grumpily.

Trey's eyes widened. "You put her in touch with Sybil?"

"Sure. Who else wouldn't push stuff she'd hate on her? Rebecca has her comfort zone. Sybil respected that."

Trey struggled with his resentment. He'd wanted to do that favor for Rebecca. And why was Zane familiar with her comfort zone? Was the kiss Trey walked in on not their first? Exactly how long had they been seeing each other?

His face must have betrayed his questions.

"I met her at the 'Hot Men of Harvard' shoot," Zane said. "Her brothers were the cover boys. I knew she was your new chef, but I swear I didn't guess you were into her. I didn't tell you about it, because I figured you'd warn me off."

Trey felt his mouth turn down as he tried to process this without anger.

"*I'm* sorry," Rebecca added, touching his sleeve gently. "I knew you were attracted to me, and it did occur to me that seeing Zane would be awkward. He just sort of . . . charmed me."

Zane chuckled, obviously liking that.

"You were attracted to me too," Trey said levelly.

"Yes." Her gorgeous mouth twisted in apology. "But you and I really couldn't date. I thought maybe he and I could squeak away with it."

"She did break it off," Zane put in. "After the first time."

"*The first time?* You and she slept together already?"

"Once," Zane said. "And, uh, in the interest of full disclosure, I also got her off in my car the day we met."

"Great," Trey said, irritation bubbling up in him.

"Too much to get over?"

Zane's blue eyes were worried but sympathetic, like he'd understand if Trey couldn't forgive this. Trey looked down at his arm, where Rebecca's hand still rested. Tiny scars marked her fingers, battle wounds from cooking. Her thumb rubbed him through his sleeve, little soothing motions she might not have made consciously. Her gaze was lowered, probably because she was more inclined to guilt than Zane. She'd feel it even when—to be fair—she wasn't obliged to.

"Do you want me as much as you want him?" Trey asked her.

Her lashes lifted, their gold blackened by mascara for tonight. Within that frame, emotion sheened her gray eyes. She appeared to understand he wanted honesty.

"I think you're awesome," she said earnestly. "I'm amazed you want me. When we had sex, I felt different things than with Zane, but they were just as strong."

"Hey," Zane said, his turn to be aggrieved. "When did *you* have sex with her?"

Trey couldn't help it. He lifted his brows and grinned.

"Shit." Zane shook his head, thankfully more bemused than angry. "I don't know whether to sock you or demand every damn detail."

CHAPTER ELEVEN

Buck House

Rebecca hadn't officially agreed to anything, but that didn't seem to matter. Trey told the valet to bring Zane's car around the back, and Zane carried her to it. Fortunately, the silver convertible was a four-door. She and Trey fit in the rear seat.

"This isn't necessary," she said as Trey arranged her with her head resting on his lap.

She was curled on her side, which seemed less helpless than lying on her back. Free to do so, Trey ran one hand soothingly down her tense muscles. His palm was warm, and it really did make her feel better. She steeled herself against liking it too much as Zane pulled out of the Lounge's lot.

"At least tell me you're taking me home," she said.

"We are," Zane assured her. "Our home."

This stunned her. "Not that mansion in Lexington!"

"What's wrong with Lexington?" Trey finger-combed her hair.

"Everybody says it's Sodom and Gomorrah, that you throw wild sex parties on weekends."

Zane snickered and shifted gears.

"If they claim that," Trey said, "they've never been invited."

This wasn't the same as saying there weren't wild parties. "I am *so* not interested in orgies."

"Not even to watch?" Zane teased.

123

"No!" she denied too hotly. She'd have watched him and Trey getting it on with each other any day of the week.

"Don't worry," Trey said, returning to making seductive passes along her spine. "Zane and I only want you to play with us. When we're really into someone, we're not inclined to share."

"How do you know?" Rebecca demanded. "You implied you've never, er, done the same woman at the same time. Maybe you'd change your mind."

Zane burst out laughing in the front seat. "You could turn worrying into a superpower."

"It's a legitimate concern!"

"Of course it is," Trey crooned. "You'll be the boss, Rebecca. Any time you want to call a halt, we will."

Calling a halt wasn't the same as calling the shots. Moreover, it suggested there'd be an activity she might want to call a halt to. She remembered the game Zane played with her and his belt in this very car. She pressed her thighs together, also remembering how she'd responded. She *thought* she'd noticed Trey's breathing accelerating as he restrained her wrists tonight. Was he into bondage too? When they'd had their wild monkey sex in the Lounge's kitchen, hadn't his style been controlling? Her pussy simmered at the flashback, a new and softer ache distracting her from the one in her back muscles.

"Uh," she said, "just how sexually adventurous are you two?"

Trey's reassuring hand chafed her shoulder. "Why don't we cross that bridge when we come to it?"

Rebecca's inner muscles twitched. She wasn't the only one to react to this conversation. The flesh her head rested on was stirring. Trey was getting an erection. So was Zane. The angle she was curled up in allowed her to see between the front seats. Zane had just tugged his trousers to give his cock more room.

The heat that poured through her then was incredible.

"Oh my God," she couldn't help murmuring.

"Close your eyes," Zane advised huskily from the front. "With all you've had on your mind, I bet you haven't slept much lately. You might want to rest up before we get there."

His words caused Trey's cock to lurch beneath her temple.

Holy smokes, she thought, her knees vised together with excitement. The reality of them wanting her and each other was sinking in. Zane and Trey were her best lovers to date. The handful of other men she'd slept with trailed far behind. To enjoy these men one at a time had set new records for her. To be taken by them both, and to watch them take each other, was bound to knock her pleasure out of the ballpark. Zane's suggestion that she ought to rest up implied a few home runs in her near future.

How little that frightened her should have been alarming.

~

Zane must have been right about Rebecca's sleep shortage. She dropped off in Trey's lap—one moment conscious and the next zonked out. Trey continued to pet her, shifting so that his legs stretched out and his shoulders rested against the door. His hard-on subsided but didn't disappear. The moment felt surreal. The woman of his dreams was with him. She was using his thigh as her pillow.

"She asleep?" Zane asked, twisting his head around to see.

"Like a baby."

Zane returned his attention to the road, fingers tapping the steering wheel. "You really okay with this? With sharing her? You've been thinking about her for a long time."

"I'm okay," Trey said, relatively sure he was. "I confess you had a tendency to creep into my fantasies about her."

Never short on ego, Zane's smile held a hint of smirk. "You've got to be the most monogamous non-monogamous guy in existence."

"Maybe," Trey conceded, amused. He went on more seriously, aware the topic was sensitive. "Are *you* ready for this, Zane? Not to sound arrogant, but whether we cross swords or brush hands or what have you, she's going to see you want me. You're going to expose what you think of as your gay side."

Zane's smirk faded—and not simply because he was concentrating on merging onto the highway. "Why don't we cross that bridge when we come to it?"

Trey pinched his lower lip. The bridge was approaching fast, no matter what Zane preferred.

~

Rebecca didn't wake so much as slide from one pleasant dream into another. Trey was lifting her from the car, his arms hooking under hers. Her body was limp, her back muscles warm and supple.

"Mm," she mumbled. "I feel so much better."

She guessed Trey expected her to sleep through him carrying her. He'd been bending to swing her legs off the floor. When she spoke, he left them where they were and straightened. Rebecca didn't mind. Her front rested pleasantly against his.

"Your back is okay?"

"Uh-huh." She opened her eyes and squinted. "It's bright in here."

"We're in the garage. We're home."

They were in a freaking airplane hanger. Everything needed to service vehicles was here, up to and including a hydraulic lift.

"Wow," she said, craning around Trey to take it in. Two limos gleamed side by side in slots: a vintage black with a fancy grill and a classic white modern. Zane's silver convertible was behind her. Its nearest car buddy was a shiny red Bugatti, low-slung and—even to her unsophisticated eyes—thoroughly sexy. After that, she noted two Harley motorcycles, some sort of giant black SUV, and a relatively sedate Mercury sedan.

She had a hard time imagining her beat-up delivery van parking here.

"We drive them all," Trey said. "Or if we don't, staff do. Zane's weirdly attached to the car he bought in college."

Rebecca smiled, endeared by his defensiveness. "They're pretty. You have no idea the silly things I'd buy for my home kitchen if I could afford them."

He smiled back, his brief tension relaxing. "My Bugatti is the prettiest."

"Oh here we go," Zane groaned liked he'd heard this before.

"Because it's red," Trey said. "And faster than his old Mercedes. Plus, its curves are sexy."

His cars' curves seemed to remind him she had some. He slid his palms around her ass, hitching her higher and closer. As he lifted her off her feet, Rebecca's eyebrows rose. Trey was all the way hard, the firm swell of his erection nudging her pelvis. Unable to help herself, she squirmed. Trey's penetrating eyes darkened.

"What do you say?" he asked in a rougher tone. "Want to get this adventure started?"

"Here?"

"Why not? This is our territory, home to our manliest man toys. And no one will interrupt us. Once we drive through our front gate, we can do and be what we please."

Having spent much of her life hiding things, Rebecca saw the appeal of that. She laid her cheek on Trey's shoulder and looked at Zane. He stood maybe ten feet away, seeming rooted to the sealed concrete floor. He was a handsome man: tall, built, and pricey in his tailored trousers and custom shirt. His expression inspired a shiver. He was watching her and Trey as if someone had cast a spell on him. Lust had him in its grip, from the parting of his bedroom lips, to the quickened rise and fall of his chest, to the sizeable hump behind his zipper. Wanting that and more, she swung her legs around Trey's hips.

"What about you?" she asked Zane. "Do you want to get started?"

"Yes," was the answer he grated out.

"Thank God," Trey whispered a second before he kissed her.

He walked with her as he did, arms tight around her and mouth hungry. Though she'd closed her eyes, she wasn't the least surprised to be laid back over the hood of his Bugatti. Happy to be there, she crossed her ankles behind his tailbone.

"Let me do the work," he murmured in her ear. "I don't want your back to seize up again."

Her back was fine, but she sensed that wasn't behind the instruction. He wanted her restricted. He got off on it. Zane had come closer while they were kissing, only a step away from the sleek sports car. One palm rested on his belly, like he was afraid or maybe embarrassed about moving it to his cock. He hadn't minded touching himself before. Trey had to be the source of his hesitation. He was opening the buttons on her blouse. Zane met her gaze and flushed.

"Zane bound my hands the first time he got me off," she said.

Trey lifted his head, breath suspended for a heartbeat. She'd spoken impulsively. From the men's reactions, this was the right topic to bring up.

"He used his belt," she went on. "He wrapped it around my wrists and went down on me."

"In his car?" Trey's voice rasped like sandpaper.

"In his car. He barely had room to move."

Air wafted over her cleavage, above the satiny bra she wore. Trey closed his eyes. "Are you saying you'd like him to bind you now?"

"I'm saying if you want, *you* could restrain me some. I didn't mind when he did it."

"'Didn't mind' isn't the same as liking it."

"Oh I liked it," she admitted.

Trey groaned like she was killing him. Suddenly, he moved in a flurry. Her blouse was gone, and her skirt, and then he pulled her panties off.

"You have amazing legs," he panted, hands cruising up her calves and thighs. She supposed they were strong. She was on them all the time. Chances were she was lucky Trey noticed them. He snapped her bra free in a second, pushing each breast up for a hard kiss. The sting of his lips pulled a gasp from her.

"Okay?" he asked, soothing her now blazing nipples with his thumbs.

She nodded, somewhat surprised for enjoying it. She couldn't doubt she had. The pulsing of her clit had just doubled in tempo. As if he knew, Trey stepped between her knees. He sat her up, yanking her to the edge of the hood with a vigor that caused her skin to skid on the cherry paint.

It didn't hurt, but it made her gasp as well. She hadn't expected her sweetheart boss to be quite this decisive. Zane did, apparently.

"Here," he said, tossing Trey a small object.

The object was a condom. Trey caught it in one hand and yanked his zipper down with the other. That left him a hand short.

"Take my cock out," he ordered her.

It absolutely was an order. Rebecca had given enough of them to recognize the tone. Nothing inside her minded, not when the order came from him. Shaking just a little with anticipation, she spread his trouser front.

His big erection pushed out his underwear. Carefully, Rebecca folded the cotton under him. She tucked the waistband beneath his balls, which resulted in lifting them. Pleased with that picture, she wrapped her hands around his hipbones, her thumbs stretched beneath his shaft. The stiffened flesh jolted with his pulse, the slit beading with pre-cum.

"I love your dragon," she said, her right thumb running over it where the pointed tail stretched up his underside. Aside from its erotic suggestiveness, the tat was beautiful in the brightness of the garage, its colors and scales vivid.

"He's going into you," Trey said hoarsely. "As soon as I get this on."

She wasn't the only one turned on by this idea. Zane let out a low moan. Trey jerked but didn't look at him. She suspected Trey would have liked Zane to roll on the rubber. Perhaps he didn't want to push his luck. He did it himself instead, quickly and with deft motions. Rebecca watched him, mesmerized.

He brought her eyes back to his by slapping his palms on the car hood beside her hips. This too was a dominant gesture. She was very aware that— of the three of them—only she was naked. Moisture trickled through her folds, hot and slick. Trey leaned forward until the crest of his penis touched her where she was wet.

"I thought about this," he said, his tone dangerous. "Every time we were together at the restaurant, no matter what else was going on, I wanted to be fucking you."

She wet her lips, her gaze caught and held by the fire in his. She touched his penis lightly, adjusting its angle to fit his wide glans to her entrance. Trey sucked in air but didn't move forward. "I wanted that too."

Her answer freed him. He pushed in: one long stroke slow enough to count as careful. As his cock disappeared inside her, Zane made the same low sound he had before. Trey stopped when his slinged-up balls met her ass.

"Come closer," Trey rasped to Zane. "Rebecca, lean back so he can see."

Rebecca could hardly help herself. The pressure of his cock inside her was delicious. She had to arch at it. When she did, the shift in position bared the veiny width just above his root. Zane's eyes totally locked on it. His fascination made her crazy, like the dial on her arousal was spun to ten. She needed to be taken as she never had in her life.

"Please," she said to Trey, her grip tight where she hung on his strong shoulders. "Please do this."

Trey snapped his reins but good. His smooth hard strokes reverbed along every nerve in her abdomen. The result was heaven and hell together— making her want desperately to come, yet also to go on like that forever.

"Rebecca," Trey gasped in that way he had, as if her name was one he knew intimately. She supposed she understood why now. He'd been dreaming of her for years.

The thought excited her even more; the crazy intensity he brought to every plunge into her. Her breasts bounced on her ribcage, drawing his eyes to them. He palmed one, thumbed one, then simply gripped her hips and churned. That must have been what he wanted most. His head tipped back with pleasure, his Adam's apple standing out. Groans issued from his chest and echoed through the garage. Rebecca dug her fingers deeper into his shoulders and timed her upward humps to his.

"Fuck," he cried, approaching some crisis. "Fuck. Fuck."

As amazing as his actions were, she couldn't forget Zane. From the corner of her eye, she saw him wrap his crotch in a killer grip. He didn't rub his bulge, but—boy—was he squeezing. New heat streaked through her at the sight of his white knuckles. Her pussy contracted helplessly around Trey's shaft.

This shot Trey to a new plateau.

Groaning, he slammed her back down onto the car. His hands caught her wrists, trapping them so he could pull her arms out and up. Rebecca's body writhed. She wasn't fighting the hold but enjoying how unbreakable it was. Trey seemed to like her faux struggle. His cock stretched and throbbed inside her, his thrusts resounding against the car's metal. His groans had devolved to snarls.

"I've got you too," Rebecca panted, pulling her heels inward for his next drive. "You're not getting away from me."

She was small, but she was wiry. She used more strength on Trey than she would have dared with another man. The muscles of his butt clenched for her, giving her heels lots of firmness to dig into. His hips began to twist with his plunges, as if he craved the strongest possible pressure on every part of his cock at once.

Maybe Zane's view of Trey going in and out wasn't as good as before. He stepped right up to the car, his free palm planted inches away from her. He was so close Rebecca registered the waves of his body heat.

Trey gasped, sweaty hands threatening to slip on her outstretched wrists. "God, you're so . . . fucking . . . tight."

He swelled one more millimeter, and that was it for her. The sensations coiling inside her sex burst in an explosion of sweet feelings. Trey jerked his cock up into her, and up into her, like he couldn't stop the motions. Bending, he caught her nipple in his mouth and sucked. He came like that, his moans of ecstasy vibrating through her breast.

He didn't release her nipple or her wrists until they'd both finished.

"God." He straightened and pressed a soft kiss into her brow.

Her arms were trembling from being stretched, but she wrapped them around him. Oh that felt good. His nice shirt was damp with sweat, his lean and powerful body warm inside it.

"Next time, no clothes for you," she slurred.

He laughed, still breathless, then turned his head to check on Zane. His friend had let go of himself and was astonishingly hard, his prick pushing out his zipper like a tent pole. A star of creases in the cloth attested to the force with which he'd gripped it. Like Trey and Rebecca, he was breathing raggedly.

"Saving that for something special?" Trey suggested.

His arch words didn't amuse Zane. "Shit," he said, sounding shaken. "I can't— I'll catch up to you two later."

"Zane," she called a second before Trey did.

Zane stopped in the middle of striding off. He turned his head back to them. "I'm okay," he said over his shoulder. His breath came out on a shaky laugh. "I guess Rebecca isn't the only one who needs to think."

"Shit," Trey swore after he was gone.

Rebecca touched his shoulder.

"Sorry," he said, maybe believing he shouldn't let her see he was upset.

"That's okay. Of course you want him to be all right with this."

Trey wagged his head ruefully. "I went at you like a crazy man. He saw how into it I was."

"It turned him on, Trey—a lot. He couldn't take his eyes off us."

"I couldn't take my eyes off you."

"I don't think that was the problem."

Trey pulled gently out of her.

"I don't," she repeated, because he remained troubled. "And I'm probably an expert on the sort of things people can have problems with."

He smiled crookedly, his fingers smoothing her hair back from her hot face. The caress was spine-meltingly pleasant. "I don't know how to hide my feelings. I don't know how to slow them down. I've been waiting too long to let them out."

God, his sweetness made her eyes sting. She stroked his hair like he was stroking hers. "You have to be yourself," she said, more than half wishing her nature was as brave as his. "Once you start pretending, you tend to get stuck with it."

He kissed her then, and helped her hop off the car. "Grab your clothes," he said. "I'll give you the dollar tour of Sodom and Gomorrah."

~

Zane and Trey's garage was bigger than most houses. Clad in brick and draped in ivy, it resembled a residence from outside. Rebecca was dressed again, at least haphazardly. Following Trey, she padded barefoot across the long stretch of grass to the house proper. A bright partial moon lit what appeared to be very spacious, very picturesque landscaped grounds. The plantings were nicer than Boston Common. No question about it: Rebecca had left the humdrum world.

Trey caught her hand as she slowed to gawk. "Do you like it?" he asked, long fingers squeezing hers.

"It's beautiful."

He smiled, seeming to hear her unsureness. "We earned it," he reminded. "I doubt we grew up any fancier than you."

His hand was warm. Though she tugged a little, he didn't allow her to pull away.

"Let me," he coaxed. "I like this kind of thing."

It seemed silly to object when he'd just ravished her atop a car. Holding hands wasn't more serious than that. She had no cause to feel self-conscious simply because the gesture might be interpreted as romantic. She didn't have to interpret it that way.

The problem was, part of her wanted to.

Trey let her in to his and Zane's mansion via a side door. Whatever staff lived in were snug in their beds. Trey and she had the plush antique-laden halls to themselves. Here and there she spotted a touch of modernity—an abstract sculpture on a pedestal, a bold contemporary painting, a streamlined chair or lamp. Mostly, though, Zane and Trey's furnishings were old. They looked comfortable to her, but they weren't what she was used to . . . or what she'd expected.

The dollar tour didn't reveal evidence of Sodom or Gomorrah. It also didn't reveal Zane. Short of opening every one of the zillion doors, Rebecca couldn't imagine how they'd find him.

"And this is our suite." Trey opened one half of a set of paneled doors on the third floor.

The doors led to a shadowy sitting room. Through the arch behind that was an orgy-sized heavy wooden bed, its design reminding her of pews in a cathedral. The suite took up the end of the floor. Tall paned windows brought in light on three sides. At the moment, the light was strictly nocturnal. No lamps had been turned on. The space was peaceful and empty. Zane wasn't here either.

Trey exhaled a small disappointed sigh.

"I should let you wait for him," Rebecca said. "Give you a chance to talk. I'll be fine sleeping in a guest room."

"I wouldn't be fine with that. I'd rather you slept with us."

Rebecca looked at her bare toes. It seemed impolite to point out that *us* didn't exist right then.

Trey repeated the quiet sigh. "If Zane wants to avoid us, *he* can take a guest room."

"I don't want to create awkwardness between you."

Trey took her face in his hands. "What do you want for you, Rebecca? What would you choose if you had no one to consider but yourself?"

The question was hard to answer. She wanted to stay with him, but she was frightened to. She was bet he'd cuddle, that he'd hold her and stroke her until she fell asleep. She also bet she'd like it.

He laughed at the length of her hesitation. "You'd think I was offering you a line of cocaine."

He was in a way, and she feared addiction. On the other hand, did she really want to live the rest of her life never risking anything? What was the point in having survived so much if she didn't move forward?

"I'd like to stay with you," she confessed shyly.

He smiled, hands sliding from her cheeks to her shoulders. "Good," he said. "I'll give you the dime tour of our suite."

~

Zane hadn't gone inside after he left the garage. His feelings were too intense, and he'd needed air. He'd strode stiff-legged and stiff-cocked to their lagoon, a small manmade lake he and Trey sometimes rowed out on. The reeds at the edge were tall, the water wavery with moonlight. Zane calmed a bit as he stared at it.

He'd expected jealousy to be his worst problem. He did have a possessive streak. To his surprise, when he'd watched Trey and Rebecca fuck on that car, he hadn't known who to be jealous of. He wanted to be taken with the animal single-mindedness that Trey was taking her, but he'd also wished her tight hot body were all his to play with.

She was so damn cute, so touchably firm and curved. He hadn't realized watching Trey's cock pump in and out of her pussy would flip his brain upside down. Her wetness had gleamed on Trey's shaft, on his swollen veins, on her engorged clit, the flow lubricating each fervent thrust. It seemed perverse that she was naked and he was dressed, like she was extra vulnerable. Her beautiful pink nipples had stood out like fingertips on her bouncing breasts. Zane had longed to suck them even as he'd longed to suck Trey's. Torqued by what he was doing, Trey's had beaded behind his shirt as if it were December.

When Rebecca pulled the trick where she hammocked Trey's balls on his underwear, she could have been trying to drive Zane insane. He was accustomed to having a strong sex drive, but from their first hungry kiss, Trey and Rebecca had shot his through the stratosphere.

He couldn't help thinking a real man wouldn't enjoy watching a friend screw the girl he wanted . . . or vice versa.

He didn't know how to handle it. He felt like he was out-of-control drunk, and someone ought to take his car keys. He couldn't join in with them. Sliding behind that wheel would be dangerous. He'd crash and break into pieces. He needed more control before he went to them.

He groaned to the clear night sky. The thought of going to them punched his cock hard again. Were they making love even now? Was Rebecca running her hands over Trey's lean torso? Was Trey's adorable ass clenched with longing for someone to fuck it?

"God," he swore, covering his face. He needed half a dozen cocks to do everything he wanted to those two.

He glanced back over his shoulder to the house. He was far enough away to see the whole structure. The windows of the bedroom wing glowed gold, the only ones lit up. He knew how sweet Trey was, how he crept into a person's heart and made them want to keep him forever. Could Zane leave Rebecca to his charms? No matter how off balance he felt right now, didn't he want to stake a claim on her too?

His erection throbbed out a *hell yeah, you do.*

Maybe Trey was right. Maybe Zane had issues about exposing his "gay" side. If he wanted to enough, he'd get over them.

"Can't do that out here," he muttered.

Squaring his shoulders, he prepared himself for battle. He kind of had to. He wanted them both too much to remain where he was.

In the end, he'd girded himself for nothing. He'd stayed out too long. Trey and Rebecca were asleep, spooned back to front in the big California king. So hard he was shaking, Zane cursed his luck. Trey slept naked, but Rebecca wore one of Trey's T-shirts. Trey's arm wrapped her waist, his chin tucked above her blonde head. Already he was putting his mark on her.

Don't be an idiot, he chided. Trey didn't think that way. He wasn't half as competitive as Zane. Rebecca probably had been cold—what with Trey's fondness for cranking up the A/C. Zane stripped down to skin. He told himself he wasn't trying to match Trey for seductiveness. This was how he went to bed. Because there was room, he slipped under the covers in front of Rebecca.

She made a kitten noise in her sleep.

Zane's cock thought it sounded sexy. An ache pulsed hard in his groin, his balls starting to draw up, which reminded him what she'd done with Trey's Calvin Kleins. He screwed his eyes shut against that image. Christ, he wasn't going to be able to sleep like this. He wasn't even certain he could lie still. Gritting his teeth, he reached for his erection. His palm was dry, which wasn't his preference, but squeezing the rigid pole still felt good. Rubbing it was *too* good. His nerves were sensitized from waiting, his stored-up come ready to boil out. Probably, he should get up and do this in the bathroom. Trying to control his breathing would be impossible.

Then Rebecca squirmed forward and snuggled him, her soft breasts flattening on his back.

Pre-cum squirted from his tip at the sudden jump in his excitement.

"Zane?" she mumbled against his shoulder.

He froze, then overruled his teenage-style urge to pretend he was asleep. "I'm awake."

Her hand followed his forearm to the pounding erection his fingers gripped. "Mm, yes, you are."

His fist let go. He turned and kissed her—soft, deep, stroking his tongue against hers and sucking. She hummed again, sleepily, her top leg sliding over his. His cock bumped her belly, the slit leaking more excitement. Rebecca might not be quite awake, but he knew he couldn't resist her instinctive welcome. He had to take her now.

"Two seconds," he said, and reached into the nightstand drawer.

The movement roused her. Rebecca came up on one elbow.

"Boy," she said, watching him cover his raging prick. "You two are quick at that."

The comparison to Trey aroused him, maybe more than made sense.

"I can't wait much longer," he warned.

She opened her arms to him.

He spread her thighs and moved between them.

He slid balls deep in a single stroke.

She was hot and soft and he could have pounded to his finish in ten seconds. She stopped him with a subtle wince.

"Sore?" he asked.

She shook her head and flushed. "What Trey did in the garage left me tender. Your penetration felt . . . extra good. I really knew you were going in."

Oh he didn't need that match tossed onto his sexual coals. Her words had the same effect as a flurry of pumping strokes. Then she pressed her hips closer.

"Fuck," he swore, the tingle of impending orgasm buzzing up his tailbone. "Hold still a minute. I am too fucking close."

She stopped mid-wriggle and smiled at him. "What if I am too?"

He didn't think she was lying. Besides the squirm she'd cut short, her sheath twitched around him in small contractions, her pussy growing wetter by the second. Her fit felt like heaven around his cock. He guessed it did to her too. As if she couldn't help it, she shifted her legs to let him deeper. The head of his cock prodded her cervix.

"*Fuck,*" he repeated, his penile skin stretched so tight it stung.

If that weren't enough to test him, Trey stirred and began waking. "Hey, buddy," he said, husky and half asleep. "You came back."

He put his hand on Zane's back, a friendly gesture that nearly took his skull off with arousal. Zane groaned at the pain gathering in his balls.

"Uh," Trey said, sensing there was a problem. "Should I back off?"

Zane shook his head tightly. "Just . . . don't do more right now. I'm about to lose it."

Trey accepted this as the reason. "Okay." His hand rubbed just a little. "You need to do your own thing with her. I get that."

Zane wasn't sure what he needed, except to come as soon and as long as decently possible—preferably without embarrassing himself.

"Roll me on top," Rebecca suggested throatily. "That'll make it easier to control your responses."

He wasn't convinced his responses *were* controllable, but her on top sounded fine to him. He squirmed around and sat her above him. Her weight pushed him really deep, which she liked enough to roll her lower lip beneath her teeth.

"Now," she said, humorously smug, "*you* keep still while I work."

"Go slow," he warned.

Trey sat up next to them.

Zane wanted to grind his teeth—and not from annoyance. Trey had one leg bent up and the other dropped to the side, making it clear to the others that he was getting an erection. Zane wanted to look and not look at the same time. Rebecca looked, smiled at Trey like they shared a secret, and then braced straight-armed on Zane's shoulders.

"You watched us," she reminded him. "In fairness, you can't ask Trey not to."

"You like him being here."

"I liked *you* being in the garage." Her tone said all this was completely reasonable. Zane's jumping nerves said it was thrilling but stressful. Trey closed the difference by reaching over to cup Rebecca's breast.

"Do you like me doing this?" he asked Zane.

He liked it all right. Trey's darker hand caressing her fair skin was nearly as hot as his cock disappearing in her body.

"I like it," he said, out of breath. His hips pressed deeper, their motion impossible to restrain. "Rebecca, please move on me."

"Put your hand on me too," she said.

He covered her other breast so that he and Trey each supported one soft globe. This must have been what she wanted, because she writhed on him.

Zane and she made noises in chorus. The wet tight friction around his cock was too good not to moan over. Leaving the hand that cupped her breast in place, he took her hip to guide her as she lifted. From there, he slid his thumb inward to pull one labia wider. This exposed her clit to his and Trey's view.

He guessed she realized this. She groaned as Trey swallowed.

"Can I touch her there?" Trey asked. "Can I pinch her clit out between my fingers?"

Rebecca's neck was arched, spine twisting as she slowly rose and sank again. She couldn't answer so Zane did.

"Yes," he panted. "Do that to her."

She came two seconds after Trey got his pinching rub on her. The ripples of her orgasm gripped his shaft. Trey milked the pleasure until she stopped shaking. Rebecca's head tipped forward again, her gaze zeroed in on Zane, though Trey was the one who'd just brought her over. Her face was beautifully flushed, her irises a lustrous gray ring around her pupils.

What his face looked like, he didn't know. Slightly crazed, probably.

"Are you ready for me to bring you off?" she asked.

Her voice was smoke, her body dripping heat down him. His cock gave a pulse hard enough to hurt. "I am ready like you wouldn't believe," he growled.

She didn't rush. She rolled to his flare, tightened her gate around him, and then relaxed and rolled down. Maybe she did the muscle-squeezing trick for her own pleasure, but it felt great to him.

"God," he said when she repeated it. "Please keep doing that."

She leaned forward, bracing more of her weight on him—and more on the two palms that cupped her breasts. With his second hand, Trey started working her clit again. His fingers bumped Zane with her down strokes.

The combination was too enticing. Zane tried to breathe deeper, easier, to hold onto the edge longer.

"Slower?" Rebecca offered breathlessly, seeing him struggle.

"No," he gasped, reluctant to give up the delectable sensations. "Keep on like that." His grip tightened on her hip, his pelvis lifting off the mattress to press into her harder. He made a noise he would have been embarrassed by if she hadn't made it back.

She couldn't keep to her pace. Both of them needed her to speed up.

"*Yes*," he said, giving her permission even as she took it.

She cried out and he did too, riding him as he bucked. He huffed for air and went crazy. Trey couldn't hold onto her. Zane shoved his fingers where his friend's had been, twisting and rubbing the slippery button as they both went over.

Heat shot from deep within his balls. His body clenched with pleasure, his cock jammed as far as it could go between her legs. His hang-ups intensified the climax, as if he'd indulged in something forbidden. He ejaculated until he simply couldn't anymore. Then he collapsed with pure mellowness.

He was dazed and dozy from the hard come. At first, he didn't understand why Rebecca lifted his hand from where it had fallen to the covers. His fingers were too limp to do her any good.

At least they were until she folded them under hers on Trey's shuddering erection.

In spite of the massive climax he'd just enjoyed, Zane's penis stirred inside her.

Trey gasped with shock and pleasure as they pulled the joined fist up him. Seeing how stiff and big watching them had made him, Zane suspected he was about to go.

"Tighter," Zane said, voice hoarse from his final shout. Rebecca's fingers immediately obeyed. Knowing Trey would like faster too, Zane dragged their fists to the crucial stretch of nerves on the upper part of his under side. Trey watched their hands slide up him, then gaped at them. Satisfied he and Rebecca were exactly where they were needed, Zane shimmied Trey's skin up and down the hot spot as fast as it would go.

This flipped Trey like a giant switch.

He moaned, every muscle in his body jerking as he spewed semen over them.

Playing voyeur must have wound him up. The fountain sprayed pretty high and went on longer than usual.

Rebecca let go before Zane did. *He* couldn't seem to stop stroking Trey's penis.

"God," Trey panted. He put his hand over Zane's. Zane did stop then and looked into his eyes.

"Thank you," Trey said so seriously Zane probably should have laughed. He wished he could laugh, but he felt serious too.

"Fair's fair," he said, wondering if fairness truly had dictated that hand job.

Before the moment could get more awkward, Rebecca lifted off him and called dibs on the shower.

~

Rebecca didn't know which man's bathrobe she'd borrowed on her exit from the sybaritic bathroom, only that it smelled heavenly. Unable to resist, she inhaled through the fluffy lapel as she padded back to the bedroom.

The bed, which was empty, looked like a hurricane had hit it. In spite of being excellently pleasured twice recently, her flesh tightened at the sight.

"Over here," Zane called from the sitting area behind the arch. "We rustled up a snack."

Rebecca's stomach growled. She'd only tasted the food in the Lounge tonight. Turning, she saw the men sprawled in armchairs in their underwear. Their snack was spread across the round table between them. She spotted sliced smoked salmon, a big tin of caviar, and two bottles of Louis Roederer Cristal chilling in silver ice buckets. Both men were toasting bread on long forks over a small gas fire.

The fireplace turned the scene into a wet dream, its flames flickering cozily over the muscled limbs of the two big men. The air conditioning justified the warmth—sort of.

"It's August!" her sensible side felt obliged to say as she walked over.

Trey flashed teeth in a grin. "We have to toast the bread. Caviar doesn't taste as good on plain."

Delicately, so as not to break the eggs, he spooned a portion onto a finished slice. He passed it to her hand like the rare treat it was.

"This is Ossetra," she said, staring at the glossy gold rounds in awe.

"Petrossian Special Reserve," Trey informed her.

Rebecca gulped. Comparable in quality to Beluga, this stuff ran upwards of a thousand dollars for a five-ounce tin. Chef though she was, it was so expensive she'd only tasted it once before.

Laughing, Zane pressed a cool flute of Cristal into her other hand. "Come on. Who better to appreciate this luxury than someone with your palate?"

"I need to sit down for this," she said.

Zane helped her into the third armchair.

"Eat," Trey coaxed, taking a bite himself.

Rebecca bit down on the loaded toast. Amazing flavors exploded in her mouth. The large-scale caviar was the perfect texture: firm, smooth, the taste a layering of butter and nuts and sea.

"Mm," she hummed, closing her eyes to absorb it. She felt as if she'd been transported to Mother Russia, to some wintry gray seashore. When she lifted her eyelids, Zane and Trey were fighting laughs.

"You look like that when you come," Zane explained.

"And you definitely need more," Trey said, before she could blaze up in a blush.

They ate the decadent feast together—laughing, licking fingers, and enjoying. The salmon was nearly as good as the caviar, the chilled champagne the perfect accompaniment. The food was gone by the time Trey popped the second bottle.

"You do that as neatly as my head chef," she praised.

"Practice." He poured for the others and settled back in his chair. "Somewhat to my surprise, Zane is a champagne hound."

Zane grinned unabashedly, likely a little buzzed. "I'm about more than beer and burgers." He stretched his bare legs until his feet bumped hers. "You're wearing my robe."

This appeared to please him.

"It smelled good," she said.

"It smells like bad boy," Trey clarified and laughed.

"Is that an inside joke?"

"We're testing a new men's fragrance," Zane said. "Called 'Bad Boy,' of course. We've both been wearing it. We're hoping to launch it next Christmas."

"It's nice on both of you," she observed.

Smiling, Trey slouched deeper in his chair, arms flung out in relaxation, feet nudging hers like Zane's were. He seemed not only amused but happy, drunk perhaps but not impaired.

This is what he wants, she realized. Trey had no hesitation where he loved. His heart's desire was to draw both of them close to him. Zane's body still held a hint of tension, not much but it was there. Like her, he didn't let down his guard easily. Also like her, he found a lot to admire in Trey.

"How did you two meet?" she asked, sensing the champagne would oil their answer.

Trey turned his head to Zane, silently offering him the option of answering. She realized something else then. Trey was more careful of Zane's boundaries than Zane was of his.

Zane seemed willing to tell the story—if warily. "We were neighbors," he said, fingers tapping his chair's arms. "And we went to the same high school."

"I was a nerd. He was a jock."

"You weren't a nerd," she said, not believing it. Trey was quirky, but too beautiful for that.

"An outsider then. Zane took me under his wing in our senior year."

Zane leaned forward over his knees. His sandy brows drew together, creating a furrow above his nose. Rebecca leaned forward too, not close enough to tell him with her touch that his private stories were safe with her.

"Did he know what your father did?" she asked gently.

Zane wet his lips. "Trey's father hit him too. For different reasons, but we found out we had that in common."

"And also liking men and women."

"And also that," Zane concurred. "One night, my dad and I had a last-straw blowout. I was convinced I was going to kill him and spend the rest of my life in jail. Trey watched the fight from his bedroom window. When I ran from the house, he followed me. I'm not sure what he thought I was going to do. Throw myself off a bridge maybe. We talked for the first time at the high school track. You could say he initiated the other half of what I wanted sexually. We got each other through our last year of school."

"And then you came here to Harvard."

"And then we came here." His lips curved as he looked at her. The smile was wry. She couldn't read the emotion behind it.

"My father never hit me," she said.

"That's not a requirement for us liking you," Zane teased.

"I didn't mean— Shit." When he chuckled, she threw a napkin at him.

Still smiling slightly, he went on. "Everything we have here reminds me my old life is behind me. Every bite of caviar is a bite of freedom."

Rebecca's breastbone pressed in against her heart. "That's a nice way to put it."

Trey reached out to take Zane's hand. Zane returned his hold with a squeeze. Zane had told his story lightly, but she guessed sharing it wasn't that easy.

"I read your brothers' interview," Trey said.

He startled her. "Oh," she said, her hand coming to her chest. Zane was looking at him as if this surprised him as well.

"What you did for your brothers, when you were so young, it can't help but mean something to people who grew up like us."

"I just . . . I didn't want to lose them."

"You protected them." Trey's tone was soft but firm.

"I protected me too. And they helped, even though they were little."

He leaned back and smiled. "I admire you anyway."

He turned his statement into a tease, the same as Zane's crack about not needing to be hit for them to like her. She felt ridiculously flattered but also uncomfortable. She was no hero.

"Well," she said. She stood and tightened the tie on Zane's robe. The table between them was scattered with plates and crumbs. "Maybe I should clean up."

"We'll take care of it," Zane assured her. "Why don't you warm the bed for when we get back?"

"You're spoiling me," she said, trying to sound as light as them. "Aren't you worried I won't want to go to work tomorrow?"

Trey drew breath as if he meant to speak. Zane stopped him with a hand on his arm. "Just be a guest," he said. "We're happy you're here tonight."

~

"You need to ease up on her," Zane cautioned.

They'd brought the food to the suite on a rolling cart. Because Mrs. Penworth was asleep in her quarters, they were trundling it back with the remains. Just in case they ran into staff, they'd pulled on what Trey teased were their Hugh Hefner robes.

"*I* need to ease up," he repeated as Zane opened the old elevator's metal gate. "That's not what a woman groaning in ecstasy signifies. Anyway, she went at you hard for the finish. I couldn't have gotten her too sore."

"That's not what I meant." Zane pulled his end of the cart into the car. Closing the gate, Trey got the mechanism going. "She's a total workaholic, way worse than me. She had the wardrobe she did because she doesn't like wearing clothes she can't cook in. I'm not sure she has a shut-off button. She won't welcome being told she can stay home from the restaurant."

"But she can. We're not opening the Lounge to the general public for a week. Unless you have business you can't put off, now is the ideal time for a sex vacation."

The elevator creaked to a stop in the basement. Neither man shifted to get out. "You realize she probably hasn't taken a vacation since her dad walked out," Zane said.

Trey opened his mouth to argue and then shut it. "Really?"

"That's my best guess. Plus, saying the *V* word sets off warning bells for some chicks. You *date* a guy you're getting to know. You *vacation* when it's serious."

A warning bell rang belatedly in his head. Shit. Had Missy assumed he was serious when he'd agreed to join her for the weekend?

Unaware of his mental side trip, Trey frowned stubbornly. "This *is* serious. And we could do it now. We could spend a whole week playing and seeing if this arrangement can work out. You said yourself you wanted to give it a try."

He had said that. As usual, Trey was a couple steps ahead of him in commitment. Zane couldn't deny the appeal of what his friend seemed to be aiming for—at least he didn't think he could. He rubbed the groove between his lower lip and chin. "You're talking long-term here? You want to make Rebecca a regular part of our lives?"

"I do." Although Trey's answer was firm, his hands gripped his end of the cart as if they might break it. Beneath his neck tattoo, a nervous pulse was beating. The enclosed space they stood in made the conversation feel even more intense. "I think you want it too, Zane, even if you're not ready to admit it. You told her things you never tell anyone. You've thought about her as a person and not a bimbette. You're trying to figure her out. Hell, you might have done a better job of it than me."

"Well, I wouldn't lay odds on that." Zane looked into Trey's face as he weighed the situation, aware Trey was watching every expression that flitted through his eyes. "You wouldn't expect me to get over all my hang-ups at once?"

"Cross my heart," Trey promised.

"She does seem to be into both of us."

"She does," Trey agreed.

"And into both of us taking her at once."

"Which we're also into," Trey pointed out with his lips curving. "I honestly believe we'd have a better chance of victory as a team."

Zane smiled at his coaxing tone. Trey was cute when he thought he'd won an argument. "All right," he said. "You and I are now partners in seduction."

That settled, Trey heaved the elevator gate open. After Trey lifted the cart's wheels over the gap, Zane pushed it into the dark corridor. A few lights burned in the kitchen, guiding their progress there.

"If we're partners," Trey said, continuing their joint train of thought, "we need a strategy. I think you're right about Rebecca being likely to resist."

Zane's groin took on weight at his words. A memory rolled across his mind: Trey humping her atop the red Bugatti, his hands on her outstretched wrists, her breasts bouncing merrily. She'd writhed at him cuffing her, just as she'd writhed for Zane when he restrained her with his belt.

"We have to show her the playroom," he blurted.

Trey halted so suddenly Zane almost bumped his legs with the cart. He turned to stare back at him. "Not right away surely?"

"Yes, right away. We knows she's afraid of relaxing, afraid of—"

"—liking things too much?" Trey suggested.

"Yes. She doesn't know how to let go and enjoy. We need to . . . provide the illusion of taking that decision out of her hands."

Trey considered this, but Zane was almost certain he'd agree. A tent was forming behind his dark blue robe, large enough that Zane perceived the thin silk shifting. His own robe had been rising already. Seeing Trey throw a boner finished the job swiftly.

"We'd start tomorrow?" his lover asked.

"Early," Zane confirmed huskily.

Trey spotted the developments at Zane's crotch. One of his eyebrows rose, but he wasn't surprised. Neither of their appetites was modest. "Should we, maybe . . ."

"No." The roughness in Zane's voice increased. "At least for a while, I don't think we should get off without her."

CHAPTER TWELVE

Bound

A motherly woman the men referred to as Mrs. P served a hot breakfast in their suite. Quiet and efficient, she also seemed good-natured.

"Let me know if you need anything you'd rather not ask these two for," she said to Rebecca. "Whatever it is, the staff or I can get it."

The scope of the offer impressed. If Rebecca asked for a spaceship, would one appear on the lawn?

For the moment, breakfast was sufficient. Zane and Trey dug in without conversation, so she guessed they weren't morning folk. That was all right with her. The food was good enough to take up her attention.

"Don't get dressed while we're gone," Trey said sternly when he and Zane excused themselves to shower. "We have business we want to discuss with you."

She'd planned to pull on her clothes and go. It was after ten by then. She wanted to stop at her house, maybe check the Internet for early reports on last night's event at the Lounge. She knew Trey's people were on top of PR, but it couldn't hurt to touch base with her contacts in the media. Though these were reasonable intentions, she didn't pursue them. The way Trey said *business* made it impossible.

Her curiosity as to whether he and Zane were sharing more than a shower also might have kept her there.

Maybe it would be okay to poke her head in, but they hadn't invited her. So what if she wanted to soap their lovely backs—or watch them soap each other's? Being inordinately intrigued by what they were getting up to was no excuse for invading their privacy.

She'd gotten the robe she'd borrowed a little sweaty by the time they emerged from the walk-in closet that connected to the bathroom. Somewhat to her frustration, she couldn't tell if they'd had sex. Though the color on their cheeks was high, they didn't wear the languor that went with orgasms.

They also weren't wearing the playboy robes they'd left in.

"You dressed," she complained. They wore white T-shirts with no sleeves and sweat shorts—Zane's in gray and Trey's black. They were so fit the simple workout clothes looked ridiculously hot. Either could have graced a spread in their magazine. *The Bad Boys get casual!* the caption might have said.

Unmoved by her objection, Zane handed her a folded pile of clothes. "These are for you, sweetheart."

Him calling her *sweetheart* almost caused her to blush. She focused on what he'd given her instead. The small bundle included yoga pants, cotton bikini panties, and a soft strappy shirt with a built-in bra—an outfit any woman could have worn for lazing around on her day off. Rebecca peered at them suspiciously.

"These are new," she said. "And my size."

"The clothes you wore last night are wrinkled," Zane not-quite-explained with a smile.

If they'd pressed her to accept a designer dress dipped in diamonds, she'd have had no problem refusing. Suspecting she'd been managed, she retreated huffily to the bathroom to put them on. When she returned, both men gave her onceovers. Their unmistakable approval heated her in places she wished she could control better.

"Nice," Trey praised.

"Very," Zane seconded.

Rebecca put her hands on her hips. "Fine. You've dressed me in formfitting sportswear. Now tell me what your business is."

"Not here," Zane said. "We need to take a walk."

He caught her fingers in his, surprising her. She'd thought Trey was the big hand-holder.

The walk took them to a vintage elevator with a folding gate. Rebecca half expected to be shoved against its wall and screwed . . . and maybe more than half wished for it. When Zane smiled at her knowingly, she snapped her head away. They got out at a sub-level, one she had the impression was under the basement. From there, they strode along a shadowy corridor, stopping at what looked like a bank vault door. Constructed of metal, its hardcore lock required a key and a thumbprint.

Rebecca bit back a tart remark about showing off their stash of gold bars. Just because she was nervous, she didn't have to be snarky.

Trey finished swinging the heavy door open. With a humorous little bow, he waved her ahead of them.

The corridor she'd entered was lined with old brick and arched. Cool and smelling of earth, the passageway bent left, then right, and then opened into a huge round room. A columned arcade circled it, each pair of arched supports dividing off a niche. High above their heads, a crude wooden wheel of a chandelier provided illumination, but not enough to make out the contents of the recesses.

"What is this place?" Rebecca asked, automatically speaking in hushed tones.

"During Prohibition," Trey said, "it was a gin mill and speakeasy. Now it's Zane and my playroom. We're completely private here. No one has the key but us."

A shiver she couldn't suppress ran through her. She realized she wasn't afraid to be alone with them. With the sense that she'd stepped to the edge of a deep canyon, she turned to look at the men. They were watching her closely. "The stories are true then. You throw orgies."

"Maybe not as wild as you're thinking," Trey answered. "We invite trusted friends here. And we all play responsibly."

"Responsibly." Rebecca wet her lips, gaze straying to the nearest shadowed niche. Was that a metal rack inside it? The sort a person could be attached to? She didn't want to think about how hard her pussy was quivering. "Why show this to me?"

"Because we believe you'll enjoy trying out our toys. We know you're thinking of leaving us today. We'd like to present the strongest possible argument that you should stay for a while."

"And you think this is it?" Rebecca didn't have to fake her surprise. "Guys, I promise neither of you needs anything like this to turn me on."

Trey's smile was crooked and gentle. He hid it well, but she sensed she'd touched a nerve. This place was important to him. "It's not about needing this to turn you on. It's about getting past the walls people build around their passions. I think you'll admit you have a few of those."

"Give us one game," Zane said, the consummate bargainer. "If you like it, we play another. We want a whole week with you, but we're prepared to earn it a day at a time."

She couldn't just say *yes*. That wasn't how bargaining worked. "If I play one of your games, do I get to choose one to play on you?"

If Trey's smile had been gentle, Zane's was devilish. "You have no idea how much Trey would like that."

"How much *Trey* would."

Zane laughed throatily. "Trey's tastes are flexible. You can play games with him or me, and he'll enjoy both."

And what if I want you to play with each other? She didn't say the thought aloud. She hadn't forgotten Trey's comment about Zane being embarrassed by his "gay" side. Trey was breathing more deeply than he'd been when they first walked in, like he was aroused and working to hide it. When he talked about walls, did he realize he had them? Meeting his eyes gave her the same rocked sensation as the night they met. The floor wasn't solid. She was falling into him.

"Nobody does anything to me if his clothes are on," she said.

"Deal," Zane agreed, and just like that, they seemed to have one.

Trey pulled his T-shirt over his head, then shoved his shorts and briefs down his legs. As he stepped out of them, he had a half-mast erection. From what she could see, the flag was running up the pole posthaste.

"Hey," she said breathlessly. Did they have to rush into this? But maybe they did. Zane was undressing too.

"You wanted us naked," he said. "We're obliging you."

His erection was beefing up just like Trey's.

"You *didn't* have sex in the shower," she exclaimed without thinking.

Zane tossed his last shoe into the pile of clothes Trey had started. "We made a rule for this week. We don't get off without you."

Boy, she wished that knowledge didn't wind her up so well. She was vulnerable enough to their attraction. Her heart pumped in her throat as Trey stepped closer.

"Don't I need a . . . a safe word?" she asked nervously.

Trey knelt beside her to pull down her yoga pants, a service Rebecca forestalled by grabbing their waistband. Trey tilted his head to look up her body. "Zane and I prefer to let 'no' mean 'no,' but we can give you one if you like."

"I've never done this before. How would I know my preference?"

Smiling, he kissed her hip and tugged the pants free of her fingers. "Trust us then. We'll pay attention to what pleases you."

She guessed she did trust them, because she let Zane peel off her top. She was naked then. They all were. Standing tall as a tree before her, Zane steadied her head between his hands. His hold was more than a reassurance or a caress. The strength of his hands kept her from looking away from him. Her breathing sped up at his control, a reaction she couldn't stop.

"I'm going to give you instructions," he said, his bright blue eyes holding hers. "Unless you tell me you don't want to obey, I'll expect you to follow them. If you want to struggle, feel free. We won't let you hurt yourself. Other than that, your words are all you need to stop this train in its tracks."

"You won't gag me?"

Zane's chuckle was sexy. "Not to be cliché, but we have better uses for a mouth as sweet as yours."

It didn't take an Einstein to figure out that implication. Rebecca's nipples beaded like he'd pinched them.

"Okay," she said, striving to sound steady. "I can go along with that."

Zane stepped back and considered her as if he were an artist and she his clay. Trey remained where he was next to her. Was Zane his boss for this as well?

"Trap her arms against her sides," he said to his friend. "Carry her to the niche behind you. I saw that one catch her eye."

When Trey lifted her as instructed, his stiffened cock pressed against her back. Rebecca squirmed but held her tongue against making noises that might be construed as *stop*. His task fulfilled, Trey set her down in the recess Zane specified, facing the shadowy apparatus she couldn't make out yet.

"Stay," he said and struck a fireplace match.

Rebecca stayed, her normally independent nature caught in the spell the men were weaving. The flame Trey held revealed two gas sconces on the brick columns to either side of her. He lit them, after which Rebecca sucked in a breath. In the dancing light, she saw what the shadows hid. The recess was about six feet wide and deep. An elaborate rack stood within it, fashioned of dull black metal in a complex arrangement. Bars supported padded rests and rings, some of which were adjustable with gears. Buckled leather restraints provided still more security. A floor length black curtain, also velvet, lined the wall to the rear, concealing who knew what additional instruments.

Rebecca had to appreciate the imagination at work here.

"Kneel on the first set of rests," Zane instructed behind her.

Trey helped her onto them. Their positioning spread her knees, and air tickled her wetness. Liking this a bit too much, she clenched her jaw.

Maybe Trey knew. "These lock," he said. He slammed a curved metal piece around her calf and into an aperture. The noise jolted through her, sounding like a jail door closing. Cream welled from her, but at least she wasn't alone in being affected. As she twisted around to watch him shut the second one, she noticed the tip of Trey's erection was stretched and shiny with arousal. A pulse beat hard in his upright shaft.

It bounced as he came around to her front again. "Left hand," he ordered.

Unable to speak, she gave him her hand. He pulled it gently along a padded rest until her wrist was stuck through a ring. Her right arm was treated to the same procedure.

"Tighten the cuffs," Zane said.

Trey turned a crank and the rings clanked smaller. He didn't stop until the segmented metal fit her wrists perfectly. She was certain there were easier means of securing her, but the noises the mechanism created were fabulously theatrical. A million shivers of excitement swept her skin. The rack was like some crazy steampunk device—custom made, she was sure. Once the cuffs were snug, Trey strapped her elbows to the padded rest with leather. Nothing pinched, but neither was she able to get away.

The arm bars were extendable. Trey pulled them toward him and locked them down with more clanking. The shift forced her to lean forward. The combination of being slightly off balance and restrained was weirdly arousing.

"Your torso needs supporting," he said gruffly.

For this he supplied a leather harness. He wrapped it around her middle like a corset. Like the historical version of that garment, it lifted but didn't cover her breasts. Unlike it, it attached by a system of straps and rings to hooks on the rack. The harness took the weight of her forward lean, holding her perfectly.

"Test it," Trey said.

She assumed he meant to pull against it so she did. The leather creaked, but nothing broke or snapped. The rack itself didn't budge, no matter how she swung her weight. Its structure must have been sunk into the floor. She guessed Trey liked the look of her moving. His right hand fisted at his sternum.

"Anything hurt?" he asked.

"No," she answered huskily.

His eyes slid down her bound body, over her breasts, down the corset, locking on the now wet spikes of hair at her sex. He let out an aroused sound, one she'd heard from him before, one he was unable to hold in. His cock stood up like a horn, his erection thicker and more brutal than any she'd seen in person. At the thought of pleasuring it in some fashion, goose bumps broke out across her thighs.

"Are you cold?" he asked immediately.

She smiled, waiting for his gaze to rise to her face again. He seemed concerned, and not entirely for her wellbeing. She thought she understood his real question. "This may be the oddest foreplay I've ever had used on me, but I confess it's working. You can stop worrying."

"But if you're cold—"

"If she's cold, we'll warm her," Zane said. His tone was authoritative as he stepped closer behind her. He'd let Trey indulge his fetish—or maybe genius —for bondage. Now he was taking charge again.

Trey didn't seem to mind.

"Draw the curtain," Zane said softly.

Trey turning to obey gave her an unobstructed view of his hindquarters. That was a lovely show, what with his wedge-shaped back and his muscular rear. She took a moment to shake off her admiration and notice what he'd uncovered.

The curtain had concealed a mirror as tall as him, framed in ornately carved dark wood. With round and startled eyes, Rebecca stared at her trussed-up reflection. Her hair was mussed, her mouth stretched into an O. The redness of her nipples above the harness was pornographic, but this wasn't all that was. In the blue-tinged gaslight, moisture glistened on her inner thighs. Her clit was so swollen it peeped out. Blood rushed into her cheeks with arousal and embarrassment.

"Good Lord," was all she could say.

Zane moved in while she gaped. His reflection was nearly as flushed as hers. "See how beautiful you are?" he murmured in her ear. "How enticing?"

He stood between the shin rests that spread her thighs. He was close enough that filling his lungs with air caused his chest to brush her back, close enough that head of his erection bumped the top of her ass. He reached through the various bars and straps to stroke the pebbled skin around her right nipple. The feathery touch drew more hot fluid from her.

Trey's intake of breath was harsh as he spotted this. Forcing his gaze upward, he looked at Zane instead of her. "Is the height all right?"

"Perfect," Zane said. "I can slide my cock right into her from here."

A shiver crossed Trey's shoulders. Did he want Zane to slide his cock into him? "I'll shift the mirror," he said, his voice gone thick. "I don't want to block Rebecca's view when she's going down on me."

"Good," Zane said. "I'll want to watch that too."

The mirror hung on a wheeled track. Trey pushed it to a new position, gauged the angles, and then returned to her. He was breathing harder, a thin sheen of sweat gleaming on his bronzed skin.

"Here are the rules," he said, not quite evenly. "You make me come, and then Zane lets you. As long as I hold back, he doesn't bring you off. Obviously, you can only use your mouth."

Was it rude to point out this could be short game, given how wound up Trey was?

"My mouth can't reach you from here," she said instead.

Trey climbed onto the frame with her.

There were places to put his feet she hadn't noticed before, and also a subway style strap for one hand to hang onto. Once he'd gripped it, Trey's cock was level with her mouth. This close, his erection filled her field of vision, rock hard and juddering. All she saw of his tattoo was the dragon's tail.

Trey cupped the side of her head with his free hand. "I can pull out if you push me too close to the edge. Because you're bound, you won't be able to stop me. As you might have guessed, I'll need the advantage."

His self-deprecating tone caused her to crane to see his face. Did he think she judged him for liking this? How could she, when her body had been creaming since her first sight of the contraption? She'd told him this bondage worked on her. Hadn't her words gotten through?

Words didn't always, of course. Sometimes convincing someone required action.

Behind her, Zane ran his hands across her shoulders and down her arms, across the leather that secured her elbows to the metal cuffs on her wrists. He caressed both her and what held her captive.

"I think we ought to start," he said.

She trembled, knowing the men wouldn't stop unless she told them to. Maybe she ought to tell them. Maybe this was too much for an uptight control freak like her . . .

She forgot every doubt the second Zane's prick nudged into her pussy.

Her tension gave way like wax melting. His cock completed her bondage, its solid length going in the key that dissolved her fears. The reaction was primitive. Irrational. Some big male taking her didn't make her safe from anything. At the moment, logic had no power over her. Zane was stretching her limits, clearly worked up like Trey. When he moaned his pleasure for the penetration, the sound rang through her soul.

Oh yes, she thought. This was what people meant by surrender.

"You like that?" Trey rasped.

Until Zane answered, she wasn't certain whom Trey was talking to.

"She's hot around me," he said. "Tight. Wet. You should try her mouth and see if it's as nice."

"I will," Trey said. "After I do this."

With his hand still cupping her face, he swung his groin forward. His erection settled against her cheek, extending from her jaw to her temple in a hot line. His skin was velvet, the throbbing hardness within it reminding her how alive this part of him was. As if his cock were another hand, he caressed her face with it: one side, the other, sighing as she turned her head to rub it. Pulses shook within her lips as his hardness brushed them, but her mouth was relaxed. Trey liked the feel of it. He dragged his cock up and down its fullness, tugging at the seam with his flare. It was a tease that made her shiver and him impatient. His hold grew infinitesimally harder against her jaw.

"Take me," he ordered hoarsely. "Open those sexy lips for me and suck."

She didn't want to resist. She opened and his cock pushed in. He didn't try to overwhelm her, but he wasn't tentative. God, he was thick. Her mouth stretched around him, watering, adjusting. Her tongue wanted to taste and rub all of him, but settled for the inches it could reach on the strut underneath his glans.

She looked sideways, seeking him in the mirror, only to have his gaze meet hers there. Like her, he wanted to see the whole picture: her corseted and strapped to the rack, hanging from the straps of leather with Zane's cock buried deep inside her. His prick held her prisoner, a spike she didn't have the means to escape. Above her, his long muscled arms gripped the rack for leverage. His abs were taut, her bottom soft and tilted to give him access to her sex. Every part of Zane was bigger than she was, causing her to seem extra feminine. The strange thing was, she felt extra powerful. Sexier. Maybe irresistible. Her forward lean caused her breasts to dangle X-ratedly.

Trey took in every bit of this—lips parting, breath hastening, totally turned on by what he saw. The journey of his eyes complete, he returned his gaze to where his erection breached her mouth. There it stopped like he was frozen. This visual might have been crudest, but she knew they both liked it. Trey's huge hard-on pulsed in the mirror and on her tongue.

"Fuck," he breathed. "Rebecca."

He sounded awed, as if she were doing him a favor rather than giving in to her own desires. She knew what she wanted then: to show him how much she accepted him, to prove it with tenderness and care. She crooned to him, the snug circle of her lips drawing back along the careful distance he'd pushed in. When she pulled free, she kissed his trembling tip.

She felt she loved him. Maybe the feeling would fade, but it existed in that moment.

"Come in again," she said huskily. "Fuck my mouth nice and slow."

Trey wasn't likely to do it rough. Not to a woman anyway. Never mind his dominant streak. If she knew him at all, he'd err on the side of caution.

She wasn't mistaken. He moaned softly and pushed back in. As if it were a signal, Zane started moving his cock inside her too. Her pussy clenched around his hardness, and that drew a groan from him. The sound was deeper than Trey's. Zane seemed more in control than his lover but not by much. Caught between them, sensing them straining to rein in their bodies' natural urges, she realized something new.

She didn't have to be responsible for herself.

If the men wanted to stop her from coming, that was on them. Her only job was to drive them as crazy as she wanted and enjoy herself doing it. She was free. They were bound by the rules they'd set. Giddiness welled in her. She gripped the end of the arm bars, using their stability to increase her control of her own movements.

When Zane thrust back into her the next time, she set the angle. He grunted, so she knew the pressure hit him in a good place. Small though it was, Zane's reaction provided too much of a charge to Trey. He pushed less steadily past her lips, then yanked out and panted.

Mouth temporarily unoccupied, Rebecca turned her head to speak to Zane. "Better bend closer if you want to watch him go. He's already having to take a break."

Zane laughed and took her advice. He'd been holding onto the rack, but now he crooked his arms up her front and gripped her shoulders. His head was next to and just above hers, making it easier to talk.

"Don't count Trey out," he said, thrusting in a fraction harder than before. "My CFO has hidden reserves."

"You could help me," she suggested. "Let him feel you panting while I suck him."

Zane thought this was funny too.

"Fuck," Trey said, less amused. Apparently deciding his break was over, he prodded her lips again.

She didn't stint. She took him in as deeply as she was able—licking, pulling, twisting her head to move the soft suction of her cheeks and tongue around him. Whatever inhibitions she had, she threw to the wind. She moaned with pleasure as she sucked him, the same as she did for Zane when he drove into her pussy. He was careful not push her over, and she let them know how wild that made her. She didn't care that she was loud, or that she writhed like a thing possessed. The men liked watching what they did to her —and what she did to them.

"You should . . . pull out again," Zane told Trey, his words broken by his thrusts. "We're supposed to make her wait. I can . . . tell you're about to go."

Trey groaned and dragged his cock out of her, but didn't retreat far enough. The next time Zane jolted her forward her lips caught the head again. Trey lost it then. He shoved between her tongue and palate like he meant it, like he could barely stop himself from plunging down her throat.

"God," he moaned. His body tensed, leather creaking as his hand tightened on the strap it held. She caught sight of him in the mirror with his head flung back ecstatically. "It feels too good. She's . . . licking me . . . so . . . good."

He began ejaculating, and she sucked him more fiercely. Before it occurred to her that this might hurt him, he made a sound so helplessly carnal, she knew she'd accidentally done the perfect thing. The edge of pain triggered him. Anticipating the effect this might have, Zane slapped his hand around the base of Trey's cock, so he couldn't slam too far and gag her. Naturally, Zane's grip excited Trey even more. He cried out and his come flooded her, his whole body arching to get closer. Though Zane didn't climax, he seemed driven by the same instinct. He shoved his length all the way up inside her, holding tight and shaking.

Rebecca was trapped between them, and she loved it. They were both straining to get deeper, maybe straining toward each other. It might be a strange thing to get off on, but she couldn't deny she did. The three of them seemed a unit, as if they all took each other.

Trey convulsed with one final shot and sighed, bringing her awareness to him in particular. Beginning to go soft, he eased himself from her clinging lips. Then she did mind being bound. She wanted to touch him as he stepped down onto the floor. She could tell his knees were shaky.

On the bright side, when he tipped her head up, she was able to look directly into his eyes. She licked her lips free of the last taste of him, an action he watched fascinatedly.

"You liked that," he said.

It wasn't a question. Rebecca smiled, the sensation that she might love him rising in her again. She wasn't frightened by it. She couldn't be in the unusual state she was in. She hadn't come, but she would. She wasn't free, but she was. She'd trusted him more than she had anyone in her life, and it was turning out all right. A hint of these thoughts must have shown in her expression. Trey's dark brows furrowed above his nose. His perplexity amused her.

"The rules of this game entitle me to come now," she said.

The corners of Trey's mouth turned up. "They do. Would you like me to help Zane finish you?"

Zane's cock jerked inside her. An imp prodded Rebecca to share the idea that flashed to her. "Do you think he'd mind if you lick my clit while he thrusts? I realize he'd feel you down there. Perhaps you'd even lick him by mistake." Her tone was intentionally coy, maybe more so than Zane could appreciate.

"Fuck," he swore behind her. His body wasn't objecting. His arms tightened around her, his cock gone steely hard in her.

Trey's eyes flicked to Zane's face and back to her, his mouth pursed with the amusement.

"I believe he'd survive the ordeal," he said.

~

Whatever doubts Zane harbored in his mind, his body was on board with Rebecca's plan.

"I have to unfasten these," he said, reaching forward to unlock and unbuckle Rebecca's arms. "She'll be at the wrong angle otherwise."

Maybe she would and maybe she wouldn't. He only knew he wanted her closer. Before she had a chance to rub her wrists, he pulled her up so that her weight rested on her knees and not the waist harness. His prick fucking loved the change in position. The pressure of her body on his underside was stronger.

He gritted his teeth against letting that push him over. If he was going to do this, he was damn well going to enjoy it for more than two seconds.

"Do her if you're going to," he said impatiently to Trey.

Trey lifted a brow at him. Submission was something he played at and not his true nature. Zane realized how possessively he was hugging Rebecca, both arms wrapped around her to hold himself deep and snug in her.

Trey kicked a convenient cushion into place under her. "Your wish is my command," he said.

Rebecca shivered—for Trey, he thought. Though it was childish, he jerked his prick deeper into her. Resentment made him hot, or maybe how hot he was made him resentful. Trey knelt on the cushion and looked up at Rebecca.

The shiver ran through her again, but this time she chafed Zane's enfolding arms.

"You're beautiful," Trey said. "Both of you. Especially right here."

He touched them with his fingertips where they joined. A shock of pleasure streaked up Zane's cock, much too strong for sanity.

Trey must have seen the reaction. He smiled subtly and leaned forward.

He didn't pretend to be avoiding Zane. His tongue dragged up the strip of shaft that bulged outside Rebecca before continuing up her folds to her clit. Zane made a noise, then she did, and then Trey swiped them both again. The joint tongue job made him crazy. His cock twitched like a mad thing, which Rebecca must have felt. He hated that he couldn't hide his reaction to Trey licking him, but part of him loved it too.

He gasped as Trey cupped his balls and pressed upward. The outside pressure added to the inner was stellar.

Trey did something to Rebecca too, because she moaned and squirmed.

"I'm going to finish her," Trey warned. "Thrust if you're going to."

Oh Zane was going to. He drew back, pulled in a breath, then drove strongly into her. Rebecca cried out with pleasure.

She groaned when Trey made good on his promise and sucked her clitoris.

Zane snarled. Her pussy was immediately wetter, and softer, and when he thrust again she thrust back at him just as hard.

"Yes," she said. "*Please.*"

Her short fingernails pricked his arms.

"Hold her hips still," Trey growled.

Zane steadied them and went at her full throttle, pumping through that sweet wet tightness as if it could save his life. He couldn't stop. His nerves screamed for release, his instincts for conquest. Rebecca let out little cries that told them how close she was. Trey wasn't teasing and neither was Zane. Together, they drove her harder, higher . . .

Her sheath sucked at him and quivered with orgasm.

She pulled his climax from him. Timing it perfectly, Trey's fingers contracted on his sac. The top of his head came off as ecstasy rushed from him—so hot, so strong, he couldn't hold back a bellow. Rebecca's head was arched back over his shoulder. He'd cupped her breast as he came, and now her heart pounded in his palm, her hardened nipple pulsing. She lifted her hand to cover his.

He couldn't hold back his contented sigh any more than he had his shout.

"Zane," she said, nuzzling him on the jaw.

He looked down. Trey's cheek rested on her pubis, his dark hair mingling with hers. Rebecca's second hand petted him.

Tears rose into his eyes, but he wasn't sure what fueled them. Not jealousy. Maybe protectiveness. Did Rebecca understand how strongly Trey could love? Would she be careful not to lead him on if she couldn't return his feelings?

Trey was the romantic. Rebecca seemed more like Zane. Could he trust her to be like him in looking out for Trey? Trey wasn't a child or anything like that. He simply didn't shield his heart as well as most people.

Confused by his own reactions, Zane cleared his throat. "Ready to get off this ride?" he asked Rebecca.

Her lips curved. "For now," she said.

~

Rebecca had never liked massages. The idea of putting herself in someone else's hands so they could relax her didn't sit right with her. If she couldn't relax by herself, she wasn't sure she wanted to.

"Stop wriggling," Trey scolded, giving her bare bottom cheeks a swat. "You'd think *this* was the torture rack.

She lay face down on a professional style table in another of the playroom's niches. Pillar candles lit this one, and soft pink rose petals strewed the floor. Both men were smoothing warm scented oil over her. She knew she ought to be enjoying it. Most likely, a normal woman would.

"I'm sorry," she said, flinching when Trey touched her foot. "Getting massages gives me performance anxiety. The masseurs all feel obliged to tell me how tense I am."

Trey snorted as Zane pressed his oiled hands more firmly into her back. He stood at her head, bending over her. When his stroke reached her butt, he drew up it again. "We're not tying you down for this, sweetheart."

"I'm not asking you to. But, um, maybe I could massage one of you instead?"

"No," the men said in unison.

"You gave yourself marks from twisting in the restraints. We want to rub them away."

This reasoning came from Zane. She knew they'd have massaged her regardless, or why the rose petals? They'd planned to do this to her. She heaved a suffering sigh.

"Oh you poor thing," Trey mocked, making smooth passes around her calves. "We feel so sorry for you."

Because Rebecca's face was hidden in the table's hole, she let herself smile a bit. "You could talk to me—you know, for distraction."

"Oh brother," Trey said at her overly innocent manner.

"You practically abducted me. The least you could do is answer a few questions."

"What questions?" Trey asked.

Rebecca hadn't actually planned that far. She curled her toes as she considered. "Have you always played games like this with each other?"

"No," Zane said. "And we don't always play them now. They're like an extra spicy meal. You wouldn't want to eat it every night."

"And when you play with other people, do you play with women or men or both?"

Zane's hands hesitated in moving down her spine.

"We invite both," Trey said. "But Zane and I only play with women and only separately."

This suggested their trusted friends didn't know they were a couple. That was a level of secret keeping worthy of her.

"That's all you've got?" Trey said when she paused. "Those are all the answers you want from us?"

"Now you're inviting trouble," Zane chided.

Maybe he was. Rebecca wriggled up on her elbows and looked at Trey. "Can I ask you something personal?"

His face tightened. She thought she knew what thought had crossed it. He assumed she wanted to ask why he liked tying people up.

"It's about your dad," she said, which maybe wasn't any better.

"Okay," he said cautiously.

"Zane said your dad beat you for different reasons than his."

"And you want to know what they were."

"You don't have to tell me," she assured him.

Trey's hands had stilled on her legs. He stood to one side of the table, working on her lower half. When his gaze met hers, it was steady but guarded.

"My dad's father abused him sexually. I never met him, and my dad didn't follow in his footsteps, but he was very weird about anything to do with sex. I wasn't supposed to date or jack off or watch certain TV shows. If I gave any indication I wasn't a eunuch, he got really uptight. In his way, I think he was trying to insure I never did to anyone what was done to him."

"He tried to teach you sex was dirty. He tried to beat it into you."

"Yes." Trey seemed relieved she understood. He smiled unexpectedly. The expression was so compassionate it awed her. He wasn't angry with his father —not like she would have been.

"I don't know why," he said, "but I never believed him. I always thought sex was good. I guess I'm lucky that was the case."

Zane reached to squeeze his arm. He didn't speak, but the depth of what he felt for Trey was clear. Trey smiled at his friend and her.

"Lie down," he said. "We're not done with you."

When she returned to her prone position, her body forgot to tense against them. For once, the thoughts she was busy thinking didn't get in the way of her relaxing.

CHAPTER THIRTEEN

Dare

Rebecca loosening up changed the rest of the day. Feeling proud of herself, she skinny-dipped with the men in their indoor pool, not even squeaking when the chauffeur walked in to ask if they'd need the car later. Aside from his initial startled look, the young man hadn't eyed her, so that was all right. Zane handled it well. He'd kept his temper as he told Owens to wait for a response to his knock next time. She doubted the man would forget. After their swim, they fed the ducks in the estate's lagoon, then enjoyed a quickie back in the bedroom suite. The sex wasn't as intense as their time in the playroom, but Rebecca liked it because both men were laughing and playful. Around four, she left a message for the twins that she was away from home.

She didn't say the *V* word. That would have alarmed them.

At four thirty, Zane and Trey checked in with their office. That was more than her restraint could take. She begged the use of a computer in their library. Scattered around the elegant book-lined room, Zane and Trey had small writing desks for guests, each with an internet-ready workstation. Palms gone sweaty, she pulled a rolling leather chair up to one.

Typing in the link to Gordon Hewitt's *Boston Eats* blog tightened every nerve she had.

You don't have to read his review, she told herself, finger hovering over the ENTER key. She knew Hewitt's experience might have been colored by having Neil Montana at his table. Moreover, Hewitt was a single set of taste buds in a world of them. People usually, mostly, almost always liked her food. The Lounge's opening had some hiccups, but overall Monday's service had been solid.

"Oh God," she moaned and clicked onto the site.

"Do Bad Boys Do It Better?" asked the anxiety-inducing headline.

"Shit," she said and forced herself to read on.

Before she'd finished the first paragraph she was grinning. Bad Boys did it awesome, apparently. Hewitt mentioned the problem with the lobster—but only in conjunction with it being fixed quickly. Her servers were praised for their knowledge and aplomb. Her clam chowder was declared sublime, her Boston beans on toast less aesthetic but still tasty. The words "creative" and "playful" were thrown around more than once. Trey earned kudos for an atmosphere as warm and glowing as fine whiskey.

Hewitt saved his most fulsome praise for the end.

"It is the dessert, however, the simple, satisfying genius of toothsome apple tart topped by handcrafted cinnamon ice cream, that deserves to become this establishment's signature creation. The blend of flavors and textures fill one with an actual sense of love. Chef Eilert cooks with both heart and skill, making for an experience that this sometimes-jaded reviewer confesses to being eager to repeat. A Highly Recommended for The Bad Boys Lounge from me."

"Oh my God," Rebecca breathed, both hands pressed tight against her mouth. Gordon Hewitt, Boston's most persnickety and respected food critic, highly recommended her. Almost unnoticed, a tear of relief spilled from her right eye.

She had to email Raoul, though he'd probably seen the blog already. Still, her head chef would be excited. This triumph was as much his as hers. She wondered if the booking service was getting many reservations for next week. Trey's people needed to highlight Hewitt's rating on the Lounge's website, maybe pull out a few good quotes.

Adrenaline flooded her, her body wanting to do everything at once. *Stop,* she thought. *Take a breath and calm down.* When she did, she knew who she most wanted to share her excitement with. She also knew the partiality meant something.

~

Zane and Trey had a private office down the hall from their bedroom suite. When they had guests, this allowed them to get work done without disturbing their company. Because they'd decided to play hooky with Rebecca on short notice, there was work to see to. As efficiently as he could, Zane checked in on a few situations he couldn't ignore. Though the office had two desks, and he'd left the door open, Trey made his calls from the sitting room.

Zane had just wrapped things up when Trey came in.

"You done too?" Zane asked, stretching back satisfyingly in his chair.

Normally, this would make Trey admire his muscles—a reaction Zane probably took for granted. This afternoon, Trey wasn't biting. He sat on the corner of Zane's desk, folded his arms, and rubbed his lower lip with one finger.

"I just got off the phone with Elaine," he said.

"Oh?" Zane prompted, unsure what emotion he was facing.

"She took a message. From Constance Sharp's grown son and daughter. They're under the impression their mother is in Boston and want to know if I've seen her. Evidently, they're worried. Elaine seemed to think you know something about that."

"Uh," Zane said. He recognized Trey's mood now: it was controlled anger. "Your aunt kind of broke into our offices Friday night. I got her out before she did any damage."

"You got her out."

"I had security escort her back to her hotel. I gave the guards strict instructions not to let her back in the building. I'm sorry I didn't tell you. I went on that weekend with Missy, and Rebecca's big do was when I came back. Then we convinced her to join us here. I didn't want to throw a damper over our nice time."

Trey's rubbing of his lower lip turned into a pinch. "So she's here in Boston."

"I guess so. Her kids wouldn't be calling if she'd gone home. I couldn't force her to leave the city. I talked to Evan. He doesn't think we have grounds for a court order."

"You thought her showing up was important enough to consult a lawyer, but not to inform me?"

"I'm sorry. I don't like seeing you upset about this."

"Fuck." Trey got up to pace, both hands shoveling through his dark hair. He really wasn't himself when it came to his aunt, which tended to knock Zane equally off kilter.

"Look," he said, hoping Trey wouldn't jump down his throat for what he was about to say. "It's totally your call, and you know I'll back your play, but are you sure avoiding her is the best solution?"

"There's no point seeing her!" Trey exclaimed. "The only thing that will satisfy her is denying my father was abused. I can't give her that—even if she's just a crazy old lady who's afraid of her own guilt. The truth is the truth. My father paid for it. *I* paid for it. And maybe she could have done something to stop the abuse. She was eight years older than my dad. I wasn't there. I don't know what the fuck happened in that house."

Zane came around the desk to sit on its other corner. He touched Trey's arm lightly. "You don't really blame her."

"I don't know whether I do or not. Kids don't always speak up, even when they could. You and I both know that."

"We do know that," Zane agreed, keeping his hand where it was. Trey was the least judgmental person he knew. Zane didn't want to see that change.

"Fine." Trey looked away and scowled at the wall. "I made your point for you. But even if I went along with her, even if I said, 'Yes, this lie you're telling yourself is true. Your father didn't abuse mine, and my dad never claimed differently to me,' do you think once would be enough? On some level, my aunt *knows* what happened. She'd need me to keep shoring up the lie. I'd never be done with it. Fuck," he finished and covered his face.

Zane moved his hand to Trey's shoulder, which was trembling. "Trey," he said. "Sweetheart."

Trey choked out a sound that let Zane know he was crying.

Zane immediately pulled him against him. "Sh," he said against Trey's hair. Trey clung to him as he rubbed his back. "I'd offer to beat up your aunt, if it weren't for that little old lady thing."

Trey laughed raggedly, forehead rolling against Zane's shoulder. "God, I love you."

Zane held him tighter and closed his eyes. When he opened them, heartbeats later, Rebecca was in the open door.

~

Rebecca shouldn't have stood there listening as long as she did. Now that she'd been discovered, the polite thing would be to excuse herself. If a person walked in on a grown man crying, and his best friend was comforting him, it wasn't right to intrude on that. She especially shouldn't intrude considering the tenderness with which Zane was holding him. This was third wheel territory, without question.

The only person who might claim differently was Trey.

She looked at Zane. His eyes weren't telling her to come or go. He'd stiffened, probably with embarrassment. Then again, despite her catching him being less than macho, he wasn't letting Trey go. The caution in his expression suggested he was waiting to see what she'd do. Was she having a fling with them—which meant she ought to stay out of this—or did she actually, maybe accept Trey's idea that they were destined to be together? Was she willing to be serious about them both?

Decide, she thought.

Not sure she had, but unable to do nothing, she walked in without speaking and put her hand on Trey's back.

Startled, he turned and wiped his face. "Shit. Sorry."

She shook her head. "You're not doing anything you need to be sorry for."

"You heard?"

"Yes." She dried a streak he'd missed on his cheek. "Sometimes you can't lie even to be nice. It would be too big a self betrayal."

Trey's wet eyes were the green of grass. "I just want her to go away."

"Who wouldn't?" she said, understanding he thought this was wrong of him. She glanced at Zane. The men were sitting side by side now, with Zane's arm braced on the desk behind Trey's back. "So, um, maybe it's not my business, but have you talked to the kids? Are they reasonable people? Could they help control their mom?"

"I don't know." This time Trey wiped his face wearily. "They're strangers to me. I hadn't met my dad's relatives before he killed himself."

"He killed himself?" She blurted out the question. Fortunately, Trey didn't flinch.

"Yeah," he said. "My mom did too when I was younger. My dad did it the same way, in a running car in the locked garage. Neither of them were happy people."

Rebecca was at a loss for words. She considered how kind Trey was, how deeply he embraced life and love. What a waste that his parents didn't have the capacity to appreciate that. But he must fear their sadness was in him. No one could come from that background and not wonder. She stroked his cheek, the skin beneath his stubble hot from his emotions.

"You know how to be happy," was all she could think to say.

He smiled, moisture glittering in his eyes again. He took her hand to kiss its palm. His lips were warm and soft.

"I can talk to your aunt's kids," Zane said.

Trey's head jerked to him. "That's not your responsibility."

A muscle bunched in Zane's jaw. "It's good sense. You send the coolest head into a negotiation."

"It's not a negotiation."

"Maybe it is. We don't know what their deal is. Either way, I'm the best person for the job."

"Zane—"

Zane crossed his arms. "I'm not negotiating with you."

"We'll talk about it later," Trey said.

Rebecca rolled her lips together to hide a smile. Given Zane's stubbornness, she doubted that discussion would occur.

"I have good news," she said, deciding the subject was ready to be changed. "The Lounge got a great review from Gordon Hewitt."

She handed Trey the printout of his blog.

"'Highly Recommended,'" he quoted, eyebrows up and reaction predictably pleased for her.

As he continued to read the review, exclaiming the best bits aloud, Zane mouthed *thank you* silently to her.

~

Zane knew Trey was more rattled than he'd let on. He took off in his—yes—pretty red Bugatti and still hadn't returned by evening. Zane could tell his absence troubled Rebecca. She joined him in the library while he power-watched the news on the multi-screen wall display. Aside from sending a few emails, she mostly wandered up and down.

He wondered if this meant she felt more comfortable being alone with Trey than him. She wasn't relaxed like she'd been this morning after their game. She felt back on her old standby, offering to whip up a quick dinner. Reminding her she was a guest didn't dissuade her.

"I'd love to play in your kitchen," she said earnestly. "You have great equipment."

"Maybe some other time." Wanting to give her his full attention, he clicked off the television and lounged back in his big leather chair. "Mrs. Penworth rules that roost. If you were cooking, I'd want to give her advance notice."

"Oh," she said, her face falling comically.

"You wouldn't want Trey to miss out on your food," he added. "We can't be sure when he'll come back."

"But *you* like eating," she pointed out hopefully.

God, she amused him: their delectable, neurotic little elf with her short blonde hair and her big gray eyes. She resembled a sprite even more in the workout clothes she'd pulled on again. He didn't know how to admit he had an entire wardrobe of clothes for her stashed in their walk-in closet—ordered through Sybil Spaulding and then hidden in the back. The discovery had raised Trey's eyebrows that morning.

Perhaps Rebecca hadn't cornered the market on eccentric behavior. Perhaps, in his way, Zane had been dreaming about her as hard as Trey.

"C'mere," he said, patting his thigh for her to sit on.

She lowered herself with her back as stiff as a board. Zane snorted, squeezed her, and she relaxed a few inches.

"Sorry," she said, wrinkling her nose. "Not a lot of lap sitting in my past."

"No trips to Santa?"

"I took the twins."

Of course she did. He smoothed a spiky lock from her brow. Hadn't her parents treated her like a kid when they were around?

"My mom must have taken me," she said as if she'd read his mind. "Or sat me on her lap. She was affectionate. I guess I don't remember that part of my life as well as . . . what came after. Just as well, I expect. I'd have missed it, and there was no getting it back." She frowned, squaring her shoulders even as he tugged her closer. "Will Trey be all right?"

Zane supposed she thought she wasn't allowed to feel sorry for herself.

"He'll be all right," he said, hoping this was true.

"He doesn't usually get upset like that, does he?"

"No."

She squirmed around to face him more directly. "He feels guilty for not wanting to see his aunt. He forgives other people's flaws, but he thinks he's supposed to be perfect."

Zane laughed softly.

"What?" she asked, surprised by the response.

"I don't know if I believe in soul mates, but I suspect there's a reason he recognized you as a kindred spirit all those years ago."

Rebecca worried her lower lip between her teeth. She didn't deny she was a perfectionist. "Do you?"

"Do I what?"

"Do you recognize me as a kindred spirit?"

"Maybe." He couldn't look away from her sweet vulnerable eyes. "I definitely feel something for you I haven't for other women. You might be like me in some ways. I don't know you well enough to be sure. Can I ask you a question?"

"Sure," she said, bracing for it.

Her reaction made him want to laugh again. "Is it easier for you to be alone with Trey than me?"

"No," she said without hesitation. "I know it might not seem the case, because I'm kind of uptight, but it's easier for me to be alone with either of you than any men in the world. Well, except for my brothers and maybe my head chef, but that's different."

"I'd hope so."

She smiled, her gaze falling to his mouth. Her fingers rose to stroke its curved edges. A tremor slid down his spine at her touch, a mini-quake that rolled out his cock and set it stirring. "Will anyone walk in on us?" she asked.

He recalled Owens interrupting them in the pool, a transgression that had bothered him more than he'd let on at the time. His and Trey's rules were clear. The man should have known better.

That, however, wasn't worth wasting brain space on now.

"No," he said, angling his head in preparation to kiss her. "No one will walk in. We can do what we like."

"I like this," she whispered and sealed his mouth with hers.

The sex the kiss sparked was quick and hard, both of them getting naked in record time. Zane began by taking her on the chesterfield, but decided it was too soft. Yanking the throw off the sofa's back, he shifted her to the floor. He didn't want her getting rug burns but, oh, he liked fucking her on a hard surface. She was strong for a small woman, and she flung herself into lovemaking—each time more than the last, it seemed.

"Oh God," he said, feeling his climax rise but unable to slow down. He had one hand on her breast and the other braced on the floor to push up his torso. Watching pleasure and desire trade places in her expression was an incredible turn-on.

"Me too," she gasped. Her heels dug into the floor, hips slapping forcefully up to his. Her hands gripped him below the waist, urging him to pump harder. "I'm close too. God, yes, grind into me at the end." She groaned as he obeyed. "I love that. I love—"

She came and it triggered him powerfully, her contractions like a fist yanking the delicious feelings out. He made a strangled sound as he let go, pressing even deeper into her. She cried out in a way that said that felt good. A second later, another set of inner flutters tightened wonderfully on his cock.

Humming with enjoyment, he dropped onto both elbows. Her nipples trembled with her post-orgasmic heartbeats, tickling where they brushed his chest.

"Nice," she said between pants for air, hands rubbing his back as she smiled up at him.

"There's a reason the missionary position is a classic."

He stroked her damp hair from her brow. Just looking at her made him happy, knowing he'd put that dreamy, slightly smug laziness in her face. Her roving fingers slid around to his front, circling his pectorals. Zane didn't think he ever wanted to pull out of her.

"What would you say to planning something for Trey?" she asked. "Something he thinks of as a classic . . . if it isn't rude to suggest that now."

Zane's cock stopped softening inside her.

"It isn't rude," he said, additional gravel in his voice. "Since we're all interested in each other."

"So what's a classic for Trey? What does he especially enjoy when it comes to sex?"

"A lot of things." He hesitated. "Would you like to go back to the playroom?"

"Would you?" Her eyes were lambent, her pussy suddenly a little wetter, a little tighter around him.

"He likes having sex there," Zane said. "He likes the Gothic atmosphere and the elaborate toys. He likes being hurt a bit. I think part of him believes he shouldn't like it, but that just gives the kink more power over him."

"And you like that," she said, her gaze locked on him.

"I *love* that," Zane admitted.

~

Trey drove down country roads for hours, trying to get his head on straight. When he returned, Zane and Rebecca were sitting up in bed, seeming to have waited up for him.

"You look exhausted," Rebecca said.

He was exhausted—and grateful they didn't press him to talk. He crawled up between them, laid his head on Rebecca's leg and passed out. His last conscious awareness was Zane rubbing his shoulders while Rebecca stroked his hair.

He felt better when he woke, but in his absence something had altered between the pair. They *looked* at each other more, both when the other knew and when he or she didn't. Twice Trey caught them having conversations they cut off when he walked in. He chose not to ask what they'd been saying. They were entitled to interests they shared alone. For them to work as a threesome, they'd probably need them. The sense of exclusion only bugged him because he hadn't thought his way through it. He was certain Zane had felt similarly a time or two.

When the pair disappeared in the afternoon without explanation, his rationale stopped working. They popped up again as he pretended to relax with a magazine on the back terrace.

"There you are," Rebecca said. She was bright-eyed and smiling. Zane looked pleased with himself as well. Whatever they'd been up to, they'd enjoyed it.

"Here I am," he agreed, turning toward them on the Adirondack chair.

He must have done a decent job of hiding his irritation, because Rebecca grinned.

"Well," she said, arms slapping her sides as she exchanged yet another happy glance with Zane. "I guess I'm off to do the thing. See you in a bit."

Trey waited until she'd walked off to explode.

"She's off to 'do the thing!' Why are you doing *things* without me?"

Zane placed a hand on his chair back and bent to kiss him. The kiss was tonguey and very nice. To Trey's annoyance, it did smooth out his temper. Zane drew back just as Trey was getting into it. He took consolation in Zane's smoldering eyes revealing he'd been affected too.

"The thing she's doing is for you," Zane explained. "She asked me to help her with a surprise."

"Really?" Guilt pricked Trey belatedly. "She doesn't have to do that. This week is about seducing her into a relationship."

Zane shook his head, amused. "You two are a pair." He held out his hand. "Come see what we did. I predict seducing you is a step on the road to seducing her. She's not the sort to want everyone focused on her all the time."

When he put it that way . . . Trey grabbed Zane's hand and rose, pleased when his friend kept it afterwards. "Is it a good surprise?" he asked, throwing him a sideways glance.

"Of course it is. I helped her pull it together."

"Not short on confidence, are you?"

"Rarely," Zane agreed.

Realizing they were headed toward the playroom put a skip into Trey's pulse. "Was this your idea?" he asked as Zane worked the elevator.

"My suggestion. Rebecca brought her own ideas into the mix."

"What ideas?"

Zane grinned. "You'll see."

He paused at the bank vault door, turning to rest both hands on Trey's shoulders. Though his lips were curved, Trey sensed his friend was about to be serious.

"This game is for all of us," Zane said. "If we all have fun, this whatever-it-is will have a better chance of lasting."

"I want it to last."

"I know." Zane squeezed his shoulders. "I think . . . so do I."

Trey's heart really started thumping then. Knowing Zane, if he admitted that much, chances were he felt more. Zane unlocked the door with his personal key and thumbprint. He was grinning again, anticipating what lay ahead.

"God," Trey said with a laugh. "I'm already hard and you haven't done anything."

Zane wagged his brows at the tent in Trey's trousers and swung the door open.

They walked side by side along the twist in the hall. Imagination running riot, Trey held his breath and stepped into the central room. His skin tingled in reaction to the tableau he found.

In the center of the room, lit by a huge movie-style spotlight, was an old iron bedstead he'd never seen before. It wasn't a fine antique. Any secondhand store in New England might carry a handful. The narrow—and new—mattress was dressed in crisp white sheets and a hand-stitched quilt so deeply scarlet it glowed. The pillows were fluffed, and a small weathered nightstand added hominess beside the head rail.

Less homey but certainly provocative were the four lengths of chain that hung from the ceiling through the wagon wheel chandelier. They ended in iron shackles, the sole component of the display with which Trey was familiar.

The contrasting images of safety and danger caused his cock to throb. Ripples of excitement joined the tingles on his skin. The whole arrangement was a stage set, awaiting only actors to walk on. *I'm one of the actors,* Trey thought. Zane—or perhaps Rebecca—understood his love of theater better than he'd realized.

"How did you pull this together?" he asked once his voice recovered.

"We rush ordered the bed last night on the Internet. It arrived in pieces and we assembled it down here. You should have seen Owens' face when I told him Rebecca's help was all I needed. Our driver seems to think billionaires and women are equally helpless."

"He's wrong there," Rebecca said, emerging from the shadows of a niche.

"I can lift hundred-pound tuna."

She knew how to make an entrance. She wasn't wearing a stitch: not makeup and not clothes. She was no vamp as she came toward them. Her walk was just a walk, not shy but maybe self-conscious. Her body was naturally beautiful—slim, strong, the faint cooking scars on her arms picked up by the strong spotlight. Her small rounded breasts jiggled like maracas, better to him than any centerfold's.

She stopped on the nearer side of the bed. The frame was tall. She rested her butt back against the mattress. His breath caught as he noticed her pubic hair was waxed. A honey brown strip replaced what had been a triangle.

"Do you like it?" she asked, noting where his gaze had gone.

He nodded, his throat choked with arousal.

"Would you undress so I can see for myself?"

He wasn't averse to making a show of himself. Aware that both his lovers were watching, Trey removed his clothes. Rebecca smiled when his erection came free of them. He stood, letting her enjoy her eyeful. If he was going to be chained like a slave—and he sincerely hoped he was—he might as well get into character.

Pleased by his behavior, Rebecca clambered onto the bed. She patted the red coverlet. "Join me up here. Zane showed me how to lock you up."

If he'd ever heard a phrase more delightful, he didn't remember it. Fighting a last unsureness, he shot a look at Zane. How much had he told her about his preferences? She could have guessed Trey's fondness for bondage from what he'd done to her.

"Go on," Zane said, waving him forward. "This game can't start until you're secured."

It had started for him. His motor was revved and his knees shaky. As he swung up and faced her, his cock was very erect. Its shaft was hard and aching, impatient for pleasure. With one finger Rebecca flicked its tip. The subtle but sharp sensation sent a deep thrill through him.

Maybe Zane had told her everything.

"Pretty," she said. "But we'll see to it later."

She attached the shackles at his wrists and ankles. She was slightly awkward, the task new to her—which only aroused him more. This wasn't some practiced scene from a cookie-cutter script. She'd be involved as this unfolded.

He tried to wrest control of his breathing, but it was difficult. The chains the shackles were attached to stretched from him to a hook on the domed ceiling. Though they allowed a good range of movement, their weight and rattle reminded him he was bound.

"Sit back on your heels," she said.

Her voice was different, not authoritative but husky with arousal. That was fine. Strictly speaking, Trey didn't need to be mastered; he was happy to volunteer. Rebecca turned on her hands and knees to open the bedside table. He didn't think she was consciously trying to display herself, but the position did. He clenched his hands, wanting to lick his way up her slit and bite that sweet little ass. Her newly groomed folds were rosy, the glistening of her sex forcing him to swallow back a groan.

She rummaged through the drawer and huffed out a curse. "I can't find anything in here. I'm pulling out the whole thing."

Trey heard Zane snort as she yanked it free and set it on the coverlet between them. He caught glimpses of objects that made him shiver.

"Sorry," she said, lifting her gaze to Trey's. "I guess I should be smoother about this."

"No, no," he demurred. "I find your inexperience charming."

He was too breathless for her to doubt the words. Her attention fell to his erection, which was pointing skyward and throbbing violently.

Grinning, she extricated a quirt from the jumble in the drawer. With a slowness designed to torment him, she drew the braided leather across her palm. "Zane tells me this is for after you're warmed up. We'll set it aside for now."

She laid the lash neatly on the bed. In his reluctance to drag his eyes away, he missed her making her next selection. She held a wooden paddle, seven inches square with a high gloss finish. The handle was wrapped in rubber to prevent it from slipping in a sweaty hand. Having been on its receiving end, Trey knew it dealt out a smack. "Zane says this is good to start with. I've decided to let him use it. His arm is stronger and, well, he knows what he's doing."

That explained, she handed Zane the paddle. He'd taken off his shirt, but was dressed otherwise. Trey guessed he was enjoying Rebecca's first performance. A considerable bulge distorted his zipper. He stretched to warm up his arms and loosen his shoulder joints. The shifting of his muscles had Trey swallowing. Sometimes he forgot just how powerfully built Zane was.

"Yes, he's something," Rebecca agreed when he turned back to her. "Makes me wonder where I find the nerve to let him have at me."

"You enjoy it," Trey burst out. "You love all that strength and size overwhelming you."

"That's true. I do." She looked so directly into his eyes that for a second he felt like he was falling. "You're big enough to overpower me. If Zane decides you deserve it, maybe he'll let you."

A stab of longing shot through his cock. "If Zane decides . . ."

She tipped her head to the side. "Don't you like him being in charge? He thought I'd make a nice reward for good behavior."

"What's to keep me from just taking you? These chains are long enough for that."

A flush crept across her cheeks, her eyes suddenly brighter. "He'd stop you."

She didn't sound sure, and Trey like that immensely. When he responded, his tone was darker than hers had been.

"Maybe," he said, "and maybe I'd shove my cock into your pussy before he could rescue you."

Any dominant but Zane would have smacked him for his defiance, but he seemed curious to hear her answer too. Her respiration had sped up, her breasts starting to tremble.

"You'd have to be careful if you took me," she said, surprisingly steadily. "You're very excited, and when you come, the game is over. I think we both know you don't want that happening soon."

She knew she had him. She didn't wait for his response, but pushed sharply at his chest. He'd been leaning into her space, and this made him back off. He sat on his heels, satisfied she'd show the spine he wanted. Satisfied with *him*, she pulled a pair of nipple clamps from the drawer.

"Do you want these?" she asked.

"Yes," he said, his earnestness not put on.

The clamps were new, chosen by her perhaps. Their business ends were rubber-coated to prevent them cutting into his skin. Rebecca attached them to his nipples. Zane must have showed her how to use them. She knew to squeeze in his areola to give them enough flesh to grip. That task accomplished, she turned the wing nuts that tightened them.

"More," Zane said from behind him. "Don't stop until our prisoner gasps."

She gave each screw two more twists and he did, unable to restrain the intake of air—or the momentary shutting of his eyes. The pain was perfect: enough to make his nerves jump but not enough to discourage his arousal. Wetness leaked from his rigid penis, tempting him to make good on his threat to simply take Rebecca. He knew he wouldn't. Waiting would make this better for all of them.

The thought of marauding was in his head all the same. When he opened his eyes, the things that were in them caused Rebecca to scoot back cautiously toward the pillows. He liked that, probably more than he ought to. She set the drawer of goodies back onto the nightstand. Looking nervous but excited, she nodded at Zane that she was ready.

Zane wasn't ready, and Trey thought he knew why. Rebecca sat with her knees pressed together almost primly. She dried her palms on her smooth pale thighs.

"Tell her to expose herself," Trey said hoarsely. "I want to see her pussy."

Startled, Rebecca jerked and looked past him to Zane.

"Our prisoner deserves encouragement," he conceded, "if he's to get through his ordeal. Spread your knees as far apart as they'll go."

Blushing furiously, she spread them.

"Now that's pretty," Trey said, observing her wet and engorged state.

"No one asked your opinion," Zane snapped, ramping up the role play. "Grab the chains higher up. Go to your knees and stay there."

As soon as Trey obeyed, the paddle landed. The sting sang through his buttocks, stirring the pleasure he never could manage to suppress—no matter how twisted that made him. A sound broke from him, low and grateful. Zane hit him again and twice on the other cheek. Trey moaned helplessly when he stopped. Zane was strong and knew what he could take. Trey's ass was hot and pulsing.

"Kiss his cock," Zane ordered Rebecca, his voice harsh with arousal. "Lick the tip very gently until I tell you he's had enough."

Rebecca bent forward. Trey tensed as she approached, chains rattling from his grip on them. This was almost too exciting. He and Zane never played together in front of an audience, much less a woman they both wanted. For that matter, Trey always took the dominant part with guests. He was naked here, and on uncharted ground. His responses were all amped up. He held his breath as the pointed tip of her tongue made contact with his glans and licked.

It felt incredible, much more intense than a light touch should.

"Shit," he said, unable to stay silent.

Zane didn't miss the reaction, though it wasn't Trey he cautioned.

"Careful," he said to Rebecca. "Don't use your lips. Just lick him around the head."

She was very serious, like she truly had to follow his instructions. Her earnestness got to Trey more than any roleplaying could. Positively tormenting him, she licked him—circles and swipes and soft little flicks across that sensitive pulsing flesh. Beads of pre-cum welled from his slit. She gathered them until he trembled, until his veins began to stand out. He couldn't hold on much longer. He wanted to give in too badly. As if he knew, Zane finally said *stop*.

Without being told, Rebecca retreated to the bed's head rail. Her eyes were wide, her breathing nearly as broken up as Trey's.

"Prisoner," Zane said, his manner all authority. "You're going to take ten strikes, and you'll count them aloud for me."

Trey counted. Each stiff blow was hard. At first they were welcome, because they helped him back off the edge, but soon they excited him as well. For whatever reason, he was wired to respond that way. His ass was on fire within a minute, his inner muscles twitching with their desire to be fucked. Zane seemed unlikely to satisfy that craving in front of Rebecca—a fact that only made Trey want it more. He wanted to fuck and be fucked simultaneously. The instant he acknowledged the desire he knew he was stuck with it. This was his obsession, the yearning no amount of wooden paddles could beat from him. He wanted Zane and Rebecca at the same time.

"*Ten*," he rasped with all the frustration he had in him.

Zane ceased swinging. Sensation throbbed through Trey's whole body.

"Do you want your reward?" Zane asked sternly.

"Yes, sir," Trey answered, a response Zane only drew from him sometimes.

"'Yes, sir,'" he repeated with the faintest wisp of a sneer. "That's polite, prisoner. I'd double your reward, except I know you prefer suffering."

"He'll need protection," Rebecca said softly. "Would you do that for me?"

She tossed Zane a condom, and he caught it. There was a little pause. "For you," he said, huskiness in the words. "I'd do anything."

He walked up the side of the bed to roll the rubber on. With absolute fascination, Rebecca watched his hands on Trey's cock. Zane didn't fumble under her regard. He was too accustomed to handling Trey. Cranked up by the whole situation, Trey's balls jerked closer to his body.

"Will that do?" Zane asked when the task was done.

Rebecca's eyes flicked from Trey to him. Did she realize she could order Zane to touch him more? He'd shown her more deference than any previous play partner. She pressed one finger thoughtfully to her cheek. Her next words flashed through Trey like a rocket trail.

"You could have caressed him more," she observed, "around the balls or shaft, but I admit he looks well prepared."

"If I'd excited him more, he might not last through his reward."

"True," she said.

"What's my reward?" Trey dared to ask.

"You took ten strokes from me," Zane said. "You can have ten strokes inside her. If you survive them without coming, I'll use the quirt on you."

Trey groaned, the reaction as unavoidable as his hard breathing. Under normal circumstances, ten strokes inside her would be a breeze. Under these, they might in truth finish him.

"Grab the head rail," Zane said. "Only your cock can touch her while you do this."

Rebecca moved down the mattress while he moved up. She'd bent her knees, but Zane pulled the leg nearest to him down. "Keep this flat. You don't want to spoil my view.

Rebecca's lips parted for a quick breath. Trey concluded they hadn't pre-planned this part, and it excited her.

"I'll aim your cock for you," Zane told him.

It wasn't all Trey wanted, but it was good. Zane's hot fingers placed his head at her creaming gate.

"There," he said. "You may push now, prisoner."

Trey pushed . . . and let out a helpless whimper as his broad crown went in. Her body gave for him easily: soft, wet, clinging to his throbbing cock all over. When he was fully seated, he looked at her.

"Please don't move," he begged in an undertone.

"I'll do my best," she promised breathily.

He took his ten strokes as slowly as he could, savoring them, gritting his teeth in places, but adoring that he could make her moan with him. She had a hard time keeping her right leg flat. Her knee wanted to come up. On the third stroke, she stretched up to grip the head rail, needing something to hang onto to keep herself from squirming. Her breasts lifted on her ribcage, her nipples tight with arousal. When Trey saw that, every cell in his body wanted to go at her full speed, to satisfy the desire her squirms signified. If this had been any other night, he'd have pumped at her and pumped at her until they both screamed with climaxes. Ignoring the urge, he pulled out carefully at ten.

Zane had been watching closely. They heard him breathing beside the bed.

As Trey's butt settled on his shackled ankles and he laid his hands flat atop his thighs, he couldn't have been more aware that he was chained and cuffed.

Rebecca released the rails and went up on her elbows. Her eyes went to the chains but didn't stay. At the sight of Trey's erection, she wet her lips. Her attention redirected his. He felt the swollen organ sticking up like a pole.

"Your skin is so dark," she murmured, her voice smoky. "The tip of your penis is almost red."

He couldn't look. He could barely stand to look at her. Her skin was rosy all over, her every motion sensual.

"I guess you'll be wanting this," she said.

She found the quirt among the covers and handed it to Zane. Zane took it, drawing the lash along his palm like she had earlier. In him, the gesture was thoughtful and not teasing.

"I have a proposition for the prisoner," he said, as if he wasn't sure of it.

"What—" Trey's throat was rusty so he cleared it. "What are you proposing?"

"I could—" Zane looked down, and Trey's pulse galloped at his hesitation. His next words came out lower. "I could whip you while you're inside her. I'd like to watch you try to hold off."

Trey wanted to bargain for more, wanted Zane fucking him as his reward if he succeeded. Zane was generally more concerned with pleasing Trey than himself when they played these games. For him to make a request was unusual. Trey couldn't open his mouth to ask for his desire. When you knew a friend was uncomfortable, you didn't purposefully push him farther than he wanted to go.

"You could have her after," Zane said. "With the chains still on and her under you. Your alluring captor, helpless to get away. Assuming that appeals to her, of course."

"No need to worry about me," Rebecca said with a breathless laugh. "I seem to like everything you do."

"Ten lashes?" Trey asked, as if this were the crucial negotiating point.

"Ten lashes," Zane confirmed.

~

Rebecca hadn't known she'd get so caught up in this. Her arms trembled as she grabbed two of the chains above Trey's head. The links were large enough to work her fingers through. Up on his shins again, Trey supported her bottom in his shackled hands. The cuffs were lined to prevent injury, but like the chain, they were heavy. Their hard presence under her was welcome. She had to squeeze Trey's sides with her thighs—without blocking him to the whip. The difference in their heights meant her knees didn't rest on the mattress.

Trey shifted her until his extraordinarily erect penis parted her labia.

"Ready?" he asked, his gaze unwavering.

"If you are."

She guessed he was. Slowly, he lowered her weight onto him. She moaned with pleasure as his length filled her. Ten strokes hadn't been enough for her.

Trey gave a little grunt when she settled as far as she could go. Her body swung slightly from her hold on the chains.

A sense of wonder overtook her. "Are you really my prisoner?"

Trey's smile was soft. "I am, Rebecca. Now and forever."

She bit her lip, liking his promise more than could be smart. With a shiver-inducing growl, Trey leaned forward and nipped her mouth.

A whistle split the air, followed by a sharp crack. Trey jerked, his cock jolted deeper into her. Zane had given him his first lash.

"No kissing your mistress yet," he said.

Startled, Trey began to turn his head.

"Don't look at me," Zane ordered, a second lash finding Trey's backside. "You keep your eyes on her. Don't close them either. Your reactions are for her to enjoy."

She would have felt guilty for enjoying them if Trey hadn't so clearly liked the harsh treatment. A low noise broke in his chest, his cock throbbing inside her. It throbbed harder when Zane struck him a third time.

Sweat broke out on Trey's face. His fingers tightened on her butt, causing the edges of the shackles to dig into her. The metal wasn't as cold as it had started out. His heat was warming it.

"No thrusting," Zane demanded, laying four and five across his ass.

Rebecca felt the air displace for these strokes, though the leather hadn't once touched her thighs. Zane had practice at this, all right.

"I'm not thrusting, sir," Trey protested, his pelvis jammed into her with all his strength.

"Are you calling me a liar?" Zane cupped Trey's presumably burning cheeks. "I say I saw you move. I say these muscles clenched."

"Just to get deeper, sir."

Zane leaned toward them, his lips an inch away from Trey's ear. "You like being inside your mistress, prisoner? You like all that heat and snugness around you?"

"Yes . . . sir," Trey managed to pant out.

He jumped suddenly. Rebecca suspected Zane had just pinched his rear.

"You have five more lashes to go, and I'm not sure you're worthy. I'm not sure you can last long enough to serve your mistress as she deserves." Zane's arm moved, his palm circling their slave's butt. "She seems to think your balls have been neglected. Perhaps I'll see to them now."

Trey sucked in air as Zane's hand found them. Whatever he was doing felt good to Trey.

"Please," he moaned, straining and squirming inside her.

"Please more?" Zane mocked, doing whatever it was again. "Or please stop before I make you come?"

Unable to answer, Trey bit his lip hard enough to turn it white.

Zane released him. "Your unworthy ass has had enough. You'll take the next five across your back."

He returned to the foot rail, drawing the short lash along his hand. Rebecca could see him now without turning, but he wasn't focused on her. The bulge at his crotch was huge, lines of sweat rolling through the golden hair on his bare chest. His big taut body was beautiful, his expression utterly determined. She was afraid and excited at the same time.

As if Trey knew Zane was readying himself, he clamped her bottom tighter and rested his brow on hers. Zane filled his lungs with air.

Sound burst from both men in tandem as the sixth lash fell.

"*Unh,*" Trey grunted for the seventh, hips twisting desperately against her.

Rebecca's nipples turned to stone for the eighth.

"God," Trey gasped as her sex melted around him.

"You don't go until I say," Zane snarled. "You don't fuck her until I say the word."

"Yes . . . sir," Trey agreed.

He gave Trey nine, and Trey's head snapped back in reaction. She knew most of that reaction was pleasure. His cock had swollen even more inside her. Trey forced his gaze to hers again. His eyes were blazing, tiny tremors making his skin twitch. They were so close she could have counted his eyelashes as easily as his heartbeats. What he saw in her eyes, she didn't know. She felt as intimately connected to him as a person could be. How much he wanted what was happening seemed profound.

Zane brought the quirt down for the tenth time.

"Not yet," he barked when Trey began to lift her up his cock to stroke.

"I want her," Trey said.

"You'll wait," Zane answered, his voice unrecognizable. "You'll fucking wait for me."

Rebecca and Trey's eyes had a second to widen. Then Zane was climbing onto the narrow bed behind Trey. A catch popped and his zipper whined downward. His hot hands covered Rebecca's where they still clenched the chains.

"Let go," he ordered her like Doom itself.

Rebecca couldn't disobey him. She was mastered. She let go reflexively.

He pushed Trey forward and she tumbled onto her back with the shackled man on top of her. The four lengths of chain were slack enough to allow this, though the metal clashed crazily. Trey was still inside her, but not moving. Maybe he wouldn't until Zane told him to. Maybe he was mastered too. Zane stretched over them both to dig in the supply drawer.

"Jesus," Trey breathed as Zane's hand emerged with a container of KY.

Zane cursed as he fumbled with the top. They heard a squirt and a slap as he rubbed the slippery stuff on his cock. Lubed all the way up and down, he kicked Trey's knees wider. Then he moved into position behind him. Zane's face was a picture she wouldn't soon forget: flushed, tense, as if he had to do this or die.

Rebecca's sheath tightened on Trey without her willing it.

"Fuck," Trey gasped, pelvis twisting at how good the contraction felt. "Please don't do that. I'm about to—"

And then Zane shoved into him.

Trey's head went back the same as it had for the ninth lash, his mouth stretched open with shocked bliss. Zane pulled back and heaved again. Pushed farther by the thrust, Trey's cock seemed to knock her womb.

"Now," Zane said, guttural and urgent. "Now you can fuck Rebecca."

Trey cried out, using his muscle power to shove back toward Zane. "Not so hard," he panted. "Between the two of us, we'll hurt her."

Zane growled in frustration but not protest.

The last thing she expected happened.

"Follow my lead," Trey said, apparently still in charge of himself. "I can feel how she's responding."

The men took a couple thrusts to coordinate but then they went like a well-oiled machine—or as well oiled as cocks so close to exploding would let them be.

She was glad they were being careful. Their combined strength could have bruised her. As it was, their combined energy—their huffs and groans and sweaty bunched muscles—drove her excitement to heights she hadn't known it could reach. She wasn't able to hold back her responses. Moaning with pleasure, she gripped Trey's side and Zane's arm and prayed the little iron bed would survive the beating it was taking.

Trey made a noise as Zane thumped something good inside him.

"Fuck," Trey said, shoulders hunched, head dropping to her shoulder.

"*Unh.* Yes. Keep fucking me right *there.*"

Zane clamped his fingers around Trey's hip to continue pummeling him at the same angle. His eyes were screwed shut, and a vein stood out at his temple. Trey found a sweet spot in her and blotted out the image.

Her spine arched off the bed, despite the men's weight on her. Trey grunted at the strength of her contractions on his cock. She couldn't stop them. She needed to work against his thickness like she needed to gasp for breath. Just when she thought the pleasure couldn't get more intense, someone's thumb compressed her clit and rubbed.

She keened, fingernails scoring skin.

The men sped up at her cry, maybe too excited not to, maybe greedy to join her. The effect of their acceleration was inevitable. Zane hissed, big body locking as he lost it and shot his climax into Trey. Trey's chest arched back from her. His expression was ecstatic. He was almost there, straining to go over even as he tried to hang on. With the last of her brainpower, she remembered a trick Zane had shared with her, one he said Trey especially got off on. She slid her hands up his heaving ribs . . .

And yanked off both nipple clamps.

Trey cried out at the sudden pain, cock jamming deep into her to spill.

"Christ," he gasped. His prick throbbed hard, shooting everything he had with abandon.

Neither man collapsed, but they probably wanted to. Thanks to the domed room's acoustics, it sounded like a dozen people were panting inside it.

"Whew," Rebecca said once she had sufficient breath. "I guess that screw we had left over wasn't important."

"What screw?" Trey asked hoarsely. A drop of sweat plopped from him onto her belly.

"From putting the bed together. Zane and I had one left over when we were done."

Trey chuckled, then sucked a breath as Zane pulled out of him without warning.

"Sorry," he said, staggering off the bed with one hand on the foot rail to support him.

In less of a hurry, Trey withdrew from her with a groan. He sat up in the clear spot between her legs. She didn't know where the men found the strength to move. To give himself more room, Trey pulled her right calf across his lap. He stroked it and her foot as he watched Zane zip up.

"You okay?" he asked.

"Of course I am," Zane said. "That was incredible."

He wasn't telling the whole truth. Though he was smiling, the creases around his eyes seemed strained. Rebecca guessed he hadn't meant to take Trey while Trey took her. He'd been swept up in the overwhelming heat of the moment—and now that heat was over.

She had no doubt Trey saw this as clearly as she did.

Discovering she could sit up after all, she laid her cheek on Trey's shoulder. "Thank you," she said to both of them.

"Thank *you*," Trey corrected. "That was a great surprise."

Rebecca rubbed his chest, suspecting he could use the comfort. For a while there, he'd had everything he wanted.

~

You're not going to run, Zane ordered himself. *You're not going to be surly. You don't want to hurt Trey that way.*

He rescued his shirt from the playroom floor but didn't put it on. God, he'd come hard. His cock was limp from it—and from going at Trey like a jackhammer. He'd loved knowing Trey was inside Rebecca, loved that each thrust into Trey's ass pushed his friend's cock harder into her. Rebecca couldn't have missed what fucking Trey did to him, how excited he got, how he couldn't have stopped what he was doing for anything. She'd gotten off on it. He shouldn't be embarrassed.

Zane needed to purge his bastard father's pronouncements on "real men" from his brain. So what if he wanted to lay his lips on Trey's that second? So what if he loved touching him as much as he loved touching Rebecca?

Zane was a real man. If he'd been completely gay, that would have been the case. His father was an asshole. After all these years, Zane shouldn't still be fighting this battle.

Dressed now, Rebecca came to him and stroked his arm. He looked at her, and she kissed his shoulder. "Don't regret what you did," she murmured.

He stroked her hair. His hand was big against her delicate cheekbone, different than when he cupped Trey's face. He started to say he had no regrets but decided the moment deserved more honesty.

"I'm trying not to," he said.

Rebecca smiled and stretched up to kiss him.

CHAPTER FOURTEEN

Last Chance

The rest of the week flew by faster than Rebecca thought possible. Each day felt more relaxed than the last, until she actually began to worry she'd get back into work mode. They made love, they played, they had lazy conversations over Mrs. Penworth's straightforward but tasty food. On Saturday, they took the yacht out, where the men finally relented and let her cook for them.

Afterwards, the night was cool enough that they snuggled in one shared blanket out on the *Bad Girl's* deck. The captain had anchored in the bay, beyond the reach of the city lights. Thousands of stars danced on the wavering mirror of calm water. The universe was big, and the three of them were small. That they'd come together was a miracle.

"This is the best," she sighed against Zane's chest, happily tucked naked between the men on an island of lounge cushions. "I'm going to remember this forever."

Trey rubbed his cheek on her shoulder. He was behind her with his arm draped across her waist. His hand rested on Zane's belly, fingers playing with his line of hair. "This doesn't have to end."

"I'm going back to work on Monday," she warned them. "And so are you two tycoons."

"Right. But we aren't going to disappear into a puff of smoke. You can see us again."

"We *want* you to see us again," Zane put in.

They sounded truthful. Rebecca wanted to believe them, but she questioned how long the inclination to keep in touch would last. This week had been intense—like erotic summer camp or the final day of high school. Emotions ran high in those situations. People were convinced they'd made friends for life. Then they went back to their normal lives, and the feelings faded. She took comfort in the fact that she'd see Trey at the Lounge now and then—at least until he got sidetracked by his next project.

"This isn't casual for us," Trey said as if he could read her thoughts. "We're not capable of loving and leaving you."

She wriggled around to face him, chest aching with the knowledge that she'd never known a man this sweet. "Kiss me when you say that," she teased, hoping to keep tears at bay.

Trey kissed her, and then Zane did, and then the stars had something new to shine down on.

She stole an hour Sunday morning to meet Raoul in Quincy Market. The young driver, Owens, chauffeured her downtown and dropped her at an open-air cafe. She and her head chef had a last few t's to cross before their official start of business, a task they were sweetening with coffee and biscotti.

Zane had dug up another outfit for her from wherever he was getting them. This one paired black jeans and a wraparound shirt printed with colorful Italian tourist scenes. A couple of the scenes were restaurants, and Rebecca hadn't been able to resist, despite the neckline baring more cleavage than she was used to. She supposed the style suited her, because Raoul's eyebrows rose.

"Something agrees with you," he observed slyly once they were done with their hugs. "Maybe to do with the fancy limo that dropped you off?"

She had to answer. Conceivably, her activities could affect their jobs. "Trey Hayworth and I hooked up," she confessed, conveying as much of the truth as she thought germane.

To her surprise, Raoul wasn't horrified. He leaned back in the small cafe chair and smiled. "I thought something like that might happen. I never saw that man look at you like he didn't want to eat you up."

"You're not upset? It is sleeping with the boss. What if—"

"—the sky falls tomorrow?" her associate joked. "Life is a banquet, *chica*. Believe it or not, there's more on the buffet than work."

Speechless, Rebecca could only blink at him, which amused Raoul. "Enjoy yourself," he said. "Whatever happens, you and I will land on our feet."

She hadn't known he thought of them that way. He made them sound unbeatable, like a team nothing in the world could knock down. So much faith was amazing.

"You know I love you, right?" she said impulsively. "I might not say it, but I do."

Raoul reached across the table to pat her hand. "I know. I only wonder if you're aware how much everyone loves *you.*"

~

Zane hadn't forgotten his intention to talk to Trey's . . . cousins he supposed they were. He'd obtained the son's number from Elaine and called him the next day. The area code was in Connecticut, the son businesslike and stiff. Just as capable of being formal, Zane explained that he was Trey's business partner and would be handling the matter for the time being.

"Your mother trespassed in our offices," he said, not inclined to mince words. "The last I saw her, our security guards were escorting her back to her hotel. She's since checked out, and I don't know her current whereabouts. If it would set your mind at ease, I can ask a private detective to track her down. Naturally, you can hire one yourself, if you prefer."

Zane's friend-slash-PI was already working on locating Constance Sharp, but Benjamin Sharp didn't need to know that. Zane figured the son's answer would tell him something about what he was dealing with. Somewhat to his surprise, the son said he'd be grateful for whatever Zane's PI could find out. He hung up soon after, leaving Zane hardly more enlightened than before. He didn't know what to make of the brother and sister coming to Boston a few days later to speak face to face. Zane's detective had looked into their backgrounds but discovered no red flags: no arrest records, no money troubles, nothing to indicate this was a scheme. To all appearances, they were simply worried about their mother.

He arranged the meet for Sunday morning in the BBC Imperial Hotel lobby. Neither sibling objected to the discussion being on Zane's home turf.

He told Trey he had a breakfast appointment he couldn't reschedule. He wasn't sure Trey believed him, but since Rebecca was out as well he didn't do more than sigh.

"It isn't Monday yet," Trey reminded him.

This was true, but Zane wasn't convinced they'd make any more progress toward a committed relationship. Rebecca seemed to care about them. She trusted them when it came to sex. She admitted she was more relaxed than she'd ever been, and Trey and Zane could see they were good for her. Those accomplishments notwithstanding, every time they brought up the future, she became evasive.

Is it me? he wondered as he parked the Mercedes in his slot at the hotel's garage. Was Rebecca hesitating because he wasn't a hundred percent at ease with their threesome? Didn't she realize the distance he'd come? Surely he wasn't expected to get over all his uptightness in a week? He loved how the three of them were together. He wanted it to continue. That had to be obvious.

He grimaced and took the stairs to the lobby level, hoping to smooth out his nervous energy. Second-guessing himself was counterproductive, as was splitting his focus. For Trey's sake, he needed to be on his game.

Though not huge, the Imperial's lobby displayed the same attention to detail and quality as all TBBC's businesses. The flowers were fresh, the dark marble floors gleaming. The furnishings were upscale but comfortable. Zane strode across a gorgeous antique carpet to the main sitting area. As he did, a man and a woman rose from an upholstered couch.

They appeared to be in their fifties and were well dressed but not showy. Before she was widowed, Constance Sharp had married the founder of a small chain of convenience stores. The son and daughter ran the business now. Their understated self-presentation suggested they wished to be taken for children of older money than they were. In his experience, 7-Eleven owners didn't go for strings of pearls and expensive beige twin sets.

"Mr. Alexander?" said the son. "I'm Benjamin Sharp, and this is my sister, Antonia. Thank you for seeing us. We're sorry to shove in on you this way."

An apology at the get-go was interesting. So was the deference Benjamin Sharp was showing a younger man. Zane nodded at him and his sister.

"I've reserved a conference room for us to talk in," he said. "Why don't you follow me?"

"Your hotel is very nice," the sister said nervously behind him.

More deference, he thought. And maybe a hint of fawning. He thanked her and held the door for them.

The conference room was a miniature of the lobby, down to the fresh-cut flowers on the side table. The siblings sat on the sofa he indicated, while he sank into an armchair. He leaned back, and they leaned forward on the seat cushions, their body language that of people hoping to please.

"You must think we're very forward," Antonia said, smoothing her skirt over tight-pressed knees. "We wanted to make sure you knew we had no idea Mother planned anything like this."

"You knew something," Zane said calmly. "Or you wouldn't have thought to call Trey Hayworth after your mother disappeared."

"Oh. Well. That was—" Flustered, Antonia touched her professionally waved short hair. "He's her latest little fixation. Mother's always been a bit . . . unpredictable."

"She's always been a nut," her brother put in gruffly. "We've got her in one of those retirement communities. You know, where old folks live in their own houses, but get assistance if they need it. I'm not convinced it's enough oversight."

"Well, Mother is independent," Antonia defended.

Benjamin's snort said he didn't consider that a good thing. He leaned farther forward, forearms resting on the knees of his conservative suit trousers. "Her doctor insists she doesn't have Alzheimer's. She hasn't wandered off and forgotten who she is. Can I ask what your detective found?"

"We'll reimburse you for his fees, of course," his sister put in.

Seeming to understand this wasn't necessary, Benjamin rubbed the furrow between his brows. For just a second, Zane saw Trey's bone structure in his face.

"She hasn't used her credit card since she checked out of the hotel," Zane answered. "Or withdrawn money from her bank. Unless she has fake ID, she hasn't bought a plane, train, or bus ticket. She also hasn't rented a car. Does she have friends in the area she could be staying with? A former schoolmate maybe?"

Benjamin heaved a sigh. "I'm not sure the old bat ever made a friend in her life. The marvel is she convinced our father to marry her."

Antonia smacked his leg, but didn't contradict him. Zane experienced an unexpected pity for them. Their childhood couldn't have been much easier than Trey's—and no wonder they playacted at coming from a different background than they did.

"If you truly fear for your mother's safety," he said, "you should go to the police."

"Oh no." Antonia wagged her head back and forth. "We couldn't. Mother would throw a fit."

Having met Constance, Zane imagined that would be daunting. "I'd like to ask you both something," he said, making up his mind as he spoke. "About your mother's father."

"You mean the saint?" Benjamin responded sardonically. "According to Mother, no man was ever as good as him. Or smarter. Or more deserving of honors the world was forever denying him."

"Did you know him?"

Benjamin shook his head. "He died before we were born. We have some older cousins who knew him. They claim he could make their skin crawl just by laying eyes on them." He stopped, drew breath, and started again. "Those things our mother is so desperate to have your business partner deny? I wager they damn well happened. I don't know exactly what our grandfather did to our mom, but she sure as hell is screwed up."

It seemed a relief for him to say it out loud. Zane wondered if he had before.

"You're not going to sue her, are you?" Antonia broke in pleadingly. "That would make such a mess."

He understood the reason for their visit then. They didn't want a scandal to crack the civilized patina they'd laid across their lives. "It's not in my immediate plans," he said.

He got up, and the siblings did as well. He shook Benjamin's hand. "I'll keep you informed if the PI turns up news."

"Thank you," the son acknowledged. "We'll be in town a few days."

His sister began to interrupt, but Benjamin shushed her with a hard look. He, at least, understood when shutting your mouth was the best strategy.

~

The meeting weighed on Zane's thoughts for the rest of the afternoon—how one man's sins affected so many. He wondered if he should tell Trey he'd met his cousins. Would Trey want to know them? Did they have enough in common beyond the blood tie? He knew he didn't have the right to shield Trey from making his own decisions but couldn't seem to stop himself. He wished he'd gotten a better bead on the Sharps, good or bad.

Rebecca returned from her appointment distracted too. Zane expected this was due to turning her mind to work. Monday was tomorrow. She'd be back at the Lounge early.

She didn't even try to talk her way into Mrs. P's kitchen to cook dinner.

Trey attempted to de-mope the mood by dragging them to the theater in the basement to watch a movie. Zane was aware of cars blowing up and the hero saving the world. Other than that, the plot slipped by him unnoticed.

"Maybe we should turn in," Rebecca said after Trey brought the lights back up. "We all have work tomorrow."

When Zane agreed, Trey muttered they were pitiful.

Back upstairs, Rebecca called dibs on the suite's bathroom. She'd become a fan of its multiple pulsating showerheads. Zane sincerely hoped that wouldn't be what she missed most about her time with them.

He glowered as he undressed. Standing with him in the roomy custom closet, Trey smacked Zane's diaphragm with the back of his hand. As intended, the sting caught his attention.

"Cut it out," Trey said.

"I'm annoyed that she's going," Zane replied.

"Going. Not gone. She's right behind that door with a dozen steamy sprays shooting over her hot body."

Zane was stripped to his boxer briefs, the stretch of which gave his cock room to twitch. "She called dibs. She wants the shower to herself."

"And you can't think of anything that would change her mind."

He could think of a lot of things, one in particular. Maybe Trey knew which, because he put his hand on Zane's shoulder. His eyes held a touch of sadness Zane didn't like. "Don't you want to end this week memorably?"

He did, maybe more than Trey knew. He ached to keep Rebecca, to add her to the wonderful portion of his life he'd been lucky to build with Trey. What did his hangups matter compared to that? Didn't he owe it to Trey and himself to make this last-chance pitch as well as he could?

He stroked Trey's forearm to his elbow, ruffling the silky hairs and causing him to shiver. Watching Trey's pupils darken lifted his prick some more.

"Finish undressing," Zane said throatily. "You're going to help me convince Rebecca she'd enjoy company."

~

Aside from the pool and the library and—as of tonight—the gilded mini-movie theater, Trey and Zane's bathroom was her favorite place in the house. Okay, the underground playroom was cool as well, plus the kitchen, from the peek she'd had at it, but the giant bath was definitely up there in her top ten.

Bigger than her bedroom at home, the bath had a glittering crystal fringe chandelier, pale green silk wallpaper, and an array of plumbing more elaborate than two American men should know how to use. Rebecca was so in love with the shower's zillion body sprays that she hadn't yet tried the freestanding, reheating soaker tub.

If she'd had this bathroom in her house, she might never get muscle knots.

She half-hummed, half-sang a Pink song as she soaped herself. She pushed aside the knowledge that this might be her last time here. She'd remember it. She'd remember everything.

Glass divided the shower space from the rest of the room, and she had her back to it. Given how many sprays she had on and the roar of the water, it was no wonder the men's entrance was drowned out.

She jumped and squeaked as two warm hands settled on her shoulders from behind.

"You're a rock star?" Trey teased her for her song choice, his lips right beside her ear. "Does that make me and Zane your groupies?"

She turned to face him. The men had stepped into the white marble enclosure, towering and naked. Rebecca became a different sort of wet when faced with their male beauty.

"Wow," she said, taking in their taut muscles and tall erections. "If you're my groupies, I really rate."

Trey's smile was beautiful. "Zane and I wondered if you could stand company."

"No," Zane corrected, drawing Trey's head around. "Not company. Not yet."

"Not company?" Trey repeated.

Rebecca's heart skipped a beat as Zane dragged a fingertip down the centerline of Trey's water-beaded chest. Maybe Trey's heart skipped too. He sucked in a gasp loud enough to hear.

"I think she'd prefer a show." Zane's attention followed his finger across Trey's navel. "The show she secretly wanted to see that first morning when you and I shared the shower in here."

Zane didn't touch Trey's erection, but it jumped anyway. "A show with just you and me?"

"Exactly." Zane looked into Trey's eyes. The mist was clinging to Trey's lashes, the sparkle making him seem dreamy. "You and me making love to each other in front of her. She can watch as closely as she wants without being distracted."

Trey's Adam's apple bobbed as he swallowed. "You sure?"

"I'm sure." Zane shifted his gaze to her. "That's something you want, isn't it?"

She'd been holding her breath without realizing. "Yes," she said on an outward gust of air.

Zane smiled, his blue eyes simultaneously hot and affectionate. "I'd kiss you," he said, "but I'm saving that for later."

He kissed Trey instead, holding his face, and then his biceps, and then Trey broke and plastered the two of them front to front in a full embrace. The move shocked through Rebecca as if it had been done to her. This was how they'd kiss if they were alone—hungry and hot and hard. In the center of the spray, the men sucked each other's tongues, their chiseled jaws and cheeks working. Trey was moaning long and low. Zane moved his hips against his lover's, rubbing their thick erections side by side.

"Shit," Trey gasped, yanking his head back for air. His hands clamped Zane's buttocks to increase the pressure.

"Feel something you like, buddy?" Zane teased him.

He undulated his pelvis and Trey groaned. Something about the sound was so uninhibited, so personal that Rebecca took a step back. She wouldn't have thought Zane was paying attention, but his left hand snapped out to catch her wrist.

"No," he said, his face streaming with water, his lips reddened from kissing. "Stay close. You can . . . you can touch us if you want. We're just not touching you right now."

She heard the unsureness in his voice. Despite setting this in motion, he wasn't completely confident about baring this side of him to her. "You're okay with that," she not-quite-asked.

"I want it," he said roughly. "Like you wouldn't believe. If you put your hands on me while I'm fucking him, I'm going to be so excited I might explode."

Her heart pounded in her throat at his intensity. For a moment, she couldn't speak.

"Would you like that?" he asked, actually worried by her pause.

"Oh yes," she assured him with a ragged laugh. "Like you wouldn't believe."

"Me too," Trey piped up, laughing like she was. "You have no idea the daydreams I've had that started just like that."

The space between the marble walls was filling up with steam. Even so, she and Trey witnessed the hot flush that darkened Zane's cheekbones.

Growling softly with longing, he bent to kiss Trey's neck. His hands moved over Trey's naked body, self-consciously at first and then getting into it. Trey touched him back, writhing as Zane stroked him. Zane wasn't afraid to manhandle him, pinching his nipples and butt, giving his balls a tighter squeeze than Rebecca would have dared to use.

Given Trey's fondness for a hint of pain, this cranked him to a very excited state. Zane's kisses shifted to his sharp little nipples, turning to love bites there. The marks he left on Trey's chest were red. Rebecca suspected they'd linger.

Unable to help herself, she touched one. Trey whimpered his oh-that-hurts-so-good sound. Taking this as a signal, Zane began to go to his knees.

"No," Trey panted, grabbing his shoulders to stop him. "I'm too close. You'll push me over. Let me suck you instead."

He dropped before Zane could stop him, water spray bouncing off his broad shoulders as he drove his wonderfully expressive lips down Zane's cock.

Zane couldn't hide how much he liked that. He forked his fingers into Trey's hair and made a garbled sound. His neck fell back and his eyes closed with bliss. His hips pushed at Trey even as he tried to control his arousal by deepening his breathing. Trey took his thickened shaft eagerly. Maybe because he had a cock himself and knew its mysteries, neither hesitation nor embarrassment marked the treatment he gave to Zane's. He wasn't deep throating him, but he had to be coming close. His hands gripped Zane's hipbones, perhaps to prevent him from accidentally forcing the issue.

The slurping noise of his lips and tongue caused her sex to tighten.

"God," Zane gasped, every muscle in his abdomen gone rigid. "That feels so good. I'm going to fuck your mouth too far."

Trey pulled free with a pop. "Hold his base," he said to her. "Squeeze your fingers around him as tight as you can."

The order startled her, but she complied. Zane's cock was incredibly hard, not only pointing upward but also arching slightly back toward him. He moaned when her hand gripped him, and louder when Trey swallowed him down again. Rebecca shuddered as Trey's lips bumped her fingers.

Zane had said they wouldn't touch her, but he couldn't resist wrapping his arm around her waist to hitch her close to him. His side was hot, his muscles bunched with tension. She guessed the squeeze she had on his base wasn't tight enough. Cursing, Zane released his guiding hold on Trey's head. He grabbed his own testicles instead, tugging his sac to keep himself from coming.

"Ahh," he sighed as the urge relaxed. He rolled his hips into Trey's mouth more smoothly. "God, Trey, that feels soo good."

She saw Trey grin around his cock. She imagined Zane felt his lips curving.

"Fucker," Zane responded, very locker-room jocular. "Jesus, you're good at that."

His trick of tugging down his balls won him a few extra minutes of oral enjoyment. He didn't let go of her as he neared his limit, but his arm began to tighten spasmodically.

"Okay," he finally said. "Enough."

Trey was already pulling off him. He came to his feet with an assist from the marble wall. Inspired by what he'd been doing, his erection was as big and upright as Zane's—though shaped differently at the head. Zane touched the broad silky surface with the hand that wasn't holding her. The skin of Trey's glans appeared to grow redder behind the swipe of Zane's thumb.

"God, you're beautiful," Zane breathed as a bead of pre-cum squeezed from Trey's slit. He smoothed the fluid around until Trey shivered. When he looked up at Trey, both their gazes were laser hot.

Trey kissed him, slow and tender and deep. Almost as tall as Zane, he only had to stretch up a bit.

"I love you," he said after he pulled back, his goldy green eyes swimming with emotion. "You've brought more sweetness into my life than anyone could deserve."

A rivulet rolled down Zane's cheek that wasn't shower water.

"Trey," he murmured, caressing the other man's trimmed stubble. His eyes said he loved Trey back, something Trey obviously knew.

Seeming amused that he didn't say the words, Trey broke into a brilliant grin. "Better bend over, baby. This rocket is ready to launch, and I'm thinking you'd like it firing up your ass."

Zane's jaw fell with surprise. Trey didn't give him a chance to make an objection.

"Oh no, boyfriend," he said, wagging his finger from side to side. "You took me in front of her already. It's my turn to show off."

"Your turn to— I wasn't— I didn't—"

"Doesn't matter why you did it," Trey said. "Fair is fair. Plus, you know I'll make you like it."

His fingers trailed down Zane's front, over his pectorals, around his navel, gathering up Zane's cock and stroking. He handled his friend's equipment with firmness and confidence, a confidence that was justified. Zane's face twisted with pleasure, the expression deepening as Trey squeezed and rubbed his glans. Over the course of the week, Rebecca noticed he liked playing with Zane's foreskin. He used his palm as well as his fingers, which earned him a sharp gasp from his victim. Satisfied he'd made his point, Trey let go with a smirk.

"Fine," Zane surrendered. "But you're not making me scream this time."

"We'll see," Trey said, pausing to wink at her.

This time? Rebecca thought, her insides liquid and pulsing. Trey had made Zane scream before?

"Why don't I, uh, grab supplies from the cabinet?" she said hoarsely.

Trey beamed at her like she was the cleverest woman ever.

By the time she returned, Zane faced the shower's longest wall, the one with the bench she used for leg shaving. He'd grabbed a pair of vertical metal handles that were anchored into the marble, maybe five feet off the floor. She'd wondered if the holds were there for sex, as Zane's action seemed to confirm. He was bent forward, butt out and back twisting sensually as Trey massaged it and licked his spine. The view of Zane's long clenching legs was pretty spectacular.

Trey was laughing at Zane's curses. "She's coming back," she heard him assure Zane over the water. "Don't be so impatient."

"Then don't tease me."

"I have to." Trey nuzzled his tailbone. "Making you crazy is too much fun."

Rebecca was a little sorry to interrupt. "Here," she said, holding out the lube.

The laughter in Trey's eyes settled into warmth as he accepted it. "Thank you."

She bit her lip, incapable of saying more. Smiling, Trey squeezed the stuff down Zane's crack. When the stream reached the spot he wanted, he pushed it gently in with both thumbs. Zane's knuckles whitened on the handholds.

"His nerves like this," Trey said in a quiet voice. He moved his thumbs slowly in and out, essentially fucking him with them. "He has a lot right around his entrance. In the right context, the stimulation is very sexual."

This context seemed to qualify. "Christ," Zane said, unable to resist arching his rear closer.

Trey fulfilled the wordless request with more stroking, seeming to enjoy massaging him. Only when Zane whimpered did he pull away. He washed his hands in the shower, then held out his palm to her. Rebecca supplied a condom, thrilling to the sight of him rolling it down his big erection.

He didn't look at her again. Letting her play voyeur, he reached up and wrapped his right hand beneath Zane's on the wall handle. He settled the other on his hip, presumably to steady him.

"Ready?" he asked his friend.

"For God's sake, get on with it," Zane snapped.

Trey grinned, taking this as praise and not insult. Since the bench was handy, he swung one bare foot onto it. This put their respective parts at the perfect level. With a casualness that stopped her breath, Trey prodded Zane's anus with his cock, adjusted, and then pressed smoothly in.

"Fu-u-ck," Zane moaned, pleasure stretching out the word.

"See how good . . . waiting makes this?" Trey said.

Zane groaned and twisted his ass around Trey's intrusion. "Do it," he ordered. "Fuck me now, or I'll squeeze it off."

Trey laughed and began to swing.

She didn't think they forgot she was there, but after a point they lost their self-consciousness. Maybe pleasure simply overwhelmed them, and they had to give in to it. She loved watching both their faces. Trey's shoulder-length hair was wet and twisted behind his neck, Zane's too short to obscure his expression. After a bit of Trey rolling in and out, Zane shifted one of his grips from the wall handle onto Trey's buff arm. Trey got more serious then, which Zane seemed to appreciate. Relying on groans and broken words, he pleaded with him to go faster.

The evidence of the men's strength enthralled her. No matter what they were doing, they were definitely male.

"Yes," Zane said once Trey had achieved a certain pace. "There. *Deeper.*"

Trey grunted and gave him a hammer strike.

"Fuck," Zane gasped, his head lashing.

The last thrust seemed to have struck its desired target, but this wasn't enough for Trey. He kneed Zane's legs wider with his own. This seemed to restrict Zane's ability to react. He was at the mercy of how deep and fast his friend chose to go. His powerful body struggled, though it also seemed to love the trap. The sounds he made were raw, the jerking of his cock frantic. Trey released Zane's hipbone to grab his balls, cupping them snug against his body. Though the men's main anchor was Trey's single handhold on the wall, Trey went at Zane so fast he could have been a machine.

"Fuck," Zane said again, eyes squeezed, face strained. "Fuck, fuck."

"Rub him off," Trey panted through his wild thrusting. "Grab his penis now."

Zane's cock was red with excitement, thick, strutted, like a horn pointing up from his abdomen. Trey's thrusts were shaking it, but she grabbed it around the middle, wanking her fist as hard and fast toward the crest as she'd seen men do in porn films.

Timing it perfectly, Trey added an extra *oomph* to his upward drives.

Zane's mouth stretched wide a second before he let out a roaring shout.

His cock convulsed in her hand. Semen shot into the shower's spray, jet after jet, like he was coming for twenty men. He made a noise like this hurt. She would have stopped rubbing, but he slapped his hand around hers, milking his ejaculation to the last drop. He didn't stop even after he started softening.

She guessed it hadn't hurt. She guessed it had felt *really* good.

Zane's breath wavered out on a sighing moan, his body bending forward again.

"Wow," he said. "That was . . ." He swallowed and had to stop speaking.

Trey let out a little laugh. "I believe the phrase you're searching for is 'hell to the fuckin' yeah.'"

He pulled out and dropped to the bench, his knees giving out temporarily.

He was nearly as hard as when he'd started. Weariness rather than an orgasm caused him to flag. Watching his prick stick up even as his head dropped with exhaustion clenched her pussy on itself. She knew exactly how she wanted to work off the excitement the men had inspired in her.

"Phew," he said. "You up for finishing this with me?"

Her eyes jerked away from his groin. Trey was looking straight at her. He laughed at her expression. "Yes, I'm talking to you. You're the one I saved this for."

"Really?"

"Absolutely. How many times does a man like me get to live out his hottest daydreams?" As many times as he wanted if the person he was asking was Rebecca. She didn't know how to say this, and he held out his hand to Zane. "A little help here, please?"

Zane helped him to his feet and also to tidy up. Zane's own hands shook with tiredness, but Trey liked his assistance. He squirmed as Zane re-dressed his erection. She suspected Zane was smoothing the latex a little better than it needed. When he stroked one finger around Trey's balls, the caress was plainly gratuitous.

"That's more help than I need!" Trey objected with a grin.

Zane grinned back. "You two put me out of commission. I want to make sure you're up for doing both our parts with her."

"Well, now I'm too up for it," Trey said, his mood just as playful. He turned to her. "I hoped you're primed, sweetheart. This isn't likely to be my finest hour."

Rebecca padded to him to twine her arms behind his neck. His hot green eyes were the only eyes in the world right then. She'd never forget their twinkle; never stop being grateful for having these memories. Seeing the emotions her gaze held sped up his breathing.

"Your finest two minutes ought to do it," she predicted.

He took her at her word. His hands hoisted her bottom, his delicious mouth dropping to conquer hers. That was better than awesome. He had no idea how she'd hungered for his tongue.

"Mm," he moaned at the ease with which his hardness slid into her. "Mm, Rebecca, you *are* ready."

She couldn't blush; she was too busy tightening her calves to pull her sheath down him. God, she needed this, needed his heated thickness stretching her sexual aches.

Maybe he sensed that. With another moan, he took two strides and flattened her into a wall.

She gasped with pleasure at how deep this drove his cock.

Trey's body trembled against and inside hers. "I held back for this," he whispered. "Zane was sweet as hell, and I wanted to go with him, but I held back to do this with you."

He made her quiver—with his words, with his rock-hard body, with his breath-stealing willingness to share his soul. Rebecca's body clamped around him, but he didn't press in farther. Instead, he drew back, sucked air, and thrust in even more emphatically.

Rebecca's nerves all moaned: *oh my God.* Possibly his did too. They groaned together, her nails digging into his gorgeous shoulders as he clenched her bottom. Neither of them could speak. Trey growled and gripped her tighter, his sea-bright eyes an inch from hers.

Now, said his lips as his erection throbbed inside her.

He didn't stop again. He pulled back for ten strong strokes—all long, all hard, all intense beyond measuring. She knew Zane was watching; she heard his quickened breathing nearby but couldn't look at him. His presence wound her up all the same. The sensations inside her pussy approached pain as her body reached for its peak. At the eleventh stroke, she came with a cry so loud it echoed around the room.

Trey groaned back and poured his pleasure out. He came not only because of her but Zane. The storm of longing stirred up by taking Zane was now buffeting her.

When he stopped shoving into her and quaking, all of them were done in.

"I need a bed," she moaned, squished between Trey and the silk-papered wall, which he was using to hold them up. "If you put me down, I promise I'll try to walk."

"You're nice and warm," Trey mumbled in complaint. "I don't want to move."

Zane added his two cents by swatting Trey's bare ass.

"Nope," Trey retorted. "Can't get a rise out of me with those tricks right now."

"Haha," Zane said. "Let Rebecca down, and I'll help you both into the bedroom."

With a few more grumbles, Trey let her go. He could walk, it turned out— better than her anyway. Zane was left to bring up the rear. He flipped off the bathroom lights and began to shut the door.

~

Zane's mind wasn't on what he was doing. Thoughts of what he'd just experienced filled his head. He'd enjoyed it start to finish, and he remained okay with it now. He wanted to do it again—though maybe not until after he'd taken Rebecca on his own. Watching Trey have her was inspiring. Zane got ideas for things *he* wanted to do to her.

With a few of those ideas occupying his attention, it was only after he swatted down the light switch that he realized Rebecca had left the supply cabinet open. The thing was a reproduction of old-style pharmacy storage. Constructed in zinc, it included glassed-in shelves for stuff like towels, and drawers for the sort of items Rebecca had brought him and Trey. Unfamiliar with where they put things, she'd pulled all the drawers open. Too interested in not missing their show, she hadn't shut them again.

The cabinet was close to the door. Zane didn't bother turning the light back on before he stepped to it. If he had, he might not have noticed the tiny red eye blinking at the back of the middle drawer's clutter.

Fuck, he thought, his chest going icy hot.

"Trey," he said, low and sharp.

Trey padded back to his side. "What is that?"

Zane slapped the overhead light on and dug out a small black box he knew he hadn't put in there. "Surveillance equipment." Feeling sick, he turned the thing over in his palm. "Wi-Fi. Sound activated. Probably a powerful battery in here. This is expensive gear."

Trey cursed. He shot a quick look over his shoulder, but Rebecca wasn't in hearing range. "Where's the lens?"

Zane's stomach clenched. "If I wanted to catch something salacious, I'd aim it where it could see the shower."

Trey immediately strode to the enclosure. Now that he knew to look, he found it in less than a minute: a thumbnail sized wireless fisheye adhered to the top of one marble wall with waterproof adhesive. Zane had been facing it while Trey fucked him. It would have seen everything.

Hands shaking, he pried open the box he'd found. As he did, the power light winked off.

Trey returned to his side to peer at its innards. "There's no storage chip in there."

"No," Zane agreed tightly. "It's sending the signal from the lens somewhere else, probably through the house network."

"It wasn't Rebecca," Trey said defensively.

"Fuck's sake," Zane snapped, still speaking in a low tone. "I know that. Rebecca wouldn't do this in a million years." He set the opened box on a stack of towels, not wanting to touch it. "It had to have been someone on the staff. Getting access is too difficult for strangers."

"They've all been with us for years."

"All except one," Zane corrected. "The one employee we didn't vet as closely as the others because he's related to Mrs. P—the staff member we trust the most."

"Owens," Trey said, hard and flat.

Zane opened his mouth to agree when Rebecca spoke from the door. He didn't know how long she'd been there, but her pallor said she'd added up the pieces she'd overheard.

"I think I know why. I just remembered where I've seen him before."

Zane and Trey responded at the same time. "You've seen him before?"

"Last Monday. At our VIP sneak peek for the Lounge. He, uh, helped that supermodel you said wasn't your girlfriend out of her limo. I wasn't paying him much attention. I assumed he was her driver."

Zane recalled the uncomfortable weekend he'd spent with her. "That wasn't Missy's limo, it was ours. I wanted to get shut of her, so I took a taxi from the airport. I told Owens to drop her wherever she liked. He knew who she was. He seemed a little star struck. I thought it was funny."

"Not so funny now," Trey said. "Missy would have been in the mood for blood, you having just dumped her. I guess your ex-not-girlfriend and our strapping young driver found mutual interests."

"That is not good," Zane said.

"That is *very* not good," Trey emphasized. He lifted his hands at Zane's look. "Sorry. I know you kind of liked her, but that glorified swimsuit hanger is poison. The first time I met her, I knew she was hoping to stash her eggs in your basket."

Zane hadn't known Trey disliked her. He'd been aware Missy had ambitions. He simply hadn't thought they were his problem. He'd been wrong about that. People like her didn't set up secret surveillance just to watch it themselves. People like her had *E! News* on speed dial so reporters could "accidentally" catch her on dates. God, he'd been stupid. Owens had probably been spying for her when he walked in on them in the pool, maybe hoping to tell his new famous girlfriend what they'd been up to. And that business with him and Rebecca supposedly needing help assembling the bed . . . Owens had wanted an excuse to get into their secure playroom. Probably Zane ought to be grateful he'd only managed to plant a sex-cam here.

He shook his head to rid it of those thoughts. Every minute they delayed was one too many. "We need to get to Owens before he sends Missy this footage."

Trey threw him a pair of pants and grabbed one for himself. "I say we need to beat Owens to a pulp, but I'll settle for shutting down his snooping."

~

Rebecca wanted to come with them, but Zane backed up Trey's opinion that she should stay in the house.

"I don't want you any more involved than you are. Don't make us waste time arguing. We need to confront Owens now."

"We won't do anything stupid," Trey promised, which he suspected was her main concern.

The chauffeur lived in the apartment above the ivy-veiled garage. If luck was with them, he hadn't been watching the feed come in and didn't know what he had. That hope died the moment they saw him behind his lit-up windows. He was hurrying from his dresser to his bed, carrying clothing to a suitcase.

"Shit," Zane said. "He's packing. He must have heard us find his equipment."

They bounded up the outside stairs with Zane in the lead. Trey's best friend didn't bother knocking. He lowered his former quarterback's shoulder and busted in the door.

The apartment was one big room. Owens spun around to them.

"Stay where you are!" he demanded in a quavering voice.

He had a dark object in his hand. He was pointing a gun at them. Trey's heart had a second to trip over itself before Zane roared and rushed Owen.

The driver was a big kid, but he had no chance against Zane's determination and athletic skill. The mere fact that 6 foot 4 worth of solid muscle was barreling toward him rendered him too scared to shoot. He froze, and Zane hit him, the heels of his palms targeting his lungs. The blow threw him back. Zane's momentum carried both of them onto the bed, on top of the suitcase. There, they struggled for about ten seconds for control of Owens' shooting hand, which Zane held wrenched above his head. Losing patience, Zane did something to his wrist. Owens cried out, and the gun clattered to the floor.

Not required for the wrestling match, Trey kicked it farther away. The weapon looked a lot smaller now that it wasn't aimed at them.

"You can't . . . kill me!" Owens panted, cradling his possibly broken wrist. "Even you'd go to jail!"

Zane sat on top of him, hands trapping his upper arms, subduing him with his greater weight. "What is your damage? We hired you as a favor."

"A favor to my fucking aunt," Owens spat, trying to wriggle free. "You and she think you're such hot shit. The famous bad boys. Ooh, how awesome to work for you! Everyone's supposed to kiss your stupid billionaire asses. The truth is you're nothing but a pair of jumped-up homos trying to pretend you like girls."

Zane growled, the sound more irritated than enraged. Owens flinched anyway.

"You hit me again, I'll sue," he blustered. "You already broke my wrist."

"You had a fucking gun in your hand!" Zane shook his head at the kid's stupidity. Trey knew then that Zane wouldn't hurt him. Owens wasn't an equal enough opponent, and Zane's history didn't allow him to play bully. That was too bad. Trey wouldn't have minded seeing the kid with at least one more broken body part. Since Zane was setting the standard, Trey stepped to the side of the bed and looked down at him.

"Where's the footage you took?"

"Somewhere you'll never find it," Owens sneered.

If *never* meant five seconds, his claim was true. The little shit's gaze cut left, where a laptop sat on a coffee table. Trey strode to it. Owens' email program was open. Trey's spirits sank when he saw the last message sent. They weren't going to catch a break tonight.

"He emailed a video file to a Mystique@Mystique.net."

"Anybody else?" Zane asked.

"Not that I can see on first glance."

"Shut it off," Zane said. "We'll go through the hard drive after we deal with this idiot."

"Hey!" Owens objected. "That's my property."

Zane gave him a look, swung off him, and retrieved the gun from the floor. Once he'd checked the safety, he tucked it into the back waistband of his trousers. Owens had just enough sense not to protest that.

"You have five minutes to finish packing," Zane said. "Since you seem a little slow, I'll explain that you're fired, and you shouldn't use me as a reference. You violated the nondisclosure agreement you signed when we hired you, and for that you can be sued."

"You wouldn't dare," Owens huffed. "I'll turn you and your ass-licking butt-buddy into laughing stocks."

Zane seemed to take this coolly, but a vein ticked at his temple. "Considering your new best friend is sure to do that anyway, that's hardly an effective threat."

Owens sat up, about to spout off again. Zane stopped him with narrowed eyes. "I don't give in to blackmail, boy. Not from you and not from her."

"She has lawyers too," Owens retorted.

"I'm sure she does, but if you think she'll pay them to work for anyone but herself, you're stupider than you look. She has what she wants from you. You'll be lucky if she returns your calls."

"She cares about me! She said I'm the best lover she ever had."

Zane simply smiled at him. Jumped-up homo or not, Trey expected that title belonged to him. "Are you planning to pack? You've got maybe three minutes left."

Owens packed, hefted his suitcase, then stomped like a surly teenager down the outside stairs. He owned a scooter, which he putted down the long drive. Thanks to his broken wrist, the machine wobbled at intervals. Trey joined Zane at the window to watch.

"Much as I hate to admit it, you did the right thing not beating him up. He's still Mrs. P's nephew."

Zane grimaced, his frustration showing now that Owens was gone. "Missy will give him his comeuppance. What do you want to bet he'll dial her the minute he's off the grounds?"

"Are you going to call her?"

"And say what? She'd enjoy it too much if I beg, and I refuse to pay her off. Money isn't what she's after anyway. This is about revenge." He covered his face. "When that film goes public, the media will have a field day."

"We have friends in the media. Maybe they'd agree to keep a lid on this."

"It won't matter. Missy can post the file on fucking YouTube or a hundred of her fan's blogs. Our lawyers might get it taken down, but not before it's seen—and copied—who knows how many times."

Zane's arm muscles were hard with tension when Trey rubbed them. Zane wasn't in the mood for sympathy.

"It's my own damn fault," he said bitterly. "I'm the one who hid what he was and gave them something to expose."

"Everyone has a right to keep their private life private."

Zane snorted. "Not me. And not you, apparently. I'm sorry, Trey. You saw what Missy was. I should have known better."

"I wouldn't have predicted she'd do this. Anyway, maybe we should worry about Rebecca. She's in that footage too."

Trey's reminder hardened Zane's face. "Damn it. She doesn't deserve this." He looked toward the house and sighed. "We should go back. Warn her what happened."

"We can't let her go home tomorrow," Trey said.

"No," Zane agreed. "Whatever it takes, we protect her until this blows over."

Unlike Owens, they went quietly down the garage stairs.

"So," Trey said, because he truly couldn't leave it alone. "Were you trying to give me a heart attack by running toward a guy with a gun?"

"He wouldn't have hit me," Zane said. "He was too scared to aim. Besides, sometimes the best defense—"

"—is a good offense. I remember."

They'd stopped on the walk at the bottom of the steps. Zane squeezed Trey's trapezius exactly the way he used to on the football field in high school, when they'd had to hide what they were to each other. The potentially lethal danger they'd just faced had shaken Trey. At the squeeze—and the reminder—emotion sheened his eyes.

Zane saw this and touched his face. "No way could I let that pipsqueak shoot you."

"Good to know," he said roughly.

Zane pulled Trey to him, holding him hard and tight. This would have been the time to say *I love you* . . . if he'd been anyone but him. Trey usually didn't mind not hearing it, but right then wasn't usual. Rather than complain, Trey hugged him back. Zane had taken a risk tonight. To expose the other side of his nature to Rebecca, and then have this happen, must have seemed like the universe reaching down to smack him. Trey himself wasn't looking forward to total strangers passing judgment on what should have been private acts. Bad enough that Owens and that bitch had seen.

He rubbed Zane's back and let go of him.
"Rebecca will be wondering what happened," he said.
To his relief, his voice was steady.

CHAPTER FIFTEEN

Fallout

Rebecca's relief when the men returned safe and unbloodied was dizzying. She jumped up from the bed and hugged them in turn.

"God," Zane said, bending to squeeze her. "I'm so sorry you're getting dragged into this."

"It's done," she responded, stroking his golden hair. His face was pressed to her neck. She looked over his head to Trey. "I take it you didn't kill Owens."

"Broken wrist," Trey said. "Confiscated laptop. Fired and gone from the house. I'm afraid he sent the file already. To Mystique, like you guessed."

Rebecca had concluded that from Zane's apology. She reminded herself she was good in a crisis. This wasn't going to break her. She pushed back gently from Zane's embrace. "I was thinking while I was waiting here. If you can't convince that woman not to use the footage—"

"I doubt we can," Zane warned.

"Then maybe you should prepare a statement. Come out as bi voluntarily. As if you're not ashamed, but you wanted to keep it private. That'll take at least half the wind out of the gossips' sails."

Zane sat on the edge of the mattress to think while Trey very carefully refrained from commenting. Zane might not like this, but he was too smart not to follow her reasoning. "I'd have to act fast," he said. "I doubt Missy will wait to deploy this bomb."

"We could call Evan," Trey said. "He's handled damage control before.

You could record something quick tonight. —Evan is a friend of ours who's a lawyer," he added for her benefit.

"All right," Zane said, his face determined. "I'll call him now."

He'd only half risen when Rebecca heard her cell phone's ringtone. She got up to get it, pretty sure someone calling her at this hour wasn't a good thing. When she answered, her brother Charlie was on the line. She returned to the bed.

"Are you all right?" she asked, big sister worry kicking in. "Did something bad happen?"

"Not to me," he said in a funny voice. "Maybe this is a misunderstanding, but someone saw a sex-tape online of you and Zane Alexander and that other guy from TBBC in a shower. He sent me and Pete a copy. I didn't watch, and I guess there was steam blocking some of it, but Pete said he thought it was really you."

"Crap." Her free hand rose to her brow. This certainly settled the question of whether Mystique was serious.

"Rebecca?" Charlie asked when she didn't say it was a mistake. His voice had jumped half an octave. He always was the sensitive one.

"Okay," she said, forced to bite the bullet. "The tape is really me, and it's really Zane Alexander and Trey Hayworth. We were filmed without our knowledge."

Trey lowered himself to her other side, both men's presence bolstering her. *Your brother?* Trey mouthed, and she nodded.

"Let me talk to him," Zane said, easing the phone from her.

Rebecca would have stopped him, but he moved away too fast. He took the cell to the arch that opened into the sitting room. From the sound of his side of the conversation, he was accepting a chewing out from both twins.

She supposed they were kicking themselves for tricking her into meeting Zane at the photo shoot.

"Let him handle it," Trey said, giving the back of her neck a squeeze. "They're your brothers. They love you. They can't curse at you the way they can at him."

"This isn't Zane's fault," Rebecca protested.

"They'll think it is. They'll think he should have protected you better."

Maybe Zane thought so as well. He didn't appear ticked off after he hung up. "I told them to come here," he said. "In case the media track them down."

Rebecca covered her mouth. Was the scandal going to be that big? Trey put his arm around her shoulders, which was comforting and not at the same time.

"Your brother Pete told me something interesting," Zane said. "The footage was posted anonymously. Missy seems not to want to admit she's the source."

"That *is* interesting," Trey agreed.

Rebecca didn't see why it mattered. Either way, the shit was going to hit their fan.

~

The boys were still angry when they arrived. They didn't goggle over the mansion the way they would have otherwise.

"We're here for *you*," Pete said to her. "Because the three of us stick together. We don't care about hiding from the press."

His fierceness took her aback, along with the fact that Charlie echoed it.

"Who you sleep with is your business. That stupid model should be sent to Siberia. In her bikini." Charlie's arms were crossed. He was glaring somewhat illogically at Trey, who'd joined her to greet the boys in the luxurious front hall. Zane was in the library with the tall dark lawyer, working out the fine points of his statement.

"We're very sorry," Trey said to Charlie. "We didn't take care of your sister like we should have."

"You didn't take care of her at all!"

"Charlie," Rebecca scolded. "That's not fair. They took . . . they took very good care of me before this happened."

"They dazzled you with their money. We thought Zane was a nice guy, but he and his buddy here just wanted you for their plaything."

"They didn't," Pete broke in unexpectedly. Charlie gaped at his brother. "They didn't. I watched that tape and—okay, I totally didn't need to see my sister doing that—but I could tell they cared about her. Anybody with eyes could. Sure, some people are going to be outraged, but some will just be jealous. Love is love, Charlie. It's not always tidy."

Rebecca didn't know whether she or Charlie was more flummoxed. Charlie's mouth worked a moment before he glowered at Trey again. "You love her?"

"I do," Trey said, the ghost of a smile playing around his lips.

"And Zane?"

"I've seen indications he feels the same."

Rebecca's heart beat faster for each statement. She turned wide eyes to Trey, who smiled angelically at her. She wanted to say she loved him too, but her mouth felt stuck. God, was she as bad at this as Zane?

If she was, Trey let her off the hook as easily as he did his friend.

"Why don't you boys pick a guest room or two?" he suggested. "Then, since I doubt any of us will sleep, maybe we can convince Rebecca to whip up a snack."

In spite of everything, she inhaled in involuntary excitement at the thought of having free rein in that big kitchen.

Charlie didn't miss the sound—or what it signified.

"Okay," he said grudgingly to Trey. "Maybe you do know our sister better than you would a plaything."

~

Evan really came through for Zane. Though it was the middle of the night, he'd driven right over . . . with his own camera equipment. He said he often taped clients to prep testimony, to coach them on how to present themselves as honest and forthright.

"Some people sound like they're lying even when they're not," he explained.

Zane guessed that wasn't his problem. Once they'd hammered out what he'd say and practiced a few times, Evan only filmed him twice before he was satisfied.

"You don't want to be too polished," his old friend said. "Then you'd come off as fake."

"Why do I feel like crap?" he asked as Evan packed up his equipment. "I'm facing my demons, spilling my guts to the world. That's supposed to make me feel better."

"Oh, I don't know." Evan smiled faintly. "Maybe because you're the sort of person who doesn't like to be pushed into doing things."

Zane supposed that was it. He rubbed his temple, hips propped on the desk where he'd been filmed. Evan had decided the library would make a respectable backdrop. "When will you send this out?"

"As soon as I get home. Best not to let other people control the spin on this."

"We won't be able to control it either."

"No, but at least you'll look like you're standing up to it. I'm guessing the networks will start airing your response early tomorrow." Evan clapped his hand on Zane's shoulder. "You were fine. Calm. Straightforward. You're not Paris Hilton, so I expect you'll be excruciatingly uncomfortable for a while, but then you'll get over it."

"All this doesn't shock you?" Zane couldn't help asking.

Evan shut his black carrying case with a snap. "I'm a lawyer. It takes more than this to make me blush." He started to go and then stopped. "It might not feel like it right now, but you're lucky. To be loved that much by two people, whoever the hell they are, isn't a privilege everyone can claim."

"Send me your bill," Zane reminded as he turned to go again.

"A huge one," Evan laughingly promised.

The rest of the night was a weird cross between going to the mattresses in a mafia movie and meeting the in-laws. Rebecca wasn't engaged to him or Trey, but having her brothers around made it feel that way. Once the twins relaxed, something they couldn't seem to help doing around their sister, the chips fell off their shoulders. They were the same smart funny kids he'd enjoyed interviewing for *Bad Boys*—decent kids, with their heads and hearts on straight.

Along with Rebecca, they brought an amazing amount of extra life into his and Trey's house.

Zane woke his corporate head of PR early, giving him a rundown of the situation and telling him to respond to inquiries with *No Comment*. He hadn't bothered going to his private office to make the call. The five of them—him, Trey, Rebecca and her brothers—were hunkered in the library in front of the wall of screens. News of the sex tape, including portions edited and blurred to pass FCC standards, filtered onto the networks for the early morning news cycle. Crumpled and tired from being up all night, no one spoke as the coverage aired. Charlie hid his face in his arm for the explicit bits, a reaction Zane wished he could imitate.

The tape cut off before Trey took Rebecca against the bathroom wall. Either the lens hadn't covered that angle, or the footage didn't suit the point Missy hoped to make. Zane's statement showed up in most cases on the heels of the tape. Seeing his face pop onto the screen was more surreal than usual. He didn't think he looked calm. To his eyes, he appeared incredibly uptight.

"As some of you will have heard," he said stiffly to Evan's camera. "A tape of myself and two people I care about has been posted onto the internet. The tape was made without our knowledge and released without permission. It's regrettable that we live in a world where people's expectations of privacy can be violated so recklessly. Human nature being what it is, some of you will watch the footage. To those who don't, I thank you in advance. While I've chosen to keep my bisexuality private until now, my personal preference isn't something I'm ashamed of. I believe it's given me a unique perspective on the world, one I hope makes me a fairer businessman and person. The freedom to pursue happiness, each in our own way and irrespective of others' approval, is important to everyone. Thank you for your time and for letting me have my say."

In the after commentary, the newscasters—for now at least—were treating him and his statement respectfully. Most felt compelled to add that it was fortunate TBBC was a private company and wouldn't have to worry about plummeting share prices. Ditto for their brand being edgy to begin with. One waggish female commentator dubbed the incident Showergate. As mockery went, Zane decided he could live with it.

Once he'd watched a fourth station air its version of the story, Zane shut off all the TVs. He felt as tired as if he'd been up for week.

The picking apart would come later: the jokes on the late night talk shows, the conservative groups frothing at the mouth, the debates over whether bisexuality actually existed. Zane had done what he could for now. That had to be enough.

"That was all right," Pete said judiciously, his words slurred by lack of sleep. "The bit about the pursuit of happiness was sort of patriotic."

Rebecca got up to kiss her brother's cheek. She came to Zane's chair next and curled up in his lap like a cat. She was easy to put his arms around.

"I'm glad I'm someone you care about," she murmured.

"Me too," Trey said, sitting on his chair's other arm.

Surrounded by the people he loved, Zane closed his eyes and let his breath gust out.

~

He let himself enjoy the respite for five minutes. Then he got up to tackle Mrs. P. Trey volunteered to speak to the house manager, but Zane preferred keeping busy right then.

"Stick with Rebecca," he said. "Make sure the boys have anything they need."

Standing close, Trey rubbed Zane's wrist with his thumb. His brows went up when Zane had to fight not to pull away. "Stop thinking about your dad and his macho code. Letting Rebecca see who you are was the right choice. Having that exposed doesn't mean you're being punished. It's just Missy being a nasty cunt."

"I know," Zane said. "In my head, I totally know."

To prove it, he kissed Trey softly on the lips—though Rebecca's brothers still sprawled sleepily nearby.

Trey pulled back from him and smiled. "Don't let Mrs. P resign."

"I won't," Zane promised, knowing as well as Trey did that she'd try.

His patience wasn't completely up to soothing the guilt-stricken woman. She *should* have mentioned her nephew was the family troublemaker before suggesting him for a job. Zane was sure she'd convinced herself the position would help Owens straighten up, and no doubt her sister had put pressure on her to put in a word for him. People lied to themselves all the time about relatives.

Though Zane didn't ask, she swore she hadn't gossiped to her nephew about her bosses' relationship. She probably hadn't had to. Once Owens was on the staff and around them everyday, he'd have sniffed it out by himself. A single glance exchanged in the car could have given them away. Lately, Zane hadn't kept up his guard as carefully.

"Trey and I didn't have to take your recommendation," he pointed out to Mrs. P and himself. "Ultimately, the buck stops with the bosses."

It took ten more minutes, but he convinced her she wouldn't improve matters by quitting. That was one load off his mind. Mrs. Penworth ran their house really efficiently.

He detoured to the terrace afterwards. He needed a few deep breaths and to remind himself that the sun had come up regardless. The birds were singing, the squirrels still scampering on the lawn. An unexpected peace settled over him. The truth was out, and the world hadn't ended. He had Trey, and Rebecca hadn't left. It was hard to imagine, considering all that remained to face, but maybe they'd come out of this stronger.

He'd set his cell to vibrate, and it buzzed in his pocket. Pulling it out, he saw the caller's ID was blocked. This was his private number. He hoped to hell the press hadn't got hold of it.

He drew one more clear breath and answered it.

"There you are," purred Missy's most seductive voice. "I'm so glad I caught you."

Zane's heart thumped so hard she should have heard it on her end. "What do you want?" he asked tightly.

"Just to congratulate you. Coming out like that was clever. I'd almost think you didn't mind."

Zane gripped the phone and tried to project calm. "Missy, what I did to you doesn't warrant this reaction."

"Doesn't it? You wasted my time, Zane, when all along you were in love with your CFO. I can have any man I want. I won't be humiliated by some bastard billionaire using me as his beard. Does your new whore know that's all she is to you? Does she realize you and your precious Trey count the minutes until you can be alone? Will she tell *her* friends she's certain you'll be popping the question any day?"

Was that what Missy had told people?

"Look," he said, "I'm sorry you misunderstood my intentions, though—frankly—I can't fathom how you could. You knew you weren't the only woman I was seeing."

"Oh, no, no, no," she said, her voice crisp and hard with anger. "You don't get to turn this around on me. I'm the victim, and you are going to pay—you and your precious gay boyfriend."

"Missy—"

"Turn on *Boston AM*," she advised, naming a local daytime talk show. "You've got—oh—about ten minutes until it starts. We'll call this 'Revenge, part deux.'"

She ended the call, leaving him to curse at no one. He glanced up the rear of the mansion to the quiet third-floor windows where he and Trey had shared so many nights. Rebecca joining them had felt natural—inevitable, even. She fit them both, and they fit her. He saw that now, as clearly as the sun beaming down on him. What he didn't see was why people like Missy needed to twist their happiness into a different shape. Couldn't they ignore it and go be happy themselves?

Because he guessed they couldn't, he went inside to find the others.

They weren't in the library. He found them in the twins' guest room, standing in a loose cluster in front of the wall TV.

"My friend Caroline called," Charlie said as he came in. "She said *Boston AM* was promo-ing an interview with Mystique."

He'd barely finished speaking when the smartly dressed female host of the show appeared onscreen. Frieda Finch, a forty-something auburn-haired woman, was as birdlike as her name. To the swells of show's theme music, she introduced her guest as the world famous swimsuit model, Mystique. Missy sat in the opposite chair, seeming to like the description. She'd dropped her recent Marilyn Monroe kick and was looking more Kim Novak in a primly buttoned but very curve-hugging light gray suit.

Finch leaned toward her sympathetically. "Mystique, you and billionaire Zane Alexander have been viewed as an item for a few years. What's your take on these recent shocking developments?"

"First of all, Frieda," Missy said, establishing their rapport and her own composure, "other people built more on that relationship than I did. You know how it is when someone's famous. Everyone they blink at must be their boyfriend. I'd say Zane and I dated casually. On the other hand, I don't deny that today I'm feeling a bit misled."

Treys snorted as Missy smoothed her snug skirt primly, not coincidentally drawing attention to her legs.

"So you don't believe Zane Alexander's claim that he's bisexual? Don't you think the tape supports that?"

"Well, I'm no expert on these things, but some might say if he really did like women, he'd have tried harder to hold onto me." Missy attempted to look modest, but wasn't selling that.

Whatever Finch believed, she maintained her poker face. "You must feel like you dodged a bullet. If Zane Alexander had pursued you harder, that could have been you in that tape."

This question was a bit sharper than Missy expected. She drew herself straighter and pursed her mouth. "I assure you, the . . . sort of activities in that recording aren't what I go in for. I have more self-esteem than that. My concern is that other vulnerable women don't get taken in by Zane or Trey Hayworth. Behind that rich bad boy glamour, the truth is unsavory."

"You're saying Trey Hayworth, CFO of TBBC, is also to blame for this?"

Missy turned her million-dollar fake-lashed eyes toward the camera, her expression oozing sincerity.

"Fuck," Zane muttered even before she spoke.

"I'm saying Trey Hayworth has his own shameful secrets. I'm saying neither of TBBC's chief officers can be trusted."

The camera cut back to Finch, who announced they had an exclusive pre-taped interview with a close relative of TBBC's CFO.

"No," Trey said, startled into it. Zane grasped his arm in support, but couldn't stop Trey's crazy aunt from appearing on the screen. Constance Sharp was better dressed than he'd last seen her—her make up professionally applied, her silver hair freshly coiffed. Despite the buff and polish, the crazy glitter in her eyes was impossible to disguise. She was posed in a high-backed chair in what looked like a nice hotel room.

"I'm not surprised by anything Trey Hayworth does," she huffed. "He ignores his family, and spreads horrid lies about my father. My father was ten times the man those limp wrists are, but my brother was just as bad as Trey. He lied too, and hit people with his toys. It's no wonder my nephew turned out the way he did."

"And there you have it," Frieda Finch concluded, her face in the frame again. "Does Trey Hayworth have a reason to be estranged from his family? Is he the victim of ill treatment or the boy who cried wolf? More mystery and scandal surrounding two of Boston's best known businessmen."

"Oh come on," Pete burst out as the station went to commercial. "This is bogus. Anyone can see that old lady is off the rails. Just like anyone can see Mystique set this whole thing up when she couldn't bag her man. She's lashing out like a jilted cheerleader in high school. It's so obvious it's sad."

"It'll only be obvious to people who want to see it that way." Trey spoke quietly, but his face had gone white with stress. Even more than Missy, Finch had put her finger on his personal angst button. Zane moved his hand from Trey's arm to his shoulder, which caused Trey to shift his gaze to him.

"I guess we know where my aunt disappeared to," he said. "Missy was hiding her."

Missy must have tracked Constance down after seeing her break into TBBC's headquarters. He gave her points for paying attention, but God what a mess this was. He supposed it helped that Trey's aunt wasn't reading from the same revenge playbook as the model—though that didn't spare Trey of course.

Aware of this, Rebecca wrapped her arms around Trey's chest from behind.

"I'm okay," he said. "Missy only wins if I let this upset me."

That he had let it upset him was apparent to everyone.

"Someone needs to school that bitch," Charlie said.

"You leave it alone," Zane advised, though he shared the sentiment. He leveled a stare at Pete too. "Both of you. This is for me and Trey to handle."

"Sure," Charlie said.

"Sure," Pete agreed.

"Oh God," Rebecca moaned, no doubt on account of knowing her siblings well.

Zane wanted to smile but worried it might encourage them.

~

Trey didn't know how long he'd have stood there, stupid and dumbstruck, if Rebecca and Zane hadn't led him to the empty guest room across the hall. The windows there overlooked the front lawn and the long tree-lined drive. Everything outside was peaceful: just another gracious country estate in rural New England.

Ignoring the allure of the air conditioning, he yanked up the window sash. Real air swept in at him, warm and grass-scented. Rebecca and Zane rubbed his back from either side.

"I don't care if people know who I sleep with," he said as steadily as he could. "I just don't want the world to view me as a victim. I want to choose who I share my past with."

He turned to rest his hips on the windowsill. Rebecca and Zane looked worried but not overcome with pity. Maybe they were downplaying their concern, or maybe they gave him credit for not being made of glass. A smile pulled at his lips without warning, prodded by a sense of humor he wouldn't have thought he'd recover this quickly.

"The swimsuit hanger might have done us a favor," he observed.

"Might she?" Zane responded, his mouth curving.

"Piling on the revelations as thick as she did means people won't know what to poke at first—or who to feel sorry for." Trey took Zane's hand and then Rebecca's, enjoying the easy way their holds twined with his. He made a decision within himself. "I'm not going to worry about us. We're going to be fine."

Rebecca looked down at his hand. Hers was small but strong, her cook's fingers battered but wonderful. When she lifted her gaze, she was smiling.

"I love you," she said. "Can I be you when I grow up?"

He laughed, his chest suddenly warmer. She'd said the words almost as a joke. Her hint of shyness let him know they were anything but.

"I love you too," he said. "I love you both."

Rebecca's eyes twinkled with mischief. "The swimsuit hanger would totally hate you saying that."

"Yes, she would," Trey agreed. "Guess I know how I'm getting my revenge."

~

Realizing Trey was okay worked on the others like a sleeping pill. The trio trooped upstairs to bed together. Rebecca dimly heard Zane making one final call—to his PI friend, she thought—and then she passed out.

She woke, hours later, with a tall slumbering man on either side of her. The sun outside the windows seemed late afternoon-ish. Her cell phone was ringing.

Zane was nearest to the sound. He cursed, fumbled around the table where she'd left it, and handed it to her.

"Yes?" she said, her voice mostly sandpaper.

"Well, hey there, chef," said Raoul. "I guess this means you aren't coming to work today."

Heedless of the body parts the men had slung over her, Rebecca bolted up in shock. "Oh my God."

Evidently not angry, Raoul laughed at her.

"Oh my God," she repeated. "I forgot to go to work. And I forgot to call you. Raoul, I am so sorry!"

"It's okay, *chica*. I've got the restaurant under control."

"But I forgot!" Rebecca never forgot work. Never, ever. Even on the rare occasions when she was sick, she called in periodically.

"I saw the news," Raoul said in a gentler tone. "I know you must have been distracted."

"Shit," Rebecca said for a whole host of reasons. Did Raoul hate her? She'd told him she'd slept with Trey, but that hardly covered the situation. "Is the staff okay?"

"The staff is fine. Some are surprised, but quite a few are impressed. Line cooks are notorious belt notchers, after all. You should prepare yourself for some teasing—you know, when you stop lazing around all day."

"Oh God."

Zane and Trey were looking at her now, but she couldn't look at them.

"I ever tell you about my threesome?" Raoul went on. "I was a hot young fry cook. Abs of steel and a knife so fast I could chop ten onions at the same time. This cute pastry chef took a liking to me. Her special friend was a very bendy yoga instructor—"

"I'm stopping you right there," Rebecca warned, recognizing a tall tale when she heard one. "You tell me anymore, I'll repeat it to your wife."

"I tell her this story all the time. You have no idea how sick of it she is."

"Damn it," she said, in spite of her amusement. "I wanted to be there for our first normal night."

"Well, it's not going to be normal here for a bit, not until the wagging tongues settle down. Let me handle things for now. You know you can trust me to do right by your food."

She did know that. "You're the awesomest head chef ever," she admitted.

"Don't you forget it. Fortunately, none of this is bad for business. We were booked solid for two weeks after our VIP shindig. Now I hear it's two months. Someone told me Wilde's is so empty crickets are chirping there."

"Maybe I should get into trouble more often."

"Maybe you should."

Rebecca was smiling when she ended the call.

"You forgot work," Trey said, one slashing brow lifted. "Being here really has changed you."

Rebecca snuggled back between the men. "You want credit for that, eh?"

"He can have half," Zane said. "The other fifty percent is mine."

~

Rebecca drifted off between them, burrowed cutely into Zane's chest. Higher up on the pillow, Trey looked across her mussed blonde head at Zane. The sun shone in Zane's face and he squinted, but—like Trey—he wasn't ready to go back to sleep. His right hand rested on Rebecca's hip, his upper leg slung across both of hers so that his bare foot touched Trey's. A pleasant low-grade arousal collected in Trey's groin—another reaction he hadn't expected to feel so soon. He was glad for it, glad for everything in a way. He put his hand above Zane's on Rebecca's waist.

"You okay?" he asked his lover.

"Yes," Zane said. "You?"

"Yes." He stroked his pinkie finger along Zane's index, delighted by the darkening of Zane's baby blues. "You want to tell me what that call to your PI friend was about?"

Zane turned sheepish. "I had Elaine route your cousins' calls to me. I met them at the Imperial the other morning."

Trey's exasperation was softened by fondness. "I figured you'd do something along those lines. And?"

"And as far as I could tell, all they wanted was to get control of their mother. I gather she's been a lifelong embarrassment. Now that we know Missy had her, Mike should be able to locate her and put the family in touch again."

"Leaving her with Missy might be a good revenge. Considering their respective personalities, they can't have enjoyed each other's company."

"I thought of that. The problem is, Missy is sure to hand your aunt off to some flunky."

Trey bent his arm and resettled his cheek on it. "Weathering this salvo has one drawback. Missy may up the ante if we don't give her the reaction she's hoping for."

Zane sighed. "I thought about that too. We'll figure some way to shut her down."

He stretched his left arm across the pillow to play with Trey's loose hair. The simple sweetness of the gesture melted his heart.

"I love you," Trey murmured, the words coming out with almost no fear at all.

"Me too," Zane returned. "I'm glad we're all in this together."

Trey's grin was as much for the effortlessness of Zane's answer as for him avoiding—yet again—his three most dreaded words in the world.

CHAPTER SIXTEEN

Operation Blue Velvet

Zane led Rebecca, whose heart was beating like a cornered rabbit, to the back of their huge closet.

"We need to be seen," he said, "as a threesome, as openly and boldly as possible."

He opened a double-door wardrobe with swirling exotic wood. Rebecca expected—or maybe hoped—to see suits for the men inside. Instead, a rainbow of expensive women's dresses hung on the rack.

"Holy crap," was all she managed to say.

Trey snickered behind them. "Zane has his obsessive side. He couldn't help shopping for you in the hopes that you'd hang around."

"I'm supposed to wear one of these?" She touched a long silk gown in pale peach. It was even fancier than the silver slip thing he'd bought for her. "These dresses are beautiful, but I'm not sure they're me."

"They're you," Zane said sternly. "The you you haven't met. Think of them as uniforms for billionaires' girlfriends."

She burst out laughing, which she hoped was okay. She looked at Zane to make sure. A muscle ticked in his chiseled jaw. Okay, maybe this was important to him. "Really," she said, patting his arm. "They're gorgeous."

"Pull out the blue one," Trey urged. "That color is exactly her."

The blue one was sapphire velvet. The skirt was cocktail length, and the neckline plunged dangerously. She believed it was the sort of dress people referred to as flirty.

"Uh," Rebecca said at the thought of wearing it.

"Please," Zane said, holding it out to her. "Try it on."

Still a little shy about undressing with the men, she took the dress into the bathroom. Naturally, it fit like a second skin, requiring that she remove her bra in order to look right in it. The skirt was snug and shorter than expected. She had booty in it. And legs. Truth be told, it made her a new woman: a glamorous, sexy, thinking-man's hot female. She didn't know whether to frown or gasp as she studied her reflection.

Both men smiled when she came out again.

"That's the one," Trey said. "Don't make her try on the others."

Rebecca was all for not trying on the others. The rest of the program she hadn't quite signed off on. "Where am I wearing this?"

"The center of the universe," Zane said.

He made her laugh in spite of her nervousness. "And that would be where?"

"New York. There's a charity function at the Whitney-Moeller Museum, to raise money for wildlife. Trey and I have been invited."

"And I'm your plus-one."

He cupped her face. "Always. For as long as you're willing."

She laughed again, because what woman could resist that prospect? "For you," she said, "I'll wear the matching heels."

~

Rebecca didn't expect him to, but Zane rustled up invitations for the twins. She was starting to feel bad about keeping them from their lives, but both boys seemed keen to come. She assumed this was because they'd be flying in a private jet, not because they loved penguin suits.

Space was also made for Charlie's geekalicious four-eyed friend. Caroline's curvaceous body was poured into black leather pants and a sparkly top. The pants made Rebecca jealous—because they allowed the girl to wear flats. Caroline carried an overnight bag and a rather beefy looking small laptop.

"Studying for a final," the redhead said when she noticed Rebecca's attention to the computer. "I took summer session over the break."

Studying on a date didn't seem right to her, but if Charlie didn't mind her preoccupation, Rebecca had no business getting upset on his behalf. The girl did take a moment to admire Charlie's James Bond-ish attire as he took the seat next to her. Pete sat in the same grouping of chairs with them, so she guessed the outing wasn't meant to be romantic. Then again, what did she know about romance for college kids?

They landed after a brief flight. A private car service picked them up. Inside the tricked-out limo van, Zane and Trey went into mogul mode. Neither made less than a dozen calls, touching base and schmoozing.

"You're letting people know we're here," she said when they finally stopped.

"Here and kicking," Zane confirmed. "Our associates in Manhattan need to know we're doing business as usual."

"Will they be at the fundraiser?"

"Some of them."

Trey was sitting next to her, with Zane on his other side. Sensing her nervousness, he took her hand. "We show up. We drink. We dance. We write a big check for charity. We act like what we are to each other is perfectly normal."

"What if I screw up?"

"You can't," Zane said. "You look too damn delectable to be anything but an asset."

Rebecca hoped cleaning up well was all tonight would require of her.

Trey saw her skepticism. "We won't leave you on your own. One of us will be with you at all times."

"You don't have to go that far."

"We do. The more people see us together, the more they'll understand there's more to us than Showergate. We're serious about each other."

Rebecca snuck at look at Zane. He didn't bat an eye at Trey's claim. She knew he'd heard it. He wasn't murmuring in his phone. He was slipping that into his tuxedo jacket's inside pocket.

"We're serious," he agreed and straightened his black bowtie. He and Trey were so stunning in formal wear she had trouble thinking straight. She definitely couldn't afford to dwell on them finding each other stunning too. Her knees wobbled badly enough in these dressy heels.

"You're not nervous," she said.

Zane's sensual lips curved in an amused smile. "I seem to have gotten over that. Maybe all I needed was something to fight against."

She supposed that would light a fire under a competitive man like him. She wished she had a cure for her nerves. She was serious too. About Zane and Trey. About building some sort of future together. The fact that it was *some sort* was what threw her. She wanted the men forever, and she wanted a guarantee. Knowing nobody got that couldn't squelch her wish for one.

Trey leaned over to kiss her cheek. "This isn't life and death, Rebecca. We get through tonight, and we tackle tomorrow when it comes."

"Right," she said, tightening her grip on his hand. When Zane reached sideways to grip it too, she actually did feel better.

~

Zane was better at hiding his nerves than Rebecca realized. He hadn't lied about feeling ready to be a threesome in public, but he had trickier irons in the fire tonight. He hoped he wasn't crazy for letting her brothers talk him into Operation Blue Velvet.

Naturally, they hadn't heeded his request to leave Missy to him and Trey.

In the confusion of the scandal breaking, Zane had shoved Owens' confiscated laptop onto a shelf in the library. The boys had found it, read Owens' name on the case, and decided to take a peek. A phone call to Charlie's brainiac red-haired friend enabled them to crack Owens' apparently pathetic security, whereupon they discovered the dismissed chauffeur had a long-term fondness for filmmaking.

Their plan for exploiting that was one Zane might have devised in his college days.

Too smart to propose the plot to Rebecca, the boys had come to him.

"It's the nuclear principle," Pete had said with frightening reasonableness. "We've got a bomb, and the swimsuit hanger doesn't. If we want her to stop taking jabs at you and Trey and Rebecca, we have to demonstrate we're willing and able to use it."

"Plus, Mystique going after you is the reason the bomb exists," Charlie said. "It's poetic justice. We'd be silly to feel guilty."

"You'll only push the button if she shows up?"

"She'll show up," Pete said. "Once she hears the three of you will be there, she won't be able to resist making more trouble. She'll dress to the teeth and try to show you what you're missing. Or play poor misled thing to anyone who'll listen."

"Or both," Charlie added. "I'm betting that's not beyond her."

That was a wager Zane wouldn't take. "I don't want you getting caught."

"We won't," Charlie promised. "No one but Mystique will guess where the bomb came from. Caroline has, like, criminal level skills."

Zane saw this didn't dampen Charlie's interest in the girl.

He'd accepted their offer with stipulations, which the boys agreed to honor. All that remained was seeing if Missy would act true to form. Knowing it was best to shelve his worries for the time being, he joined Trey in helping Rebecca out of the limo van.

She looked better squirming to get comfortable in her blue velvet dress than Missy could in a hundred designer gowns—with or without photo retouching. The model would never understand why he and Trey preferred their shared lover, why *her* wobbly ankles were the most alluring, why *her* happy grin made their hearts stutter. Rebecca was a beautiful woman, but she was also a big bright soul. Being seen with her made him proud, no matter what anybody thought.

To his surprise, now that the truth was out, being seen with Trey had rather the same effect.

A man who'd won over those two had something to brag about.

"Watch the curb," Trey laughed as their date almost tripped on it.

"Damned heels," Rebecca muttered, holding tight to their hands. "I hope you two are giving me brownie points."

She forgot her grumbling the moment she saw the illuminated mansion behind the iron fence. The noise of nighttime Manhattan was all around them: the rush of traffic, the machinery of tall buildings. Other guests of the event stepped out of taxis and limos, chattering with their companions. Zane watched all of that fall away for Rebecca. Her face lit up at the fairytale house before her, her lovely eyes going wide.

"Wow," she said, her delight instantly becoming his. "This is cool!"

The turreted Whitney-Moeller Museum had once been a residence. Back in the twenties, the family donated it to the city, along with its extensive art collection and period furnishings. Today, it was a popular venue for charity events, thanks to its magnificently preserved turn of the century ballroom.

To escort her to it, Zane and Trey each offered her an elbow. The place was too packed for this arrangement to draw more than a glance or two. Rebecca, bless her, was too busy gawking to notice.

"Look at those tiger ice sculptures!" she exclaimed, understandably taking note of the catering. "I have to find out what artist supplied them."

Trey shot an inquiring look over her head at Zane, who nodded a go-ahead.

"Why don't we ask?" Trey said. "And maybe grab some champagne."

He steered her in that direction, leaving Zane with the other terrible trio. Caroline was already scoping the terrain for a likely place to set up her gear. The ballroom was long and tall with a painted barrel ceiling and a balcony on either end. The orchestra would claim the more distant perch. The nearer was arranged with fancy white-clothed tables.

"Up there?" Zane asked, nodding his head toward it. "If you blew out your table's candle, you'd be very hard to see."

"That'll work," Caroline agreed. She turned back to him, her eyes owlishly fascinating behind her thick glasses. "Switch on your earpiece, Mr. Alexander, and I'll hear everything you say. It'll only take a few minutes for me to be ready to make the delivery. All I'll need then is your signal that it's a go."

Zane squelched the childish thrill this cloak and dagger talk inspired. Charlie's nineteen-year-old friend was much more blasé than him. "Thank you, Caroline," he said soberly. "Charlie, why don't you make sure she gets into place safely?"

Charlie leaped to do it, inspiring the teensiest blush in Caroline. For Charlie's sake, Zane was glad to know she wasn't nonchalant about everything.

Pete laughed under his breath as he watched them go. "She is so out of Charlie's league."

"Maybe not," Zane said. "Charlie seems to have his own criminal tendencies."

Pete laughed at that as well, probably because he had them too. "Becca didn't mean to raise us sneaky, but we sure learned to be." He paused to narrow his eyes at Zane. "Don't let her down again."

"Not while there's breath in my body," Zane swore sincerely.

Pete nodded and then craned around the crowd. He touched his hidden earpiece to activate it. "Target entering the ballroom."

Zane stifled amusement even as his heart rate kicked up a notch. He wasn't the only person enjoying playing spy.

Missy was indeed coming in. On her arm was a hot young actor from one of the TV shows currently shooting in New York. Missy sure knew how to pick her dates. As irony would have it, Zane had heard some very underground rumors, from people who ought to know, that the stud was in the closet. That, of course, wasn't Zane's business. He waited until the actor peeled off toward the bar to approach Missy.

He had no trouble pasting on a severe expression. Seeing the model brought back more unpleasant memories than she probably imagined.

Always aware of her best angles, she leaned picturesquely against a column at the edge of the glittering room. She'd gone Roman tonight in a deep ruby gown gathered with a ribbon beneath her breasts. The shade suited her brunette coloring as perfectly as the style did her height and shape. One knee-high gladiator sandal peeped through a long leg slit, no doubt intended to declare her readiness for war. Her rich red lips formed a curve as he halted in front of her.

"Miss me already?" she asked archly.

"Probably as much as you miss Constance Sharp, now that her family's collected her."

"I enjoyed the old bag's company while I had it. It was useful."

"You'll find that particular usefulness has a price."

Missy toyed with the ruby pendant in her cleavage. "Men like you know what everything costs, don't you? What's it costing your little friend Trey, I wonder? His aunt raised such speculations about his childhood before her children whisked her away. Do you suppose Trey's mean old daddy explains why he turned out the way he did?"

Zane had heard those speculations. He supported Trey in his decision not to address them publically. If people discovered how he and Trey were raised, so be it, but for every person who understood there'd be ten like Missy who'd twist the facts somehow. The world might enjoy putting them under that microscope, but it wasn't their business.

No one should be forced to share their history.

"Careful," he said to the model. "You sound like you're implying bisexuality is a condition that needs explaining."

"It would need explaining, if it hadn't been invented by people who can't admit what they are. If you're gay, just be gay. Don't lead honest women like me on."

Zane let out a sigh, knowing this conversation was pointless. "I'm here to give you a warning. Leave off bothering me and mine, or I'll make you sorry we ever met."

"You're threatening me?" she asked in mock horror. "That's hardly cricket, Zane. I'm only here to support this fine charity."

He looked straight into her eyes, waiting an extra beat for her to understand he was serious. "You don't matter to me. Not as a supposed girlfriend and not as an enemy. Cause me the slightest inconvenience, and I'll cut you off at the knees."

This brought true anger into Missy's expression. Face hard, she opened her mouth to speak. She was too late. He'd given Caroline the signal. The phone she always carried in her clutch purse rang.

"You'll want to get that," he said.

She dug it out with a muffled curse. It was a videophone, of course—the latest, smartest model available. The minute she answered, the file Charlie and Pete had found on the chauffeur's laptop began to play. It showed her and Owens in bed in a hotel room. The picture was excellent, the sound a testament to Owens' skill at concealing microphones. Missy gasped—and not because of the video's graphic nature. Quite obviously, she hadn't known she was being filmed. As she rode her young panting lover, not as gracefully as she thought, she gave him instructions for planting a camera to spy on Zane in his home. She called Zane a revolting cocksucker and Trey a flaming queer. Owens negotiated an additional payment for his risk, and Missy agreed to pay. If this got out, GLAAD would have her ass on a platter—and never mind Zane's lawyers.

This, however, wasn't the worst the footage had to reveal—or not from Missy's perspective.

Excited by the topics she and her lover had been discussing, Missy tossed back her hair and came.

A sound like a dying walrus issued from the phone's speakers. Missy might not mind the world seeing her naked, but she'd damn well mind them knowing the noise she made when she climaxed.

Missy jabbed her phone off, but not before half a dozen people turned curiously toward the noise. "You *wouldn't*," she hissed, her eyes shooting flames. "That . . . that is a private thing!"

"I would," Zane said, hard as steel. "What's more, I want you to know I can. Anytime. To anyone. Any damn where you go. If you want *your* privacy respected, you need to stop violating other folks.'"

"No." She grabbed for his sleeve, her fury tinged with pleading. "Don't do this."

Zane shook her off and touched his earpiece. "Make the delivery," he said to Caroline.

Thankfully, this event was packed with people who didn't turn off their lifelines for anyone. All around the ballroom, hundreds of phones in purses and pockets chirped and buzzed and played an endless variety of tunes. Attendees laughed, cheery from the free-flowing booze and food, assuming the charity had arranged a stunt to entertain them and raise money. As they opened the message they'd received, a chorus of moaning walruses succeeded the previous cacophony.

"Damn you," Missy cursed, humiliation tears in her eyes.

Zane caught her wrist before she could storm past him. "It's a cartoon."

"What?" she said, tugging to get free.

"They're watching a cartoon. Not your face. Not the rest of the vitriol you spouted. It's a cartoon woman having sex, making that sound you do. The caption says, 'What's more generous than a big fat O? How about a check with a lot of O's that helps save endangered tigers?'"

"I don't believe you," Missy said.

Zane turned his phone around to show her. "This is your only warning," he said as she took it in. "Pull anything against anyone I care about, and this will seem like child's play compared to how I'll go after you."

She looked from the screen to him.

"Child's play," he repeated.

He saw the intelligence he'd once admired come into her face. "You mean it," she said, searching his expression.

"I will do *whatever* it takes to protect the people I love."

Hurt flicked across her eyes an instant before she looked away. She shoved her own phone into her spangled purse. "I won't bother you again," she said.

~

Rebecca and Trey snagged a small stand-up table to sample the hors d'oeuvres. She'd meant everyone to share it, but they seemed to have disappeared. Most troubling, after Mystique's big entrance, Zane had strode across the ballroom in the same direction.

Rather than give in to paranoia or jealousy, Rebecca frowned at the cell phone she'd just shut off.

"That was weird, huh?" she said to Trey. "Who knew the wildlife people were such pranksters?"

"Mm," he said, attention focused where the well-dressed crowd might be concealing Zane and Mystique. He didn't seem worried, but like he was distracted.

"They had to hack everyone's phone to do it."

"Maybe they had people's numbers from their fundraising."

"They didn't have mine."

Trey finally looked at her. "We'll get you a new one, with better security."

"*I'll* get me a new one. Don't you remember what you pay me?"

He smiled with soft eyes and a hint of wickedness. "I'm sure I barely scratch the surface of what you're worth."

A ripple among the partygoers stopped her from coming up with a smart remark. "That's Mystique," she said. "She's leaving without her date. I hope whatever Zane said to her didn't rile her up even more."

"I wouldn't worry," Trey soothed. "He's pretty good at encouraging people to cut their losses."

Something in his tone made her brows lower. "You know what he said. Her being here wasn't an accident."

"And there's the man himself," Trey announced as Zane's warm hand settled on her shoulder.

Rebecca turned at the touch. "Zane. What have you been up to?"

He smiled the way Trey had—like a mischievous angel. "What I've been up to is looking forward to our dance. I noticed the orchestra taking their seats on the balcony."

Rebecca wasn't that easily fobbed off. "Where are Pete and Charlie? Why *did* Caroline bring her laptop in here?"

He shrugged. "Maybe they're helping her study. Those summer courses can be a bitch. Come on, Rebecca. Aren't you going to dance with me?"

She was, and after that she'd dance with Trey, an arrangement she was secretly looking forward to. Apart from chaperoning Pete and Charlie, she'd skipped the proms in high school. In the interest of making up for that, she let her suspicions drop.

"No dipping," she stipulated. "Balancing on these heels is hard enough."

Zane's seductive grin broadened. "If I dipped you, you'd just have to hold me tighter."

"Oh God."

"Trey's the one you need to watch out for. He can dip *and* spin his partners."

Despite her trepidation, she let Zane lead her onto the dance floor. The music that started up was waltzy. Thankfully, Zane simply pulled her close, put his arms around her, and coaxed her head against his big chest. When he sighed, she felt tension run out of his whole body.

"What's wrong?" she asked.

"Nothing," he said, stroking her short hair. "Nothing now that you're here."

She couldn't spoil a moment like that—or the ones that followed when Trey took over. The men danced with her like no one else existed. Their care for her was wonderful and humbling at the same time.

Zane drew the line at taking a turn on the floor with Trey.

"He steps on my toes," he joked. "And he's way heavier than you."

She couldn't complain about his limits, not when he'd bent so far. Zane touched Trey nearly as sweetly as he touched her. He wasn't shoving people's faces in their relationship, but neither was he hiding that they all were romantically involved.

The people who knew the men appeared to take this in stride moderately well. Their trio wasn't avoided or whispered about where they could see—any snarky remarks being saved for elsewhere. Some of the folks who stopped to talk were stiff, but no one was impolite. The worst the awkward ones could be charged with was that they didn't know what to make of them. Rebecca understood that. Although arrangements like theirs weren't unheard of, they weren't generally public.

Rebecca's biggest surprise was how natural being with both men felt.

You've come a long way, she thought. Her former worries about sleeping with the boss seemed quaint by comparison.

"What are you smiling at?" Trey asked as they enjoyed one last twirl around the dance floor.

"You. Zane. How lucky I turned out to be."

"We're all lucky."

His soft sweet kiss was better than a cherry on a sundae.

~

Rebecca knew the college kids wouldn't admit to being up past their bedtime, but all three slept through the flight to Boston. Once there, the twins decided it was time to return to their own lives.

Rebecca hugged them on the pavement outside their idling cab.

"Love you," Charlie said, sliding into the back seat where Caroline waited.

"Love you," Pete seconded.

"You have enough to cover the fare?"

"Yes," Pete said. "As long as you stop hugging me sometime in this century."

She held his face a moment longer. Apparently, her brothers had left off worrying about her. More than anything, that told her they'd been involved in scaring off Mystique at the fundraiser. The question was, did she really want to know what they'd done? Whatever it was, they—and her two bad boys—wanted to spare her the responsibility for their actions. Maybe, just this once, it was enough to know her life was blessed with truly amazing men.

"Go home and enjoy your hunks," Pete encouraged. "We'll call you before the next Sunday dinner, to find out where it is."

That startled her enough to let go. Sunday dinner was always at the row house. She waved as the cab drove off, noting that the boys also waved to the men beside her.

"Sunday dinner?" Trey asked.

"The boys and I have one together once a month."

"We could have it at our place," Zane said.

Rebecca turned to look at him.

She guessed he interpreted this as doubt. His jaw hardened stubbornly. "We're not putting you in a cab. You're coming home with us. And not just tonight, either."

She smiled. She understood how Trey knew Zane loved him—with or without the words. An impulse to truly open to the miracle they were offering prodded her to speak.

"Could we stop at my place first?" she asked.

"Promise it's not pick up clothes."

"You're horrible!" she accused, unable to keep from laughing. "What if I need fresh underwear?"

"The stuff I bought for you is nicer. It's even comfortable."

Zane was right, so she relented. "I have another reason for wanting to stop. It'll just take a few minutes."

The sun came up as Zane drove, waking the old-new city with a wash of gold light. Rebecca's street was a quiet tunnel of leafy green, the trees at their peak of late-summer growth. As Zane parked his beloved silver convertible at the curb, she realized the construction dumpster was gone. Jesse must have finished the basement apartment.

What she'd feared would be a source of anxiety now barely made a blip on her nerves' radar.

"Should we come in with you?" Trey asked.

"Please," she said.

She unlocked the old scratched front door that held so many memories. She hadn't been away long, but the house smelled foreign—part staleness and part sawdust. She went to sit on the steps to the second floor. The snugness of her blue velvet dress meant she had to do this carefully.

"I thought you needed to get something," Zane said in confusion.

She patted the steps next to and below her. "I want to tell you a story. And to show you where it happened."

Trey lowered his narrow butt next to hers. Zane chose to lean against the opening to the living room. He'd pulled his bowtie open at some point. Looking tired but insanely hot in his formal wear, he peeked in at the old couches—curious to see how she lived, she supposed. She was no decorator, and there wasn't much to see. Most of their furniture came from bargain stores.

She clasped her hands on her knees, refusing to give them a chance to tremble. "You see that door?" she said. "Where we just came in? That's where my father stood before he left."

Trey laid one hand around her forearm.

"It's funny how vividly I remember it when it was so long ago. His overnight bag was at his feet, right there on the penny tile. His shirt had a stain on it that hadn't come out in the wash. My mom had been dead a week, and he hadn't figured out the machine."

Zane was looking at her now, his eyes sad and serious. Rebecca shook off that consciousness. Pity wasn't what she was after.

"He told me he couldn't handle Mom being gone. He told me when I tried to cling to him, all he wanted to do was run."

"Shit," Zane said softly.

"I don't know if I'd been clingy or not. I was sixteen. Dad had never done much parenting, so maybe me needing anything from him was too much. I remember how he shuddered when he said it, like I disgusted him. When I saw that, I was so angry, I swear I'd have killed him if I'd been able to. I refused to beg him to stay. When he did go and didn't come back, I thought maybe I should have pleaded—for the boys' sake, at least. I expect it wouldn't have made a difference. He told me to call child services. He said there'd be a family who wanted Charlie and Pete."

Trey breathed a curse like Zane had. Rebecca turned on the step to him.

"One of the last things my mother told me before she passed was to be patient with our dad. She said he needed us kids to love him. I still don't know if she was right, only that he needed even more to escape."

"We need you," Trey said, taking her hands in his. "We need you to love us."

"I do," she said. "That's why I'm telling you this. For most of my life I was convinced I'd never trust my heart to a man. Absolutely, I'd never let myself need one. You two did an end run around my fears. You made it easy to love you."

Trey's eyes spilled over, and hers did too.

"You need to sell this fucking place," Zane broke in.

She and Trey let out matching laughs.

"I mean it," he said, glaring at their amusement. "Your brothers shouldn't even live here. Those memories are bad mojo."

"I have good memories too. Raising Pete and Charlie here was great."

"Make new good memories with us. Move in with us. There's plenty of room for your brothers whenever they want to stay. Trey, give her the thing."

She looked at Trey, who smiled crookedly. He took one hand from hers to dig in his pocket. "We hadn't decided when to do this, but I guess now is a good time."

He handed her a plain square box with a lid. A quick glance at Zane showed he was frowning—not an angry frown, more like a worried one. He wasn't sure she'd like this. She lifted the lid carefully.

A ring of keys lay on the white batting.

"Front door," Trey said, touching one with his fingertip. "Garage and master for all the cars. This one opens the door to our flat in Paris—"

"You have a flat in Paris!" she couldn't help exclaiming.

"We do. With an awesome view and a balcony. Remind Zane to speak

French for you sometime. Trust me, it's super-hot."

"I bet it is." The leering grin she exchanged with Trey was all the more entertaining for the power it had to embarrass its subject.

"Show her the last key," Zane ordered Trey gruffly.

The final key was beneath the others and dangled from a golden chain. The links were hand-fashioned and looked a bit Medieval. The key itself was modern, but more complex than the others.

"The playroom," she breathed, knowing instantly.

"We'll put your prints into the system," Zane said. "That plus those keys will give you access to anything in the house."

Rebecca dropped the gold chain around her neck. The weight of the key fell gently between her breasts.

"Thank you," she said, her heart beating fast and strong. "I accept your very kind offer to move in with you."

"Good." Zane's blue eyes met hers with breath-stealing directness. "Let's go home and fuck ourselves silly."

CHAPTER SEVENTEEN

The Cherry on the Top

Rebecca deserved a medal for not attacking the men in the car. They seemed to expect it. Both had erections when they got out.

"We've done the garage," she said airily, though her body was simmering. "Please follow me to the house."

Zane chuckled behind her. "Have something in mind?"

She didn't answer, just smiled to herself. Inside, the mansion had its usual nocturnal hush, twinkling with just enough tasteful lights to see by. She was carrying her heels and consequently dared to add an extra sway to her hips. It would have been a shame not to. The formfitting dress was made for it.

"Look out, Trouble," Trey said, apparently liking what he saw.

She stopped outside the elegant period elevator.

"Have you swept the place?" she asked Zane.

His focus took a second to travel back to her face. He'd been distracted by the dip of her neckline, in which the key now hung. "You mean for surveillance? Yes. Top to bottom. Nothing's here apart from the security that should be."

Smiling, she turned to Trey, where her eyes widened. She'd caught him tugging the crotch of his trousers to make room for his bulge. "When you're done there, big boy, could you work the door for me?"

"It's been a while," he explained, grinning.

"Not since Showergate," she agreed.

Trey laughed and opened the folding gate. Feeling like a femme fatale,

Rebecca sauntered into the car. The walls were dark wood with art deco detailing. She pressed her back to one age-tarnished handrail and dropped the shoes she'd been holding.

"Please join me," she said to the men.

Zane stepped in cautiously, like he thought she might bite. "You sure you don't want to wait until we get to our bed?"

"I have elevator fantasies."

"Trouble," Trey repeated, his eyes twinkling.

Now that she had the men's attention, Rebecca shimmied the bottom of her short skirt to her hips, where the velvet's slight stretch held it. For the first time in her life, she wore honest-to-God silk stockings and a lace garter belt. She'd found both in the stash of clothing Zane bought for her. Her tiny black panties matched, though she wasn't flashing that much of them.

Zane swallowed at the visual. "You have the best girl thighs in the world," he swore.

She grinned, appreciating the distinction. Trey had nice thighs too, after all. She noticed Zane's tuxedo jacket was slung over his forearm.

"Please give that to Trey," she said.

Neither man seemed to mind catering to her whims. Trey accepted Zane's jacket. "Shall I shut the door?" he offered.

She nodded, and he closed them into the wood-lined space. He knew better than to take them to the third floor. They weren't leaving here just yet. Already caught in the spell, Zane couldn't look away from her. He wet his sumptuous lips, seeming nervous and excited. If she had her way, she'd turn the heat up under both reactions.

"Unzip," she said, the order husky, "but don't unbutton."

Wincing at the trickiness of the task, Zane lowered his zipper tab. His pleated shirt was tucked in. His big erection pushed a stretch of white through the slit.

"Reach back for the railing," Rebecca said. "Don't let go unless I tell you."

Behind her, Trey's breathing hitched and then sped up. He liked this game where she was the boss as much as she'd hoped he would. Lips turning up with pleasure, she stepped toe to toe with Zane. His eyes went dark as she dug through his shirt and into his briefs for the hot silk of his organ. His arm muscles bulged in his sleeves as he restrained his impulse to move them.

"Nice," she said when she found and stroked his erection.

She pulled it gently through the opening in his trousers. She knew Zane enjoyed that, but he controlled himself.

"This isn't fucking each other silly," he pointed out almost evenly.

"Fucking each other silly is the main course. This is the appetizer."

Because her dress's skirt was already hiked, she had no trouble kneeling in front of him. The carpet was soft and padded, like it had been designed for mischief. She wrapped her fingers around Zane's base, her thumb on the bottom to rub the raphe. The dark veins that fed his stiffness created a very masculine image.

"You're too tall for me to suck comfortably," she observed. "Please plant your feet wider."

He moved his long legs apart, his breathing going ragged in synchrony with Trey's. The sympathy between the men thrilled her, the fact that arousing one stirred up the other. She sensed Zane looking at his friend across the enclosed space.

"I want him down there with you," he said, more request than demand. "I'd like him teasing you while you're teasing me."

His manners earned him consideration. She glanced back around at Trey. He was a hot picture too. He had one hand clamped around his hard-on, like it needed extra confining.

"That would gun my motor," he admitted.

The rasp in his voice heated her pussy to overflowing. "You won't take control?"

"No," he promised, then broke into a grin. "Zane and I will save that for dessert."

She couldn't repress her shiver. Green eyes gleaming, Trey sank to the floor behind her. He yanked down his zipper, shoved the nice trousers to his hips, and took hold of the wall rail. He slipped his second hand down the front of her silk panties.

"Mm," he said, rubbing her outer folds with two fingertips. "You're all plumped up and hot."

The light strafing tingled more deeply rooted nerves, making her pussy clench. He brushed the tip of her clitoris, and she sucked in her breath sharply. She was swollen and sensitized. Each glancing touch felt incredible. He must have known. He took her bud between his thumb and finger and pinched gently.

"Trey," she gasped as sensation shot through her.

He bent to nip her earlobe, growling with enjoyment. "Better suck him now," he advised. "Before I destroy your concentration."

He could destroy it. His arm had shoved the blue dress higher, while his hand pushed her panties down. His cock throbbed hot and thick along the cleft of her bottom cheeks. He felt heavy, the aliveness of him exciting her. She suspected Zane saw him there.

When Zane licked his lips, she knew he did.

"Please," he said, hands fisted around the rail. "Rebecca, put your mouth on me."

She put her tongue on him first. Up the head she licked, lap after lap, until he quivered uncontrollably. Her lips were next, their nerve endings perfect for savoring how soft the skin that wrapped him was. She wasn't as bold as Trey, but she didn't neglect the ring where excitement had drawn back his foreskin.

When she finally opened her mouth for him, he moaned like he was dying and pushed inside.

Trey chose the same moment to slip one finger inside of her.

Her lovers were both so careful and yet so tense with longing. She closed her eyes and took Zane's cock further, as if he were a delicious dish whose ingredients she needed to analyze. Thickness slid across her tongue. Heat. Strength that pulsed like a heart. She creamed around Trey's gently stroking finger.

Moved by that, Trey's body pressed harder against her back.

"Don't," she said when Zane's hand came to cup her head.

He'd forgotten himself. He returned his grip to the brass railing.

She sank down his shaft and drew up again, tightening her lips, working him with her tongue. Sweet fluid oozed from him.

"Christ," he said, his hips wriggling helplessly.

Rebecca pulled free and looked up his tall body. His eyes weren't exactly focused, but he looked straight at her.

"That was *so* fucking hot to watch," he confessed.

Rebecca smiled. "I bet Trey would like us both to watch him."

She leaned to the side so Trey could lean in, which he seemed happy to do. This was better than a ringside seat. She was so close to the action she could feel Trey's exhalations fanning Zane, could practically count how many degrees their temperature had gone up. A bead of pre-cum squeezed from Zane's championship hard-on.

"Keep steadying him," Trey directed her. "Zane, don't move your hands from where they are."

Trey licked him like she had, then brushed him with his lips. When he swallowed him halfway down, both men moaned with pleasure.

She guessed it got to them more than they planned.

"Fuck," Trey said, pulling free shakily. He moved his hands to lacy sides of her panties. *No, he's not*, Rebecca thought, but he made a growling noise and ripped them off.

"What are you doing?" Zane panted.

"Can't resist." Trey caressed her thighs to urge them wider. "She is too damn sweet."

Air fluttered across her naked pussy a second before blazing hot skin nudged her. Trey pushed, and groaned, and filled her inch by arousing inch. Oh he was thick, stretching and throbbing as he went in. She couldn't control her neck arching back. Luckily, that wasn't required of her.

"Jeez," Zane breathed, admiring her reaction.

Trey pushed into her to his balls and pulled down her low neckline. Her breasts spilled free, sharp-tipped and shaking. Trey covered them with both hands and rubbed.

Again the men groaned like they were the same person.

"So pretty," Zane said as Trey pulled her nipples out.

If she'd had breath left, she'd have said the same when Trey leaned across her shoulder and slid his mouth down Zane's shaft. He got Zane wetter than she had, sucking him harder and more noisily. He undid the waist fastening to Zane's trousers, exposing more of him to work on. Rebecca decided that was good. His drawn up scrotum was perfectly in reach.

Zane made a pleasure-pain noise when she squeezed it.

"God," he moaned, hips twisting to get closer to both of them. His body arched like they had it on a rack. It seemed to be a good rack. He didn't ask them to stop until he couldn't stand anymore.

"Please," he said then. "I need a breather."

Trey drew back and panted, his cock hard as stone inside her. Zane wasn't the only one on the edge. Trey hadn't moved in a while. With a reluctant groan, he pulled out of her.

"Me?" Zane asked.

"You," Trey acquiesced.

Zane released the rail and held out his hands to her. His burning eyes told her if she took them, she'd pass control to him. She was ready for that. Actually, she was eager.

He lifted her to her feet.

"Arms around my neck," he said.

She put them there, and he boosted her by the bottom—which thanks to Trey was now bare. She hooked her stocking-clad legs around his waist.

"Jacket pocket," he said to Trey. "Right side. There's something in there for you too."

"Look at me," he added, when she would have turned to see.

Trey reached between their bodies to roll on Zane's rubber. Pleasure shifted Zane's facial muscles, but his gaze stayed on her.

"The other thing," Trey said. "Is it for you or her?"

Her eyes felt as wide as saucers. Zane studied them calmly.

"For her," he said. "No reasons she shouldn't get a taste of what this feels like for us."

Whatever *this* was—and certainly she could guess—Trey decided her dress ought to be peeled off first. This left her in the black stockings and garter belt, plus the key on the golden chain. Probably she looked like a French sex slave. Zane bit his lip and smiled.

"Rub your breasts on my shirt," he said.

The cloth was smooth, the starched pleats supplying the perfect chafe for her tight nipples. She guessed Zane liked the friction too. The vein at his temple pulsed more quickly.

"Ready?" he asked like he really hoped she was.

"Yes," she said, meaning it all the way through her.

His strong hands tightened on her bottom, pulling her sex up and over him. The trip back down was with him inside her.

She adored the groan he let out for that.

She almost didn't notice the rustle of Trey taking off his shirt. Bare and warm from the waist up, he returned to nuzzle the back of her neck. His cock felt like it was sheathed.

"Don't be scared," he whispered.

His heart pounded into hers through his chest. Both men's did, the wall of powerful male on either side of her more exciting than anything they'd done to her before.

"You wouldn't mind if I was a little scared," she whispered shakily to Trey. "You'd like it a tiny bit."

His laugh was a broken breath on her shoulder. He enjoyed that she'd busted him.

"It's the edge," he said, hands smoothing around her thighs to the place where her pussy and Zane's cock joined. "Riding it makes sex better."

His touch explored their meeting until they squirmed with longing. Breathing even harder, Trey returned his caresses to her back and then his hands left her. She heard something squirt and twitched in reaction. Trey was lubing his erection, running his fist up and down. His body was close enough that his knuckles bumped her spine.

"That feels good, doesn't it?" she asked.

"It does. But not as good as this."

The lube trickled down her crack. He smoothed it with two fingers over her anus, which itched pleasantly as he rubbed.

"Rock her on you," Trey said to Zane. "She needs to be more relaxed."

Zane rocked, and she couldn't help moaning. She might be nervous, but— God—she wanted this. Her body craved an orgasm. Satisfied with the change Zane's small motions had effected, Trey positioned his cock to enter her.

"I'll only give you what you can take," he said.

Taking him was easier than she expected, perhaps because they'd prepared her, or maybe she simply trusted Trey that much. He pressed into her, all the way, with only a few back and forth attempts.

"God," he said, one arm around her waist while the other still gripped the rail. His body trembled with excitement. "You okay?"

"More than," she said breathlessly.

Both her passages were throbbing, both stretched and hot and electrified. A current seemed to pass in waves between the men's erections. She was nearly too full, but she loved the sensation. Surrendering to it, she reached back to hold Trey's head.

The pads of Zane's fingers dug deeper into her cheeks. "I can feel him," he said, sounding awed by the realization. "The pressure of him in you is pressing me."

His face bent toward her as she looked up. Sweat glittered on his brow and his knotted jaw, his gaze intense with emotion. That she was the only woman they'd done this with moved her.

"I like being taken by both of you," she said, arousal shaking the words. "I love having the pair of you in me."

Zane slid one hand from her ass to the key that dangled between her breasts. "You're ours, Rebecca. You belong to both of us."

She believed him. The wonder of it drew tears into her eyes.

Zane's lips curved when he saw. "We'll be careful with you, sweetheart."

Trey kissed her shoulder from behind.

"You move," Zane said to him. "If we both thrust, we might hurt her."

Zane trusted Trey that much too. She gasped at his first cautious movement, unable to believe how good it felt. Talk about electric. A net of sensation she hadn't known existed suddenly connected her pussy, ass, and vulva.

She couldn't speak. She could only groan.

Trey thrust in again slowly.

Zane liked that, gasping and grinding close.

"Jesus," Trey said. "I think I just . . . felt your dick get bigger."

"Go in again," Zane said. "God, she's so fucking wet."

She was at their mercy: held up, pleasured, titillated from her ears to her curling toes by the men's actions. For a while, Trey went in and out by himself, but before too long Zane couldn't remain passive. He didn't pump, only moved enough to savor the squeezing tightness of her pussy.

"Bring her over," he said to Trey, his face twisting with pleasure. "I want to feel her clamp on my cock."

She cried out as two of Trey's fingers searched out her clitoris. He rubbed the hood over it, up and down, side to side, naturally not shy about touching Zane in the process. She felt the men swell harder.

She couldn't resist what that stirred in her. Her head went back, and the ache in her sex flashed hot. She came so hard it felt like her moan was kicked from her.

"Shit," Zane gasped, finding that too stimulating for his control.

"I'll . . . stop," Trey offered, his teeth grinding. "You go ahead and pump."

Zane grabbed the permission like it would save his life.

"Ah," he cried, pulling back and plunging deep. "Ah, ah—" He held on for five more strokes, for ten. Then he simply seized with pleasure, his gorgeous mouth shaping out a silent *fuck*. His cock jerked and shot inside her, her weight held up by his pelvis's final dramatic lift.

Feeling him go like that was amazing. He took a while to slide back from the peak.

"Fuck," he breathed, his cheek next to hers. "Trey." His hand stroked up Trey's bicep.

"I'm good," Trey rasped. As if to prove it, his fingers resumed their stroking of her clit. "Can you come again, honey?"

She nodded, not up to speaking then.

"Good." He pulled back and forged in with a pleasured growl. "I want you to go with me."

She was swimming inside, so excited she could hardly stand to wait. Zane grunted as Trey slung in, firming up a bit inside her. She wondered if he might come again as well. As Trey thrust with increasing speed, she clutched Zane's shoulders, her fingernails surely pricking him.

"Yes," Trey said, registering her rise in tension. "Yes, honey, go for me."

His movements jolted her into Zane's hot chest—harder, faster, the lube beginning to click in her. Zane held her and touched Trey too. Pressure swelled within her from her closeness to orgasm, from the crazily throbbing erections of the men. A noise tore from her as the sharp-sweet imminence spiked too high to contain.

Trey had been holding back too long. He snarled with pleasure, with determination to join her. He powered in to his limit and shot, his climax heightening hers. Once he let go, he came and came, like a demon had hold of him. Someone squeezed her breast at exactly the right moment. She was pretty sure it was Zane.

The glow that spread through her was headier than wine.

"Wow," she said, trying twice before her vocal chords cooperated. "I think my climax had a climax."

"Me too," Zane said with a shaky laugh. "Trey, old friend, you are inspiring."

Trey might have wanted to speak, but what came out was a sated moan. His cheek rested on her shoulder, his arms wrapped around her midsection.

"I'll take that as a 'you're welcome,'" Zane teasingly told him.

~

Trey didn't want to let go of Rebecca. Of the two of them, Zane had more stamina. Nonetheless, Trey felt a need to carry her to their bedroom. Zane didn't argue, pulling down the sheets and helping Trey settle her. She seemed so precious, now more than ever. She was the second half of Trey's dream come true.

When he laid his head on her breast, she stroked his hair.

"I love you," she said, exactly the words he wanted to hear.

"I love you," he said back.

She kissed his brow and held him. "Beautiful man."

Zane wriggled down on her other side. He reached across her, chafing the shoulder of the arm Trey had draped over her stomach.

"I think I need to see my aunt," Trey announced.

"She won't change," Zane warned. "She needs to believe what she believes about her father."

"That doesn't matter. I need to face her for me. If I don't, I'll worry I didn't talk to her because I was afraid."

"Don't lie to her," Zane said. "Your integrity is important. You can't pretend just to make her comfortable."

"I won't."

Zane leaned over Rebecca to kiss him.

Trey saw Rebecca was smiling. He let his past go—at least for then. It didn't weigh on him so heavily anyway.

"How did you like what we did tonight?" he asked her.

"Oh come on," she said. "You know I loved it. If I were a man, you'd totally turn me gay."

He laughed, something he hadn't known was tense giving way in him. "So you think you'll like living here?"

"I know I will. You will have to give Raoul a raise."

"I will?"

"He's been filling in for me more often. I confess I'm eager to go back to work. I can't help being excited about running our restaurant. Sex fiends that you are, though, you probably won't want me at the Lounge every night."

This was truer than she knew, though not only because they liked having sex with her. "Maybe you'll enjoy work even more when you do it a little less . . . and when you have us to come home to. Any other demands?"

"You should design a perfume that I can wear. Your Bad Boy cologne and sweat is all over me. If you bottled a smell like that, females would line up for it."

"Bad Girl," he said, testing out what he knew she meant.

"Absolutely." She poked her finger into his sternum.

She did smell good, homey and sexy at the same time. She squirmed around and up onto one elbow. Her fingers traced the dragon tattoo on his stomach. That felt so nice, he didn't realize her lazy exploration included being observant.

"There are initials in this design," she exclaimed. "It's a 'Z' and a 'T.'"

"It is," he confirmed. "That was my commitment to Zane way back when."

"Aw," she said, laying her palm on it.

God, she was cute. "Guess I'll need an 'R' in there now."

"Really?"

"Really. Zane wasn't speaking out of turn. You belong to both of us."

Grinning a little smugly, she settled down against him.

"Jesus," Zane huffed. "Trey isn't the only romantic here."

Rebecca turned her head to him. "I don't know, Zane. I haven't heard you say those three special words."

Zane cursed and stomped out of the bed.

"Where's he going?" Rebecca asked.

"The closet, I think."

"Uh oh. He's got crazy things hidden there."

Trey laughed. She felt like his ally and Zane's too, the piece that fit their puzzle more snugly together.

Zane returned with a black leather jewelry box. The image of a pair of hands holding a crowned heart was stamped on it in silver.

"They're Claddagh rings," he said, thrusting the box at Trey.

Three nestled in the velvet slit, one in each of their sizes, beautifully fashioned in platinum. Seeing them, Trey's eyes filled up with hot tears.

"They're hokey," Zane accused himself.

"They're perfect," Trey contradicted.

"Say the words," Rebecca urged softly. "Trey pretends he doesn't need to hear them, but he does."

"I love you both," Zane said. "I love you both a lot. I want us to be together for a long time."

Trey looked from the rings to him. Time folded back to the night they'd become friends and more. That was the night his life began. "How long is a long time?"

"Forever," Zane swore, his eyes as blue as sun-struck sapphires.

Trey smiled, reaching sideways to grasp Rebecca's hand.

"Forever will do," he responded.

# # #

ABOUT THE AUTHOR

Emma Holly is the award winning, *USA Today* bestselling author of more than thirty romantic books, featuring vampires, demons, faeries and just plain extraordinary ordinary folks. She loves the hot stuff, both to read and to write!

If you'd like to discover what else she's written, please visit her website at http://www.emmaholly.com.

Emma runs monthly contests and sends out newsletters that often include coupons for ebooks. To receive them, go to her contest page.

If you like threesome stories, you might try *Hidden Depths* or *The Assassins' Lover*.

Thanks so much for reading this book!

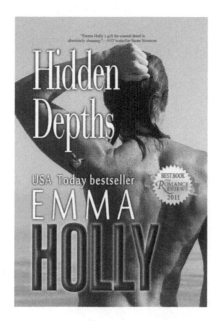

J ames and Olivia Forster have been happily married for many years. A harmless kink here or there spices up their love life, but they can't imagine the kinks they'll encounter while sneaking off to their beach house for a long hot weekend.

Anso Vitul has ruled the wereseals for one short month. He hardly needs his authority questioned because he's going crazy from mating heat. Anso's best friend and male lover Ty offers to help him find the human mate his genes are seeking.

To Ty's amazement, Anso's quest leads him claim not one partner but a pair. Ty would object, except he too finds the Forsters hopelessly attractive.

"The most captivating and titillating story I have read in some time . . . Flaming hot . . . even under water"—Tara's Blog

available in ebook and print

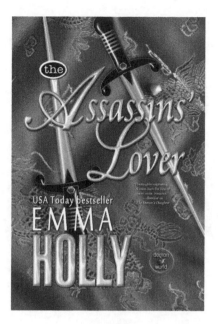

In the alternate Victorian earth the Yama live in, secrets are tantamount. This supposedly demonic race doesn't believe in expressing emotions—or in giving their hearts away.

Assassin-guards Ciran and Hattori were bred to live by that code, until Hattori's too-moral twin is imprisoned, and Ciran falls in love with the grieving man. Both have illegally altered genes that heighten sexual needs, making those needs a challenge to satisfy. Theirs would be a match made in heaven, if only Hattori's heart could stretch that extra inch toward Ciran.

Katsu Shinobi isn't your typical demon princess. As tenderhearted as she is lovely, she seems an unlikely match for these dangerous men—until a dangerous enemy orders them to kill her. The trio can't forget the erotic interlude they once shared . . . or give up the chance to build a lasting future, together.

available in ebook and print

CPSIA information can be obtained at www.ICGtesting.com
Printed in the USA
LVOW04s1617110914

403633LV00017B/1186/P